BRUTAL CALLOUS HEIR

DUET THREE

HEIRS OF ALL HALLOWS'

CAITLYN DARE

Copyright © 2024 by Caitlyn Dare

All rights reserved.

No part of this book may be reproduced in any form or by any electronic or mechanical means, including information storage and retrieval systems, without written permission from the author, except for the use of brief quotations in a book review.

Editing and proofreading by Sisters Get Lit(erary) Author Services

BRUTAL CALLOUS HEIR: PART ONE

HEIRS OF ALL HALLOWS' BOOK FIVE

1

RAINE

"Fancy," I say as my gaze sweeps around the decent sized room.

"You have one of the en suite rooms," Trudy, my social worker says. "Hopefully you'll appreciate your own space." I raise a brow and she lets out a weary sigh. "Raine, come on—"

"Relax, T, I got it." I run a finger over the desk, taking it all in again.

There's a small double bed tucked in the corner of the room, a bedside table, a matching desk and wardrobe, and a small bookshelf with a flatscreen TV mounted on the top.

It isn't much and yet, it's more than I've ever had.

"What do you think?" she asks as I meet her gaze, giving nothing away.

"It's fine."

"Can you try and at least be a little bit excited? It's your last chance to—"

"I know, okay. I know." Everything tightens inside me. I don't need a reminder of what my arrival at All Hallows' signals.

The posh school on the edge of Saints Cross is the last

place I want to be, but Trudy managed to pull some strings with the Deputy Head, her brother, and get me a place.

I don't relish the idea of repeating my first year of sixth form. But it's not like I have much choice in the matter. I'm still seventeen which means I'm still under the care of the Local Authority. And after a string of suspensions and a couple of run-ins with the police, being shipped to All Hallows' is better than being dumped into a young offenders' institute.

"This is your shot at something better," Trudy goes on. "You're a bright girl, Raine. You just need to focus on what's important."

Yeah, like keeping my head down, playing the game, and waiting until I age out of the system.

The second I turn eighteen, I'm gone.

"Your pocket money will be transferred into your account weekly. I'll check in with you every few days at least until you're settled. And Miss Linley expects you at her office first thing Monday morning."

Ah yes, the other requirement of my stay at All Hallows'.

Therapy.

Fuck my life.

"She'll be providing me with regular updates. You're here to attend class. Keep your head down. And pass your A Levels."

In other words, stay out of trouble.

"Got it." I give Trudy a small salute and she rolls her eyes. But after four years together, she is used to me by now.

"I guess this is where we say goodbye then."

"I'd say thanks for everything but we both know it would be a lie," I say, flashing her a wide grin.

"Raine..."

"Yeah, yeah. I got it, T. I can do this."

Not long and then I'll be free.

"All Hallows' is a good school. I really think you can make it work here."

"That's the plan."

"Okay. If you need any—"

"You're hovering," I point out, desperate to wrap things up.

"Good luck, Raine." Trudy makes for the door. "I know that you're not used to this"—she glances around the room—"but it could always be worse. Don't forget that."

As if I can.

With a stiff nod, I watch as she disappears out of the room and leaves me all alone.

Damn.

I'm here.

I'm really here.

At some posh boarding school for Oxfordshire's spoiled rich kids.

What the hell was the board thinking when they agreed to send me here?

I drop onto the end of the bed and take in the room once more, a strange sort of anticipation ripples through me.

The last group home I was in, my room was barely much bigger than a walk-in wardrobe, and I had to share a bathroom with five other kids.

Five.

Having my own bathroom—even if it is only a small toilet and shower—will be worth it.

At least that's what I tell myself as I sit there, in a strange room, in my posh new school, and try not to freak the fuck out.

I'm unpacking the last of my meagre belongings when there's a knock at my door. As I make my way across the room, I half expect to see Trudy standing there, ready to impart more of her words of wisdom.

I don't expect to find a pretty girl with gorgeous eyes and a warm smile.

"Hi, you must be Raine. I'm Tallulah. Mr. Porter asked me to stop by and check in on you."

"Tallu—"

"You can call me Tally." She smiles. "I'm Head Girl of All Hallows'. I—"

"You don't need to do this," I say, trying to spare us both the awkward tension crackling between us.

"Do what?" She frowns.

"This. Pretend to care. I'm not here to make friends so you can run along."

"Good thing for you I'm not here to make friends either then, isn't it?" She stares me down, not missing a beat. "I came to give you the tour. It'll be a whole lot easier doing it now while campus is quiet."

"The tour?"

"That's what I said, didn't I?"

"I'm not sure—"

"Look, I get it. You don't want to be here. I don't particularly want to be here either, but Mr. Porter expects me to give you a tour, so that's what's going to happen." She takes a step back and arches a brow.

"Fine," I find myself saying. Because something tells me she isn't going to run off with her tail between her legs until I've at least stepped foot out of my room. And I guess it would help to get the layout of everything.

"Great." She flashes me a victorious smile that makes me bristle.

"Great," I mutter, pulling my door closed and following her down the hall.

"So this is the girls' dorm. But I'm sure you already know that. There's a common room, a communal kitchen, and a laundry room all at the end of the hall." She points behind us. "Mrs. Danvers is the Dorm Aunt. She's pretty chill. If you have any problems, you can go to her. Just don't try and sneak in any boys after curfew. That's a hard line for her."

"Not going to be a problem," I mutter.

"The dorm is right next to the student welfare building. We're super lucky to have a state-of-the-art facility. Swimming pool, therapy rooms, a studio." She glances at me and smiles. "It's pretty great."

"Great, right."

"Miss Linley is really nice too."

So she knows. It shouldn't really surprise me. The headteacher probably spilled all my secrets while assigning her to babysit me.

"Then in the other direction toward the main building is the boys' dorm."

"What's that building?" I ask, pointing to a church style building in the distance.

"Oh, that's the Chapel."

"The Chapel. So it's a church?"

"Not exactly," she murmurs. Before I can ask her anything else, she says, "Let's check out the sixth form building. I can get you up to speed on where all your classes are and show you the cafeteria."

Tally takes off toward the school and I traipse after her, unable to shake the feeling that all is not what it seems with the Chapel.

But I'm not surprised. All Hallows' is old, steeped in tradition and elitism. It reeks of money. Places like this are always full of corruption and secrets.

"What are you studying?" she asks me as I fall back into step beside her.

"English, psychology, and sociology."

"I'm sure you'll fit right in."

"I think we both know I won't."

"Raine, that's—"

"Save it." I cut her off.

Tally studies me for a second but chooses to swallow whatever bullshit is on the tip of her tongue.

I'm grateful.

Because I meant what I said.

I'm not here to make friends.

I'm here because I have to be. And when I age out...

I'm gone.

After forty minutes of strained conversation and Tally's attempts to get me excited about life at All Hallows', she finally lets me return to the dorm.

I refuse her offer to show me the way back. I've got it. The campus might be a vast sprawling place surrounded by perfectly tended lawns and fenced off by an ominous looking forest on three sides, but most of the buildings are clustered together, making it easy to remember the route back.

When I reach the entrance, I spot a young girl huddled by the door, arms wrapped around herself, practically holding herself together. Alarm bells go off in my head as I slow my approach, taking in her skittish appearance.

Don't get involved, I urge myself. *Just keep walking.*

She lifts tear-stained eyes to mine and a life's worth of trauma rises inside me. But I push it down. Force it back into its box.

I'm not that girl anymore.

I'll *never* be that girl again.

But I can't do it, I can't just walk past her without saying something.

"Hey, are you o—"

Her bottom lip quivers and she darts inside the building.

Okay then.

I frown, giving a little shake of my head.

When I finally force myself to go inside, there's no sign of her. My stomach growls and I decide to check out the communal kitchen.

I don't expect to walk straight into someone as I enter the room.

"The fuck?" A deep voice growls. "Watch where you're going."

I step back to look at the boy. Man would be a better word for him. He towers over me, his eyes full of fury and fire as he glares down at me.

"Who the fuck are you?"

"Someone who belongs here more than you," I spit, my hackles rising at the violence rolling off him.

He falters, eyes flashing with confusion. But then his icy mask slides back into place. "I don't know you."

"No shit." I fold my arms over my chest, arching a brow. "Stealing from the girls' dorm?" My narrowed gaze drops to the stash of snacks and sweets in his hands. "How original."

"Get the fuck out of my way."

"Not until you tell me what you're doing with all that."

I know boys like this.

Arrogant.

Entitled.

Spoiled.

"Move," he barks, literally vibrating with anger. But he doesn't scare me. Not one bit.

Why would he when I've been dealing with guys like him since I grew boobs. Even before then.

"Make me."

The words detonate between us, surprise flickering over his expression.

"You don't know who I am," he muses.

"Should I?"

A slow, wicked smile curls at his mouth, sending a ripple of heat down my spine.

Jesus, this boy is hot.

Hot... and dangerous.

"Theo Ashworth." He leans into my space, his warm minty breath fanning my face. "It would do you well to learn that name. And remember it."

"Oh my God." Laughter peals out of me. "Does that line actually work?"

"Who the fuck are you?" he asks again.

"Raine." I get all up in his face, smirking with amusement. "It would do you well to learn that name. And remember it."

"What—"

"THEO!" Someone yells, and his entire demeanour changes.

"Fuck," he mutters, grabbing my shoulder and yanking me away from the door.

"Hey," I sneer, spinning around to give him a piece of my mind.

But he's gone.

And for as much as I hate it, all I can think is who the hell was that boy?

2

THEO

Every single inch of me vibrates with anger. It's been the same every single fucking day of the holidays.

Christmas is meant to be the best time of the year. When you spend it with those you love. Laugh, eat, drink, and be merry.

What a load of bollocks.

With my arms locked around whatever snacks I could find in the girls' kitchen, I walk back to where I left Millie, desperately trying not to crush everything to dust.

"What took you so long?" she asks, stepping out of the shadows still with tears clinging to her lashes.

I hate it.

I hate the life she's forced to live. I hate the shit she's forced to witness. I hate that I can't protect her in the way I really want to.

"I got what I could find. It should tide you over until I can get to a store tomorrow."

"I could have just stayed at home," she argues quietly.

My teeth grind as I fight to bite back my response to that comment.

Millie doesn't get it. Well, not all of it.

She might think I'm just an irritating, overbearing big brother. But it's more than that.

She didn't hear the argument between Dad and Maria because she was in her room with her headphones on. But I did. I heard the barely veiled threats; the way Dad was starting to lose his control as his anger surged.

There was no fucking way she was sleeping under that roof while he was in that mood. Even if I was there too.

It has been brewing all Christmas, but something happened tonight that shattered through the mask he'd been wearing.

I could try and figure out what it was, but experience tells me that it would be pointless. It could be something as simple as a piece of fluff on the floor. His temper is like a switch. The second it's flipped, something explodes. And if he's been drinking, it only gets worse.

Unease washes through me that we've left Maria there to deal with the fall out. But I find it increasingly hard to really care.

She married in. She knew the kind of man he was, yet she chose to be there anyway. More fool of her if you ask me.

Not waiting for a response, she continues toward her room on the second floor of the girls' dorm building.

She's been boarding here since she started year seven. Thankfully, Dad didn't argue. He was more than happy to have the house to himself. But she still goes back at the holidays. If I had my way, she'd never step foot under that roof ever again. But we have to keep up appearances, for now, at least. He's the mighty Anthony Ashworth. One of Christian Beckworth's best lawyers. Can't say I'm surprised. He's the master at covering up indiscretions and fighting for the guilty, even more so if it's himself.

It's why it's going to be so sweet when I knock him off his pedestal.

The red haze lessens a little as Millie unlocks her door and steps into her own space. She's safe here. His vicious words and hot temper can't touch her. I can sleep tight at night knowing that she's doing the same.

"Message me with anything you need and I'll get it all for you tomorrow," I say, lowering the armfuls of food I have to her chest of drawers. "Do you have homework to do before school starts?"

"I've got it, *Dad*," she teases. "We're not all bad students, you know."

"You're going places, kid. Get yourself some epic grades and the world is your oyster."

"It can be yours too, you know," she says with a small smile.

"You know that's not how life is going to go for me." Heirs of the founding families in Saints Cross have their futures mapped out before they're even born. And I have another reason to stick around here. I've got justice to serve. The time is getting closer to when I can finally expose the truth both Millie and I deserve about our past.

"Theo," she sighs.

"Not now, Mills. It's been a long arse day. I'm ready to kick back and enjoy what's left of the holidays."

"Easy for you to say, you're about to go home to friends. I'm now stuck here alone."

"And that's worse than being stuck at the house?"

"Well, no. Not really. But..."

I raise a brow, waiting for her to finish that thought but she decides against it.

"Forget it. I'm just going to find a series on Netflix to binge and make the best of it."

"Things will get better," I promise her. Tomorrow her friends will return ready for the new school term to start. Things will return to normal. As normal as things ever get at All Hallows'.

"Lock the door after me," I demand.

"I'm not a moron, Theo."

"Shit. I know. I'm sorry, M. Sometimes I forget that my baby sister is growing up," I confess, wrapping my arms around her and holding her tight.

"Don't I know it," she mutters against my chest.

"She's a smart-arse too," I counter.

"Go and have fun with your friends. Just remember how hypocritical you sound when you don't let me do the same."

My lips part to explain but she holds her hand up between us. "I've heard it all before, Bro. Just go. I've got this."

With one more hug, I leave her to it, although I don't go far. I loiter in the hallway until I hear the click of her lock.

Happy that she's safe, I take off, more than ready to find my boys, a bottle of vodka and a joint.

Yeah, Millie is right. I am a fucking hypocrite.

I jog down the stairs to the ground floor, and march back toward the kitchen where I found the girl with the dark hair and mesmerising violet eyes.

It wasn't just the fact she was standing there that startled me, it was that she was so fucking beautiful but not in the classic All Hallows' way. She was different. Darker, more mysterious. More... enthralling.

It's just a shame she was in the fucking way and gave me nothing but lip and attitude. If the situation were different, I could have made better use of that smart mouth. But not while Millie was waiting for me. Despite my reputation, I do have some fucking morals.

Besides, she seems like a girl who will take a little more convincing than the Heir chasers I'm used to.

Bring it fucking on, I'm all about the challenge. It makes the inevitable win so much fucking sweeter.

My skin prickles as I turn toward the exit. Looking over my shoulder, I search the hallway for a set of eyes—violet eyes—

but I don't find anyone. Not that that means she isn't there. This old building has plenty of hiding places.

If I were feeling a little more patient, I might play her game. But tonight is not the night.

So without looking for her again, I focus on the doors and make my way home.

My real home.

"I didn't think you were coming back until tomorrow," Elliot says the second I crash into the Chapel like a raging bull.

The short walk from the girls' dorm was just long enough to replay the day and it made my anger surge to the surface once again.

"Change of plans," I bark, making a beeline for the good shit.

"Hey," Elliot complains when I steal one of his expensive as shit bottles of vodka. Pretentious fuck.

"Eat shit," I grunt, twisting the top and taking my first shot of the liquid that promises some reprieve from the last few days.

"What happened?" he asks, jumping up on the counter and watching as I pace back and forth.

"Normal shit. It has been brewing all week, but the pin was finally pulled. I brought Millie back, got her settled in her room."

"Does she need anything?" he asks without missing a beat.

"Nah, I stole what I could from the kitchen. I'll go get her everything else tomorrow."

"You could have brought her back here for the night, you know."

I glare at him. It's not the first time he's suggested it but just like every single time he has, I shoot it down.

"Not happening."

"Mate, we're just hanging out. It's not like—"

"I said no. She's not coming here. The less she gets involved in this life the better."

"You can't smother her in bubble wrap forever. She's twelve. She's going to be partying and meeting boys. You can't stop that. It's part of teenage life."

"Watch me," I snap. "She's getting out of this place at the first possible opportunity. And she certainly isn't ending up with some All Hallows' prick."

He shakes his head. "We're not all that bad," he mutters.

"Aren't we? I saw photos from the basement the other night," I tease.

I swear, his face turns fucking purple.

"You what? Who fuck would be stupid enough to take—" Apparently able to read something on my face, his words abruptly cut off. "Fucking prick."

"Yeah. Fucking gave yourself away there though, didn't you? So go on, give me all the juicy details. Hell knows it's been a few days too long since I've seen any action."

"Fuck you. We don't all like to share the details."

"Seems like none of you do anymore now those two motherfuckers are all loved up. Everything is changing. I don't like it."

He's silent for a moment. "Yeah, it is. Can't say it's for the worse though."

"Holy shit, was it Abi?" I gasp.

His brows pinch together in confusion, and my heart sinks. For a smart guy, the clueless prick can't see what's right in front of his face.

"You're an idiot," I mutter, taking his beloved bottle with me to the sofa. "I need to beat the shit out of something. It's either you, or a zombie. Your choice."

"Right now, I'll take the zombie. But tomorrow we can hit the ring if you want."

"Fuck yeah, I want." I crack my fingers, my muscles twitching to throw a punch and hear the crack of bone beneath my fist, although it's not Elliot's face I picture but one that is a little more similar to my own.

I load up the game, taking a shot of vodka every few minutes before we get into it. It might not be the physical outlet I could do with, but it's a good enough distraction as we slay zombie after zombie like goddamn pros.

I lose track of time but eventually, the front door to the Chapel opens and laughter from our missing friends hits my ears.

"Where the fuck have you all been?" I ask without taking my eyes off the TV.

"Cinema and dinner. Why? Did you want to be our fifth wheel?" Reese teases as he falls onto the sofa, pulling Liv onto his lap.

"And watch the four of you hook up in the back row of the cinema? No fucking thank you."

"Theo," Tally gasps.

"Prim," Oak teases. "No need to be shy. You shouldn't be after those four orgasms I gave you back there."

"Jesus," Elliot mutters. "You four make me sick."

"And you're a jealous motherfucker," Reese announces happily. "You know you'd have rather been knuckles deep in a certain girl tonight than sitting here playing Xbox like a loser."

"You're a pig," Liv hisses.

"Maybe so, but you weren't complaining when you beat Tally by one tonight."

"Fucking hell, I need to get laid."

"So what are you waiting for?" Elliot asks. "Send one message and you know you'd have a queue outside the front door in two minutes, tops."

I pause the game, thinking about his words. He's not wrong. The chasers of All Hallows' are that fucking desperate.

Desperate and too easy.

I don't want easy, not anymore. The excitement of that has more than dulled.

I want a challenge.

Someone who is going to fight me at every turn.

And I think I know just the girl.

3

RAINE

Starting over isn't something new to me.

Being in care is like that.

If it wasn't a new foster home, it was a new school. New friends. New family. Sometimes even a new town.

I've spent the weekend holed up in my room refusing to come out unless absolutely necessary. The babysitter stopped by again, offering to hang out with me. I saved her the awkwardness and declined. I'd like to say I was polite, but I wasn't, practically slamming the door in her face.

Besides, something tells me I won't fit it in with the likes of Tallulah Darlington and her posh school friends.

By the time Monday morning rolls around, I'm ready to climb the walls. Mrs. Danvers dropped off my uniform yesterday. The godawful black and green tartan skirt and black blazer make me want to vomit but I suck it up and play my part. I draw the line at the knee-high socks though, opting for a thick pair of black tights instead. I'm sure the headteacher will take pity on the outcast.

Grabbing my timetable and my bag, I decide to head out early, before Tally appears and tries to take me under her wing.

I have to meet with Miss Linley, the school counsellor, first thing but I want to get a lay of the land. Maybe check out that weird Chapel place again.

There was something about it... something ominous. I've always been into creepy shit. Horror films. Urban myths. Anything scary and a little grotesque. I didn't grow up plucking the wings off bees or the legs off spiders or anything. But death and the macabre has always kind of fascinated me.

I spent my early teens in a pretty hardcore goth phase. Probably had something to do with my boyfriend at the time.

When we broke up, I traded my black biker boots and black lipstick for tartan skirts, chains, and pink hair dye.

I bounced between styles like I bounced between foster care homes.

Now I'm older and my style has settled somewhere between grunge and geek chic. I gravitate to dark colours. Love anything baggy and oversized and live in my tatty old black Dr. Martens.

A far cry from the prep school uniform I'm expected to wear.

Still, I want to make a good impression on my first day. Or, at least, avoid getting summoned to the headteacher's office.

For as much as I don't want to be here, in a strange new school, among a bunch of rich kids who I doubt have known hardship, it's my chance to regroup. To make a plan for when I age out of the system.

A chance to breathe without constantly looking over my shoulder.

A violent shudder rolls through me but I shake it off. I'm safe here. All I have to do is keep my head down and my nose out of trouble.

Famous last words.

Campus is quiet but then, it is only a little after eight.

A fine mist clings to the ground, giving the entire place an eerie vibe. One I embrace as I roam between the buildings toward the Chapel in the distance.

I don't get very close before three figures emerge, laughing and shoving each other. Straining my eyes, I watch the boys head toward another building on the opposite side of campus. A fourth boy appears, jogging after them. Something about him seems familiar but they're too far for me to get a better look.

Shaking off the odd feeling, I decide to get a closer look at the Chapel. My heart crashes against my chest as I approach the small yet impressive structure.

Set away from the main cluster of buildings, it's cloaked on two sides by the dense woods along the perimeter of campus.

Surely those boys don't stay out here. Unless it's an extension of the boys' dorm. But it doesn't look big enough for that.

I'm about to move closer when voices fill the air.

"I have to go check on the new girl."

"Hopefully it'll go better than the other day."

Shit.

My spine goes rigid as I press myself against the wall, hoping to remain invisible to Tally and whoever she's with.

"I'm not holding my breath. She was... difficult to say the least."

"If anyone can reach her, it's you."

"I'm not so sure. Abi might have more of a chance."

The girls emerge and cut a line toward the main buildings, oblivious to me sandwiched between the wall and a huge tree.

Anger bubbles inside me as I catch the tail end of their conversation.

Their conversation about me.

"She doesn't belong somewhere like All Hallows'."

"Tally, I'm not sure..."

Their voices drown out against an icy gust of wind.

But I heard enough.

Tallulah-up-herself Darlington is exactly the judgemental, stuck-up bitch I assumed her to be, and part of me wishes I was in my dorm room to witness her confusion when she realises I'm not there.

With a smug smirk, I double back toward the buildings and make a beeline for the student centre. My appointment with Miss Linley isn't until eight forty-five but maybe I can find somewhere quiet to hang.

The Darlington Centre for Student Welfare is clearly new. Pristine doors welcome me as I slip inside, the smell of fresh paint permeating the air. There's an unmanned reception desk and a long hallway off to the side.

Unsure of where I need to go, I take one of the seats in a small cluster around a low coffee table and pull out my sketch pad and a pencil. It's about one of the only personal effects I brought with me. Years worth of sketches and doodles scratched into the pages.

I've always loved to draw. To lose myself in the sound of lead against paper. I don't overthink it, I let my muscle memory lead as I flip it open to a new page and start drawing.

I don't have raw talent. My art doesn't end in a masterpiece. But it's a part of me. And I take some measure of peace in it.

I'm so lost in the process, that I don't hear anyone arrive until I sense someone looming over me. My eyes flick up, connecting with a petite redhead.

"Hello," she says softly.

"Hey." I dismiss her, going back to my sketch.

"I'm Abi. You must be Raine."

Is everyone so goddamn persistent here?

My mouth twitches.

"You got me."

"You're very talented," she adds, leaning over me to get a better look.

With an irritated sigh, I snap my sketchbook closed and twist around to face the girl but before I can get out some snide reply, she says, "You're here to meet with Miss Linley?"

"Did they put out an announcement or something?"

"Sorry, what?" Her brows crinkle.

"Well, everyone seems to know my business."

"Oh, sorry." A small, uncertain smile lifts her mouth. "I volunteer here, and I have therapy with Miss Linley too."

"Right."

"Tally said you were a tough nut to crack."

"Tally... let me guess, she's the queen bee of All Hallows' and you're just one more of her willing minions."

"I... that's... it isn't like that." Something passes over her expression. "Tally is a good person."

"I'm sure she is," I scoff.

"You know you really shouldn't judge people until you get to know them."

"Whatever, you can go now." I give her my shoulder again, really wanting to be done with this conversation. Like I've said before I'm not here to make friends and I certainly don't need Little Miss Goody Two-Shoes trying to put me in my place.

The girl—Abi, I think she said her name was—drills holes into the side of my head and finally, I relent, unable to stand her heated stare any longer.

"What?" I snap, hating that she's looking at me like she sees straight through my façade.

"You know, Raine, we all need a friend now and then."

"I don't need anyone."

She regards me for a second longer, murmuring, "We'll see," under her breath, before she turns and walks off, leaving me alone.

She's wrong. I don't need anyone. I learned that the hard way.

Agitated, I shove my sketch pad and pencils into my bag and tap my foot on the floor, my gaze darting around the fancy centre.

I don't belong here, that is dreadfully obvious, and I still don't know what Trudy and the board were thinking sending me here.

But it's only a few months. I've survived worse.

I'm about to bolt, to say to hell with it when a girl enters the building.

A girl I recognise.

"You," I say to the girl I saw crying outside the dorm the other day.

She cuts me with a scathing glare and continues walking.

Okay then.

I'm about to shout after her, to ask her what the hell her problem is when a young woman appears, fixing her warm smile right at me.

Great. This must be the counsellor.

"Raine?"

"The one and only." I stand, throwing my bag over my shoulder.

"It's so lovely to meet you. I see you found the place okay."

"It's literally across from my dorm," I deadpan.

Her lips twitch. "Yes, well, why don't you follow me to my office, and we'll get started."

"Great." Not.

"How are you liking All Hallows' so far?" she asks as I follow her down the hallway.

"It's... different."

Soft laughter bubbles out of her. "I thought the same thing when I first started working here. But it's a good school. I'm sure you'll flourish here."

I barely refrain from choking on my disbelief. "I think we both know that isn't going to happen."

She hums her disapproval, stopping outside a door at the end of the hall. "This is me," she says. "Shall we?"

I shrug. I'm here under duress. Nothing more.

I've done the therapy thing. I've talked to shrinks and counsellors and therapists. Sat in their chair while they try to help me unravel my past, the trauma I've fought hard to bury.

None of it made a difference, and I don't suspect Miss Linley's attempts will be anything different.

I'm broken.

And some broken things can't be fixed.

4

THEO

"Have you seen her yet?" Oak asks, dropping into the seat next to me and tearing into his packet of crisps.

"Glad to see you're taking Coach's advice seriously when it comes to healthy eating," I mutter, pointedly ignoring his question.

"What are you talking about?" he balks, lifting his shirt, showing off his abs for the chasers who are already looking this way.

He's off the market. That news has spread far and wide since he openly announced his relationship with Tally at the end of last term. But it hasn't stopped the most desperate ones from continuing to bat their lashes at him.

I, however, am totally free and single, and more than happy to distract them from their heartache with an orgasm or two.

I jerk my chin at our audience as Oak smacks his abs. "This machine is in top working order, I'll have you know."

"Not what you were saying when we were out running yesterday. Is your poor quad feeling better?" I ask in an annoying baby voice.

"Yep, good as new thanks to Tally's expert massage. She does this thing where she oils me up and—"

"Hey, beautiful. Long time no see," I say when Keeley leads her group of whores over.

"It's been the holidays, silly," she squeaks, sounding like the airhead she most certainly is.

Flicking her glossy blonde hair over her shoulder, she presses her small tits together in an attempt to impress me.

Pushing my chair back a little, I spread my legs wide and gesture for her to sit. She might be annoying as all fuck, but I'll take a little attention. Especially if it means Oak will knock off his questions about the new girl.

Tally told us all about her when we were hanging out at the Chapel last night. Basically, she explained exactly what I already knew from my few seconds in the girls' kitchen with her.

She's an angry bitch who doesn't belong at a school like this.

Fuck knows who thought it was a good idea to let her attend. But if she's as bad as we've both experienced, then I've no doubt that she won't be hanging around long.

Keeley's hand slides down my chest, her fingers bumping over my tense abs making her squeal in delight. I have no idea why she's so surprised. It's not like she hasn't got closer than this before.

I'd be tempted to say it was probably the best night of her life the evening I took her down to the basement. Sadly, it was nowhere near mine.

Turns out, she's all confidence and bravado when she's surrounded by her friends. But strip her naked and tie her up, and she turns into a timid little mouse. She tried telling me that she wasn't a virgin, but I wasn't convinced. She looked about as terrified as one as I prowled toward her with my dick in my hand.

"Do you mind?" she asks, reaching for my abandoned

banana that's sitting on the table before me with her free hand. The other is quickly heading for my mostly uninterested dick. Who knows, maybe a little pet will wake him up and force him to get with the programme.

"No, go for it."

"Oakley, be a doll, would you?" she asks, handing it over. "I'm a little busy."

She nods down to where she's stroking me, forcing Oak's eyes down to my crotch as well.

"Sure. I'd hate for you to stop. Theo looks like he's *really* enjoying that," he quips, wiping his greasy fingers on his trousers and opening the banana for Keeley.

He passes it back and she immediately locks eyes with me as she parts her lips and pushes the fruit inside.

"You're a tramp, Kee," Reese says as he joins us and falls into a seat next to one of Keeley's less handsy friends. That or she's smart enough to know not to go near Reese. The cat fight it would start isn't worth it.

"Ugh, Theo," the girl in question complains. "There seems to be a skank on your lap."

Keeley ignores her jibe and continues her show, biting off a piece of banana in a way that makes me wince.

I know her blowy skills need a little improvement but shit.

"I don't hear Theo complaining," she purrs.

"He's also not about to blow his load either," Oak points out. "Hey, babe," he says, his tone changing completely as Tally appears at his side.

Ignoring Keeley, I study Tally for a beat.

She's looking good. On the outside, she seems to have put everything she went through before Christmas behind her. I know the invisible scars she's been left with might be a little harder to banish, but at least with her bruises gone, the gossip around the halls of All Hallows' has almost stopped. Well, that and she's a fully fledged member of the Heirs now. Something I think she's still trying to come to terms with after her many, many years of hating everything to do with us.

But what can we say?

Under it all, we're a loveable lot.

"Keeley, you look like a cheap whore," she sneers at my playmate.

Unfazed by her words, Keeley continues chowing down on my banana.

"At least she's a healthy whore," Oakley quips, balling up his crisp packet and throwing it on the table in favour of pulling his girl onto his lap.

She shrieks in fright, but he soon silences her with his lips. Although, much to his irritation, she fights him.

"Prim," he growls.

"We can't do this here," she argues.

"Why? Because everyone still thinks you're a good girl?" he teases. "I hate to break it to you, babe. But you're with me. Everyone knows that you've been fully corrupted."

"Oakley," she gasps.

"Pull that old stick out of your arse, Prim."

As they glare at each other, movement behind them catches my eye, and suddenly, my little soldier isn't so uninterested in the hand stroking him. And I'm not the only one who immediately reacts to the sight before them because New Girl abruptly pauses, causing those behind her to crash straight into her back.

"What the fuck?" one of the football team complains before darting around her and toward their table. The rest of his crew follow, giving her death glares. Not that she notices, she's too focused on us.

With my temperature finally spiking and my cock swelling, I wrap my fingers around Keeley's wrist and bring my banana to my mouth for a bite. But I keep my eyes on her.

New Girl.

Her lip peels back, clearly disgusted with the show we're

putting on before she glances to the side and straight at Tally. Then her brows pinch in confusion as Tally finally caves to Oakley's plan and kisses him back.

I get it. She'll have met Head Girl Tally. She probably has no idea that she spends her nights taking one of the four best dicks in this place.

It takes her a few seconds but finally, she rips herself from the trance the sight of us put her in and remembers what she's meant to be doing and takes off across the room to an empty table.

Dumping her bag on the top, she pulls out a book and pencil, and starts doing something. But every few seconds, she glances up at us.

She probably thinks she's being discreet but she really fucking isn't.

Keeley leans forward, her breath rushing over my neck, making a shudder run down my spine. But it's not for her. She's the easy I don't want. I'm pretty sure if I pushed it, I could take her right here in front of almost the entire sixth form. But while a little exhibitionism is fun, it's not what I want right now.

That isn't what's making my dick hard.

"You want to go somewhere a little more private?" she whispers in my ear.

"No, not really," I confess, making her gasp.

She's probably thinking exactly the same thing I was a second ago.

"Theo, I don't think—"

"We're done here, Keeley. Thanks for the entertainment."

She gasps again but this time, it's not with shock, but anger. "B-but I thought—"

"You thought what? That I wanted you? That you were special?"

One of my boy's whistles at my harshness. Fuck knows why. They've both said worse things to the chasers before now.

"It sure feels like it," she squeezes my dick, making my teeth grind.

Yeah, her touch does feel nice. But I'm pretty sure Elliot's would if I closed my eyes too. Doesn't mean I fucking want him, either.

"Keeley," I hiss, ripping her hand from my dick and shoving her from my lap. "Your time is done. Take your little friends and fuck off."

She stares down at me, and I swear her bottom lip trembles.

"Fine. But don't come running to me when you need to finish that off later," she sasses, jutting a hip out and flicking her hair over her shoulder.

"Don't worry. I have hands, too," I call after her as she stalks through the common room.

"Brutal," Elliot says with a smirk as he grabs one of the chairs the chasers were sitting in, spins it around and sits backward on it. "She can't be that unqualified, pretty sure Reese trained her."

"Ow, fuck. He's joking, sweet cheeks," Reese whines after Olivia smacks him around the head.

"He's not, though, is he? Don't forget, I hear all the bathroom gossip."

"That was the old me," he pleads. "I'm a changed man now. The only girl I can see right now is you."

Elliot laughs. "Isn't it amazing what shit a guy will spew to ensure he continues getting laid?"

"Something you clearly know nothing about," Oakley pipes up having stopped trying to suck Tally's face off. "When was the last time you saw some action, oh fearless one?"

"None of your fucking business."

"Aw, leave him alone. We all know he's got a little crush," I tease.

"Fuck off, Theo."

"Maybe you should try your luck with the New Girl. She

might need someone a little... darker than Prim and Abs to bring her out of her shell," Oakley suggests.

At his mention of her, my eyes dart toward where she is, and once again, I find her watching us.

"She was rude to Abi this morning," Tally explains.

Elliot's shoulders tense at the mention of the timid girl he seems to be so taken with. "What did she say?" he asks, sounding possessive as shit.

When I glance at Oak, I find him smirking, thinking exactly the same as me.

"Not much. Just brushed her off like she did me."

"It's tough being new," Olivia says. "And as you said, she doesn't exactly look like she's used to a place like All Hallows'."

She's fucking right there.

She might be wearing her uniform... kind of, but it still doesn't cover up that fact that she's clearly not All Hallows' material.

Her make-up is heavy, giving off major don't talk to me vibes that only adds to her unfriendly aura. And it's that that makes me want to walk over there and see if I can get a reaction out of her.

She was so unfazed by me the night I found her in the kitchen. But I know there's so much more. A depth, a darkness that I'm desperate to discover.

Elliot looks back around having studied her. "I think I'm good. Not my type."

"Oh really?" Reese asks, beating me to it. "I thought you loved a challenge. Surely the New Girl isn't too much for the great Elliot Eaton."

"I swear to God, if you guys start a bet then I'm leaving you, Reese Whitfield-Brown."

"What the hell did I say?" he argues, but it doesn't work, and she narrows her eyes on him in warning.

"We might not have been together all that long, but I've

known you lot all your lives and I know exactly how you work. She's new, be nice. Do not put her in the middle of a bet. I'm warning you." Olivia pins us all with a look before Reese twists his fingers in her hair and claims her lips in a filthy kiss.

"My sister is a bore."

"Don't even think about it, Beckworth," Tally warns making Elliot, and I laugh.

Is it wrong that a part of me is disappointed that those two whipped motherfuckers will obey orders and ruin our fun?

5

RAINE

Theo Ashworth.

That was his name.

The boy I'd bumped into at the girls' dorm. The same boy I'd watched maul a girl earlier in the cafeteria as he watched me with smug amusement.

Conceited arsehole.

Apparently, he's a rugby player and an Heir. Whatever the hell that means.

I'd heard the same whispers all day.

Another Heir bites the dust.

Two down, two left for the Heir chasers.

Wonder who will fall next. Theo or Elliot.

It was obviously rich kid talk. Code for some stupid elitist little gang or something.

I didn't ask anyone to explain because I didn't care.

Not that I had anyone to ask. Everywhere I went, kids gave me a wide berth as if brushing past me or acknowledging me might tarnish them.

"Watch it," a girl hisses at me as she shoulders me out of the way.

"Stupid bitch," I murmur, rubbing my arm where her bag caught me.

"What did you say?"

The venom in her voice gives me pause. I really don't want to do this. Not here. Not now. Not when I'm so close to getting through my first day without any drama.

All day, I've done what Trudy and Miss Linley asked of me. Kept my head down and my mouth shut. But I'm not about to stand by and let some stuck-up princess act like she didn't just mow me out of the way.

"Come on, Keeley, she's not worth it."

"She called me a bitch."

I turn slowly, taking the three girls in, recognising the one who shoved me as the girl draped all over Theo earlier.

Lovely.

She's not only a bitch but a desperate whore.

I barely resist the urge to roll my eyes.

"What?" she snarls.

"You do know you walked into me, right?"

"Because you didn't move."

Is this girl for real?

From the way she's glaring at me I guess she must be. Jesus.

"I'm sorry, I must have missed the sign that said this is your hallway."

"Look, tramp." She steps forward, getting all up in my space. I'm vaguely aware we're drawing a crowd, a low ripple of chatter going up around us as more and more students stop to see what's happening. "I don't know who thought it would be a good idea to let you enrol but you don't belong here."

"Hardly something to cry about," I scoff.

Her teeth grind as she looks for a dent in my armour. But the thing is, I've survived a lot worse than some mean girl who wants to put me in my place.

"Keeley, come on—"

"You should listen to your friend, *Keeley*," I drawl her name, taunting her. "Walk away before you start something you won't finish."

Her cheeks flame. "Is that a threat?"

"More like a promise."

"Who the hell do you think you are? You can't talk to me like that."

"Run along now, princess." I smirk, going to walk away but the crazy fucking bitch grabs my bag and yanks. Hard. "What the hell?"

My arm shoots out, my elbow connecting her chest.

"Ow, you psycho. You hit me. She hit me," she starts screaming like a banshee as I try to wrestle free from her hold.

"Let me go then, stupid—"

Strong arms wrap around me, hauling me backwards.

"What the— You." I glare at Theo as he steps in between us.

"Oh, Theo; thank God. She attacked me. The crazy bitch attacked me."

He arches a brow, sliding his gaze to me and back again. "Not how I saw it go down, Keeley."

"W-what? She came at me. Ask anyone." She motions to her friends who nod.

Of course they fucking do.

"She goaded Kee," one says, and I bark out a bitter laugh.

They all glance over, Theo included.

"What?" I shrug. "She started it, and she knows it."

Keeley tsks, and if looks could kill, I'd be six feet under.

So much for a friendly welcome.

"You should take off, Keeley. Before you make things any worse."

"M-me?" Disbelief coats her voice. "But I told you, I didn't—"

"Keeley," Theo snaps, an air of authority in his voice that

makes me wonder who the hell this boy is and why people call him an Heir.

"Come on, Kee." Her friends tug her away and Theo glances around the hallway.

"Show's over," he practically growls the words, and the place becomes a hive of activity once more.

"I see you're making friends."

"She came at me."

"Keeley is... a handful." He runs a hand over his jaw.

"I got that memo earlier."

"Jealous, New Girl?" Something flashes in his eyes, and I frown.

"That would be a resounding no."

Theo takes a step closer, and another, until I have no choice but to retreat, his presence sucking the air from around us. "You sure about that?" He reaches out to snag a piece of my hair, but I immediately go on the defensive, swatting his hand away.

"Don't. Touch. Me." I tremble, the memories I fight to keep locked away rattling against their cage.

"You should be fucking honoured I'm even talking to you," he spits. "Do you know how many girls would kill for me to swoop in and save them?"

"Save me? Wow." Anger vibrates inside me. Who the hell does he think he is?

"The airheaded bimbos you're used to might fall for your cheap attempt at chivalry, but I can look out for myself, thanks." I barge past him, needing to get away. From him. From the strange tension crackling between us.

"Hey, New Girl," he calls after me and stupidly, I pause, twisting back to meet his narrowed gaze. "I'm not someone you want to make an enemy out of."

"Is that a threat?" I cock a brow, unwilling to play his games.

He slides his hands into his pockets and leans back against

the row of lockers, looking every bit the roguish posh boy he is. "Call it a friendly warning."

"We'll never be friends," I state, and then I turn away and get the hell out of there.

My mood is in the pits when I walk through the doors to the student welfare centre. As if it wasn't bad enough meeting Miss Linley this morning, my first group therapy session is this afternoon.

I can hardly wait. Sitting around with a bunch of other damaged students, sharing stories of our childhood trauma and pain. Just what I don't want to spend my Monday afternoon doing.

Something tells me our stories might be a little different given they attend this school.

Ignoring the handful of students gathered in the hall, I make my way to the meeting room Miss Linley showed me earlier. It's a light and airy space with a huge window overlooking the woods beyond the campus perimeter.

"Ah, Raine, you made it."

"Didn't have much choice," I murmur.

Miss Linley just smiles. "How was your first day?"

"I stayed out of trouble." Mostly.

She doesn't need to know about my run-in with crazy Keeley.

"Glad to hear it. Why don't you grab a drink and find a seat. We'll be starting soon."

I glance around the room, eyeing the girl over by the refreshment table.

It's her. The crying girl from the dorm.

Her eyes lift, landing on me and her brows pinch as she darts her gaze away.

Okay then.

I don't bother getting a drink, taking a seat instead. There are eight chairs positioned in a circle, Miss Linley's chair at the head. I know it's her chair because she's draped her pale pink cardigan over the back.

She greets the other students as they enter the room and before long, I'm sitting between a girl and boy who don't do much as acknowledge me.

"Millie, would you like to join the circle now."

The girl I came across at the dorm joins us, taking the empty seat opposite me but like everyone else, she barely looks twice at me.

"I hope everyone enjoyed some downtime over the Christmas break." Miss Linley joins the circle, taking her seat. "However, I know the holidays can be a trigger for some of you. So today I want to spend some time exploring that.

"It's been a few weeks since we last met as a group, so I want to remind you that anything you share today or in our future sessions is confidential. This is a safe space."

I press my lips together, trapping the urge to groan. Therapists sure love the sound of their own voice.

How many times had I heard the same bullshit over the years?

Talking about it will help.

It's good to explore our feelings.

Your experiences don't define you, Raine.

Funny that, because my experiences have done nothing but define me and my life. And talking about them hasn't changed a damn thing.

So..." She clasps her hands together. "Would anyone like to share how their break went?"

Her reassuring gaze roves around the room, until it lands on me. But I remain silent. There's nothing I want to share. Not today. Not next time. I'm only here because I have to be. My presence is the only interaction she's getting.

"Millie, what about you? Anything you'd like to share today?"

Millie stares at the ground, folding her arms around herself.

"I know you were particularly worried about going home for the holiday?"

"It was fine," she murmurs.

"Fine. Do you want to expand—"

"No." Her head whips up and she glares at Miss Linley. "I don't want to talk about it."

"I know it's hard—"

"You don't know anything." She doesn't spit the words, she just lets them spill out in a soft defeated manner.

I see it again, the hurt in her eyes. The pain.

"I'll go," another student says.

"Thank you, Chloe."

"My sister was home for the holiday, so I might not as well have been there. Mum and Dad were so wrapped up in her being there it was like I didn't exist."

"And how did that make you feel, Chloe?"

"Angry. Bitter... Sad. But it's happened so much over the years, I'm used to it by now. I guess more than anything, it just makes me feel numb, you know?"

"That must be very hard for you?"

I tune out, staring at a blank spot on the wall.

But my eyes drift back to Millie as she stares at the floor.

There's something about her. A tug I feel. A sense of familiarity.

Maybe it's just that I see myself in her a little. Or maybe this place is already getting to me.

Whatever it is, I don't have time for it.

Besides, putting yourself out there—trying to make friends—isn't worth it.

Letting people in makes you weak.

It makes you vulnerable.
And I'll be damned if I let anyone walk all over me again.

6

THEO

"Pick it up, ladies. All those pigs in blankets aren't going to burn themselves off," Coach bellows as we run drills up and down the pitch.

Sweat pours from my body, mixing with the mud from the waterlogged ground beneath us. My heart races to the point I'm pretty sure I'm one more length from an actual heart attack.

Someone—I have no idea who—roars in pain a little farther up the row of exhausted and pissed-off rugby players.

"Just because the first half of our season has gone okay, it doesn't mean the rest will fall into your laps," he continues. "You want those scouts here, you need to look like you want it."

"We can't win if we're all dead," Oak pants beside me as he touches the line and takes off in the other direction again.

"We're not at the top of the league, and if you want to secure that championship place then I need to see more."

"Fucking hard-arse," Reese seethes.

I fucking love rugby. And I'd like to think that I'll be playing and watching it until the day I die, but right now, Coach is making me question everything.

Sucking in a deep breath, I focus on my body, focus on pumping my legs, on making my muscles move in the way I know they can. Exercise—sex included—has been the only thing that's got me through some of my worst times over the past few years. That and the three boys at my side, of course.

Without it—without them—I'm not sure I'd be the person I am right now.

There have been times that I've been so consumed by the darkness, by the secrets of my past that I haven't been able to poke my head above water.

I've had to, though. Because as much as I want to drown and never come back, I've got someone relying on me. Someone I need to protect as if my own life depends on it.

Thoughts of Millie spur me on and I get a fresh boost of energy.

Everything I do. Everything I'm going to do, it's all for her. I want her to have the life she deserves along with the justice we both need. Not that she's aware of that. I've kept everything I know locked down.

Her life is hard enough without having the truth eating at all the goodness inside her just like it does me. She's sweet, innocent, pure, and I have every intention for her to stay that way.

"Yes, Ashworth," Coach booms when I take off ahead of the others.

He forces us to go five more before he blows his whistle.

Middleton and Ainsworth drop like fucking rocks making both Coach and Elliot groan.

"Get the fuck up," Elliot barks, kicking Middleton in the ribs while Oak sets his sights on Ainsworth and Hickman who's also gone down. "I'm not leaving my school or my team to a fucking pussy like you."

"Get out of my sight, the lot of you," Coach demands. "And if I were you, I'd come back here tomorrow ready to show me you belong here, instead of the netball team."

The four of us stare down the rest of the team before we take off in the direction of the locker room, leaving them all behind to cry like little girls.

We're almost at the door when movement across campus catches my eye. Previously, the pathways surrounding what used to be the old pool were deserted. The building ignored by almost every person at All Hallows'. But that has all changed since Oakley convinced his dad and the school board to renovate it at an eye-watering cost to impress his girlfriend.

I mean, I get it. Tally's campaign to improve student welfare wasn't a bad one. The flaw was the fact she wanted to use the Chapel—our fucking Chapel.

But Oakley being Oakley managed to make her happy and get back in her knickers all in one swift and very expensive grand gesture. It is now a state of the art hub for students who need extra support. And one of those students just so happens to be my little sister, who's just practically ran from the building like her arse is on fire.

"Millie," I shout, but my voice is swallowed by the gale-force wind that whips around us. "MILLS," I try again.

But nothing.

"Fuck."

I take off running, my need to surround her in bubble wrap in the hope no one hurts her is all-consuming.

"You can't fight all her battles for her," Elliot calls after me, making me pause as red-hot fury floods my system.

I spin around and get right in his face before slamming my palms down on his chest. "What the fuck would you know about it?" I growl, getting so close our noses are almost touching. "Do you have a little sister?"

Elliot's nostrils flare, his jaw clenching with anger, but he doesn't answer my stupid question. I know as well as he does, that he doesn't have a little sister. Just a twisted fuck of an older brother who's tortured all of us enough in the past for shits and giggles.

"Theo, just leave it. Give her some time, then go and check in on her," Reese says.

"She's a good kid," Oak joins in. "She was probably just running to get out of this shitty weather."

Shoving Elliot away from me, I spin back around to continue toward the locker room. "Fucking unbelievable," I bark. "It's like you don't even care."

It's not fair to accuse them of that. I'm more than aware. They care more than anyone. They're the family that Millie and I have needed over the years, not that she knows.

They've got her back just as much as they have mine, and the four of us are the sole reason her life here is as smooth as it is.

Everyone is too scared to go up against us. And in turn, that means anyone with even half a fucking brain cell won't go anywhere near my little sister.

Overbearing? Sure. But she fucking deserves to be treated like a queen. I refuse to allow people to use her to get to me, or any of us. She's too good for that shit.

No sooner has the door slammed back against the wall do I have my locker open and I'm pulling my shit out.

"The showers are that way," Elliot deadpans, a smug as fuck grin on his pretty boy face.

Flipping them all off, I march back out still covered in sweat and mud. By the time I get to the girls' dorms, the rain has started, and I'm also soaked through and dripping all over the place. Something that will make Mrs. Danvers have a fucking cow. But what the fuck ever. My sister is more important than her expensive parquet flooring.

Taking the stairs two at a time, my muscles burn like fuck, reminding me of just how hard Coach pushed us this afternoon.

The second I pull the door open to the corridor that will lead me to Millie's room, I stumble across a group of girls. They stare at me in horror. But the second they see through the mud and dirt, their demeanours completely change.

"Hey, Theo," Lauren purrs, looking me up and down like she's considering jumping me like this.

"You look like you've put in a good workout this afternoon," Sophie adds, stepping up to her friend. "I bet you could use a massage. Lauren and I can work magic with our fingers," she confesses, running said fingers over the low neckline of her tank, showing off even more cleavage than she is already.

"Maybe another day, yeah? I've got plans."

"Oh, Theo. Come on. We'd have so much fun."

"I'm sure."

Turning my back on them, I take off, my ears bleeding as they continue to whine like dying cats about the lack of attention I'm giving them.

My heart jumps up into my throat the second I turn the corner and find Millie's door slightly ajar. She should know better than to leave herself exposed, even in a building that should only inhabit female students and a couple of well-trusted teachers. But there are way too many rule-breaking cunts like me and my boys who have been known to sneak into more than a few dorm rooms here over the years for a whole host of things. Most of which end in some kind of high.

My teeth grind as I lift my hand, ready to slam my palm down on the door and scare the living shit out of Millie just to prove a point.

I pause, forcing myself to breathe, to calm the fuck down. I might want to teach her a lesson, but I don't need her to see me losing control. If she lives her entire life believing that I can keep a lid on my anger, my darkness, that won't be a bad thing.

Once I've got the untamed beast that lives inside me reined in, I finally push the door open, letting it slam back against the wall to reveal what's happening inside.

I swear to fuck, despite everything I just told myself, if

she's in here with a boy, any fucking boy, I will end him with my bare hands.

Millie shrieks in shock as I storm into the room, ready to strangle the fuck out of some little tosser who's trying his luck. But when my vision clears, I don't find a boy standing in front of her, protecting her.

Oh no.

Instead, I find *her*.

In my little sister's fucking dorm room.

New Girl stands in front of Millie as if she needs to hide my own sister from me.

"What the fuck are you doing in here?" I seethe, my voice low and deadly.

"Theo, leave it," Millie says, jumping out from behind New Girl.

Despite her telling me not to forget her name after she told it to me in the kitchen the other night, it had left my head long before I walked away from her irritating brand of sass and arrogance.

"What have I told you, Millie? Only your friends should be in your room."

Millie doesn't get a chance to say anything because she's cut off by New Girl as she throws her head back and laughs like I just told the world's funniest joke.

"Oh, I'm sorry. Is my presence amusing you?" I ask, taking a step closer.

The second I do, her perfume fills my nose. It's not sickly sweet and overpowering like most of the girls at All Hallows'. Instead, it's subtler, almost... bitter.

A smirk curls at my lips. Yeah, that fucking suits her.

"Nothing amuses me about you, big man," she teases. "Although, I'm sure plenty must laugh when you get your teeny weeny out like it's something to be proud of."

My eyes widen.

Oh no, she fucking didn't just insult my dick.

I close the last few inches separating us, and despite the mud that's coating almost every inch of me, she doesn't so much as flinch.

"Get out of my little sister's room, New Girl. You are not welcome here. We're not friends, remember."

Her eyes narrow as she juts her chin out in a move that few would be brave enough to do. "No, if I remember rightly, you're gunning for enemies."

My nostrils flare as I suck in a deep breath, desperately trying not to strangle the bitch right here and now. "Leave. Now."

"Only because you asked so nicely," she sneers. "Millie, if you need me, you know where to find me," she says sweetly to my sister, although she never once rips her eyes from mine.

"No," I bark. "You're not going anywhere near Millie again."

She smiles. But it's not a friendly one. It's full of bitterness and challenge.

"Try and stop me."

7

RAINE

I storm out of Millie's room fuming.
Who the hell does Theo think he is?
Entitled, arrogant, cocky—
Get a grip, Raine. He's not important.

But the fact Millie is his little sister throws a spanner in the works. When she'd run out of the therapy session crying, I'd gone after her. Followed her all the way back to the girls' dorm, unable to let go of her pained expression as Miss Linley encouraged to share how her Christmas break had been.

There's something about her. I only wanted to check on her, to make sure she was okay.

But that was before I knew she was Theo's little sister.

Jesus. Less than a few days at All Hallows' and this place is already getting under my skin. I don't like it. I need to keep my head down and my nose out of other people's business.

Easier said than done.

I head straight for my room, but sense someone following me.

Glancing over my shoulder, I arch a brow at Theo as he stalks behind me. "What the hell are you doing?" I seethe.

"We need to talk."

"No, we really don't." Hurrying, I unlock my door and slip inside. But he's quicker, slamming his palm into my door.

"Theo!" I hiss.

"You need to stay away from Millie."

I yank my door open, a smile curling at my lips as he stumbles forward a little. But Theo is quick to right himself, his eyes simmering with unrestrained anger. "I don't want her anywhere near the likes of you."

Everything inside me goes still.

"What do you mean, 'the likes of me'?"

I know exactly what he means but I want to hear him say it.

"Come on, Raine," he drawls my name, smirking. "We both know you don't belong here. That someone on the admissions board took pity on you and probably—"

"You don't know the first thing about me." Despite the venom in my voice, my body trembles. "And I don't appreciate the threat."

"Stay away from Millie and we won't have a problem."

"That's going to be a bit difficult when we have therapy together."

Something flashes in his eyes, but it's gone as quickly as I saw it.

"You really don't want to play games with me," he warns.

"Why? Because you're big bad Theo Ashworth? Because you're a Saint? An Heir?" I snort, hardly able to tamp down my amusement.

Theo takes a step forward, forcing me to back up. And another, until he's in my room. My space.

The air thins between us. Stretching taut like a bowstring.

He takes a lazy perusal of the room, pure arrogance radiating from him.

"You need to leave," I snap.

"Scared, New Girl?" He pins me with a dark look. "Because you should be."

I glare at him... and then explode with laughter, making his expression turn murderous.

"You think this is funny?"

"You do realise how ridiculous you look, standing here caked in mud, threatening me?"

"But—"

"But nothing." I get in his face close enough that I can smell the earth and dirt, jabbing my finger toward his chest. "I'm not scared of you, Theo. I'm not—"

His fingers close around mine, holding me there as electricity crackles between us. "You should be."

More laughter bubbles in my chest and his brows pinch with irritation. "You can leave now," I sass. "Don't let the door hit you on the way out."

"Stay away from Millie. I mean it."

"Yeah, yeah." I give him a little shove toward the door.

He glares at me, and I brace myself for his snappy comeback. But instead, he turns and yanks the door open, murmuring something to himself about the 'crazy new girl.'

I can live with that.

If it means he stays out of my way and stops his weird little obsession he has with me.

The door slams behind him and I flinch. Remembering how my stomach had dipped at his proximity. The fact his gaze had dropped to my mouth more than once.

Shit.

I drop my head back against the door and inhale a shuddering breath.

Theo Ashworth might not scare me, but something tells me he's trouble.

And I've always had a problem with steering clear of that.

The next day, I oversleep. I want to say it's because I slept so well that I couldn't bear waking up when my alarm went off.

But it wasn't.

I barely got any, since I kept tossing and turning. Theo's smirk haunting the corners of my mind.

The Ashworth siblings clearly have issues, and I'd do well to stay away from them both. But Millie is in my therapy group —she's in my dorm—it's going to be hard to avoid her.

Besides, something tells me she might need a friend.

After snoozing my alarm, more times than necessary, I finally drag myself out of bed and pad into the small en suite. I'm not used to this kind of privacy.

In a group home or busy foster home, stealing more than ten minutes alone time in the bathroom was a luxury. Yet here I can take my time. I can enjoy a shower without worrying that someone might pick the lock and slip inside. Or that someone might try and rifle through my belongings while I'm out of my room.

I'm used to always looking over my shoulder. Keeping one eye on the door. Never letting my guard down.

I'm not used to... to *this*.

But I relish it. Take time scrubbing my skin, my hair. I'm already late for my first class so I might as well enjoy it.

By the time I'm done, I'm clear-headed and ready to face the day. But that all goes out of the window when I slip out of my room and spot Millie in the communal kitchen.

Walk away, Raine. Don't get involved. Don't—

"I can feel you staring," she says quietly, lifting tired eyes to mine.

"Sorry. I didn't expect anyone to be here. I'm late."

"I'm... yeah." Her shoulders lift in a small, defeated shrug. "I'm sorry about yesterday. Theo is... well, he's an overbearing idiot. But he's a good big brother."

"I can handle Theo," I reply, and her eyes widen a fraction. "Oh, I didn't mean..."

"Don't worry. You're not his type."

Ouch.

"Oh no, I didn't mean it like that."

"It's fine." I brush her off.

"I just meant Theo likes girls who fall in line. He doesn't appreciate being challenged."

"I hadn't noticed."

"Of course you hadn't." Her lips twist in amusement, and I realise the younger Ashworth sibling sees a lot more than she perhaps lets on.

"So, he's an Heir…" I regret the words the second they're out. But I can't deny I've wondered exactly what it means.

Millie scoffs. "Stupid, right?"

"What does it mean exactly?"

"What do you know about Saints Cross and All Hallows'?" she asks, adding a thin layer of jam to her toast. She cuts it into four triangles and offers me the plate.

"I'm good, thanks."

"More for me." Millie shoves a whole piece into her mouth.

I wait for her to finish. She grabs her juice, drains the contents and wipes her mouth with the back of her hand. "Saints Cross is built on the money of some of the oldest and most influential families in Oxfordshire. Lawyers. Judges. Politicians. The kids of said families attend All Hallows' and then Saints Cross U to follow in their parents' footsteps. It's just a way to keep the legacy alive."

"And when you say kids…"

"Sons. I mean, their sons. Welcome to the twenty-first century, where women have equal rights so long as the men say it's okay." She rolls her eyes.

"How old are you again?"

Because she seems so wise beyond her years.

"Don't let my age fool you." Millie flashes me a wry smile.

"So Theo and his friends are all Heirs. The other students treat them like they're royalty."

"Because they practically are here."

"Sounds like loads of rich kid bullshit if you ask me."

"It's just how it is and always has been." She shrugs again.

"And the Heir chasers?"

"Ugh." Another eye roll.

"Not a fan?"

"It's disgusting, the way they throw themselves at my brother and his friends. Reese and Oakley are off the market now, but it doesn't stop them. I suspect we'll see a few bitch fights before the year's out."

"Tallulah Darlington goes out with Oakley, right?"

"Yeah. Nobody saw that coming. She's always hated the Heirs. But I guess love and hate are two sides of the same coin or something."

"Right."

"What about your brother and Keeley..."

"Keeley Davis? Please. She's nothing more than a desperate slut. My brother would never get with somebody like her."

I'm not so sure about that but I swallow any more questions I have.

"All Hallows' isn't so bad if you stay under the radar."

"Is that what you do?" I ask, and Millie nods.

"I try to. Although my brother makes it impossible sometimes."

"Why do you board here if your family lives in Saints Cross?"

Her whole demeanour changes, her gaze dropping to the floor.

"Millie, what's—"

The door to the kitchen flies opens and Theo steps inside, his heavy stare going to Millie and then me.

"You," he spits.

"Leave it, Theo. I'm fine. Raine was just—"

"You're supposed to be in class, Mills. You can't keep doing this. You know Mr. Porter has to inform Dad when you don't show."

"Relax, I'm going. It's only tutor group. It's no big—"

"Get out," Theo barks at me, and I bristle.

"Excuse me?"

"You heard me. You might not give a shit about following the rules but Millie is—"

"Theo, you're being ridiculous."

"No, Millie. She's... she's—"

"What? What am I?" I'm pissed, yeah. But it's more than that. The way he's looking at me. Casting judgements he has no right to make.

"A bad influence," he spits. "I don't want you anywhere near her."

"Theo!" Millie snaps but I'm already moving around him to get to the door.

"Raine, wait—"

"It's okay," I say with a forced smile. "I'll see you later."

"Like hell you will," Theo starts but I'm already gone, walking down the hall and away from their family drama and his anger.

But I'm not far enough away that I don't hear Millie say, "What is your problem? That was rude and uncalled for."

Or to hear Theo answer, "She's trouble, Millie. She doesn't belong here and if you think for a second I'm going to let her tarnish your reputation, you're wrong. Dead wrong."

8

THEO

"Are you actually serious right now?" Millie shouts, her fists curled so tightly her knuckles are white.

"Yeah, Mills. I am. Deadly fucking serious," I assure her, taking a step forward.

"Unbelievable," she breathes, throwing her arms out from her sides before grabbing her toast-filled plate and throwing the lot in the bin.

"What are you doing? You need to eat," I argue, storming after her when she runs through the door. "You'd better not be chasing after her."

She stops abruptly before the stairs. "Don't you dare follow me," she seethes.

"You need to get to class."

"And you need to stop pretending to be my father. I'm old enough to look after myself."

"No, you're not. And this morning proves it. You're late. You've just binned your breakfast, and you were talking to her when I specifically told you not to."

She shakes her head as a bitter, disappointed laugh falls from her lips. "I don't need you following me around and giving me opinions on every aspect of my life, Theo. It is overbearing and unnecessary."

"I'm trying to look after you."

"You're smothering me. If I'm hungry, I'll eat. If I oversleep and am late then I'll take the punishment. If I want to talk to someone, then I will. I'm allowed friends, Theo. I'm allowed to at least try and have a normal life."

"You can have friends. Girls in your own year who aren't already practising to be Heir chasers, yeah."

"They all want to be Heir chasers and you know it." She scoffs. "So what? I'm meant to be lonely and friendless for my entire time here? Is that what will make you happy?"

"Millie, that's not what I'm saying," I sigh, hating that we seem to spend more time fighting than anything else these days.

All I want to do is protect her. To allow her to live a life that isn't tainted by the bullshit that surrounds us.

"So what are you saying exactly because I think I'm missing the point?"

"Just stay away from her," I repeat, dragging my hand down my face in frustration.

Why her?

Of all the people at All Hallows', why does my little sister seem to want to befriend her?

"Why? What do you know about her that I don't? Why is she such a bad person to spend time with?"

My teeth grind as I stare back at a pair of eyes that are freakishly similar to mine. "She... she..."

Fuck.

Words escape me.

"You're unbelievable, Theo."

Before I manage to come up with any kind of answer, she's gone, running up the stairs and away from me.

The temptation to follow and continue is strong, but I'm aware that I don't have anything solid to say as to why she shouldn't be spending time with Raine other than a bad feeling. So I spin in the opposite direction and throw the front door to the Bronte Building as if it personally offended me.

"Fucking great," I bellow when I'm met with a face full of rain and a bitter wind. Just what I fucking need.

By the time I get into the Orwell Block where all the sixth form classes are held, I'm soaking fucking wet. And just because the universe hasn't shit on me enough already today, the first person I lay eyes on is Raine.

She's standing next to her locker, staring at me with a wicked smirk playing on her lips. She's bone dry, her dark hair still styled perfectly, and her make-up as immaculate as when she first applied it. But it's not her appearance that draws me in, it's the anger in her eyes that captivates me.

Pushing my sodden hair from my brow, I drag it back, keeping my eyes locked on hers as students move between us ready to start the first lesson of the day.

"Whatever it is you're playing at with Millie. I'm not going to let it happen."

Blindly, she grabs something from her locker before kicking it shut with one of her boots—those definitely aren't part of the All Hallows' uniform—and takes a step toward me. Totally ignoring the stream of people who are forced to step aside for her.

"You know, for someone who apparently rules this place, you sure do spend a lot of time rocking the hobo look. What happened? Lost the key to your castle, Theodore?"

Amusement curls at her lips as anger surges through me. My fingers itch with my need to wrap them around her throat and squeeze the life out of her.

"Theo," a sweet, irritating voice calls from somewhere down the hall that makes Raine's spine straighten. "Oh, look at you, you're all wet," Keeley says the second she wraps her hand around my upper arm.

My first reaction is to rip myself from her clutches, but

then I see the way Raine's eyes narrow in frustration, I hold steady.

Leaning in closer, I brush my lips against Keeley's ear. "Bet I'm not as wet as you."

"Give me strength," Raine mutters while Keeley purrs like a needy kitten at my words.

"I'm glad you found me, Kee. I've got a job that I think you're going to really enjoy."

"I'll give you anything you need, baby."

"Careful, she might give you a few extra gifts while she's there. Fuck knows where she's been."

"Careful, New Girl. You're starting to sound awfully jealous."

It's not until Keeley's tittering laughter floods through the hallway that I realise how much it's emptied out. And those who are left, are watching the three of us like we're putting on a show.

"Jealous? Of you and her? Puh-lease. My next class is in that direction and you're both standing right in the middle of the corridor. If you'd kindly fuck off, I'll happily put thoughts about both of you where they belong."

Tugging Keeley to one side, she crashes against my body, ensuring she rubs her tits against my chest as if it'll make me more interested in the whore.

"Ugh, I don't like her," she soothes, trying to fix my hair.

"She won't be here long," I assure her.

"So..." She bats her eyelashes at me as everyone who was loitering waiting for something to kick off disperse. "What did you need me for?"

Her hands resting on my chest quickly drop lower as excitement glitters in her eyes. I catch them before they descend to my cock. I might not like Keeley all that much, but she probably doesn't need to know just how uninterested I am right now in what she can offer me.

"Come on," I say, taking her hand in mine and tugging her

in the direction of the common room that should be almost empty as the bell for class rings around us.

She squeals in excitement as I kick the door closed behind us.

"There are still people in here," she points out, nodding to a couple of the nerds who are too focused on their laptops than us. "But I'm good with it if you are."

"I'd rather not have an audience," I mutter, taking a seat and tugging the chair in before she gets a chance to jump onto my lap.

"Uh... o-okay," she whispers, looking confused as she lowers her arse into the seat opposite me. "So what can I help you with? I'm not the right person to ask if you need someone to do your homework for you."

I can't help but laugh. "Don't worry, Kee. I'm more than aware of where your skills lie."

She licks her lips like the shameless whore that she is.

"The new girl. What's the deal with you and her?"

Her top lip peels back, exactly like I was expecting. "She doesn't belong here. I've no idea who allowed it but I've asked Daddy to look into it. We don't accept people like her here."

"What did she do to piss you off?"

"Other than show her face? She called me a stupid bitch," she huffs, crossing her arms under her breasts.

It takes every ounce of self-restraint I possess not to laugh.

I hate to admit it, but that might be something that Raine and I have in common.

Leaning forward, I rest my elbows on the table and study her. "You want revenge?"

A wicked smirk curls at her lips.

"Hell yeah," she agrees. "What are you thinking?"

I abandoned Keeley to brainstorm ideas, then headed to my first class of the day half an hour late. Not that the teacher dares to say anything as I pull my chair out and fall into it.

"Where the fuck have you been?" Elliot hisses.

"Just sorting out a few things."

"Millie okay?" he asks, aware that I darted off to find where she was when I was alerted to the fact she didn't turn up to tutor first thing this morning.

"She's good. Overslept. We had a fight," I confess.

"You need to back off, Theo. I know it's hard to take, but she's not a kid anymore."

"Don't start. I've already heard it all this morning."

I don't need to look over to know he's studying me, my face burns with his assessing stare.

"What else has happened? You're on edge."

"It's nothing," I grunt, hating that he can read me so easily.

"Okay, sure. Play that game if you want. You know I'll find out eventually."

"Whatever." Flipping my book open, I grab a pen and start copying down the notes from the projector screen.

If I were listening, I might have a clue as to what they're about, but I'll figure it out. Contrary to popular belief, I don't actually need anyone to do my homework for me. I'm not as dumb as I look.

No sooner have I walked into my second class of the day do I realise that Keeley has already rallied her band of bitches.

I remember what they were all like when they turned on Tally before the Christmas break. If I want Raine out of Millie's life, then the chasers are the fastest way to make it happen.

"What the— Get your fucking hands off me, bitch," Raine's voice rings down the corridor, and when I look over, I find three of Keeley's friends trying to look innocent as Raine pokes at something in her hair.

Chewing gum. Not exactly what I asked for, and not the

kind of actions that's going to make her run back to wherever she came from, but I guess they've got to start somewhere.

With a smirk, I walk past them and slip into my class, excited to see what's going to be next.

One of the best things about our lives here at All Hallows' is that none of us need to lift a finger when there's something we want.

By the time lunch rolls around, rumours of the chasers having a new target are rife throughout year thirteen.

"What's going on with the new girl?" Tally asks as her and Olivia join our table.

"She called Keeley a bitch yesterday morning."

"Of course she did," Olivia mutters.

"I warned her to stay away from the chasers," Tally states.

"And you think a girl like Raine would listen to that kind of advice?" Oak asks, amusement dancing in his eyes.

"Well, no, I guess not. But... well, I tried."

"I think she's strong enough to look after herself," Olivia says.

"Who can look after herself?" Reese says as him and Elliot complete our group.

"Raine," Tally explains.

"She can. I just saw her going up against a couple of chasers by her locker. We've nothing to worry about there. She—"

"Theo," Keeley squeals across the common room, cutting off whatever Reese was about to say.

Before I know what's happening, she's on my lap, her lips next to my ear. "Are you ready, baby? The fun is just about to begin."

Shivers race down my spine, but they have nothing to do with her and everything to do with the girl who's just walked in with a group of chasers closing in behind her.

Getting comfortable, I shift her on my lap and wait with a smirk for what's about to go down.

9

RAINE

A ripple of awareness goes through me as I step into the cafeteria. Theo watches me like a hawk, making no attempt to disguise the contempt in his eyes.

Wanker.

Today has been fucking awful. So much so, I contemplated skiving off and going back to my dorm. But I refuse to let Keeley and her mean girl bitch friends get the upper hand.

Gum in my hair, vile notes in class, vicious rumours… it's all child's play compared to the shit I've put up with over the years.

Sure, it stings a little, knowing that they've put a target on my back when they don't even know me. But I'll never let them see that.

I can sense a group of them behind me. Their cruel whispers and taunts brushing up against me like a cold, bitter wind.

She should just take the hint and leave.

All Hallows' is no place for a charity case like her.

Maybe we should just take out the trash ourselves.

Anger pulses underneath my skin; roiling like a living, breathing thing inside me. I knew All Hallows' would be a hellhole full of judgemental bitches and egotistical, entitled arseholes. But Trudy was adamant it was better than the alternative.

Right now, as I glance over at Keeley, I'm not so sure.

She smirks right at me, pressing in closer to Theo, staking her claim.

Doesn't she realise, she's welcome to him?

Just looking at his smug grin irritates me. He thinks he's won. He thinks this little game between us is over. Not that I wanted to play in the first place—I didn't.

I don't.

But I can't deny I'm not wholly in control when he's around, and I'm not afraid to admit he is easy on the eyes. Tall, dark, and annoyingly handsome. He's a conceited, entitled rich boy wrapped up in a pretty package. But everyone knows that pretty things can still be rotten on the inside.

With a little huff, I keep my head down and quicken my pace, making a beeline for the queue snaking around the far wall.

I don't see the boy barrelling toward me until it's too late.

He collides into me with such force I yelp, losing my footing and slip on the shiny cafeteria flooring, falling right into the cleaning trolley, sending the dirty, discarded trays everywhere. They clatter to the ground like dominoes scattering as a sharp pain shoots through my side. I throw out a hand to steady myself only to take the nearest bin down with me, emptying the remnants of half-eaten lunches all over me as I go down.

I sit there for a second dazed as silence descends over the room. Until someone yells, "Oh my God, look at her."

Laughter erupts, drowning out the roaring in my ears.

"Shit, I'm sorry." The boy looms over me wearing an insincere smile. "I didn't see you there."

"You didn't... whatever." I bite back the urge to lash out. To give him a real piece of my mind.

Fucking idiot.

He gives me a little shrug and moves around me, avoiding the disaster zone as the laughter continues, making me bristle.

As if the embarrassment curling in my stomach isn't enough, I make the fatal error of looking up only to find Keeley staring right at me, victory gleaming in her eyes. But it isn't her expression that makes my heart sink, it's Theo's.

He looks so bloody smug as if he had a hand in planning my downfall.

Then it hits me.

He did this.

Maybe the boy who mowed into me wasn't so innocent as he might have had me believe.

A fresh wave of anger surges through me as I try to get to my hands and knees, retching as my fingers slide through all sorts of food waste. Of course it just had to be spaghetti and meatball day, the bright red pasta sauce is smeared all over my white shirt and smattered in my hair.

I look like something out of a crime scene. I don't even want to think about what else is mixed in there.

Retching again, I manage to clamber to my feet, every single person in the cafeteria staring at me as if they've never seen someone covered in cafeteria food before.

My lips purse as I try my best to pick off the dead spaghetti and slimy, congealed bits of sauce.

"Well, that's one way to take out the trash," one of Keeley's friends says loudly enough that at least half the room overhears.

I grit my teeth at her, a low growl bubbling inside me.

God, I hate this place. I hate the people and the—

"Raine?"

I whirl around to find the redhead—Abi, I think—staring at me with a mix of sympathy and pity.

"Come on, let's go get you cleaned up."

"I can manage."

"But I want to help."

"Why?" I spit the word, barely aware of the regret pinching my heart. I'm so angry and embarrassed, I can barely see straight.

"Because we all need a friend sometimes. And because I don't want to see them win." She flicks her head over to where the Heir chasers stand gawking at us.

Me.

I should tell her that I don't want or need her help. But I don't. Instead, I follow her out of the cafeteria with my head held high, the whispers and laughter nipping at my heels.

"Is this a trick?" I ask once we're in the hall.

"What?" She glances back at me, confusion crinkling her eyes.

"Well, you're friends with them, aren't you? Tally and Olivia?"

"Yes, but... you think I'm one of them." A soft sigh slips from her lips.

"Aren't you?"

"I'm friends with them, yes. But... it's complicated."

"Because they're going out with Heirs?" I hate the way the word sounds rolling off my tongue.

It's so stupid. And yet, no one intervened just now. Not the teachers dotted around the room or the lunch ladies.

Not anyone except Abi.

I guess that has to count for something.

"Keeley Davis is a scheming bitch," I spit.

"You're not wrong there. The Heir chasers can be... brutal."

"You sound like you're speaking from experience."

"Not directly. But I've seen first-hand what they can do. You shouldn't have gone head-to-head with her like that."

"I'm not going to cower. Besides, Keeley is nothing compared to—" I stop myself, surprised that I let myself even speak the words.

"Compared to what?"

"Nothing."

Abi studies me for a second but she lets it go. "We could tell Miss Linley," she suggests. "A lot of the school staff won't intervene unless absolutely necessary but—"

"I'm not a rat."

"I thought you might say that. Just ignore them and they'll lose interest eventually."

"Yeah."

But it's too late. I'm already plotting how to get them back.

Only, I'm not going after Keeley and her friends.

No, I'm going straight to the source.

I'm going after Theo and the Heirs.

"You didn't have to wait," I say the second I step out of my bathroom and find Abi sitting on my bed.

"I wanted to make sure you're okay."

"I'm fine." Towelling off my hair, I drop down on the desk chair and let out a small huff.

"You don't find it easy to let people in, do you?" she adds.

"In my experience, it isn't worth the hassle." I shrug.

"I used to think that."

"What changed?"

"I made friends with Tally and Liv."

"If you're here to convince me—"

"I'm not." Her hands shoot up. "I'm just saying that, sometimes, if you give them a chance, people might surprise you."

She doesn't know that I've had enough surprises to last me a lifetime.

I'm about to send her on her way but then it hits me, she has a direct link to Theo and the Heirs. Maybe she can be of use to me, after all.

"I guess," I reply, offering her a glimpse of a smile.

"We can start small." She beams, and I feel a flicker of guilt.

Abi has been nothing but nice to me. It isn't fair of me to put her in the middle of this thing between me and Theo and the Heir chasers. But I don't owe her anything, and if it came down to it, I'm pretty sure I know where her loyalties would lie.

"Yeah, okay." I say, sealing our fate.

"Great. How do you feel about cake?"

Hanging out with Abi was more fun than I anticipated. The fact she'd snuck me off campus might have had something to do with it.

It's the first time I've seen Saints Cross in the daylight and it's exactly as I expected. Quaint and wealthy, with a long high street of expensive boutiques and exclusive restaurants and bars.

We got milkshakes and cake at a little place called Dessert Island and talked about everything and nothing. But there's something about Abi, a shadow in her eyes every time the conversation turned on her. I didn't pry though. I know what it's like to have secrets and I have no plans on sharing mine.

I'm back in my room now, lounging on my bed as I scroll through social media. Abi friend requested me earlier so I can see all her photos, although there weren't many before a few months ago.

Now her account is littered with photos of her and Tally and Liv, the odd photo of the boys too. My gaze snags on one of Theo. He's unaware he's being photographed as he stares at something, or someone, off camera. His brows are drawn together, his lips pressed into a thin line in contemplation. Or anger.

Either way, I can't help but wonder what he's thinking.

Why do you care? I shove the annoying little voice down.

I don't care.

But I also have eyes, and I can appreciate a good-looking lad when I see one.

Even if he is an absolute dickhead.

Still, the only thing I'm interested in where Theo Ashworth is concerned, is revenge.

10

THEO

Satisfaction rolls through me as the room explodes with laughter around me.

Every single set of eyes is trained right on Raine as she squirms around in the contents of the trolley and bin.

I couldn't have done better if I'd done it myself.

Ripping my eyes away from the human meatball, I glance at Keeley who's preening like a fucking Cheshire cat on my lap.

She should be proud, that was fucking epic.

So why do I want to hurt her for looking so fucking pleased with herself?

Clenching my fists, I grit my teeth as I allow her to wiggle about on my lap while the scene continues to play out. But the second Raine walks out of the cafeteria with her head held high despite the fact she's got spaghetti stuck to her arse, I shift her forward.

"Theo?" she whines.

Leaning forward, I whisper. "Go and wait for me in that storeroom down by the hall. You know the one?"

Of course she knows the one. She's probably blown

seventy-five percent of the male population of All Hallows' sixth form in there.

She licks her lips as she looks back over her shoulder at me, her eyes burning with desire. "Perfect way to celebrate," she purrs, her hand trailing down my chest until she's blatantly palming my dick.

Not that Keeley has ever cared about being discreet.

"I'll be ready." She hops off happily and takes off running.

"Of course you will," I mutter, rearranging myself and turning toward my friends.

"What did you say to her to make her run like that?" Oakley asks.

"Told her she could suck my dick," I confess.

"And it tastes that bad?" Olivia laughs as she turns around just in time to see Keeley disappear from sight.

"No, it fucking does not. She's just that excited," I state smugly.

"Or," Tally pipes up. "Keeley is just that much of a..." She trails off.

"You can say it, Prim, we won't judge." Oakley smirks.

"Tramp," she finally says, making Oakley laugh.

But Tally doesn't find it amusing, nor does Olivia as they both keep their eyes on me.

"What?" I bark, irritated with their judgey looks.

"That was you, wasn't it?"

I smile. "Who offered to let Keeley blow me? Yeah, what about my last comment didn't you understand? She's waiting for me in the storage cupboard by the hall dripping wet for me right now."

Both Liv and Tally's faces screw up in disgust.

"And you're still here, why?" Reese asks before Liv slaps her hand across his mouth.

"Not that. I couldn't give a fuck what you do with Keeley or any of the chasers. I meant that," she states, throwing her arm out to indicate the mess Raine left behind.

"So what if it was? You suddenly her bestie or something?"

"No," Tally huffs, clearly annoyed that Raine hasn't toed the line with her.

She might only be on day two of being back at school since her ordeal, but she's returned not just as Head Girl, but as Head Girl with an Heir on her arm. There aren't many people who are going to defy her now. Clearly, New Girl didn't get the message. Although, after this afternoon's performance, something tells me that she might be starting to understand.

"But that... that was too much."

I shrug. "We can agree to disagree."

"Theo," she gasps, looking back at Oak for back up but Liv is the one to speak. No surprise there.

"She's right. That was harsh."

"She was rude to Keeley, and she's been sniffing around Millie. I don't like it."

"Firstly," Liv starts. "Who the fuck gives a shit about Keeley? That bitch can look after herself. And secondly, it's Raine's second day. Can you give her a break? So what if she was nice to your sister?"

"We don't know if she was nice. She could be trying to get Millie to do anything," I sulk.

"Are you actually serious?" Tally balks. "Have you met your sister? She might be sweet, but she'd never do anything she didn't want to do."

"And how exactly do you know that Tallulah?"

Oakley's body tenses at my tone and he sits forward ready to fight for his girl.

I shake my head at him. Not so long ago, his first instinct would be to fight for me. For us. Now, him and Reese are all about putting their girls first.

Well, fucking good for them.

"I'm done here," I state, shoving my chair back so it makes an obnoxiously loud screech on the parquet flooring.

"Careful, Keeley doesn't bite it off," Liv snarks.

"Maybe avoid her and go find Raine to apologise instead."

"Why? It's not likely that she'll suck my dick."

"You're a prick," Liv calls after me, but I'm done.

So fucking done.

Walking around the mess Raine made that three lunch assistants are now cleaning up, I take off in the opposite direction of the storage cupboard and head toward my next class. I might be early but fuck it. I'd rather sit alone like a loser right now than have to deal with my self-righteous friends.

The room is empty as I storm inside and find myself a seat.

Slumping down in the chair, I stare at the projector which is already showing the topic of this afternoon's lesson. I'm already fucking bored and Miss Pearce isn't even here yet.

Maybe I should have gone for a quick, albeit sloppy blowy in the storeroom. At least I could have put Keeley where she belongs. On her fucking knees.

But my dick doesn't show an ounce of interest as I consider how she'd look down there.

A girl with dark hair and violet eyes though... oh yeah, now the little man wakes up.

I let my mind wander. I bet she's back in her room now, has probably stripped off her filthy clothes and stepped under the spray of her shower.

Spreading my legs wider, I palm my cock through my trousers, imagining what she might look like with her guard down and her body bare.

I wonder what it would take to make her break?

What would I have to do to discover if deep down, she's not all that different to the whores who walk these halls.

I bet I could do it.

I bet in a few short weeks I could have her on my knees for me.

Fuck yeah, the thought of those eyes staring up and me, as I stretch her lips wide with my dick, gets me fucking going.

She shouldn't have such a smart mouth then, not while she's choking on my—

"Mr. Ashworth, you're keen today," Miss Pearce says as she marches into her classroom with a stack of books in her arm.

I clear my throat, scrambling to sit up before she clocks the fact I was about two seconds from pulling my dick out and coming all over her floor.

"You know me," I say, my voice unusually rough considering I'm talking to a teacher. A very average, unhot one at that. "Always ready to learn."

How soft and wet her mouth would be...

Damn it, Theo.

Lock it down. Lock it the fuck down.

You achieved your goal, the entire sixth form will now think of her as nothing but part of the rubbish.

Get her out of your fucking head.

I stand in the rain, a-fucking-gain, as I stare up at my sister's window. Her light is on, so I can only assume that she's up there like she should be. What I don't know is if Raine is with her. Or worse, is she tricking me into thinking she's there but is actually up in Raine's dorm room trying to cheer her up after what happened this afternoon?

It's exactly what she'd do. She's all caring and sweet like that. It's one of the ways we're different.

She thinks our issues can be fixed with some love and a hug. I, however, know that more drastic action needs to be taken.

Shoving those dark thoughts aside, I take off toward the main entrance and tap my hip to the panel that will read my card and allows me entry into the holiest of places on campus.

The girls' dorms.

I take the stairs three at a time in my quest to find out what my sister is doing.

I'm at her door in only a few seconds. My fingers wrap around the handle and I twist.

Nothing happens.

I should be pleased that she's following orders and locking herself in, but it also could mean that she's hiding something.

"Millie," I boom, pounding my fists on the door. "I know you're in there. Open the door."

"Go away," she shouts back, confirming my suspicions. "I don't want to talk to you."

Irritation rolls through me.

"I know what you did. And I'm not talking to you until you apologise to Raine."

I scoff before taking matters into my own hands and tap my master keycard to the pad once more. I twist the handle and shove the door open.

But it doesn't fucking open.

"Millie," I growl, throwing my weight into the door, but whatever she's wedged behind it doesn't shift even an inch.

"I'm not messing around, Theo," she warns. "You're being an unreasonable prick and Raine doesn't deserve it."

"Fucking pain in my arse," I mutter.

"And make sure it's a really good heartfelt apology or it doesn't count."

A defeated sigh falls from my lips. "Fine," I bark, throwing my hands up in defeat and stepping away from her door.

Glancing down the hallway, my eyes land on one of the very final doors on this floor.

Sucking in a deep calming breath, I take off in that direction. Although it's yet to be seen if I'll do anything like offer up an apology. Right now, it's more likely that I'll throttle her for the way she's managed to worm her way into my head without permission.

I linger outside her door, trying to get my shit together. But my need to make Millie happy finally wins out and I lift my hand to knock. She's always been my weakness, and she damn well knows it.

Just like before, there's no response.

"Raine?" I shout. Not that I think hearing my voice will make her answer the door.

I knock again.

"Just let me the fuck in so I can say what I need to say." I shake my head at myself. There's no way she's letting me inside.

Once again, I repeat my actions from down the hallway, unlocking her door.

After all, this card isn't just for the entrance and Millie's door, it's for every single one in the building.

This time when I unlock the door and attempt to throw it open, it actually does, revealing a very bare room inside. Without a second thought, I step into her room, studying her space.

Her bed is made tidily, there are no clothes on the floor or posters on the walls. If I didn't know better, I'd think no one was actually living in here.

Where are all her things? Photographs of her friends and family, trinkets from home? Jewellery and make-up? All the things that litter every other room in this dorm.

"Where are you?" I mutter, walking around as if the room is going to provide me with answers.

Stepping into the bathroom, I find just a few pieces of evidence that she's been here. The shower is wet, and there are a couple of products on the shelf, along with a toothbrush next to the basin. But still no sign of her.

Figuring that she's going to make this harder than I was expecting, I walk back out. I consider leaving the door open to give the chasers easy access to her personal space, but remembering Millie's words about apologising, I pull it closed and lock it again before taking off.

If I'm lucky, I'll find her hiding out in the shadows somewhere.

A smirk curls at my lips. She seems like the kind of girl who wouldn't be scared of the dark woods that line the All Hallows' campus.

11

RAINE

I can't stop my smile as I head back to my dorm building. Theo and the Heirs think they're so untouchable.

But he's clearly underestimated me and the type of girl I am, if he thinks I'm just going to—

"Well, well. Look who finally decided to show up."

Theo pushes off the wall and stalks toward me, my heart crashing in my chest.

Shit.

He's been waiting for me. I figure I have two choices, ignore him which might only make him dig his heels in all the more or try and throw him off the scent.

Or...

I shut *that* thought down.

"Stalking me, Theodore? Not very original." I go to move around him, acting aloof, but he grabs me by the arm and yanks me around to face him.

"Don't touch—"

"Where were you?"

"Excuse me?"

"I've been waiting a while, sunshine. And I don't like to be kept waiting."

"Number one: don't call me that. And number two: who the fuck do you think you are?" I glare at him as irritation rolls through me.

"Did I touch a nerve, sunshine?" He leans in, taunting me.

"My name is Raine."

"Raine Storm." His lips curl. "What kind of fucking name is that anyway? Your mum a hippy or something?"

I go still, blood roaring between my ears as I try to swallow over the lump in my throat.

His brows pinch but before he can latch on to my sudden change in mood, I spit out, "No worse than Teddy."

"T-Teddy?" he chokes out. "No one calls me that."

"Maybe they should. Maybe I will. Kinda has a nice ring to it, don't you think, *Teddy*?"

"Seriously, do you have to be so fucking annoying? I came to apologise but—"

"Hold up, apologise? You came to apologise?" Laughter peals out of me. That shit is the funniest thing I've ever heard.

"What's the catch?"

"Catch?" His frown deepens.

"Yeah. Something tells me Teddy Ashworth doesn't apologise ev—"

"I swear to God, sunshine. You do not want to call me that again."

"Oh yeah? Why?" I give him my best saccharine sweet smile, jabbing my finger at his chest. "What." Jab. "Are." Jab. "You." Jab. "Going." Jab. "To." Jab. "Do." Jab. "About." One final jab. "It?"

He silently fumes, glaring at me with the heat of a thousand suns. Another laugh bubbles in my chest, but it's cut off when he grabs me around the throat and pushes me up against the wall.

I'm so stunned, so fucking shocked that all I can do is gawk at him.

He leans in, a wicked smirk curling at his lips. "You were

saying, sunshine?" he drawls the annoying nickname, aware of exactly how much it gets under my skin.

Bastard.

But underneath all the anger and urge to kick him in the balls, is something else.

Something I refuse to acknowledge. Because he's... and I'm...

Jesus, what is wrong with me?

Well, I know what's wrong with me. I'm broken. Defective and damaged. All thanks to a piece of shit boy not too dissimilar to the one currently smirking at me like the cat who got the cream.

"Nothing to say, my little rain cloud." His laughter is sharp. All thorns and poison. He's enjoying this, getting off on it even.

He thinks he's won. He thinks he's caught me off guard so beautifully that he's got the upper hand. But that's the problem with boys like Theo. Like Vaughn. They're so self-absorbed, so cocksure, that they couldn't possibly ever consider that someone—a girl—could one up them.

Theo's fingers flex around my throat, and I swallow, inhaling a ragged breath.

"Please," I drop my voice an octave, giving him my best puppy dog eyes.

"Please, what?"

I tip my head a little, coaxing him closer. Like a moth to a flame, he follows, leaning in until we're almost nose to nose. It's so quiet out, darkness and shadows enveloping us against the side of the building.

"Harder," I whisper.

"W-what?" He falters, confusion flitting across his expression.

"I know it shouldn't feel good. But it does. It feels so good." I lift my hand to his and cover his fingers, making him squeeze my throat tighter, letting a moan slip free.

"Shit, that's hot," he murmurs, forgetting himself.

In my mind, I'm celebrating. Men are nothing if not predictable.

"I'm so turned on right now," I whisper. "Theo, I need—"

"Shh." He presses the length of his body against mine, trapping me there. His hand still pinning me in place. "I know what you need, sunshine," he drawls.

"Kiss me," I breathe, fluttering my eyelashes for good measure. "I need you to kiss me." Hooking my finger in his waistband, I pull him closer, laying the trap.

"I knew you were desperate for some Heir dick."

"Mm-hmm," I nod, brushing my mouth over his while my hand slips down to his crotch. The obvious bulge there.

A little bolt of lust shoots through me. But it isn't because I want him. It's just the power I have over him. It's heady and a reminder that I'll never let another boy deceive me again.

"You're so big and hard," I preen, stroking him through his trousers.

"Shit, Raine. That feels... fuck," he chokes out, dropping his hungry gaze to my mouth. "I'm going to fucking ruin you." He kisses me the exact moment I grab a handful of his dick and balls, squeezing as hard as I can.

"The fuck?" He jerks away, snarling at me. But I have him in a vise.

"Don't ever touch me like that again."

"You fucking bitch. You played me... you— Ow. Shit. Stop, okay. Just stop."

"Promise me."

"I promise. Fucking psycho. You think I want anywhere near your pussy after this. It probably has teeth."

With a little shove, I release Theo and he staggers back, staring at me with utter disbelief.

"You're crazy."

"I bite too." I bare my teeth at him with a little wink. "This little game between us, ends here. You stay out of my way, and I'll stay out of yours."

"Fine by me."

"Good." I nod.

"Good," he grits out. "Just do me a favour, yeah, and tell Millie I apologised so she'll get off my back."

"Consider it done."

It's his turn to nod. He drags a hand down his face and for a second, I think he might say something else, but he thinks better of it, and takes off in the shadows.

Another smug smile falls over my lips. He made it so damn easy. He's also as gullible as shit if he thinks I'm really going to walk away without getting revenge for what happened in the cafeteria.

"Raine, wait up," Millie calls after me as I head out of the dorm building the next morning.

I slow down a little, waiting for her to catch up.

"I heard about yesterday." Her expression darkens. "I'm so sorry. That was a really shitty thing to do."

"I've survived worse." I shrug, giving nothing else away.

"Well, I just wanted to say sorry again. My brother can be—"

"Relax, I don't judge people on their siblings. Even if they are complete arseholes."

She smothers a laugh. "He apologised though, right? I told him I wasn't going to talk to him again unless he apologised."

"Yeah." The lie is bitter on my tongue. "He apologised."

"Good." She nods once, falling into step beside me as I head toward the main buildings. I guess we're walking together.

Silence blankets us for a moment but then she says, "I can't imagine what it must be like, coming to a place like All Hallows' halfway through the year."

Better than the alternative, but I don't tell her that.

"Oh, I don't know. It isn't so different to public school."

"What was it like?" She hesitates. "Being in care?"

"It wasn't all bad, if that's what you're wondering."

"I just... My dad isn't very good at being a parent. Sometimes I wonder if I didn't have Theo if he would have given me up."

"I'm sure that's not true. Some adults just don't know how to put someone else's needs above their own needs. My mum was the same."

"I can't even remember my mum." Millie leaves the words hanging and I read between the lines. For whatever reason, she wants to talk about this with me.

And despite Theo's warnings ringing in my ear, I can't find it in myself to change the subject.

"She died, right?" Millie had alluded to it in group therapy.

"She killed herself when I was four."

"Shit, I'm sorry."

"Theo was nine. He changed after it happened. He'd probably hate me telling you this, but he wasn't always this cold, angry boy. He used to be easy-going. He used to smile."

"Grief does funny things to people."

"Yeah, I became withdrawn. I couldn't understand how she could leave us. I still can't. And sometimes I'm so angry I can't see straight."

"You know it's bullshit when they tell you time will heal you."

"Yeah, I figured as much."

"Time doesn't heal you, it just dulls the pain."

"Look at us, bonding." Millie grins up at me. "Theo will love this."

"Maybe we should keep this between the two of us."

"You really don't like my brother, huh?"

"The feeling is mutual."

"I wouldn't be so sure about that," she says.

"What is that supposed to mean?"

"Nothing." She shrugs.

"Hmm. It's almost first bell, you should probably hurry. You don't want to be late."

"I'm always late." Millie grins wider.

"Well, I can't afford to be late unless I want Miss Linley and Mr. Porter breathing down my neck, so I'll see you at group tomorrow, okay?"

"Or we could hang out later?"

"I'm not sure that's a good idea, Millie."

It's one thing to walk to class with her and see her in group but I don't want to provoke Theo anymore than I already plan to.

Not after last night.

"Because of Theo?" There's a teasing lilt in her voice.

"Among other reasons."

"Name them."

"Excuse me?"

"The reasons we can't hang out. Name then."

"Fine. You're Theo's sister. His little sister. I'm five years older than you. We're in group therapy together. And I don't do friends."

"One. Theo is my brother, not my keeper. He doesn't get to say who I do or don't hangout with. Two. I'm asking you to hang out, not engage in an illicit relationship with me. You're pretty and all, but I like boys. Sorry."

My mouth falls open at her audacity, and she chuckles.

"Three. Being in therapy together means we have a common interest which gives us a legitimate reason to hang out. And four. Perhaps it's time you did do friends."

"You're kind of scary for a twelve-year-old."

"Why do you think I drive Theo up the wall so much?

Please say yes. I find it hard to make friends too and being an Heir's sister isn't exactly easy."

"He won't like it," I remind her.

"All the more reason to do it."

She does have a point.

I make the fatal mistake of smiling and she catches it. "A-ha. You're thinking about it, aren't you?"

"I... fine. We can hangout. But let's keep it low-key, yeah?"

"You mean a secret. I can totally do that. See you later, friend," she calls, taking off toward the main school building.

This is a bad idea.

But there's something about Millie.

It must be those Ashworth genes.

12

THEO

A loud groan rips from my lips as my phone vibrates on my bedside table, waking me up and letting me know that the whisky last night was a really fucking bad idea.

Fucking good night though.

With this weekend's party planned for this evening, we just hung out as a group here and got wasted. Or at least I did.

What the fuck else was I meant to do while being the fucking gooseberry?

Again.

Liv and Reese, Tally and Oak, clueless fucking Elliot and Abi, and then me. All alone nursing a glass of whisky with only the promise of my right hand for company when they all started slipping off to bed.

Well, that's not entirely true. I have a whole heap of numbers in my phone that would have gladly walked away from whatever they were doing to have a little fun down in our basement. But the idea didn't appeal. Not one bit.

The only person who seems to get my dick stirring in any way right now is her.

And it fucking shouldn't because I'm sure my poor little soldier is still sporting an injury from the first and only time she's ever touched him.

I shift in my seat as my balls ache, remembering her vice grip all too well. Doesn't fucking stop me from getting hard for her though.

The way her eyes darkened the second I wrapped my hand around her throat, her thundering pulse, and the way she begged for me to hold harder.

Fuck. If she weren't fucking playing me, it could have been up there with one of the hottest moments of my life.

But she had to go and fucking ruin it.

It wasn't all fake though. That desire... it was real.

When I had her pinned against the wall with my body pressed against her smaller, curvier one, she wanted me. I'd put everything I own on it.

The vibrating starts up again, reminding me of why I'm fucking awake this early on a Saturday morning and finally, I reach for my phone.

It's probably not, but the thought of it possibly being Millie means I'm forced to wake the fuck up and rip my eyes open.

The reality though, is so much fucking worse.

The temptation to ignore him is strong. But it's already rung off once. If I allow it to happen again then...

"Dad," I bark the second I've connected the call and hit speaker.

"I had to call twice, Theodore," he chastises.

Glancing at the clock, I find it's only seven-thirty. Why the fuck is he so surprised?

"You're meant to be at the golf club. We agreed—"

"No, we didn't," I say, finally finding my voice.

"I instructed Katherine to email you to make you aware."

Every single muscle in my body locks up.

Daily. I get emails from my father's fucking personal assistant daily.

Demands, requests, fucking bullshit that I don't give one single shit about.

"I've had a busy week. I'm not up to date," I say, already aware that no excuse will be good enough for Anthony Ashworth.

"What exactly do you think the rest of your life is going to be like, Theodore?"

Fucking awful, I think to myself.

"I'll call you when I'm there, you can let me know what hole you're on."

He grunts his irritation down the line, but it could be worse. I could refuse. But as much as I might want to do just that and roll over in bed to sleep, I know my life wouldn't be worth living. It's only been just over a week since we experienced the darkest side of our father's personality. I'm not willing to be the trigger to drag it out again. And I certainly won't be the reason for him turning up at All Hallows' and demanding to see me or worse, Millie.

Nothing more is said, and when I pick my phone up from my chest, I find that he's cut the call.

Cunt.

With a grunt of my own, I throw the covers off and get to my feet. Any high I might have felt remembering my few moments with Raine the other night has been long forgotten.

It's for the best. She's certainly gone out of her way to ignore my existence ever since.

It's what we agreed on.

I'll stay out of her way, and she stays out of mine.

So why... why do I feel like I'm missing out on a fuck load of fun by turning the other way whenever I see her?

'Harder. Kiss me.'

Her breathy voice is as clear as if she's standing right in

front of me as I step into my shower and lift my face to the spray of water.

She was right there, her lips right beneath mine, her hand stroking my dick.

Absently, I reach out and wrap my fingers around my hard length.

Yeah, maybe I did a really shitty job of forgetting about her with that phone call.

'You're so big and hard.'

"Fuck yeah, sunshine. You've no idea," I mutter as I work myself harder, desperate for some kind of relief before I'm forced to face my father.

In only a few minutes, with her breathy voice in my head and the vivid memory of how hard her heart was racing with my proximity, I come into the shower tray.

For a few seconds, I'm lighter. My muscles relax and I forget about the bullshit. But all too soon it comes back, after cleaning up, I turn the shower off and head out.

I'm only putting off the inevitable. If I'm even later then I risk pissing him off more than I already have.

What I need to do is toe the line. Be the son he expects me to be, and apparently read my emails. My day will come. I just have to bide my time, confident that everything I've planned will ruin him and his reputation.

The Chapel is dark and silent as I make my way down the stairs. I'm hardly surprised, it was long past midnight when Tally and Oak disappeared upstairs to continue alone, quickly followed by Liv and Reese.

Padding through the room, I locate the fridge and rip it open in the hope of finding an energy drink.

We don't have a game until next weekend so Elliot's healthy shit shouldn't have invaded it yet. But even still, I come up empty and am forced to choose between a bottle of water or a smoothie.

The door is almost closed as I spin around, pissed off with the options and I startle when the light from the fridge illuminates a body sitting at the table.

"What the fuck are you doing?" I bark, glaring daggers at Elliot.

"Drinking coffee," he states as if it should be fucking obvious.

"In the dark like a fucking psycho?" I accuse. "Why aren't you sleeping?"

Lifting his mug, he takes a sip. "Abi is asleep in my bed," he explains.

"And you're not in it with her because..."

He shakes his head and takes another sip.

"Since when do you let anyone in your room? We're barely allowed in there, yet Abi is sleeping in your bed alone, again."

"She's different," he whispers.

"You don't fucking say," I mutter with a smirk. "You should go up there. I bet she's lonely."

Scrubbing his hand down his face, he stares down at the table for a beat. "She's too good for that."

"When the fuck has that ever stopped you in the past?" I counter.

"Like I said, Abs is different. Where are you going?" he asks, changing the subject.

"Golf with the old cunt."

A grunt of disgust rips from his lips. "You can say no to him, you know."

"And where the fuck would that get me, exactly?"

Elliot shrugs.

There's a girl in his bed. A girl he blatantly wants and yet he's sitting down here having a pity party for one.

There's only one person in this world that Elliot is truly scared of. None of us know the truth behind why, but we've all got pretty solid imaginations. But that person isn't a quiet, pretty redhead who is wrapped up in sheets that smell like him right this second.

Abi might be shy. Hell, the complete opposite of the girls we usually spend time with, but she's not scary.

Well, unless there's more there than him wanting to fuck her…

The drive across town to the golf club is quick, quicker than I want it to be.

Dread sits heavy in my gut as I pull up beside my father's Range Rover. There are a few guys off in the distance standing around while one of their group tees off, but other than that, the place is quiet.

Saturday mornings are usually the same, the time reserved for the wealthiest of the town to come and make their business deals and talk dirty tactics while trying to one-up each other out on the course.

Pushing the door open, I grab my clubs from the boot and make my way toward the course, putting off calling my father for as long as possible.

"Theo," someone calls, and when I look up, I find Whitney rushing out of the reception with a wide smile on her face.

"Fuck my life," I mutter under my breath as she bounds up to me and plants a kiss on my lips like she fucking owns them.

"No," I bark, pressing a palm against her chest, forcing her back.

Her bottom lip pops out in a pout and her brows draw together. "I've missed you. I thought you'd be in more over the holidays," she whines, forcing me to remember the fucking irritating noise she makes when she comes.

Yeah, there was a fucking reason I avoided her when I showed my face over Christmas.

"I'm meeting my dad. You seen him?" I say, pulling my phone from my pocket.

"Yeah, he was here first thing. Must be halfway around by

now," she explains, chasing after me like a desperate little puppy.

"Don't you have a job to do, Whitney?" I snap as the call connects.

"About time. Did you have to do your hair and make-up?" Dad snarks.

"What hole are you on?" I demand, in no mood for his bullshit.

"Eight."

Of fucking course.

"I'll get a buggy and meet you." No fucking chance am I walking all the way over there. I cut the call before he says anything and take off, leaving Whitney to watch.

"Come find me when you're done, yeah?" she shouts like a desperate whore.

No fucking chance.

There's only one girl who's in my head and under my skin and it's not fucking Whitney or any of the chasers. It would be so much fucking easier if it were. I could have fucked them and got them out of my system by now.

I'm so fucking agitated and hungover that I push the buggy to its limits, racing across the course in my need to run away from everything that's buzzing around in my head. But it only means I get to him faster.

For some reason, I thought he'd be alone. But I soon find that I'm wrong.

The thought of spending time with him in any sense puts me in a bad fucking mood. But dealing with him when he's schmoozing and trying to act like the perfect fucking citizen that I know he's not is even worse. I'm pissed off and gunning for a fight before I even step foot off the fucking buggy.

"Theodore," he announces happily, holding his arms out as if he's going to fucking hug me.

My spine straightens as I vividly remember the last time I saw him. The night I forced Millie to pack up her shit sooner than planned and get the hell out of his house before he reminded her of the monster that lingers just under the surface.

She deserves better than a cunt like him as a father.

Hell, we both do.

I might not be able to replace him. But I can sure do something else about his presence in our lives.

13

RAINE

"I should go," I say for the third time in less than twenty minutes.

"Come on, Raine. Just a little bit longer." Millie pouts as she stuffs another spaceship into her mouth and throws the dice onto the game board. "You're worrying over nothing."

I'm not worrying, but I can't exactly tell her that.

"My brother and his friends are all at the party, probably doing things I do not want to be thinking about. No way he'll turn up here tonight."

If he does it would throw a serious spanner in the works. But it isn't likely.

True to his word, Theo has stayed out of my way, and I've returned the favour.

"I heard the Heirs' parties can get kind of crazy," I say.

It's all anyone's talked about all week. Abi even invited me. Of course, I said no. But not before pumping her for some information to aid my cause.

I still don't know how to feel about the fact she's friends with them. She's so... and they're so...

It's a little hard to understand. But she's one of the few people at All Hallows' who has tried to get to know me.

My eyes dart from our game of Monopoly to the clock on the wall. "It's getting late."

"It's barely even half ten," she protests.

"Late enough."

"But I'm dominating. We can't end it here."

"We can pick it back up tomorrow."

"For real?" Her eyes light up at that little tidbit.

"Yeah." I chuckle. "For real. I had fun tonight."

It's the truth, I did.

Who knew playing board games with a wiser-than-her-years twelve-year-old, while eating our body weight in sweets and popcorn would be a good time.

But Millie makes it easy, and I genuinely enjoy her company. Probably something to do with the fact that despite the shadows in her eyes, she doesn't pretend to be something she's not. She's real. Honest. And I appreciate that.

Between us, we manage to move the game board and our little piles of fake money over to her desk.

"You'll definitely come back and finish it tomorrow?"

"I said I would." I offer her a reassuring smile.

"Okay, then. I guess I am pretty tired." A yawn rumbles in her chest as she stretches her arms above her head.

"You never go home on a weekend?"

"Sometimes." She shrugs. "When I'm summoned."

Millie's expression drops as she follows me to her door.

"Sounds like you're better off here."

"Oh, I definitely am. But—"

"But what?" I ask, sensing her discomfort.

"It doesn't matter. I'll see you tomorrow, Raine."

I could push her, try and coax the truth from her. But I get it. Some things are too hard to talk about—too hard to admit. So I don't.

"Thanks for tonight."

"Until tomorrow." She offers me a weak smile, some of the light dimmed in her eyes.

It's too early to put my plan in motion yet but I need everyone to think I'm here. Which is why I make a quick stop in the communal kitchen, grabbing a can of pop and cereal bar, before heading to my room.

Once inside, I close the door behind me and flop down on my bed, checking social media. A stream of photos fills the screen. Keeley and her friends, the Saints rugby team... the Heirs.

The party is in full swing by all accounts and part of me still can't believe that the faculty allows such things to happen on campus. But I guess money talks—and buys silence.

Theo proved that this week when he demanded everyone to get off my back. I didn't witness him give the direct order but it's the only thing that makes sense. I've seen the frustration in Keeley's eyes, the desperation to go another round with me. But she's held back. Her and the bitch brigade resorting to whispered insults and the odd death stare.

I haven't allowed myself even an inch to think about how Theo felt pressed up against me that night, his fingers wrapped around my throat. Or what it might mean. Or the fact he wasn't the only one turned on at the burning hatred and anger swirling between us.

He's everything I hate.

Entitled.

Rich.

Cocky.

I'd have to be an idiot to ever forget that.

Glancing at the wall clock, I huff a little sigh of frustration. It's going to be a long night.

Worth it though.

I wait until almost a quarter to midnight, slipping out of my window and shimmying down the wooden trellis, trying my best not to tear down the climbing ivy growing on the side of the building.

The entire campus is littered with security cameras but the one on this corner of the building has a blind spot right where my room sits.

It was one of the first things I checked out when I arrived. An old trick I learned bouncing from foster home to foster home. To always know at least one escape route... just in case.

Dressed head to toe in black, the shadows gobble me up, providing enough camouflage for me to make it to the edge of the woods without being spotted.

Adrenaline pumps through me, making my heart gallop in my chest and my palms sweat. I pull the straps of my backpack a little tighter as I cut through the trees, sticking to the periphery. This route should bring me out alongside the Chapel while giving me enough coverage.

I hear the music and laughter before I see the building. It's not the crowd I expected from the photos earlier, which suggests either everyone's still inside or people have started to leave.

Either way, I plan to be in and out and tucked up in my bed before anyone even realises I'm here.

Spotting the row of sickeningly expensive cars, I drop to my knees and sling my bag off my shoulders, emptying out the contents. Uncapping the lid of the paint pen and shoving a second in my pocket, I slip out of the tree line and dart in between the BMW and Maserati. It seems like a shame to ruin such beautiful machines. But needs must.

Besides, they deserve it.

After inhaling another deep breath, I break my cover and head toward the Subaru.

Part of me feels a little bit guilty targeting Oak, Elliot, and

Reese's cars too. But I need it to look like an indiscriminate attack.

Without second-guessing myself, I get to work. Every second is torture, but I smile the whole time as my hand moves the thick-tipped pen in broad strokes and swishes. The music spilling from inside the Chapel is a haunting backdrop to the moment.

Despite my concentration, I can't help but think of him.

Theo.

Is he with a girl? Who am I kidding... he's probably with Keeley. I've heard the stories. Whispers of the basement beneath the Chapel and what goes on inside it.

Sex dungeon indeed, my nose wrinkles with disgust.

But something else coils inside me. Something sticky and bitter.

Jealousy.

I'm jealous. It's a human reaction to being surrounded by people who have everything at their fingertips. The kids partying beyond the ornate chapel doors have more money than sense. Most of them won't have known a day's hardship in their posh, entitled lives. They look down on people like me. People with so many invisible scars I feel stitched together sometimes.

I shouldn't be lusting after one of them. I should be getting angry. Furious.

I am furious.

I finally get to Theo's Maserati and hesitate. If I do this...

Who the fuck am I kidding?

He deserves it.

For sitting there and watching that guy shove me over. For laughing along with the rest of the students at All Hallows'. For constantly warning me to stay away from Millie. For letting Keeley stake her claim on him.

For making me want him.

I suppress that particular thought. That's my own stupid

fault. I'm clearly not wired right. First Vaughn, and now a conceited, cruel boy like Theo Ashworth.

When will I learn?

When will I realise that despite my situation, my childhood, I deserve more?

By the time I'm done, I fall back onto my arse and inhale a shuddering breath. It's not my best work but it'll do.

Voices fill the air, laughter making my hairs stand on end. I freeze, my breath lodged in my throat as I wait for the group of people leaving the party to take off.

Eventually, it goes quiet again and my shoulders sag a little.

I stay low as I hurry back to my backpack, sling it over my shoulder and slip into the trees, letting the shadows swallow me.

Like I was never even there.

By the time I get back to my room, it's late. But I still have one more thing to do.

I change into my pyjamas, grab my glass and head for the kitchen. The two girls chatting and laughing go silent when I enter.

"Oh, it's you," the blonde says.

Lovely.

I move around them to refill my glass with water. "Aren't you a little overdressed for bed?" My brow arches.

"We were at the party," the other says, earning her a hard look from the blonde.

"The party..." I play dumb.

"It doesn't matter."

"Right."

"It was invite only."

"Cait!"

"What? It's not like she has anyone to tell." The girl with the loose lips shrugs.

"Trust me, I don't care about any party."

"Everybody cares about an Heirs' party."

I barely refrain from rolling my eyes.

"Like you wouldn't jump at the chance to be with Theo or Elliot."

"We're not all desperate whores," I sneer, leaving them both speechless.

Without another word, I walk out of there with my head held high and return to my room.

I can't stand it. The way they assume they know me. The way they judge me without even knowing me.

It doesn't matter though. The whole interaction was a means to an end.

My alibi is tight.

At least, I hope it is.

Because something tells me, when the sun rises, and the Heirs see my handiwork, all hell will break loose.

14

THEO

"I think I'm dying," Reese complains from his spot on the sofa where he's resting his head in Liv's lap. Although he doesn't seem to be getting the sympathy from her he wants.

"I told you not to do those shots. What the hell did you expect?" she barks.

It would be easy to believe she's the righteous one listening to them. But one look at her face and it's clear she's suffering almost as much.

Oak and even Little Miss Prim don't look much better. And while Elliot is yet to appear, I'm pretty confident he'll be a wreck too.

He was the soberest out of all of us. But then something changed.

Abi left early and her disappearance flipped a switch in our leader. One I'm sure he's regretting right now.

With my head spinning and my stomach turning over, I make everyone coffee, hoping it fucking helps. The machine grinds away while I rest my palms on the counter and hang my head.

Just like last night, disappointment and irritation drips through my veins, poisoning me from the inside out.

My day with Dad was exactly as I predicted. He was a smarmy, pretentious cock and I had to laugh at his jokes and blow smoke up his arse as his equally dick-ish colleagues did the same.

It was awful. And it only got worse when they left us in the clubhouse to 'catch up.'

The second they were out of the building, he turned his dark, evil eyes on me and demanded to know everything about school this week, why he was getting alerts about Millie being late for class, and demanding to know why we insisted on going back early instead of spending the rest of the holidays with him and Maria.

Completely delusional to the fact that he is the reason we left early, I spewed some bullshit about assignments, deadlines, and exams and tried to move on.

The only thing worse than dealing with Dad's fiery temper is bringing it up in conversation. I'm pretty sure he blacks out when he fully loses his shit, either that or he's got a very fucking selective memory.

"Dude, it's finished. Bring it the fuck over," Reese demands, forcing me to lift my head up and discover that he's right.

"Fucking prick," I mutter, grabbing the mug and delivering it to Tally instead.

"Hey, I thought I was your ride or die, man. I'm fucking right dying here."

"Maybe if you stopped being such a whiny wanker, he would have given you the first one," Oak deadpans.

"No wanking here, bro. My girl makes sure I don't have to — ow," Reese complains when a coaster flies toward his head. "How is that making this any better?" he mutters, rubbing the sore spot.

"Stop talking about my sister."

"She's right here," Liv pipes up, the coaster in her hand as if she's going to send it straight back.

"Can you stop fighting?" Tally asks. "My head hurts too much for this."

Oak's expression completely changes as he turns to his girl and presses his lips to her temple.

"Sorry, Prim."

"Pussy," Reese scoffs, making Liv roll her eyes.

Oakley doesn't care though, he lets Reese's comment roll off his back as he takes Tally's chin in his hand and finds her lips, fully distracting her from her hangover.

I stand there and watch them with a weird tight feeling in my chest as the disappointment I was trying to ignore in the kitchen comes flooding back.

She didn't come last night. Almost all the sixth form was here, apart from those few we've banned from our parties for one reason or another.

It was our first one since she started here, and she didn't come.

I truly believed that her curiosity would win out. That she'd show her face just to see what all the fuss has been about.

But she didn't.

All night I watched, waiting for my moment to strike. To forget about the truce we'd agreed to because I knew the moment she stepped in here that all bets would be off.

But she never fucking came.

I shouldn't be pissed. I had enough chasers to keep me company.

More than I can count suggested that I take them down to the basement to show them a good time.

But I didn't.

Not a single one of them.

Like a fucking pussy, I stayed up here waiting.

Waiting for the girl who never came while I let others who were more than willing to choke on my dick pass me by.

What the fuck has happened to me?

"Film it if you want, you can enjoy it later when you're alone," Liv quips as I continue standing there, staring at one of my best friends suck his girlfriend's face off.

Screw it, what the fuck happened to us?

Only a few months ago, we were excited to be starting our lives as Heirs. Planning the parties, the girls, the epicness that our year was going to be and yet, here we are.

These two pussies are loved up, Elliot is walking around with a perpetual boner for a girl he probably shouldn't be anywhere near, and I am... I'm obsessing over a girl I can't stand.

Yeah, yeah. You keep telling yourself that.

You're just as delusional as your cunt of a father.

Ripping my eyes from the happy couple, I make my way back to the kitchen to finish everyone's coffee. Letting the job at hand distract me from my fucked-up issues as much as possible.

We sit in silence drinking, letting the caffeine flood our systems and hopefully perk us up a little when there's a knock at the front door.

"Who the fuck is that at this time?" Reese complains.

"It's past lunchtime," Tally helpfully points out.

My eyes catch on Oak's, concern passing between us. Elliot never sleeps this late. Ever.

"I'll go then, shall I?" Liv offers when no one makes an effort to move.

"Thanks, sweet cheeks. Love you," Reese mutters, making Oak gag.

Liv's voice floats around us as we wait to see who it is but before we find out, footsteps pad down the stairs before a rough-looking Elliot appears in a pair of sweats.

"Morning, boss. Looking good," Oak teases.

"Fuck off," Elliot grunts, combing his fingers through his hair before taking off toward the kitchen. Although he comes to an abrupt stop when Liv leads our visitor into the room.

"Red?" he breathes.

"M-morning."

I turn around just in time to see her cheeks heat as she tries not to look at his half-naked body.

"What's up, Abs?" Tally asks, turning her attention to her friend.

"Umm... have you guys been outside yet?" she asks hesitantly, hiding behind her hair as if she's scared of us again. I thought she'd got over that habit a while ago when she discovered that our bark is worse than our bite.

"Nah, we barely made it down here," Reese says, as if it isn't obvious from the state of us.

"Okay, well. I think you probably need to come out and see something."

"What is it?" Elliot demands, stepping closer to her.

Lifting her hand, Abi smooths her hair over the scarred side of her face. "I had nothing to do with it, I swear. I just... you need to see."

"Abs, whatever it is, we know it wasn't you," Liv assures her, wrapping her arm supportively around her shoulder.

"Grab some shoes, let's go see what's going on," Elliot demands, marching around Abi toward the front door.

"Holy fuck, it's cold," I complain the second we head outside.

Our breath clouds around us and there is still frost on the ground.

"Not our fault you're incapable of grabbing a coat," Liv quips.

I glance at her with hers wrapped around her, Tally too, while the four of us are barely dressed.

"This better be good," Oakley mutters as Abi leads us toward where we all park our cars.

Elliot moves faster, his concern for his baby getting the better of him. My curiosity burns red hot, and I keep up pace with him until we burst through the trees.

"What the actual fuck?" I bellow as our cars appear before us.

The usually pristine black paint is covered in graffiti.

"Ruling All Hallows' with their daddy's trust funds, giant egos and tiny dicks," Liv reads aloud, barely containing her amusement as if the rest of us are incapable of doing it ourselves.

"Who the fuck did this?" Elliot seethes quietly while Oak and Reese race around to the front of the cars.

"They don't even look like us," Oak barks, making Liv and Tally rush around to see what he's talking about.

"Oh my God," Liv roars in amusement. "They're amazing."

"My nose is not that big, and you know it."

Following their lead, Elliot and I come to stand in front of our vandalised cars.

"Whoever it is is a fucking idiot because they got the wrong cars," I say as my heart pounds and the need for vengeance burns through me as I stare at what is obviously meant to be a caricature of me on the bonnet of Elliot's Aston Martin.

The air crackles around the four of us while Liv and Tally laugh and Abi chews nervously on her fingers.

"Find out who the fuck did this. I want them," Elliot demands.

"You got it," Reese agrees, his entire body vibrating with anger.

"And call the first years. They're washing this shit off."

Without another word or even a glance in our direction, he takes off. The red haze of anger that surrounds him quickly following.

"I-is he okay?" Abi whispers, staring after him as if she wants to follow.

My lips part to suggest she go after him but Reese's eyes meet mine and he shakes his head, stopping me.

"Yeah, he'll be fine. Just needs to cool off. Seriously, though. Who the fuck would be brave enough to do this?"

"Huxton?" Liv asks, hesitant to mention our local rival team.

"Nah, they went to ground after all that shit with Dale."

"Aren't you playing them again in a couple of weeks?" Tally asks.

The three of us look at each other, silently discussing if the girls are right. But while it makes sense. I don't think this has anything to do with the Huxton Harriers. I think it's closer to home.

"Are you really going to make the year twelves clean all this off?" Abi asks innocently.

"Hell, yeah," Oak agrees. "They haven't had any tasks yet this year. Maybe we make them do it with their tongues."

"You're a... a—"

"Sick fuck," Liv offers when Tally's good side gets the better of her.

"Idiot," she settles on making everyone laugh.

Everyone but me.

I've got someone in my head. Again.

Someone who I doubt would think twice about starting a war with us.

With me.

"Theo, where the fuck are you going?" Reese barks when I take off.

I wave them off before stuffing my hands in my pocket and marching in the direction of the girls' dorms.

By the time I get there, my jaw is locked with irritation and my short nails are cutting into my palms with my need for answers.

I'm so adamant that it was her that I throw the front door open, barely seeing any of the faces I pass as I take the stairs three at a time and race down the hall.

The second I'm at her door, I unlock it without a second thought and throw it open.

Her scream of shock barely registers in my ears, but I sure as shit notice the fact that she's fresh from the shower and standing before me in only her underwear.

"What the fuck did you do?" I growl, surging forward until I'm right in her space.

I want her to be scared, intimidated but she barely fucking flinches and fuck, if it doesn't make my dick hard.

15

RAINE

Theo glares down at me, hard and unforgiving.

"Mind telling me how the hell you got into my room?" I ask, unable to keep the disbelief out of my voice.

I expected him to hunt me down eventually. But not like this.

"I'm an Heir, nowhere is off limits to me."

I snort, I can't help it.

He's so arrogant, so freaking cocky that it irritates the life out of me and yet...

No, don't go there.

Don't you dare go there, Raine.

His dark thunderous gaze drops to my mouth and a flash of lust shoots through me.

"Like what you see, Teddy?" I ask with a saccharine smile.

"You're a fucking cocktease." He rakes his eyes down my body, lingering on every curve. The heat in his gaze is at odds with the hatred in his voice.

"And you're in my room. Uninvited. Again."

"I know it was you," he spits.

"You're going to have to be a bit more specific than that, Ashworth."

"Don't fucking play games with me." His hand snaps out, wrapping around my throat as he pushes me back, slamming my body against the wall.

"We already danced these dances. And if I remember correctly." I grin. "You lost."

"Who the fuck are you?" Confusion clouds his expression and for a second, I think he might back down.

But of course, I'm wrong.

"I know it was you, sunshine."

"I don't know what you're talking about."

"Elliot is out for blood. What do you think he's going to do when he finds out it was you, huh? You might not be scared of me, but you should definitely be scared of him."

"I'm not scared of anyone."

"Big words given your current predicament." He flexes his fingers against my throat, cutting off my air. I force myself not to panic, to breathe through my nose and focus.

He won't really hurt me; he's just trying to intimidate the truth out of me. But that's a hill I'll gladly die on.

"Seriously," I implore, "I don't know what you're talking about."

"So you were here last night, all night?"

"Yeah. Where else would I be?"

Theo's brows crinkle as he studies me, searching my face for answers.

Answers I'll never give him.

"You can ask around," I add. "I hung out with Millie. Chatted to a couple of the girls in the kitchen. I was here all night. Check the CCTV if you need to. I didn't leave the building."

"I don't believe you."

"Not my problem." I attempt to shrug but his grip on me tightens. "But I'm not lying."

"Maybe you need a little more motivation."

"What—"

The words die on my tongue as he steps into me, pushing his knee right in between my thighs.

"Theo, what the fu—" I swallow a whimper as he grinds against me, his lips dropping to my ear as he cages me in.

I'm in my underwear, barely a scrap of material protecting my modesty... or my pussy.

Crap.

"I know it was you, little liar. I don't know how you did it, but I'll find out. I'll prove it. And when I do, even I won't be able to protect you from Eaton's wrath."

His hands slide around my arse, dragging my body closer so I'm practically mounted on his leg.

Jesus. It feels good.

Too good.

"Theo," my voice cracks, "don't."

"Don't what, sunshine? Don't do this?"

He moves, holding me right there sending a delicious rush of friction through me.

"Oh God." My head drops back against the wall, powerless against the intense sensations.

I shouldn't like it—I definitely shouldn't want more—but I know all too well that sometimes the body overrides conscious thought. Acting on some primal need deep inside.

"This is fucked up," I whisper, rocking against him, seeking more.

"Yeah, but it feels good, doesn't it?" He chuckles darkly, licking the shell of my ear before biting down hard.

"Fuck," I breathe, pleasure firing off around my body.

"Tell me how you did it," he coaxes, somehow applying even more pressure to my clit. He's like a freaking magician. He hasn't even touched me yet, not really, and I'm already so close.

This is not good.

Not good at all.

But I can't stop.

"I already told you... I don't know what— ah, God, Theo. That feels—"

A growl of frustration vibrates deep in his throat as he pulls away enough to shove his hand between us. "Fuck, you're soaked." He rips my underwear aside and spears two fingers inside me so quickly, I'm stunned.

"Now, this is how it's going to go," he drawls, staring at me with eyes as black as night. "I'm going to fuck you with my fingers and I'm not going to stop, until you tell me the truth."

He says it like it's a threat.

Like his fingers don't feel good inside me. Thick and long and curled in a way that tells me all I need to know about Theo Ashworth's experience with the female anatomy.

"I already told you," I sass, "I don't know what you're talking about."

"We'll see." He smirks, rolling his thumb expertly over my clit as he sinks his fingers deeper.

I melt, trying desperately to smother the moan building inside me. But it feels so good. He doesn't kiss me, but he watches me the entire time, his hungry gaze darting from my eyes to my mouth and back again.

Theo might be trying to unravel me, but I see how difficult it is for him to restrain himself too.

It shouldn't matter but it does, it gives me a strange sense of satisfaction knowing that I affect him as much as he clearly affects me.

"Tell me the truth, Raine."

"I don't know— ah," I cry out as he pushes another finger inside me, stretching me. Filling me.

Jesus. He's good at this.

Too freaking good.

"You were saying?" Victory dances in his eyes and I can't resist taking the bait.

It's always been my downfall so why should this be any different.

"From where I'm standing, the only person losing here is you."

"How do you figure?" He practically pants the words, his expression growing darker and hungrier by the second, the sexual energy and hatred crackling between us a toxic, heady combination.

"Because you're assuming I don't like this."

He falters.

Mr. Entitled Rich Boy himself actually falters.

"Cat got your tongue, Teddy?"

"Shut up, just shut the fuck up." The air shifts, his touch becoming cold and clinical as my words sink in.

I almost regret it but I'm so close that it doesn't matter.

My hips rock against his hand as I chase the euphoria building inside me. The inevitable fall I know is so, so close.

"God, yes," I murmur, eyes closed, mind drifting as pleasure saturates every cell in my body.

"Such a dirty fucking whore." My eyes snap open, my body vibrating with anger. But I'm almost there. So close I can feel—

"What the hell?" I snap as Theo pulls abruptly away from me.

He might as well have doused me in a bucket of ice-cold water.

"What the fuck was that?" A violent shudder goes through me.

"Tell me the truth, sunshine, and I'll finish what I started." His smirk is so fucking smug, it only fuels the anger bubbling under my skin.

"Get out," I snarl, suddenly realising how ridiculous I must look, standing here in my underwear, in some lust-drunk haze.

"I know it was you." He pins me with a knowing look.

"Just because you keep saying something over and over doesn't make it true. Now get out."

"Or what? What will you do, little liar? You have no friends here. No allies. If—*when*—the truth comes out, you're done here. You get that, right? Make an enemy of the Heirs, make an enemy of the entire school."

"You think that scares me? You think I give two shits about your pathetic little posh boys' club or this fucking school? I didn't ask to come here, and I certainly don't plan on staying."

Something passes over Theo's face as he closes the distance between us again.

"You made a real stupid mistake pulling that shit. Watch your back, sunshine." He storms over to my door and grabs the handle, throwing me a final warning look over his shoulder. "And stay the fuck away from my sister."

"So, I heard a rumour this morning," Millie says as we finish our game of Monopoly.

I hadn't wanted to hang out after Theo's little visit, but she wouldn't take no for an answer.

And for the last hour, it's been fine.

Safe.

She hasn't once mentioned her annoying brother or his friends.

Hasn't stopped me thinking about Theo though. His body pressed close to mine, his fingers moving inside me. The obvious hunger in his eyes.

Jesus. I hadn't expected that this morning.

And then the sneaky bastard left me high and dry.

"You did?" I ask, shaking the unwanted thoughts out of my head.

"Yeah, I was in the kitchen and Poppy and Cadence were

in there. Apparently, someone tagged the Heirs' cars last night."

"They what?"

"Tagged, you know, graffitied."

"I know what tagged means, Mills." I roll my eyes.

"Someone drew caricatures of them all. Freaking caricatures on the car bonnets. I would have paid to see Elliot's face. He's so fucking weird about his precious Aston."

"Hey, language," I scold, and she pokes her tongue out at me.

"Anyway, everyone's talking about it. Whoever was brave enough to pull a stunt like that must have a death wish." She gives me a strange look.

"What?" I ask.

"Nothing. Although... I noticed you always have a sketchbook with you at therapy."

"Oh, that's nothing. I like to doodle. It's a good mindfulness exercise."

"Mindfulness exercise, right."

"Is there something you want to say, Millie?"

"No. Nope." She presses her lips together. "I know you'd never be stupid enough to do something like that."

"Of course I wouldn't."

"And even if you were—"

"Which, I'm not."

"Right." Her mouth twitches. "So it's a moot point."

"It is," I agree, hoping she'll drop it. But I probably should have expected this. Millie sees things. Far more than her brother or anyone else gives her credit for.

"So I guess we should talk about something else."

"We should."

"But you know, if it was you, I wouldn't tell. I can keep a secret."

"Well, it wasn't me. I was here all night with you, remember? Then I went up to my room."

"Right. Well, whoever it was, they'd better watch their back," she says ominously. "Because if there's one thing my brother and his friends don't like… it's being made to look stupid."

16

THEO

I blow through the house like a storm, the sound of my name being called follows me. But I don't turn around, and I don't say a word.

I can't.

I'm so fucking angry.

So fucking horny.

She was right there.

Right there for the taking.

Her pussy was so wet, so fucking wet and needy as she sucked my fingers deeper, drowning them in her sweet, sweet juices.

She was desperate for it, I didn't need her to tell me how much she loves my rough, vicious treatment to know that.

I could have taken her.

Hell, I could have done anything I wanted with her.

Forced her to her knees. Bent her over the dresser. Throw her to the bed. Or I could have just fucked her right there and then against the wall. Take exactly what my body was craving.

Just one brutal and hard fuck to get her the hell out of my system.

That's all it'll take.

It's all it ever takes.

I've had good pussy. Fucking great pussy. But by the time I stick my dick into it, I'm bored of the person it's attached to.

It'll be the same with Raine.

So why didn't you just take her?

Use her and dismiss her like all the others.

I hit the stairs, taking two at a time as I lift my fingers, breathing in her scent.

My cock is still rock hard and desperate to sink deep inside of her and that move certainly doesn't fucking help.

So sweet.

Pushing them past my lips, I suck, desperate for another taste of her. Anything.

I storm into my room, slamming my door so hard behind me I wouldn't be surprised if it shook this ancient building's foundations.

Dragging my bedside table drawer open with way too much force, the entire thing crashes to the floor sending condoms, lube and a few baggies of all sorts sprawling across the floor.

"Fuck it," I bark, reaching for the biggest bottle of lube and taking it with me to the bathroom.

Slamming it down on the counter, I strip out of my clothes before slathering a more than generous amount of lube down my cock and wrapping my hand around myself.

A loud groan falls from my lips as I hold myself tight and start moving exactly as I like.

It's good. But it's not that fucking good.

It's not her heat, her wetness, her tightness.

Fuck was she tight.

You're a fucking moron, Theo. She could have been either choking on or strangling your dick with her cunt right now if you stayed.

"NO," I roar, my pace increasing with my need to blow off some of this desperation.

Sweat beads across my brow, every muscle in my body is locked up tight as I replay those moments with my fingers inside her in her room over and over.

Her little moans and begs for more repeats continuously in my mind as I bring myself to the edge.

"Fuck. Fuck... Fuuuck," I cry as my release slams into me. My cock jerks in my hand, adding a decent amount of cum to the pile of lube that's already covering the floor.

You'll probably break your neck on that mess later, prick.

Ignoring it, I walk around the spillage and turn the shower on, needing to wash her scent from my body.

I turn the dial up and step under the burning hot water.

Pain surges through me, the need to step away is almost too much to bear but I force myself to endure it before turning it in the other direction and blasting myself with cold, willing it to fix me.

To stop me from wanting her.

No matter how good that release just was. It was unfulfilling, pointless.

My balls still ache, my cock is still hard, and my head is still full of her.

It was her; I know it was. She's the only one ballsy enough to pull a stunt like that.

She has to be.

Everyone else knows us and our reputation well enough not to be so stupid.

But she doesn't care. She isn't scared. Of me. Of Elliot. Of any of us.

And fuck if that doesn't only make her hotter.

With my teeth chattering, I finally turn the ice-cold shower off and step out, grabbing a towel and rubbing it over my hair as I move toward the door.

"What the fuck?" I bark when I find not one but three people sitting on my bed staring at me as if I've grown two extra dicks while I was in the bathroom.

"You can come closer if you want to get a better look," I offer, moving my hips from side to side to make my semi wave at them.

"What happened?" Elliot demands, pushing to his feet and holding my eyes.

"Nothing happened," I grunt, moving toward my drawers to find some underwear but his demanding cold tone stops me.

"So you often come in like that and jerk off alone in the bathroom?"

"Yeah, actually. I do. Don't you?"

"You fucking know he does," Oak says behind him. "Moans Abi's name as he does it too."

"Will you shut the fuck up?" Elliot barks in irritation. Although the truth is, Oak has probably just touched a little too close to home. Elliot hates being seen and understood, even if it is by us.

He prefers to live his life behind closed doors where he can keep his monsters and issues hidden.

We've tried talking to him about it, forcing him to open up, but he won't. Something tells me that he'll take some of his darkest secrets to his grave.

I get it. I do, I just wish... I wish he'd let us help him.

"Talk, Theo. What the fuck is going on?" he seethes, stepping closer.

His dark eyes hold a deadly warning, one that most would take seriously, but not me.

"I went out to get laid, she wasn't up for it."

"Bull. Shit," he snaps. "Who did you go and see? And why were they so important you ran off like you did."

"Like you even noticed," I quip, remembering him storming off like the hounds of hell were chasing him.

"I noticed," he growls.

"Oh yes, because Elliot fucking Eaton sees everything," I tease, getting right in his face.

"You know who it was," he accuses.

"Theo?" Oak and Reese ask simultaneously.

Elliot holds our stare for a few more seconds before I break it.

"I thought I did, yeah. But it turns out she has an alibi," I confess, finally ripping my drawer open and pulling out a pair of boxers.

"Who?"

I hesitate.

Why? Fuck knows.

I should have no issues selling her out, especially if she's right and there is no evidence of her leaving the dorms last night.

"Raine," I finally admit.

Elliot's brows pinch together.

"Raine. New girl, Raine? Why would she—"

"She hates Theo. That would be reason enough for some," Oak says.

"And she didn't know which car was his, so she went for the whole set," Reese surmises.

"Can she draw?" Elliot asks.

"Fuck knows. She's drawn Theo in good if that little one-man show in there was anything to go by."

"Fuck you," I snap at Oak when he sits back and smirks at me.

"She says it wasn't her."

"And you believe her?" Elliot asks incredulously.

"Fuck no. Go and get your laptop and get the campus CCTV up."

His brows lift at my demand. His lips part to rip me a new one for even considering bossing him around but Reese cuts him off.

"Just go get it, man. Then we can get our answers."

"Fine," Elliot grits out before marching from the room.

The two idiots who are left lounging on my bed continue to study me.

"What?" I bark.

"You fucked up if you left there without getting between her thighs, man," Reese helpfully supplies.

"I don't want her," I seethe.

"So that's why you're standing here with us still tenting your boxers, huh?" Oak grins. "You're still thinking about her."

"She let you get close and slammed the door in your face." The smugness on Reese's face makes my fist clench.

"I don't want her."

"Okay, we'll rephrase. You want to fuck her, and you can't cope with the fact that, unlike every other girl on campus, she hasn't immediately spread her legs for the great Theodore Ashworth."

"Shut the fuck up, you've no idea what you're talking about.'

"Do we not?" Oak teases as Elliot returns with his laptop in hand.

Ignoring the tension in the room, he pulls out my desk chair and drops into it. "Where are we looking then? I've got the girls' dorms."

"Round the left-hand side. Her room is on the second floor," I say, moving in closer.

"How about we start with the front door? Assuming this girl isn't some fucking nighttime ninja who scales the building to escape the cameras," Oak suggests.

Silently, Elliot plays the footage of the main entrance from the time school finishes until the girls begin returning from our party. But there is no sign of her.

"Do the side of the building," I demand, earning myself another scowl from the devil.

But again, other than the movement of the trees and bushes from the wind, there is nothing.

"Can you get the communal cameras inside?" Reese asks,

already aware that he can. This isn't the first fucking time we've hacked into watch girls.

A smirk twitches at my lips as memories of times gone by fill my head.

"Can I get the camera's inside," Elliot mutters like an arsehole.

"Alright, smart-arse."

Elliot taps away before the image of the girl's kitchen appears.

"There look," Reese says as my breath catches in my throat when Raine appears in the kitchen standing right in sight of the camera.

It's almost as if she knows exactly where it is...

"What time is it?"

The guys continue discussing it but all I hear is white noise as I watch her clearly have an argument with two chasers.

My fists curl up and my cock thickens once more with my need to go over there and force her confession from her lips.

"Follow her back to her room. I want to see her go in."

"She fucking goes in. We just watched the whole night, she doesn't leave the building."

I can't argue with the evidence, I just watched it clear as day just like they did. But I still don't believe it.

I refuse to believe it.

It has to have been her.

It has to.

"See. Door closed and locked for the night," Elliot says as the hallway falls silent with her departure.

"So if it wasn't Raine, who's next on our hit list?" Reese asks as Elliot sits back and crosses his arms over his chest.

"I have a few ideas," he confesses.

"And did you want to share those findings?" Oak barks.

"No, not really. Let's see what tomorrow brings then maybe I'll give up my theories. But in the meantime," he says, turning to me and staring me right in the eyes. "Leave Raine the fuck alone."

"Whatever. Can you all get the fuck out of my room now?" I demand, marching to the door and pulling it open.

"Aw, you need to spend a little more one on one time with your tiny dick?" Reese teases.

"Get out," I hiss.

"We're going, man," Oak says, but he pauses when he gets to me and clamps his hand around my shoulder. "Just shout if you run out of lube. I don't need my stash these days. Tally gets so fucking wet, bro. I can just slide straight on—"

"What he's trying to say is that she's not let him do anal yet," Reese explains. "Unlike my girl. She fucking takes it so—"

Smack.

"Dude, I'm just trying to tell you how fucking awesome your sister is."

Finally, Elliot shoves them both out of my room but not before he pauses in front of me too.

"I mean it, Theo. It wasn't her so stay the fuck away."

I glare right back, the muscle in my jaw ticking with tension.

"We'll see," I mutter just before he finally closes the door behind him leaving me with nothing but silence and my regrets about what didn't happen in Raine's dorm room.

17

RAINE

"You know, Raine, this will go a lot smoother if you actually engage with the process."

I glare at Miss Linley, hoping she'll get the idea and leave me the hell alone. I'm not in the mood. Not today. Not after a morning of Theo watching me like a hawk.

It all started when the sixth form were herded into the hall for an assembly about the upcoming exams. Somehow, I ended up seated two rows in front of him which meant I had to spend the best part of thirty minutes with his heated stare burning into the back of my head.

As if that wasn't enough, at morning break, he followed me into the cafeteria and watched me like some weird creepy stalker.

He knows the truth.

He just can't prove it.

But there's something else in his gaze, something predatory, something that calls to the dark corners of my heart.

Why did I have to get tangled up with him?

It's the last thing I need.

He's dangerous. And he's not going to let this thing between us go, I realise that now.

Maybe part of me even banked on it.

Stupid girl. You know what happens when you play with bad boys...

I shut down *that* little voice.

"Raine, come on, these sessions are here to help you. It's a safe space. Anything you share is confidential." I arch a brow at that, and she releases a heavy sigh. "You don't trust me, I get it. But I am here to help."

"Do you know how many times I've heard that before?"

"I've read your file."

File.

God, I hated that word. I hated that my life was reduced to a series of events and incidents. Dates on a page.

"Okay," she says. "I can see this is difficult for you. Why don't we start off with something easy. How are you settling in at All Hallows'?"

"It's fine." I shrug.

"Fine." Her mouth twitches. "Have you made any friends? I've seen you talking to Millie Ashworth."

"We're in the same dorm and both attend therapy, so..."

"So, not friends?"

"I guess. In the loosest sense of the word."

"How about anyone in the sixth form? In your classes, perhaps?"

"I'm not really looking to make friends."

"And why is that?"

"Because I don't plan on being here long."

"You don't think it'll work out here?"

Another shrug. What was there to say? I couldn't tell her the truth. That as soon as I turn eighteen I'm done. Gone.

I don't want to be here. And I'm sure as hell not planning on accepting any of the ageing out support they offer.

"Look, Raine, I know All Hallows' is a certain kind of school."

I snort at that. Is she for real?

"No one is asking you to pretend to be someone you're not. But it's important for you to try and assimilate—"

"And how do you expect I do that?" I ask. "These kids aren't like me. And it's abundantly clear I'm not like them."

"You could try—"

"Please, save me the speech." I slouch back in the chair, folding my arms over my chest.

"You sound angry."

"I'm not. But I am hungry. Are we done?"

Her eyes flick to the clock. "No, we have another ten minutes."

"Great."

"Raine, it's my job to provide the board with a report."

"What happened to, 'everything you say here is confidential.'"

"It is. But you know I have to report on your participation."

"I am participating. I'm here, aren't I? I attend the group therapy."

"You attend, yes. But you're not present."

"Sorry, I don't know what you want me to say." I stand, done with this session. "It's my therapy session, isn't it?"

"It is."

"And I can choose what to share or not share."

"You can."

"Then I don't see what the problem is. I'm fine. I've settled in fine. I attend my classes. Keep my head down and get on with it."

Her lips twist again, and I sense she wants to argue. To counter with some typical therapist bullshit about engaging with the journey and process.

But instead, she surprises me.

"I'll see you next time."

With a stiff nod, I haul my bag over my shoulder and get the hell out of there.

By the time I get back to the dorm, my mood is infinitely worse.

I hate therapy.

I hate that Miss Linley thinks that talking about my life will change anything.

It won't.

My mum was a drug-addict whore who cared more about her next fix than protecting her own daughter from the revolving door of strange men who kept money in her purse and heroine in her veins. No amount of talking will ever change that.

I made my peace with it a long time ago. Some of us get dealt a shitty hand and that's just how it is. The only person I can count on—the only person I trust—is myself.

And come my birthday, I'm leaving this place and never looking back.

I just have to survive the likes of Theo Ashworth and his dickhead friends first.

I blow through the building, making a beeline for my room. But when I reach the door, I notice it ajar.

"What— You!" I sneer at Theo as he slams my drawer shut.

"Busted." He smirks, the idiot actually smirks. And I see red.

Marching straight over to him, I yank his arm down and spit, "What the fuck are you doing?"

"Nice to see you too, sunshine."

"Theo!"

"Raine." His brow arches with amusement.

God, he's infuriating.

"How did you even get in here?"

"I told you before, nowhere is inaccessible to the Heirs."

"You love that, don't you?"

"What?"

"That stupid pretentious title."

"Jealous?"

"Uh, no."

"You keep saying that, and yet, you've been watching me."

"You think I've been watch... wow." Bitter laughter spills from my lips. "You're so fucking full of yourself."

"You could be full of me. If you fess up."

"Go to hell, Theo. It's been a long day and I'm not looking to go another round with you." I shoulder past him to the small bathroom.

But the arrogant tosser follows me.

"Seriously, get out."

"How'd you do it?"

"We've been over this. I didn't do shit." I start undressing, not caring one bit that he's standing there.

Boys like Theo get off on power. Intimidation. If I give him none, he can't use it against me.

"What the fuck are you doing?" he growls as I stand there in my underwear and lean into the shower to switch on the jets.

It feels like déjà vu. Him in my room. Me half naked. But this time, I'm not in the mood for his bullshit.

"Taking a shower. You can either stand there and watch or get the hell out. Either way, I don't care."

Grabbing a bobble off the vanity, I pull my hair into a messy bun and reach around to unhook my bra, smiling a little to myself as I catch Theo's dumbstruck expression. He doesn't take his eyes off my body though, drinking his fill as I strip naked and slip into the shower.

I keep my back to him as I slather myself with shower gel, enjoying how the hot water feels sluicing over my body.

The door clicks shut, and my smile grows.

Raine: One.

Theo: Zero.

Feeling smug, I turn around. Only to be met with his hungry stare.

Shit.

Shit.

I hadn't actually considered that he might stay.

He leans back against the door, dragging his thumb over his bottom lip as he watches me. There's a challenge in his eyes. A flicker of satisfaction that fuels the fire inside me.

He thinks he's won.

That he's beat me at my own game again.

A normal girl might scream. Might grab the nearest thing and attack him with it.

But I'm not a normal girl and I was done being a pawn in someone else's game the moment I left Brewton.

The same electricity that exists whenever we're in the same room sparks to life, tugging something deep inside me.

I'm trapped. My own fault really. But Theo is good. A little too good, maybe.

But I'll be damned if I lose another round to him.

How far am I willing to go though?

That's the question.

Keeping my eyes locked on his, I trail a finger down my chest, gliding it over one breast and twirling it around my nipple. Lust pools in my stomach but I ignore it, trying to focus on the goal and not my own pleasure.

Theo's nostrils flare as he drops his gaze to my finger, following it. Tracking it.

'Fuck.' The word forms on his lips as I move to the other breast, touching myself with a featherlight stroke.

One I feel all the way down to the tips of my toes.

Theo licks his lips, his hunger turning the air thick and heavy. Much like the outline of his dick beneath his sweats.

My mouth twitches at that.

I shouldn't like this game we play. But I do.

I need to keep the upper hand though. I need to keep my wits about me.

Bloody hell, Raine, what have you gotten yourself into?

I quiet the thoughts, focusing on the rush of the water, Theo's heated stare, how nice my fingertips feel dancing down my stomach, toying with the fine hairs between the juncture of my thighs.

I hesitate, teasing myself. Teasing Theo.

'Show me,' he mouths. "Let me see that sweet pussy."

I can't resist his dirty words, spreading myself open a little and letting my finger slide over my swollen clit.

"Fuck yeah." His lips curve, his eyes narrowing in right at that point. He licks his lips again as if he's imagining tasting me.

I know I am. Imagining him on his knees, worshipping me.

The tidal wave of sensations carries me away as I play with myself, putting on a show for him. He makes no attempt to move, to wrestle back control.

For all I know, he could be filming this. Ready to use it against me.

The sudden thought gives me pause as I search his body, his hands for his phone. But there's nothing. Just one hand inside his sweats, stroking himself.

Fuck. That's hot.

My head drops back against the tiles as I push two fingers inside myself, riding my hand as he takes out his cock and fists himself.

Jesus, he's big. Thick and long and perfect. And I know without a shadow of a doubt that this won't be enough. I need to feel him.

To know what it's like... just once.

It's my turn to lick my lips and when my eyes lift back to his, a knowing glint sparks in his gaze.

'Come for me,' he mouths.

And this time, I do exactly what he says.

18

THEO

My grip on my cock tightens as her body quakes.

The heat that was colouring her cheeks floods down to her chest, and if it's possible, her nipples get even harder, even more desperate for my touch.

My tongue sneaks out, licking across my bottom lip. My need to taste her is almost unbearable. Irresistible.

Her chin drops and her eyes shutter as pleasure takes hold.

Beautiful. So fucking—

"Fuuuuck," I growl as my own release slams into me from almost out of nowhere.

My cock jerks violently in my hand as I spurt jets of cum onto her bathroom floor.

The pleasure, while it lasts, is fucking epic. Just with her in the room, it's so much more than anything I achieved alone since my visit here yesterday morning. But the second the high fades away, I'm left with the realisation of what I've just done.

I've just caved. I've just let her win.

Anger descends like a red haze.

Raine studies me closely, probably able to see every single one of my thoughts now my mask has slipped. I'm pretty sure

I've never felt more out of control or vulnerable in my entire life.

My heart pounds and my hands tremble as I put my cock away and push from the door.

"Theo?" Raine whispers, her brow pinched as she tries to figure out my next move.

If she thinks I'm about to throw her up against the wall and fuck her into the middle of next week, she's going to be disappointed.

As I get closer, my lips peel back in disgust. "You're nothing but a filthy fucking whore, sunshine."

I don't get the response I wanted. Not anywhere close.

Instead of shock, I get a smirk. A smug fucking smirk.

"Didn't stop you from enjoying the show though, did it, *Teddy*?"

A growl rumbles deep in my throat and my arm twitches at my side with my need to lift it and wrap my hand around her throat. "You need to watch your back, Raine."

"So you keep saying," she taunts, tilting her head to the side.

With a sneer, I take a step back and storm out of the bathroom.

I should continue and blow out of her room, but something stops me.

Something I can't quite put my finger on but I'm pretty sure it has something to do with the sweet scent of Raine in the air, or possibly her angry growl and the following thud that can only be her fist against the wall.

She thinks I've gone, and she thinks it's safe to let her walls drop.

And it's that which seals the deal, stopping me from marching toward the door and leaving her with nothing but her regrets over everything she's done since she turned up here.

The shower cuts off after a few more minutes and my

heart kicks up another notch. Pulling my phone from my pocket, I place it on the chest of drawers before leaning back and waiting.

Despite my recent orgasm, my cock is already starting to tent my sweats again. Watching her fall wasn't enough. Nowhere fucking near enough.

I hold my breath the second the door opens, and it isn't until she steps out wrapped in only a tiny towel. She shrieks in shock when she finds me standing here waiting for her when I finally let out the air trapped in my lungs.

"Shit," she curses, holding her towel tighter around her body.

"No point hiding now, sunshine. I've already seen it all," I taunt, pushing from the chest of drawers, prowling toward her as I let my eyes trail down her body as if the towel didn't exist.

"You need to leave."

"Yeah, you're probably right," I confess. I'm under no illusion that right now, I should be far, far away from here. But I'm not.

I'm standing before her, not ready to leave.

It's fucking terrifying, but I never have been good at telling myself no when I want something. And right now, I want her clenching around my cock and crying out my name like I'm her fucking god.

A smirk curls at my lips.

She'll fucking hate that. But we both know it'll happen.

"But I don't think I will," I state.

Reaching out, I grab the towel. In one swift move, I rip it from her body, leaving her standing there bare for me. She doesn't cower or show any kind of embarrassment. In fact, I'm pretty sure her shoulders widen and her chin lifts with confidence.

Damn, who is this fucking girl?

Taking one more step forward, she's forced to tip her head

back to hold my eyes and she gasps the second my shirt-covered chest brushes her still-hard nipples.

"That wasn't enough, was it, sunshine?"

"Fuck you."

Licking across my teeth, I smile again. "Yeah, that's exactly what I was thinking. But not until you beg."

"Then you're going to be disappointed because that is never going to happen."

Reaching out, I finally grasp her throat. Her eyes darken with desire, and when I tighten my grip, a quiet whimper spills from her lips.

"You want to bet?" I sneer, my nose brushing hers, our lips a hair's breadth from connecting.

My chest heaves, my temperature soars and my cock fucking aches.

Fuck that release in her bathroom, it's long forgotten.

She slams her lips closed and swallows roughly, refusing to take the bait.

I get it. She doesn't want to lose.

Who does?

"Exactly as I thought."

"Theo," she screams as I throw her back onto the bed.

The second she lands, I'm on her. My thighs pinning her hips and my hands restraining her wrists above her head.

"Look at you," I taunt. "So brave going up against me, trying to be all high and mighty, but look where you've landed."

No words fall from her lips, just an angry growl.

"Right on your back just like all the others. And the second I give you the chance, you know you're going to spread your legs for me, beg me to eat your cunt, cry for me to fill you so full of my cock that the only name you'll remember is mine."

"Never," she screams, thrashing beneath me as best she can.

"That's it, sunshine. Fight. It makes it so much fucking sweeter."

"You're fucked up, Teddy," she cries.

"Yeah. Takes one to know one though, doesn't it?"

Ducking my head, I focus on the soft skin of her throat, my mouth watering for a taste. But just before my lips land on her, she jerks her head to the side and her brow collides with my cheek.

Pain explodes across the side of my face. "The fuck?" I bark, glaring pure hate down into her eyes.

"I warned you, Teddy. I bite."

"Yeah, but so the fuck do I."

Forgetting about her throat, I go straight for her lips.

She gasps in shock, allowing me to plunge my tongue into her mouth and the second I do, she sinks her teeth into it.

"Oh, sunshine," I pant. "You're something else."

With pain still burning my face, I take her mouth again in a wet and filthy kiss. The vicious nips from both of us ensure that the coppery taste of blood fills both our mouths as we continue to battle for power.

It's a real shame she's already lost because she's putting up a good fight.

"Oh my God," she gasps, when I finally release her in favour of kissing and biting down her neck and onto her breasts. "FUCK," she screams when I suck on one of her nipples, ensuring the teeth marks I've left behind continue here.

"You want more, sunshine?" I ask, looking up into her burning violet eyes.

Fuck me, they shouldn't draw me in as much as they do.

Before she gets a chance to answer, I take her other breast into my mouth, sucking on her nipple before branding the underside with my brutal kisses.

Her back arches off the bed as she thrashes beneath me.

"I thought you liked the pain, sunshine."

She can barely catch her breath by the time I release her.

"You're so fucking wet for me right now. I can smell it."

"No. No," she chants, her head thrashing violently from side to side.

"Clearly, I've got more work to do then."

Taking a risk, I release her wrists in favour of dragging my shirt from my body. Unsurprisingly her hands fly toward me, and I don't stop her. She's not the only one who craves the pain.

Her fists slam into me but that all soon changes when I claim her mouth again and release her hips in favour of sitting between her legs.

"Fuck. The heat of your pussy is burning through my sweats," I groan into our kiss as my cock begs to sink inside her.

She moans, my name trapped in her throat.

I'm going to fucking get it though.

Her restraint might be strong. But my need to win is stronger.

The second I rub my fingers through her folds, coating myself in her juices, her nails sink into my shoulders.

I smirk, fucking loving that she's a scratcher.

Hell yes, sunshine. Shred me to fucking pieces.

"Oh shit," she gasps when I plunge two fingers inside her. But I don't give her what she needs. Instead, I pull them back out just as fast, and I lift them to my lips.

"Fuck. Th—" She cuts herself off before my name falls free.

"More? I've got plenty more."

"Dropping to my front, I get an up close and unobscured view of her pussy. It's fucking perfect, and I fear that I'm already addicted, and I haven't been inside it yet. Not really.

"OH MY GOD," she screams as I lick up the length of her, arse to clit.

Her fingers sink into my hair, dragging me closer with such

force I'm sure she's about to rip it clean out. Her hips lift from the bed, seeking more as our eyes hold over her body.

Me begging her to let go, her still adamantly refusing that she wants this.

Well, I'm about to shatter that belief into oblivion.

Sucking on her clit, I push two fingers inside her tight pussy and search for her G-spot.

I know the second I find it because she gushes and screams.

Oh hell, yeah.

I eat her like a man possessed, pushing her right to the edge before pulling her back.

"Come on, please. Please," she begs when I pull back once more.

Her entire body is slick with sweat, her limbs trembling with her need for the release I'm withholding.

"You know what I want, sunshine. Give it to me or I'll walk out that door and leave you high and dry again."

"No, keep going. Please."

Happy she's lost her approaching release again, I dive back in.

"YES," she screams. "Yes. Yes. Please... Yes. Theo please."

And there it fucking is.

"THEOOOOOOO." Her cries of pleasure bounce off the walls around me as she shatters.

Usually, I'd let her ride it out, but I'm too fucking desperate.

Abandoning her cunt, I push up onto my knees, shove my sweats over my hips and rub the head of my dick through her folds, soaking myself in her wetness.

"Theo, please," she begs as I push just the tip in, loving the way her greedy pussy tries to drag me deeper.

"Fuck, sunshine," I groan, teasing both of us.

"C-condom," she gasps."

"Don't have one. I'm clean," I confess.

"Like I fucking believe that," she pants.

"Unless you have one, you're going to have to because I'm not stopping now."

Her eyes widen and her hips roll.

Done deal, sunshine.

You're mine now.

I thrust forward, filling her in one swift move. "Holy fucking shit," I groan, feeling her against me with nothing in the way.

Fuck. I've been missing out all this time.

"THEO," she screams again, her nails clawing at my back.

Oh yeah, I'm not just a little bit addicted to this pussy. I'm fucking gone for it.

19

RAINE

"Fuck, you feel good." He pounds into me, fingers digging into my hips, his body plastered to mine.

I can't speak, can't think.

Can't bloody process what's happening because he's everywhere.

His cruel touch, his dirty, wet kisses, his weight pinning me to the bed, his glorious, perfect cock filling me to the hilt, stretching me.

Jesus, sex has never been like this, and I want more.

So much more.

My fingernails drag down his back as he fucks into me like he hates me. "Yes," I cry, lifting my hips, meeting him thrust for thrust.

"You're so fucking tight," he lifts my leg around his hip, grounding against me, creating the most delicious friction against my clit.

"Oh my God," I whimper, holding on as he destroys me.

Because I have no doubt that's what this is.

My ruination.

My downfall.

But what a way to go.

"Fuck, sunshine... *fuck*," he groans, lifting my arse off the bed to slam into me.

He's close.

We both are.

"I'm going to fucking ruin you," he breathes the words into my skin, sealing them with a kiss as he sucks at my throat, letting his teeth graze my pulse point.

It's intense. Intimate in a way I hadn't expected.

But before I can analyse the strange rise of emotion inside me, his hand slips between our bodies and he slaps my clit. Hard.

My orgasm hits like a freight train, rolling through me like an unrelenting wave.

I cry out but he swallows his name, grabbing my throat as he kisses me. Devours me.

"Fuck, fuck, fuuuuck." Theo stills and then comes hard with a little grunt of satisfaction.

He collapses on top of me, the air turning cold as ice.

We had sex.

I had sex with Theo Ashworth.

A barrage of shame washes over me. Shame mixed up with anger and frustration and... nope, not going there.

"Get off me." I hiss, trying to shove him away, trying desperately to ignore the ebbing waves of pleasure rolling through me.

"Because of course she chooses to kick me out after I fucked her senseless," he mutters, rolling off me and flopping down beside me.

"Theo, I'm serious. You need to leave. You need to—"

"You're freaking out." He glances over at me. His hair is all dishevelled, his eyes hooded, and skin flushed.

He looks thoroughly fucked. I suppose I look the same.

I trap a groan behind my lips. This is bad.

Really fucking bad.

Except, it was also good.

Really fucking good.

God, I'm a mess.

"We hate each other," I point out.

"We do."

"It was a bad idea."

"The worst." His mouth twitches.

"You really need to leave."

"I will," he says. "Any minute now. Any—"

"Theo!" I snap, panic swelling inside me.

"Jesus, you're a barrel of laughs after sex."

"And you're a prick."

"You weren't complaining a minute ago when you were crying my name. *Oh, Theo. More... more... yes... right there.*"

"You are such a pretentious wanker."

"And you're a sour-faced bitch but you don't see me complaining."

"Get out. Now."

I gather the sheet around my body, sit up, all while glowering at him.

Finally, with a little huff, Theo climbs off the bed and begins scooping up his clothes and pulling them on. Grabbing his phone off the dresser, he shoves it in his pocket, and heads for the door.

"Thanks for the ride." He winks—the bastard actually winks—and slips out of my room like it doesn't matter if anyone sees him.

Shit.

I flop back against my pillows and let out a frustrated sigh.

Well, that escalated quickly.

But maybe it's a good thing. We fucked. Now we can move on. Forget all about the electric chemistry between us.

Something tells me it won't be that easy, but it doesn't matter. Because I meant everything that I said to him. I don't want to be here and as soon as I can, I'm gone.

I don't belong here and I'm sure as hell not stupid enough to think that something might become of me and Theo.

This was nothing more than hate sex. The chance to claw each other out from under our skin.

But as I lie there with his fingerprints on my hips and his bite marks on my neck, I'm not sure it was enough.

By Tuesday morning, the post-sex glow I felt when Theo collapsed on top of me is well and truly gone.

Instead, anger swirls in its place.

I'm angry at him. Furious that he let himself into my room and baited me into another fight. But most of all, I'm just angry with myself.

Theo Ashworth gets under my skin like no other. And part of me enjoys it, I can't deny that. But I can't afford to give any more pieces of myself to boys who will only squander them, and I felt it last night.

A split second where we didn't hate each other. A brief moment where we understood each other.

That shit is dangerous, and it isn't real. Because boys like Theo don't care.

They can't.

And even if he did... it doesn't matter.

All Hallows' isn't my home, it will never be my home. It's just another place I'm passing through.

A knock at the door startles me. I assume it's Millie because she's become quite my little shadow these last few days.

But it isn't Millie at all.

"You," I frown at Tally.

"I figured we should try again."

"Try what exactly?"

"Come on, we both know you're not that stupid. We should go if we want to make it back in time."

"Sorry, am I supposed to know what you're talking about?"

"Breakfast with me and the girls."

What the hell?

My face must say it all because she lets out a soft laugh. "Don't look so worried. Abi is coming."

"Abi... right."

"Let's go." She pushes the door wider and flicks her gaze to the hall.

"I'm not going with you." I fold my arms over my chest. "You can't—"

"Look, we got off on the wrong foot before. And Abi vouched for you. So come to breakfast. We're going to Dessert Island."

"I—"

"Please?"

"Why?" I spit.

"Because something tells me you need a friend, or three."

"Did Theo put you up to this?"

"What?" Her brows knit. "Why would Theo... interesting." A slow, knowing smirk tugs at her mouth, making my stomach sink.

Shit. I gave too much away just then.

"Fine. Let me get my bag," I say, hoping to distract her from whatever dots she thinks she's joining.

Barging past her, I blow down the hall and stairs. Tally catches up with me though.

"So you and Theo..."

"Me and Theo nothing," I snap.

"Right." She chuckles and I don't like the insinuation at all. "You know, I've been there."

"Been where?"

"At an Heir's mercy. Telling myself it didn't mean anything. Telling myself I didn't care."

"It doesn't mean anything, and I don't care."

Shouldering the door, I spot Abi's car and head toward it. She gives me a little wave but the other girl—Olivia—looks less enthused to see me.

I grab the front passenger door and slide inside.

"Hey, that's my— never mind." Tally climbs in the back beside Olivia.

"You came," Abi flashes me a bright smile.

"Not through choice."

"So why are you here?" Olivia asks with a hint of distrust.

I get it.

Her brother is an Heir and she's with one of them.

"Liv, come on. You said—"

"Yeah, I know. But she could at least try and be a little nicer."

"Why?" I look over my shoulder, meeting her hard gaze with my own. "I don't owe you anything."

"We just want to help," Abi offers as she backs out of the parking bay.

"Help, with what?"

"Come on, Raine." Tally scoffs. "It isn't exactly a secret you and Theo are waging some kind of war with one another. You're playing a dangerous game."

"I don't know what you're talking about." I stare out of the window, trying to shove down the strange emotions swelling inside me.

I've never had girl friends.

Not really.

It's hard to get close to people when you know it's only temporary. When you know they'll probably only stab you in the back the second you turn around.

Olivia snorts, but I don't give her the satisfaction of acknowledging it.

"Liv," Tally warns quietly.

I sense Abi watching me and slide my eyes to hers in

question. "Shouldn't you be watching the road?" My brow arches.

"I'm glad you came," she says, giving the road her full attention.

But I don't miss the spark of humour in her eyes. Mischief even. So at odds with her quiet, meek persona.

Like Millie, there's something about Abi that resonates with me.

As we drive the rest of the way in thick silence, I realise she's probably a little broken.

Just like me.

"God, this is good," Tally groans a little too loudly as she licks the cream frosting off her muffin.

"Okay, Tally. We don't need to hear your sex noises before nine," Liv teases.

"Like I haven't heard yours plenty." Tally flashes her a smug grin.

"Bitch."

"Whore."

"Are they always like this?" I ask Abi who smiles around her caramel latte.

"It's been worse since Tally and Oak became official. They're in some kind of contest—"

"Sex contest?" I ask with a frown.

"No," they both answer as Abi squeaks. "Yes, something like that."

The blush she wears is adorable, and I hate to admit it, but I like Abigail Bancroft. I like her a lot.

"We are not in a sex contest. But when your twin is with one of your best friends, things can get... a little weird, I guess."

"That's because they're all sex-obsessed," Abi adds.

Damn.

This is harder than I thought it would be. Sitting here, pretending that Theo wasn't in my room last night, fucking me so hard I saw stars.

"Raine?" Abi's voice startles me.

"Y-yeah?" I croak.

"Where'd you go just now?"

"Uh, nowhere." I smile. Fake. Forced. But enough of a distraction that she doesn't push it.

"So back to Theo..." Olivia says. "What's going on with you two?"

"Like I said before, nothing."

"Nice try, but I don't buy it. He's out for blood. Your blood." She pins me with a knowing look.

"How do you know... Reese." I deduce.

I guess the Heir bro code doesn't apply to girlfriends.

"Honestly, they're worse than a bunch of girls." Tally chuckles.

"I don't know what to tell you..."

"You could try the truth?" Abi suggests.

"Really, there's nothing to tell. It's just a silly rivalry."

"He's an Heir. Nothing is silly where an Heir is concerned. They'll wear you down until you don't know which way is up. We should know," Tally adds.

"Speak for yourself." Liv glowers.

As I watch them bicker and joke about their boyfriends—about the Heirs of All Hallows'—I realise that perhaps I was wrong about them at first. They're not the shallow, vapid girls I assumed them to be. Like Keeley and the other Heir chasers.

But I still need to be careful.

"Look," Olivia says, "Tally and Abi are too scared to ask but I'm not. Was it you?"

And there it is.

The reason I'm sitting here. The reason they invited me to breakfast.

"Me?"

"Come on, you know what I'm talking about. Their cars. Did you do it?"

"Hate to disappoint you, but it wasn't me."

She studies me and for a second, I think she's bought my lie. But then her lip curls with amusement. "Oh, you're good. I'll give you that. And it's admirable, it is. But also stupid. Because once they figure it out. Once Theo can prove it, they'll ruin you."

I neither deny nor confirm her accusation. But I do ask, "Why are you telling me all of this?"

"Because"—she glances at Tally and Abi and they nod—"we want to help you."

20

THEO

"Don't go," Raine begs, her small hand wraps around my lower arm, trying to drag me back to her.

I should leave. I shouldn't have even caved and fucked her. But shit. I can't fucking regret it.

I'll never tell her, but I'm pretty sure that was the best shag I've ever had.

I fucking know I've never come that hard before. Ever.

It was because you're a dickhead and fucked her bare.

And you're going to fucking do it again, aren't you?

I swallow thickly, battling with what I should do with what I already know I'm going to do. "I shouldn't be here," I mutter, trying to do the right thing.

Walk away. Pretend it never happened.

You hate her.

She fucked up your car.

Punish her.

"No, you shouldn't. But it's a bit late to grow a conscience now, isn't it?" Her grip tightens, her nails that I know have already scratched up my back digging into my skin.

That little bit of pain shoots straight to my dick. I'm still rocking a semi just from the memory of being inside her. He really doesn't need any kind of encouragement.

"You'll regret it," I warn.

"Teddy." She chuckles. The fucking stupid nickname makes my teeth grind. "There aren't many things in my life I don't regret. Fucking you barely scratches the surface. I'm sure I'll forget all about yo—"

Her words are cut off when I twist around, grasp her by the throat and pin her back against the bed. Her hungry violet eyes widen, and her chest heaves with desire.

"You desperate for my cock again already, sunshine?"

She gasps down greedy breaths but she doesn't answer me with words, not that I need it. Her eyes, her pebbled nipples and I'm sure how slick her cunt is, is all I need.

"You're a desperate whore, aren't you, Raine? You're no different from all the others. Once you get a taste of Heir cock, it's all you can think about."

"No," she cries, violently shaking her head from side to side.

I smirk. "Argue all you like. We both know the truth."

Releasing her throat, I flip her over and drag her arse up.

Crack.

She screams as my palm collides with the porcelain skin of her backside before my handprint blooms.

Fucking beautiful.

"Look at that," I say, dipping my fingers to her thighs, coating them in my cum that's running from her.

Having only ever fucked with a johnny on before, this is something I've never experienced. And fuck if I don't want to see it again and again.

"You're making quite the mess here. I think you need to clean it up." With my fingers glistening, I grip the back of her neck, lifting her face from the pillow before I thrust them inside. "Lick, sunshine. Taste us."

Her body jolts and I expect her to either try to push them

out or bite them off. But I quickly find that she does neither, and to my absolute shock, she follows orders.

"Good girl," I praise, making her whimper. "Oh, you like that, sunshine? You like pleasing me and being a good girl?"

Dragging my fingers from her lips, I drag her arse back exactly where I want it and rub the head of my cock against her entrance. She wiggles her hips, trying to force me inside.

"Desperate little whore," I mutter, before bringing my hand down on her glowing arse cheek once more.

Mine.

You are fucking mine.

"Theo, please," she begs. The sound is like music to my fucking ears. "Theo. Theo."

Sucking in a breath, I surge forward, but I only get the tip in before the rug is pulled from beneath me when a loud crash makes my eyes fly open and I discover—devastatingly—that I'm actually in my bedroom, not Raine's, and I'm alone.

Or I was until those three smug tossers threw my door open and stormed in.

"You're alone," Reese states, staring down at me with my cock in my hand like it's just another day.

I guess it is for us.

"Yeah," I grunt. "Apparently, I fucking am. Do you mind?"

Reese's chest puffs out like he's considering staying to watch the show, but Elliot speaks for all of them. "We'll give you a minute. But we're talking before school."

"I'll need more than a fucking minute," I mutter. Although, it's a big fat lie. With the memories of that vivid dream still playing out in my mind, I'm already riding the edge. Even with them trying to ruin it.

Fisting the back of Reese's shirt, Elliot pulls the wanker out of my room and slams the door behind them.

The low rumble of their voices fills the air, as my hand starts moving, I push it all aside in favour of the high I was chasing in my dream.

When my cock jerks, spurting cum all over my stomach, I quickly realise it was a pointless exercise. The release is hollow and unfulfilling.

Goddammit, Raine.

Sitting up, I throw my fist into my pillow a couple of times in the hope it'll help rid my body of the frustration. But it does little to help.

I shower and dress on autopilot. Hoping that if I'm slow enough, the others will have fucked off to school and forgot all about the little meeting they want to have with me.

Yeah. Wishful thinking, I know. Reese and Oak might get bored, but there is no fucking way Elliot will.

He's out for blood, and he's not going to stop until he gets it.

I just wish I had evidence to nail Raine for this.

Or... do I just want to nail Raine again? There's a question.

Sadly, and predictably, when I finally get downstairs, dressed and ready for another fun-filled day at All Hallows' all three of them are waiting for me.

"What? No girls in attendance this morning?" I ask, noting the absence of at least one girlfriend who is usually here.

"They went out for breakfast," Oak says, sipping on his coffee, his plate and the other's already empty.

Pulling my chair out, I drop my arse into it, my stomach growling as the scent of what's probably cold bacon wafts through my nose.

Grabbing my knife and fork, I ignore all their stares and embark on devouring my breakfast. I'm starving. I mean, I did work up quite an appetite last night...

"So?" Elliot prompts after long silent minutes.

"So, what? I've got nothing to say," I argue, still keeping my eyes downcast.

Elliot's evil laugh rings through the Chapel. "You run off seconds after we discover our cars got hit. You've been walking around with a scowl for fucking days, and then you try sneaking in looking like you've been attacked by a rabid dog last night. What fucking gives? Who was she and who hit our cars."

"I don't know," I seethe.

I should just give up her name. I know that.

But if I'm wrong...

"Yes, you fucking do," Elliot roars. "Who tagged our fucking cars, Theo?"

Shoving my plate back, my chair screeches against the old stone floor as I stand, glaring at one of my best friends. "I don't fucking know."

"Okay, different question," Oak pipes up. "Who the fuck were you dreaming about this morning? I'd have put money on you talking to a real-life person before we stormed in."

Throwing my hands up, I storm away from the table.

"Where the fuck are you going?" Elliot barks.

"To school. I don't fucking need this bullshit."

I only get halfway to the door when Elliot speaks again. "Say hi to Raine for us." His words cut through me.

It's no secret that I suspected her, but there was no evidence. There *is* no evidence. Just a feeling deep down in my gut that I'm not going to confess to. Not to these motherfuckers anyway.

If anyone is going to break her down and get the truth, then it's going to be me.

"Stay the fuck away from her."

"Oldest trick in the book, man," Reese teases.

"What?" Spinning around, I hold his eyes, desperately trying to ignore the smirk playing on his lips. It makes me want to punch the fuck out of him.

"Using her pussy to make you think what she wants you to think."

"If we find out it was her—" Elliot starts, but I quickly cut him off.

"You'll stay the fuck away from her," I repeat.

"Or what?" he asks, taking a warning step toward me.

My teeth grind, my fists curling up.

"She's playing you, Theo," he warns, hitting me where he knows it'll hurt. "Playing you, just like *him*. Befriending Millie, reeling you in." He shakes his head. "If she is the one doing this, I'll fucking end her."

"She's not," I state, sounding way more confident than I feel.

But what if she is?

Refusing to hear any more of what he's got to say, I spin on my heels and storm out of the house.

My first instinct is to run. To run as far and as fast as I can away from here. Away from her and away from *him*. But I can't. I made myself two promises. A promise to look after my sister no matter fucking what. And a promise to ruin the life of the man who fucked ours up. And in order to do that, I need to wait just a few more weeks.

The walk to the Orwell Building is short and the second I get there, I discover students everywhere. Lifting my arm, I look at the time.

With a sigh, I turn toward our tutor room ready to get the day started. But I only make it a couple of steps before four girls at the other end of the hallway make my steps falter.

"No," I breathe, unable to keep my reaction to seeing her with them inside.

I run my eyes over each of them.

Liv, Tally, and Abi look exactly as they always do. Happy, in control—okay, maybe not Abi so much—but they're settled, they know they belong here.

And then I find Raine. The fourth member to their new little quartet.

My heart pounds as confusion wars.

She isn't friends with them.

She doesn't like them.

I've heard the girls moaning about her attitude and refusal to accept their friendship more than once.

What the fuck are they doing?

"Good morning, Theo," Tally sings when I get close enough to them.

"Did you have a good night?" Liv asks, but I ignore the not-so-subtle undertone of her question as I step up in front of Raine. Toe-to-fucking-toe.

I realise my mistake instantly. Her scent fills my nose, and the warmth of her tempting body burns into mine.

I want to say that she's as affected by my presence as I am hers. But there isn't so much as a flicker of recognition in her eyes.

"What the fuck are you doing?" I seethe.

Her lips twitch up into a smile. "I went for breakfast with the girls," she explains smugly.

"But you hate them," I point out.

They hear me and while two gasp, one has a more violent reaction, smacking me around the head. Liv, I assume. But I ignore her. All of them in favour of the pig-headed girl glaring up at me like she might actually win this fight.

"No, Teddy," she says with a laugh. "Don't be silly." I frown, hating the fake, high-pitched tone she uses. It sounds way too much like Keeley but as fast as I register that, it's gone. Her expression changes and her amusement is forgotten. "I hate *you*. Now if you'll excuse me. I've got somewhere I need to be. And if it's anywhere away from you, thank fuck."

She ducks around me and takes off down the hallway.

It takes a couple of seconds, but eventually, I hear the slow clapping coming from beside me.

"What?" I sneer at Liv, finding her to be the culprit.

She stops and smirks. "You really told her. I bet she's quaking in her biker boots."

"Fuck off, Liv. Just... fuck off."

I make it about six feet before the doors in front of me open and my boys walk in.

They find me, then look over my shoulder at the girls.

"What happened?"

"Get out of my way," I grunt, continuing forward.

There's no point in me saying anything. We all know that Liv is about to do it for me.

I remember a time when it was just the four of us against the world. But now, bro code has been well and truly smashed with the arrival of Liv and Tally.

Nothing is ever going to be the same again. And as much as I love our lives, I fucking hate it.

21

RAINE

"We need to talk." Theo appears out of nowhere, blocking my path as I leave the dorms.

"No, we really don't." I shoulder past him, a smug sense of satisfaction skittering through me when I hear his muted groan.

Serves him right.

Throwing his weight around like a toddler having a tantrum.

"Don't fucking walk away from me." He grabs my arm and wrenches me backwards.

"I have therapy. I can't be late or Miss Linley will ask questions. Questions I'm sure neither of us want to answer." I glare at him, dropping my gaze to where he's holding me. With a heavy sigh, Theo releases me and takes a step back, putting some much-needed distance between us.

"Why were you with the girls this morning?"

"Ask them." I shrug, walking off toward the welfare centre.

"I did."

"And..."

"And they hardly told me anything."

"Well, don't look at me. It wasn't my idea to kidnap me and take me for breakfast."

"Seriously, they—"

"Tally was very insistent. I think I misjudged her."

"You're not fooling anyone, sunshine, and what do you think they'll do when they realise you're using them—"

I whirl around, snarling at him. "Why do you even care?"

"Because they're part of my inner circle. You're not. I don't want you coming around, messing things up."

"So you're warning me off to what, protect them?"

Theo glares back at me, making anger bubble in my veins.

"Get over yourself." I sneer. "They invited me because they've noticed your little scheme to make my life a living hell."

"You weren't saying that when I was balls deep inside you." He steps closer and the air thins around us.

"Theo." It's supposed to be a warning, but it comes out more of a resigned sigh.

"Don't pretend you didn't love every second." Twisting his fingers into my hair, he searches my eyes. "Your pussy was dripping for me."

"My pussy isn't choosy."

His brows draw together. "Are you calling yourself a whore?"

Shit, he's got me there.

"No," I backtrack. "I'm saying that you were a sure thing. Why wouldn't I want to see what all the fuss was about for myself."

"Fuss..." He gawks at me, and a giant smirk traces my lips.

"You were good, but I'm thinking Elliot is probably the Heir with the—"

His hand snaps out, cutting off my taunt as his fingers wrap around my throat. "Don't even think about it," he spits.

"You sound awfully jealous…"

"Raine, I'm serious. Elliot is off-fucking-limits."

"Relax, I wouldn't do that to Abi."

Theo relaxes, his hand falling away from my neck. "You noticed that too, huh?"

"I see a lot of things."

His expression darkens again. "What the fuck is that supposed to mean?"

"Nothing. Nothing, at all. Are we done here? I really need to get to therapy."

He stares at me, through me, and I wonder if I've broken him. With a little shake of my head, I take off, leaving him behind.

But Theo calls after me. "We're not done yet."

I lift my hand and give him the middle finger over my shoulder.

"I mean it, sunshine. This isn't over."

"Theodore Arthur Ashworth, I swear to God if you're tormenting Raine again, I will—"

Millie's high-pitched shriek dies out as I reach the centre, and I glance back to find her all up in her brother's face.

My mouth twitches. She's a force to be reckoned with, and I can't help but think she reminds me of someone I know.

Except, we're not the same, not really.

Millie has people looking out for her. She has Theo. He might be an entitled, pretentious arsehole but he cares about her.

It's a damn sight more than I've ever had.

With that depressing thought, I leave them to their sibling squabble and slip inside the centre.

Telling myself that I don't need anyone anyway.

―――

Theo is relentless.

The next day, he marks my presence, tracking me all over campus.

It's borderline creepy.

Except every time I feel his gaze, it's accompanied by a rather annoying swarm of butterflies.

Theo infuriates me as much as he excites me.

And that is a problem.

But I'm determined to stay strong and give him the cold shoulder.

So we had sex?

It was a mistake. A one-time thing to exorcise the strange chemistry between us. I'm not looking for a repeat.

Even if the boy has all the right moves.

Damn him.

He couldn't be a two-pump chump, could he?

Shaking the thoughts out of my head, I enter the cafeteria surprised when Tally waves at me.

'Join us,' she mouths.

I hesitate because Oakley and Reese are with them which means Elliot and Theo won't be far behind. It will only throw fuel on the fire if I join them unless...

With a forced smile, I cut across the room to their table. "Hi."

"Hey. Come, sit."

"Uh, Prim"—Oakley frowns—"what are you doing?"

"Inviting Raine to sit with us."

"Yes, I can see that." The muscle in his jaw tics. "But why?"

"Because... she's my friend."

Reese smothers a laugh and I narrow my eyes at him. "Problem?" I ask, smoothly.

"Nope." He holds up his hands. "Not at all."

"Ignore the boys," Liv says. "They're just upset we prefer eating in here to their private dining room."

"You have a pri— of course you do." My eyes roll so hard it hurts.

I squeeze in next to Tally and Oakley glowers at me. "You shouldn't be here."

"Oakley Beckworth!"

"Babe, she's—"

"It's fine," Elliot appears. "Let her stay." He gives me a hard once over and then sits down at the other end of the table.

"Well, isn't this cosy?"

"Where's Abs?" Tally asks him.

"How the fuck should I know?" He hasn't taken his eyes off me yet, and I can see why he's the leader of their little Heir club. He's an impenetrable fortress and for the first time since tagging their cars, a little pang of fear goes through me.

But I lock it down tight. So what if I messed up his beloved car, it isn't like he doesn't have the means to get it fixed. Mummy and Daddy will probably foot the bill.

"Funny story, our boy Theo thinks you're to blame for the other night."

"Other night?" I play dumb. But I notice how still the girls go.

Shit.

"Brave. Or really fucking stupid," he mutters.

"Relax, Elliot," Liv says, jumping to my defence. "She didn't do it. You know that."

He doesn't get a chance to answer because Theo arrives and... He. Is. Furious.

"What the fuck is she doing here?"

"Nice to see you too, *friend*." I flash him a feral grin.

There's just something about pushing his buttons.

"Leave."

"Theo, don't be so rude," Tally cries.

"She doesn't belong here."

"It's the cafeteria. It literally belongs to all students."

"Not this table. This table is ours."

"Did you really just say that?"

Reese and Oakley struggle to hide their amusement, watching the two of us sling insults.

"Just sit down and eat," Elliot demands. "At least here, we can keep an eye on her."

The urge to flip him off burns through me but I tamp it down. Something tells me Elliot isn't the kind of boy you mess with. And I've already done enough of that.

Theo keeps one eye on me while they talk about the latest rugby scores.

"That was... intense," Tally whispers. "So much sexual tension."

"Please, I wouldn't touch Theo if he was the last man on earth."

His eyes snap to mine and I flush all over.

Shit.

He heard me.

And from the challenge glittering in his eyes, I just laid the gauntlet.

"Been there. Tried believing that lie. And now Oakley owns me in every way possible." A dreamy expression falls over Tally, and Liv fake gags.

"God, you two are disgusting."

"Speak for yourself, Liv. You and Reese—"

The sudden vibration of my phone startles me. No one has my number except for Trudy and Miss Linley.

Everything fades into the background as I open the text message, careful to keep my phone hidden in my lap.

My eyes almost bug at the video.

Theo fucking into me like a man possessed.

He filmed us, that two-faced fucking tosser filmed me.

Quickly, I exit out of the video, and shove it back in my pocket.

Theo doesn't so much as look at me, but I sense his smugness from across the table.

Well, two can play at that game.

"God, I miss good sex," I blurt, pretending that I've been listening to the girls' conversation.

A quick glance in his direction tells me I have Theo's full attention.

"The last guy I slept with was so sure of himself, yet he barely knew how to..." I lean in closer, whispering the words.

"Oh no, that's awful," Liv says. "What did you do?"

"Fake it." I shrug. "Twice. But he tried so hard, I didn't want to dent his self-esteem."

My phone vibrates again, and I smile to myself.

"I have English with Callum Johnson, he looks like he knows his way around the female body."

"Fucking hell, Ashworth, what did you do that for?" Oakley complains and we look over to find his drink spilled everywhere.

"Sorry," Theo mumbles. "I thought I saw a spider."

I bite down on my lip to stop myself from laughing.

Men. So predictable.

Theo doesn't want me. Not in the way girls want to be wanted, at least. But he's still arrogant enough to protect his fragile ego.

"Oh crap, is that the time? I've got a meeting with the career's advisor," I lie. "But I'll see you tonight?"

"Tonight?" The boys all say in unison.

"Yeah," Tally explains. "We invited Raine to hang out with us."

"I'm going to teach them some yoga," Liv adds.

"Yoga," Reese pouts. "But I thought you saved all your best moves for me."

"Too much fucking information, Whitfield," Oakley groans.

I offer the girls a small wave and take off, hurrying out of the cafeteria and ducking into the girls' bathroom.

It's only in the safety of one of the stalls, I dig out my phone and open up Theo's latest message.

Teddy: You're playing a dangerous game, sunshine. Keep pushing… and you might not like what you find.

Raine: Is that a threat?

I hit send and wait. But when his reply comes, it isn't fear that saturates my veins, it's something else entirely.

Teddy: No, Raine. That's a promise.

22

THEO

The guys all chant around me, celebrating our epic win tonight. But despite the high of fucking ruining the other team from the second the whistle blew, it's not enough to banish the growing tension within me.

Playing helped. Throwing my entire body weight into Penworth's defence definitely helped. But it's not enough.

Nothing fucking is.

Reaching into my bag, I pull out my AirPods and stuff them into my ears in an attempt to block all the happy out.

We're at the back of our team minibus, but Elliot, Oak and Reese are happily ignoring me as they celebrate with everyone else.

My thumb hovers over my music app. I need something heavy and angry but at the last minute, I don't open it. Instead, I open my camera roll and find our video. The thought of watching it finally wakes me up a little. Or at least it does my dick.

I'm embarrassed to admit how many times I've watched it since Monday night. And since playing my hand and sending it to Raine, I can only hope that she's watched it just as many times. I can picture her so vividly sitting back against her headboard with one hand holding her phone, the other between her thighs as she strokes her clit and pushes two fingers inside herself, disappointed that it's not my cock.

The last few days have been the biggest fucking tease of my life.

Okay, so I probably haven't helped myself as I stalked her around school, keeping tabs on her every move in the hope I'd figure out how she managed to tag our cars without leaving any kind of evidence.

Elliot is still trying to find the culprit. But whoever it was covered their tracks. There's a part of me that wants to be proud that she's managed to tie the mighty Elliot Eaton up in knots with this conundrum. But mostly, I'm just pissed off.

And horny.

Really fucking horny.

"Theo. Oh fuck. Yes. More," Raine moans in my ear as I watch the video again.

My cock swells, but I ignore it. Even as sick and twisted as I am, I draw the line at jerking off at the back of a bus full of sweaty rugby players.

Pausing the recording at one of my favourite parts. I make a copy and crop it out. With a smirk, I pull up our conversation and send it to her.

> Theo: We won tonight. Gonna need to celebrate with someone screaming my name like this.

> Sunshine: I'm sure all your adoring fans will be waiting to meet you off the bus. If you're lucky, they'll have lower standards than me and won't have to fake it to make you feel good.

> Theo: You're full of shit. You'd never fake it to make me feel good. You hate me too much.

Mentally, I do a little fist bump as the audio of us together continues to play out in my ears.

Sunshine: I never said you were the last guy I slept with.

Theo: Oh, that's right. You're a self-confessed whore.

When she doesn't start typing a reply, I panic that she's going to leave me high and dry and shoot off another.

Who's the desperate whore now, huh, Theo?

Theo: What are you doing right now?

Sunshine: Trying to ignore you.

Theo: How's that going for you?

Theo: You know what you should do?

Sunshine: Enlighten me.

Theo: You should shower, make yourself smell less bitter and twisted, pull on some sexy lingerie and send me a video of you watching our little porno.

Sunshine: And why exactly would I want to do that?

Theo: You might claim to be a whore, but do you really want the rest of the school to see you begging me for it?

Sunshine: Are you threatening me, Teddy?

Theo: Nope. Just concerned for my fellow classmates. I'd hate for them to get tangled up with a poisonous bitch like you.

Sunshine: Bitch? That really the best you can come up with? I thought you were more creative than that. And you're forgetting something…

> Sunshine: I don't give a shit what anyone thinks of me. Especially not the stuck-up, pretentious, entitled dickheads of All Hallows'. You can all kiss my arse.

My eyes widen at her little rant.

Touch a nerve, did I, sunshine?

> Theo: I'll kiss your ass. Right before I slide my coc—

"What the fuck are you doing?" I bark as my phone is ripped from my hand by a smug-looking Oakley.

Ripping my headphones out, I reach to snatch it back.

"Just want to know who has you smiling for the first time in days. We fucking obliterated Penworth tonight, man, and you barely even grinned."

"I'm plenty fucking happy," I grunt.

"You are now that you're thinking about fucking this girl's arse."

"Whose arse is Theo fucking?" Reese pipes up.

"Did you want to share with the whole fucking bus?" I mutter, reaching for my phone again.

I might have threatened to share that video of me fucking Raine into next week, but I don't actually have any intention of doing so.

Whatever is going on between us is exactly that. Between us.

This time, Oak lets me take it back, and I lock it before they see anything else.

"If you want. Although I'm not sure anyone really cares."

"I bet the girl he's threatening to fuck with that little dick does." Reese laughs.

"Fuck you. You should know better than anyone that girls love me taking them up the arse." I hold his eyes, giving him little choice but to remember the girl we tag-teamed not all that long before he started secretly hooking up with Liv.

"Nah, man. She just said all the right things to make you feel better. She was screaming because of my dick. Ow, what the fuck was that?" Reese balks when Oakley punches him right in the face without warning.

"Don't talk about fucking someone who isn't my sister right in front of me," Oak seethes while Reese holds his cheek like a pussy.

"But you don't like me talking about fucking her. Who the fuck's pussy can I talk about?" Reese asks, exasperated.

"No one's."

"Oh great. So you can tell us how tight Tally is. You can brag about fucking some girl's arse," he says, pointing at me. "You can—" he turns to Elliot. "Forget it, you're too busy pining after a girl you apparently don't want. What the fuck can I talk about?"

Silence falls as Reese waits for an answer and Oakley sulks knowing that he's just lost that round of arguments.

"Excuse me," I mutter, stuffing my AirPods back in and opening our chat again.

> Sunshine: You can threaten to stick your pointless cock anywhere you want. I can promise you, none of them will be enough to make me want a repeat.

> Theo: So. Full. Of. Shit. You dream about getting a chance to bounce around on my dick again and we both know it.

My cock aches as I wait for her reply. This banter shouldn't get me as hot as it does. But since I sent that video the other day, our little back and forth has become the highlight of my days.

Fuck. I'm turning into a pussy.

But it never comes.

She never replies.

And by the time the minibus pulls up outside the locker rooms at All Hallows' my mood is in the fucking pits.

"Aw, look at him pout. Doesn't she want your teeny weeny?" Oakley taunts.

With a glare in his direction, I jump from the seat and storm down the aisle, shoving more than a few teammates back into their seats when they stupidly get in my fucking way.

The second I have two feet on the ground, I send a message confirming my arrival and take off.

"Theo, wait," Reese calls, but I don't so much as look back as I head toward the main gates.

They know where I'm going, and they know better than to stop me once I've set motions in place.

Keeping to the shadows, I head to our usual meeting place, instantly pissed off when I'm there first. With the thick tree cover above, I can barely see the stars that are twinkling above me, I sure as fuck feel the ice-cold wind that whips around me.

"Where the fuck are you?" I mutter to myself.

I didn't set this fucking meeting up to stand around waiting to be fucking caught.

A twig snapping behind me is my first sign that I'm not alone. But when I spin around, I don't find my usual contact.

"Who the fuck are you?" I bark, instantly on edge that I don't recognise him.

"Theo?" he asks, confirming that he knows who the fuck I am.

"Depends."

He smirks before stepping closer. "Rich is currently... indisposed."

"What kind of fucking dealer uses terms like indisposed?" I seethe.

"This one," he counters. "Now, do you want what I've got for you or not?"

Pulling his hand from his pocket, he lets me see before waiting for me to make a move.

"It better be as good as Rich's shit."

"Same. Just delivered with a little more class."

I snort, trading the weed and pills for cash. "Whatever."

I take off, more than ready to get fucked up and forget everything for a few hours.

"Wait," he calls before I disappear into the trees.

I pause. Fuck knows why. I don't owe this prick anything.

"I've only got a handful of Rich's contacts. Any chance you could hook me up?"

Spinning around, I stare at him. Right fucking at him. "Why should I trust you?" I ask, closing the space between us again.

"Because you've got the best gear you've ever had in your hand."

"What's in it for me?"

"You want a cut?" he asks.

I shake my head. I couldn't give a fuck about the money really. In a few weeks, I'll have more than I know what to do with anyway.

"Free gear?"

I shrug one shoulder.

"Fucking give me something here," he sighs.

"We're having a party tomorrow night. If this shit is as good as you say it is, you can come. But I'm gonna want the best you got. Always."

"Done," he says without thinking.

"You know where we are?"

"Yeah, I know who you are."

"Great."

I take off, thankfully, without being called back this time.

By the time the lights of the dorm buildings appear before me, I've got a joint rolled, between my lips and ready to light. But something stops me. Or should I say, someone?

Pulling my phone from my pocket, I find our conversation.

> Theo: Last chance to pull on some sexy lingerie.

> Sunshine: *middle finger emoji*

With a laugh, I take off in her direction.

The dorm is buzzing with activity, seeing as we're not holding our party until tomorrow night, all the girls who haven't snuck out to the boys' dorm, or smuggled one into their own room, are all at a loose end.

More than a few proposition me, but no one so much as stirs interest, and I soon leave them all behind in favour of someone on the second floor.

> Theo: Oh, sunshine, you're going to really regret that. Ready?

I unlock her door and throw it open as she shrieks in shock. Although, I'm pretty sure it's all an act.

She was waiting for me.

If what she's wearing isn't evidence enough, then the heat in her eyes sure gives her away.

23

RAINE

Theo stares at me with hunger.

"You do know that if you keep letting yourself into my room, I'm going to start thinking you actually ca—"

"Nice outfit."

"I think you mean pyjamas." I glance down at my tiny sleep shorts and thin camisole.

He takes a step closer, his gaze darkening as he takes a leisurely sweep of my body. "You expect me to believe you sleep like that."

"Uh, yes." I frown.

"So you didn't dress up... just for me."

"I hate to disappoint but no."

"Shame." He shrugs with indifference, but his expression is anything but.

Swinging my legs over the side of the bed, I sit up. "Why are you here, Theo?"

He falters for a second, the momentary slip telling me all I need to know.

He can't stay away.

This push and pull between us is more than simple hatred. We both know it.

It's why, if I had any plans to stick around in Saints Cross, I'd stay away. Because I know without a doubt that it's foolish to get tangled up with a boy like Theo. But as it happens, I won't be sticking around. So it doesn't matter if I let myself enjoy this... whatever it is.

Heavy silence fills the room, neither of us willing to admit what's going on here.

Theo is the first to speak but it's the last thing I expect him to say.

"Want to smoke?"

"You burst in here like some kind of stalker to ask me if I want to... smoke?"

Pulling a baggie of weed out of his pocket, he dangles it in front of my face. "It's good stuff."

I bet it is.

"Nothing but the best for an Heir." I roll my eyes.

"You in or what?"

"Fine. But we'll have to crank the window." Standing, I slip around him and open it as far as it'll go.

Theo pulls a pre-rolled joint from the bag and joins me on the window seat.

"You want to do the honours?" he offers it to me, and I take it, putting it between my lips.

He produces a lighter and sparks the end.

It's been a while since I got stoned but I don't hate the acrid smoke as I take a deep hit, letting the chemicals roll through me.

"Shit, that's good." My head drops back against the window, and he chuckles.

"Why does this not surprise me."

I flip him the bird, feeling a strange stab of hurt that he thinks he's got me all figured out. "What? Are your Heir chaser sluts too prim and proper to get high?"

"I didn't mean—"

"Yeah, you did. Forget it." I wave him off, accepting another toke as an apology. This one hits me harder.

"Good, right?" Theo grins at me, and I find myself grinning back.

"Did you really come here to get high?" I ask.

"What do you think?"

"So what happened?"

"I remembered I had a pocketful of premium weed."

"Ouch."

I laugh it off, but it stings all the same.

"Do I need to be worried that you videoed us having sex?"

"Relax." He takes a long, deep drag on the joint, holding it in his lungs before slowly letting the smoke curl from his lips. "It's for my private collection."

"You're a real pig sometimes, you know, right?"

"Doesn't stop you from wanting to bounce on my dick again though, does it?"

I bite down on my lip because he's got me there.

"Thought so." Deep laughter rumbles in his chest.

"Wanker."

"Bitch."

Poking my tongue out seems like the best comeback but it only sparks interest in his dark gaze.

"I don't think I've ever been sucked off while getting high. Want to claim that first?" He drops his eyes to his crotch, the very noticeable bulge there.

"Do our verbal sparring matches turn you on?"

"I'm not used to girls standing up to me. It's... different." He shrugs.

"You like it." I smirk.

He neither denies nor confirms the accusation. But I know the truth. We both do.

"What's your story, sunshine?" he asks, and that does surprise me.

We're not supposed to be bonding. Sharing our secrets and hopes and dreams for the future. That's not how things work between us.

"I'm pretty sure you've got me all figured out." I laugh off his intense stare.

"Come on, give me something. You're in therapy, right? So there's got to be a few skeletons in your closet."

"Nice, arsehole," I mutter, accepting the joint again.

This isn't like the weed I used to smoke with Vaughn and his friends. I can already feel it saturating my bloodstream, dulling my senses. But there's something else too. A tingle over my skin.

Shit.

I'm high and horny.

"What's that look for?" Theo asks, a knowing glint in his eye.

"Nothing." I wave him off.

"You feel it, don't you?"

"You know, you didn't need to get me high to fuck me."

His eyes flare. "Is that what you want?" He picks up my legs and drapes them over his lap, his hands smoothing over my ankles.

It feels good.

Too fucking good.

"You want me to fuck you?" His fingers walk higher, pushing between my thighs.

"Theo..." I warn. Or maybe I beg.

Everything's a little hazy.

"You're in my head," he admits.

"The feeling is mutual."

Something crackles between us.

"So what are we gonna do about it?" His thumb rolls over my damp underwear, forcing a whimper to crawl up my throat.

Jesus.

This boy.

This infuriating, cocky, gorgeous boy.

I am so screwed.

He takes another couple of deep hits on the joint before offering it back to me.

"If I didn't know better, I'd say you're trying to get me high as a kite."

"Feels so good though, am I right?" He flashes me a smile full of dark promise as he continues toying with my underwear.

"If you're going to touch me, stop teasing and do it."

His brow lifts with mild amusement. "You want me, sunshine? Beg."

Laughter spills out of me as my head rolls back.

"What?" he asks.

"You're something else."

"Apparently your pussy likes it."

"I already told you, my pussy isn't choosy." I hold his gaze, daring him to push.

Suddenly, this feels like more than just two frenemies sharing a joint, trading flirty insults.

Theo leans out the window a little, stubbing the end on the sill before flicking it into the night.

He lingers for a second and panic rises inside me. Maybe it was a bad idea letting him stay, not that he really gave me a choice.

But before I can kick him out, he hooks my knickers to the side and sinks two fingers inside me.

My breath catches at the sudden intrusion, but the flash of indignance quickly gives way to pleasure as he works me.

"You like that?" His eyes are dark as the night while he watches me, his hungry gaze darting between my face and his hand.

"Y-yeah," I murmur, arching into his touch. I'm so high, I

can barely think straight but my body knows what to do. She knows what she likes.

"Need to taste you." He grumbles, slipping off the window seat onto his knees so he can pull my shorts and knickers down my legs. Hoisting my legs over his shoulders, I scramble for purchase as he lowers his mouth to my pussy and devours me.

"Theo!" I cry out. Everything is heightened, my blood heating in my veins as he unleashes his tongue on me.

"Ride my face," he demands, yanking me closer and holding me there.

I can barely move, let alone ride him. It's too much. The drugs in my system, the delicious sensations coursing through my body, the way his fingers and tongue work together in perfect synchrony to push me closer to the edge.

"Fuck," I breathe.

"Good plan." Theo rips his mouth away from me and staggers to his feet before dragging me off the window seat and throwing me over his shoulder.

"What the hell—"

Thwack.

Pain sears into my arse, sending a lick of anger down my spine.

"Did you just... spank me?"

"Yeah, you love it." His dark laughter curls my stomach.

I want to deny it. But I can't.

He throws me onto the bed, and I land with a little huff. "Stop manhandling me." I protest.

But the snap of Theo's belt silences me as I watch with rapt fascination as he unbuttons his trousers and pushes them down his hips, revealing his perfect dick.

"Hands and knees," he orders.

"So bossy." I smirk. Because we both know I'm not going to deny him.

I want this as much as he does, and it scares me.

"Sunshine," he warns as he fists himself, pumping slowly a couple of times.

I lick my lips, desperate to taste him. To devour him the way he devoured me.

But ever the bossy wanker, Theo mouths, 'Hands and knees. Now.'

Rolling my eyes, I flip onto my stomach and give him my ass. He leans over me, dragging me back onto my knees and runs his hand down my spine, grabbing a handful of my arse before spanking me again.

A harsh cry catches in my throat but then he's there, rubbing his hand down the crack of my arse to dip his fingers inside me again.

"Fuck, you're soaked." He withdraws his fingers and I moan at the loss. Every nerve ending is alive, my body's singing with pleasure.

I curl my fingers into the bedsheet, bracing—

"God," I cry as he slams into me.

Curling his strong, lean body over mine, he grabs me by the back of the neck and fucks into me like a man possessed. "Shit, you feel good."

Theo doesn't let up, pounding into me fast and hard, almost like he hates me.

Or hates to want me.

I don't really care at this precise moment. He feels too good. And I'm close.

So damn close.

"More." I demand, rocking back against him.

"Greedy little thing, aren't you?" He slows his pace, grinding against me as his hand slips around my body to find my clit.

Pleasure shatters inside me, and I come hard, tightening around him.

"Fuck, yeah. Come all over my cock."

His grip on my neck tightens and then I'm being wrenched

back against his chest. He wraps his arm around me and nuzzles my neck, licking and sucking the skin there.

"You take me so fucking good."

His words shouldn't matter. I shouldn't care. But a broken part of me lights up.

"Fuck... fuuuuuck." He drives into me twice more before filling me with his cum.

We stay like that for a second, him holding me tight, his dick pulsing inside me, and then Theo pulls out of me and flops down onto the bed with an exhausted sigh. "That was…"

"Yeah." I lie on my side and drink him in.

His eyes are closed, the rise and fall of his chest evened out. He looks peaceful.

Too peaceful to wake.

So I break all my rules and curl up beside him and close my eyes.

Telling myself we'll just sleep for a little while.

24

THEO

Best fucking sleep ever.
I nuzzle into the pillow as my limbs sink into the memory foam mattress.

The exercise from the game, the high of the win, the best fucking weed that can be found in Saints Cross... fuck yeah. I'll take some of that every night of the week.

I lie there, enjoying the pure relaxation that comes with the lingering high. Or at least I do until someone moves beside me.

My breath catches and my eyes flicker open.

Oh. Holy. Fuck.

Rubbing my eyes, I stare at Raine's dorm room, trying to remember how I got here.

Unfortunately, it all becomes very clear, very fast.

Finding her dressed in her sexy pjs. Watching her lips purse as she toked on my joint. Eating her on the window seat. Fucking her from behind.

The only thing that's really hazy is our conversation. Please, for the love of God, don't let me have said anything stupid. Like, confess just how much I've thought about her pussy since the last time she let me inside her. Or worse... that I can't stop thinking about her.

She doesn't belong here. She's not one of us. And I fucking know even without evidence that she was the one who fucking tagged our cars. But even still... I can't fucking stop.

Even now, in the midst of a freakout, I'm hard as fuck for her.

With my head pounding and my temperature soaring, I risk looking at the girl on the other side of the bed. "Holy shit," I gasp when I find a pair of violet eyes staring right back at me.

No chance of slipping out like it never happened now, arsehole.

"Good morning to you too," she whispers, her voice all rough and sexy.

I swallow nervously, wracking my brain for a time this has happened before but... Nope. I have never still been in a girl's bed the next morning. And I don't know what the fuck I am meant to do now.

I stare at her, unblinking as my brain races.

Thank her for the ride, and get up and walk out?

Suggest she takes care of my morning wood before leaving her high and dry?

Indulging completely and not coming up for air until someone out there wants us?

They all sound like pretty viable options. The latter two are way more pleasurable and appealing.

I don't think I've ever been sucked off while I'm getting high...

My confession from the night before rocks through me.

Fuck, I want that.

I want to watch as she wraps those pretty red lips around my cock.

I—

"FUCK," I bark the second her delicate fingers connect with my dick.

Oh, hell, yes. I'm not the only one horny this morning. Bring it the fuck on.

"Sunshine," I groan as she slowly strokes me.

"You're still here," she says, her brows pinched.

"Good weed and good sex will do that, I guess," I confess, my tongue running away with me. "Fuck, anyone would think you like me," I groan as she tightens her grip, making my head spin.

"I like your dick," she confesses. "The rest of you I'm not so keen on."

"Bullshit. You think I'm hot. My dick would be nothing without the rest of me."

"Arrogant prick."

"Complain all you like, just don't fucking stop."

Shoving the covers off both of us, she sits up still only wearing her thin tank from the night before and no knickers.

"You wet for me?" I groan as she shifts between my thighs, my aching cock resting well up onto my stomach. She smiles coyly at me. "Fuck yeah, you're fucking soaked, aren't you?"

Resting back on one hand, she throws her leg over my thighs, opening herself up to me.

"Fuck, sunshine. You have the prettiest cunt."

"What do you want me to do with it?" she drawls, making my cock jerk in excitement.

What a fucking question.

Everything. I want every-fucking-thing.

"Let me watch you. But I'm going to need all of you first," I say, my eyes lifting to where her tits are covered. Although from how thin the fabric is, I can already see the darkening of her nipples, and I certainly know that they are already hard.

Her lips part as if she's about to argue, but thankfully, she thinks better of it and drags her top from her body, exposing her incredible tits to me.

"Now show me how you do it." Reaching out, I take myself in hand, giving her a little show in encouragement.

Resting back on one elbow, she lowers her hand between her legs. "Oh shit," she gasps.

"Sensitive, sunshine?" I ask, smug as fuck.

"Fuck you," she hisses, rubbing her clit in circles as I stroke myself.

"That's pretty much the idea. Can't get a better start to the day than a screaming orgasm, don't you think?"

"I wouldn't know. You haven't given me one yet," she teases.

I don't respond, I can't.

She looks incredible.

Hitting exactly the right spot, her head falls back on a cry.

"Eyes. On. Me," I demand.

It takes a second, a second where I think she's going to defy me. But then her head lifts and her heated, violet eyes find mine.

"Fuck I need inside you."

Her eyes flash with something and before I know what's happening, she's off the bed and backing toward her bathroom.

"Sunshine," I warn. "Are you trying to run from me?"

Biting on her bottom lip, she shakes her head, looking at me through her lashes. "You want my pussy, Theo?"

Pushing from the bed, I stand tall and take a step toward her.

"Then I'm going to need to hear you beg," she breathes.

Irritation flares within me, but I'm too fucking horny and desperate for it to really grow legs as she darts into the bathroom. Cornering herself.

"What game are you playing, sunshine?"

I trail after her, kicking the door closed as I step inside the small room to find her resting back against the basin.

Lifting her leg, she places her foot on the toilet beside her and bares herself to me. "Want it?"

My mouth waters as I remember just how sweet she tasted last night.

"You fucking know I do."

"Then you know what to do to get it."

Dragging my eyes up, they lock on hers as we embark on a battle of wills.

She wants me to beg. To get on my knees and be vulnerable for her.

Her pussy is good. But is it that fucking good?

"You're playing a dangerous game here, Raine," I warn. But unsurprisingly, she doesn't take the bait.

"Fair enough. I don't need you anyway." Pulling out the top drawer of the unit under the basin, she reveals a dildo. "Do you mind, me and my little friend here are going to have some alone time?"

Lifting it to her lips, I'm forced to watch as she deep-throats it, lubing it up before lifting her leg again and placing it at her entrance. "It's not too late for this to be your cock, Theo."

A deep, rumbling growl rips through the air. It takes a hot second to realise it came from my throat.

But when I don't say anything else, she pushes the head inside her body.

I could march over there and overpower her, easily. But what would be the fun in that when she is clearly feeling playful?

"Fuck, that's hot," I mutter, my hand absently moving up and down my dick.

"Could be better."

Fuck, yeah. It could be.

Before my brain has registered the move, my knees hit the warm tiles at my feet.

Her eyes flash with accomplishment as I move closer. "Would you look at that," she taunts. "I've got an Heir on his knees just for me."

When I'm in front of her, she pulls the plastic dick from her pussy and holds it out for me.

And like the fucking addict I am, I lean forward and lick it.

The second my tongue makes contact, she snorts and reality hits.

Reaching out, I wrap my hand around the base of the dildo before I rip it from her hand and throw it across the room.

It hits the wall with such a thud that something on the shelf above crashes to the floor, shattering behind us. Glancing back, my breath catches when I spot her phone resting on the shelf, the camera directed right at us.

Sly fucking bitch.

Keeping my expression neutral, I turn back to her with a smirk.

"I guess this is mine now."

But she's faster than me and before I get a chance to wrap my hands around her thighs and force her to ride my face, she's jumped away and into the shower.

"Oh, sunshine. You're not nearly dirty enough yet."

I get to her before she has a chance to reach for the dial and I slam her against the wall.

"Fuck," she gasps as I knock the wind out of her.

"Time to play is over, Raine. I'm taking what I'm owed," I warn darkly.

"Fuck you, Teddy. I don't owe you anything."

Reaching out, I wrap my hand around my throat and lean in closely. "Got on my fucking knees for you, Raine."

Her lips curl in victory. "And they say that the Heirs bow to no one," she mutters.

"You're going to pay for this."

"Do your worst, Teddy Bear. I'm ready for whatever you've got."

A scream rips from her throat as I lift her up the wall before impaling her with my cock. "Theo," she screams, her nails digging into my shoulders and no doubt piercing the skin.

I fuck her hard and fast, but the second I sense she's about to fall, I slow. Refusing her the release she's woken up so desperate for.

"No. Fuck. I hate you," she screams, slamming her heels into my lower back to try and get me to move.

"You're not in control here, sunshine. It's about time you learned your place."

She growls at me like a wild fucking animal.

To be fair, after this and the way my back is burning, I'm pretty sure I will look like I've been mauled by one.

Her pussy clenches around me and I'm powerless but to start up again, my own release right on the periphery.

Fucking her bare is everything. I know it's dangerous and reckless, but it is so fucking good.

"Yes," she hisses in delight.

But the second her release begins to crest, I pull out of her and shove her to her knees. Jerking my cock roughly, it only takes two strokes for my orgasm to claim me.

"Only one of us should be on our knees," I roar as I come all over her. "Now you're dirty enough to shower."

Reaching out, I turn the dial to cold before jumping out and allowing her to get blasted with ice-cold water.

"You're a fucking cunt," she screams, scrambling around to turn the water off, but all she manages to do is slip and crash to the floor.

Marching across the small room, I reach for her phone. "Credit where credit is due, Raine. You could have got away with this if you were smarter."

"Fuck you," she seethes, finally getting the water to warm.

"Just did. It was good. Thanks for the fuck. Great warm-up for our party later. Here, you might need this," I say, throwing her dildo at her before I drag the door open and walk out.

"Get back here," she cries. "Give me my phone."

She emerges from the bathroom with a towel clutched to her body as I shove my feet into my shoes and drag my hoodie on.

"Nah, this is mine now. Laters, sunshine."

I leave her door wide open like the prick I am and take off through the quiet dorms with a smug as fuck smirk on my face and her phone burning a hole in my pocket.

One way or another, I'm hacking into that thing and discovering all her secrets.

25

RAINE

"You should come."

"Yeah, that's not going to happen." I grimace, wondering how I ended up at Dessert Island with Abi and Tally again.

But they turned up at my door an hour after Theo left and refused to take no for an answer.

I want to say I hate it, hate them, but the truth is, I don't.

Tally is nothing like I first thought, and there's something about Abi that makes it impossible to dislike her.

I won't ever admit it aloud, but I actually enjoy their company.

"It's only a party." Abi shrugs, digging into her muffin.

"An Heir party," I correct.

"So, they won't care if you come."

My brow lifts at that. I know at least one Heir who would care.

I still can't believe Theo pulled that shit this morning. But then, I guess I deserved it. The opportunity had been too good not to get him back for filming me.

I had no intention of using it against him. At least, I didn't until he went and ruined a perfectly good morning.

Wanker.

"Are you sure you're okay, you seem a little... tense." Abi studies me and I don't like it. The way she seems to know that I'm seething on the inside.

Theo Ashworth can go to hell.

I'm so annoyed with myself for letting him trick me with his skilled tongue and magic fingers and that annoyingly perfect dick of his.

I'm such a cliché.

Ugh.

I smother the groan building in my throat and stuff my mouth with pastry instead.

"Did something happen with Theo?" Tally asks, a smug little smile on her face.

"Nope."

"You know, you can tell us if—"

"I said no."

"Okay, whatever you say." She shares a knowing look with Abi.

"If you'd have warned me this was an interrogation I wouldn't have agreed to come."

"If you come to the party, you can get him back for whatever stupid stunt he pulled this time," Tally adds.

"He didn't—" I stop myself because it's pointless. She knows something is going on between us. They both do.

Pressing my lips together, I consider my options. I could go to the party. But I could be playing straight into Theo's hands. Maybe that was his plan all along. To get me to drop my guard long enough to get one over on me.

Sneaky bastard.

"You're thinking about it, aren't you?" Tally grins.

"Why do you care so much?"

"Because Theo could do with being brought down a peg or two."

"And you think I'm the girl to do it?"

"I don't see anyone else lining up for the job."

"Keeley—"

"Keeley is an Heir chaser. She doesn't have what it takes to bring him to his knees."

Images of Theo on his knees flood my mind. I didn't really think he'd do it. But God, if he didn't look good down there, gazing up at me with that dark, tortured expression of his.

Another groan crawls up my throat but I take a large sip of water to chase it away.

"What?" I ask Tally, a little defensively.

"You like him."

"No, I really don't. I can barely tolerate him."

"Been there, got the t-shirt and the boyfriend who says otherwise."

"You and Oakley are... compatible."

She's filthy rich. He's filthy rich. Her family are lawyers. His family are lawyers.

They're a literal match made in heaven.

Abi sniggers at that, and we both glance at her.

"Something you want to share Abs?"

"I was just thinking, imagine if Raine had been here when you launched your hate campaign against the Heirs."

"We would have made a formidable duo." Tally concurs, shooting me a sly look. Just then, the bell chimes and Liv appears.

"Sorry, I'm late."

"Everything okay?" Tally asks her.

"Yeah, Reese wouldn't let me... do you know what, forget it." Her cheeks burn earning her a chorus of laughter.

"Didn't expect to see you here," she says to me, and I shrug.

"We were just grilling her on Theo, but she remains tight-lipped."

"Because there's nothing to tell."

"Word of warning?" Liv says. "Those boys can be relentless."

"It's true." Tally grins again.

"Think long and hard about whether you want to go there with Theo because once you do—"

I stand abruptly, suddenly feeling very uncomfortable with this conversation. "I appreciate the advice but honestly, it isn't needed. Thanks for the pastry but I've got to go."

"If you wait, we can give you a lift back," Tally offers.

"It's fine. The walk will do me good."

"If you change your mind about the party, let me know."

I don't tell her that I can't... because Theo stole my phone.

"See ya." With a small wave, I slip out of the bakery and head toward the high street.

If Theo thinks he's won this round, he's sorely mistaken.

And tonight is the perfect opportunity to show him.

I lay low for the rest of the day. Millie stopped by to see if I wanted to hang but I made up some lame excuse.

Hanging with her after spending the night with her brother felt a little icky. I like Millie, I do, and I sense she has a lot of really bad shit going on, which is why I don't want her to get stuck in the middle of this thing between me and Theo any more than she already has.

By the time the sun sinks into the tree line, I'm almost climbing the walls. It's foolish to try and infiltrate their party and get my own back but then, I never claimed to be smart.

Pulling on my black hoodie, I grab the backpack I picked up from a charity shop in town and go over to the window, cranking it open.

It's a risk, sneaking out again. But I refuse to let Theo think he's won.

I can't.

Something inside, the jagged, broken pieces, won't let me.

It's bitterly cold tonight, and the frigid air makes my lungs smart as I shimmy down the trellis.

I take the same path as last time, but this time, I don't feel the same buzz of adrenaline.

Because you care.

I shut down the little voice. So what if a part of me likes Theo. It doesn't change the fact he's everything I should hate. And given half the chance, I don't doubt he would ruin me if he thought it would help him climb the sickening hierarchy this place is built on.

When the Chapel finally comes into view, my heart is a runaway train in my chest, making me a little light-headed.

Avoiding the front of the building, I slip around the side until I find the back... and the electrical box. Yanking my bag off my shoulder, I crouch down and pull out my supplies. Some gloves and a pair of wire cutters.

The party sounds in full swing and I hesitate for a second, a trickle of guilt rolling down my spine. Abi is in there. Tally and Liv too. But we're not friends, not really.

Besides, this isn't about me. It's about Theo.

I wrench open the box and grab the small torch, shining it inside. I don't exactly have a solid plan but after a quick Google search earlier, I'm pretty certain I can make it work.

A smile curls at my lips as I imagine the chaos that's about to ensue. But just as I lift the cutters, voices stop me in my tracks.

His voice.

Dammit.

Dropping the tool, I edge along the side of the building to get closer. It's risky, but I can't help myself.

Is he with the boys or a girl? Keeley maybe?

A lick of jealousy goes through me.

"This is some fucking good shit," Theo says.

"Damn straight," a muffled voice replies.

Not Keeley then.

At least, I hope not.

Because the idea of her touching him, being anywhere near him, makes me murderous.

"I was a little worried there for a second, but you came through."

"Said I would."

I straighten, a strange sense of awareness rattling me.

It can't be.

My mind must be playing tricks on me.

Breathe, Raine. You're freaking out over nothing. Vaughn doesn't know you're here, remember.

Forcing myself to calm down, I decide to risk peeking around the corner to put to bed the silly idea that Vaughn has somehow found me.

I spot Theo first, looking every bit the entitled arrogant prick he is, as he smokes a joint. Two other boys I recognise from school stand with him, the fourth has his back to me.

Relief sinks into me.

Of course it isn't Vaughn.

I'm losing it.

Theo has got me all twisted up in knots to the point where I'm hearing things that aren't there.

Get a grip, Raine.

I double back to the electricity box and give myself no time to second-guess myself as I gently tug the wire free and cut it cleanly in half.

Screams and yells go up as the Chapel plummets into darkness. But there isn't time to stick around and enjoy my victory because I need to get back to the dorm building to make sure I have an airtight alibi.

So I shove everything back in my bag, sling it over my shoulder and run.

By the time Theo turns up, I'm tucked up in bed, the bag well-hidden and my window locked.

He stands in the doorway like a furious dark prince, his face illuminated only by the strip lighting in the hall.

"How'd you do it?" His voice is a low growl.

"D-do what?" I play the sleepy victim to perfection.

"You know what the fuck I'm talking about."

"No, I really don't. I was asleep before you—"

"Fuck," he grunts, slamming his palm against the door. "Fuck."

I fight the urge to grin at his frustration.

Oh, Theo.

You really picked the wrong adversary.

"If there's nothing else, get out."

His eyes narrow to dangerous slits and for a second, I wonder if I've pushed him too far.

"Yeah," he breathes, "whatever." He grabs the handle and turns to leave but I call after him before he can slam my door shut.

"Oh, and Theo," I say.

He pauses but refuses to look at me.

"I want my phone back."

He blows out of there without so much as another word, and I inhale a sharp breath.

I should feel happy. Smug even.

But I can't deny the stab of disappointment that he walked away so easily.

26

THEO

"Yessss," I hiss, quietly celebrating when I finally find the code that unlocks Raine's phone. It wasn't exactly rocket science, but it's taken me longer than I'd like.

Although, that's possibly due to the anger that's blinded me since our party was plunged into darkness. The fucking cables were cut.

Who the fuck would do that?

I shake my head. I know exactly who did it.

The girl who tried to convince me that she was fast asleep in bed the whole time. The girl I left high and dry on the floor of her shower yesterday morning.

There isn't anyone else brave enough or stupid enough to pull such a move.

My free fist curls as I tap on her messages app. I am so fucking ready to discover how she's been doing all this.

Sneaking across campus to tag our cars, and then again to wipe out our party, all while apparently being in her dorm building.

It doesn't make any sense. Unless she has someone helping her.

But the second the app opens, I deflate. There are only two message threads. One with... Teddy. My teeth grind as I stare at this little nickname. And the other...

I open the thread and read a couple of messages.

Her social worker?

Interesting.

Although, the whole thread throws up more questions than it answers.

What I need is her transfer file. Elliot could get it for me in a heartbeat if I were to ask.

There lies the problem...

I have to ask. And asking means looking interested.

I could claim that I'm trying to prove her guilt. But seriously, what kind of evidence about tagging our cars would be in her file?

That would be her past. The schools she's attended, the places she's lived. That would tell me little about her guilt and a whole lot about where she came from. It would help me understand the woman who seems to have this hold over me to make me do exactly what she wants.

I got on my fucking knees for her.

I licked... Yeah, probably best not to go there.

Not finding any damning evidence, I switch to her emails. Once again, I find nothing of any excitement, so I head for her socials. And that's where I come up blank.

She has none.

I've searched for her multiple times and come up empty in my need to scroll through her images and get my fix of an addiction I really need to kick. But I never found her. I assumed that was because she had some dumb username and was hiding in plain sight. But apparently, I was wrong. She just doesn't exist.

What kind of teenager doesn't have at least one social media account?

One with secrets...

I'm about to dive into her passwords to see if she's ever stored one when my own phone rings on the bed beside me. The second it starts up I groan. The ringtone sends a chill through me.

It's been radio silence since teeing off with him last weekend, but apparently, he's remembered I exist again. I stare at his contact, letting it ring out for as long as I dare. But eventually, I hit connect and lift it to my ear.

"Father," I grunt.

"We're having a family meal this afternoon. Get Millie and be over here by two at the latest."

"What if I have plans?" I don't know why I ask, I already know what his answer will be.

"Cancel them. Maria wants you here."

That's bullshit and we both know it. Maria only wants and does exactly what Dad says. I want to say it's pathetic. That she needs to grow a backbone and stand up to him. But I can't because I fully understand why she doesn't.

He's a chauvinistic, controlling piece of shit. Life wouldn't be worth living for her if she stuck her head above the parapet.

That's why it's down to me to finally release us from the hold he has over all of us.

In only a few weeks, I'm going to expose everything I know about the man who controls all our lives and I'm going to laugh my fucking tits off when he gets everything he deserves.

Finally.

"I'll see what I can do," I say, although we know exactly what that will be.

A couple of minutes before two, I will be walking through the front door to a house I'd happily never step inside again to have a bullshit family meal.

You're doing it to protect them. Just a few more weeks, a little voice pops up.

I hang up before he gets a chance to respond. Probably a

mistake I'll end up paying for later but right now, I'm too pissed off to care.

Opening my messages, I tap out a one to Millie, letting her know what's going on before abandoning Raine's phone in my sheets and marching toward the shower. The temptation to turn up stinking of last night's whisky and weed is strong, but I won't do it. Millie and Maria deserve more than me poking the beast any more than I already have.

A little less than two hours later, Millie is sitting in my passenger seat wearing an Anthony Ashworth-approved dress and wringing her hands in her lap.

I can't deny that I'm on board with her dressing like a nun. At twelve, she's quickly developing into a beautiful young woman with curves that I know will soon bring any red-blooded male in the vicinity to his knees. Add the innocent eyes and smart mouth she often unleashes on me, and I just know that I'll have my work cut out for me if she were wearing anything more revealing.

I think about next year. About the fact I'll be at Saints Cross U while she's still here without me watching her back. Sure, I'll task the next Heirs to keep a very close eye on her. And as much as I hate to think it, Raine will still be here. I might not be overly happy about their friendship, but something tells me that Raine would throw a punch or two if anyone disrespected my little sister.

I shift in my seat as the image of Raine taking down some horny little fucker who wants a chance with my sister takes root in my brain.

Fuck, that would be so fucking hot.

Millie's curious stare burns into the side of my face and I internally cringe. I should not be getting hard while my sister is sitting in my passenger seat.

Then maybe you shouldn't have stormed off last night like an angry bellend and instead tried to fuck the truth out of Raine.

My grip on the wheel tightens. "We'll have dinner, then we'll be gone," I promise, aware that spending time in this house is something akin to Millie sticking forks into her eyes.

"It'll be fine," she mutters sadly.

"We'll see."

Dread sits heavy in my stomach as I pull up in front of the colossal house. It's huge. Almost too big. But Anthony Ashworth needs to show the world just how much money he has and how important he is. It's pretentious and obnoxious.

All the things Raine accuses you of being...

Slamming that thought down, I kill the engine and let out a pained sigh as the two of us stare up at the house.

"What kind of mood was he in when you spoke?" Millie asks, wanting to walk through the front door prepared for what is waiting on the other side.

"Normal."

She snorts. "Liar. Nothing about him is normal."

"True, but he didn't sound angry. Not yet at least."

"Please try to keep a lid on it," she begs, aware that I'm often the one who pushes Dad over the edge.

"I'll see what I can do. Ready?"

"Never," she replies sadly before throwing the door open and stepping out.

Following her, I step beside her and together we walk toward the front door. Her in her demure knee-length high-necked deep red dress and me in dress trousers and a shirt. Anyone would think we were going somewhere fancy to celebrate something. Not just to the parentals for a Sunday roast.

Sucking in a deep breath, I twist the handle, open the door and walk into hell.

Silence ripples around the formal dining room where we're eating.

The table has been laid as if the King himself is coming. All the best china and crystal is out, and there is some kind of irritating classical music twinkling in the background.

Spearing a piece of, what to me, looks like a perfectly cooked piece of roast beef with my fork, I push it past my lips as the air continues to crackle with awkwardness. I chew, barely tasting it as I watch Millie opposite me push her own meal around her plate with a downtrodden expression on her face.

I hate it.

I hate that he barely pays her any attention.

She's his child too. And just because she was born with a vagina, it doesn't make her any less of a child. So what she'll never be and Heir or a Scion? She's still an Ashworth. She's still worthy of his attention.

Millie is fucking epic. He should be proud to be able to call her his.

"This beef is overcooked," the man in question barks, cutting through the oppressive silence as he pokes his slices of meat with his lip curled back in disgust.

"It was cooked for the exact time for how you like it, Anthony," Maria says, her voice small and terrified for what might come back.

"No," Dad barks. "You did it wrong."

My stomach knots as Maria swallows nervously.

"Yes, maybe I did," she instantly concedes even though three of us sitting around his table know she didn't. She wouldn't dare.

"This isn't good enough," he scoffs, shoving his plate back.

Maria flinches, waiting for whatever is going to come next.

Millie, who's sitting beside her—Dad is obviously at the head of the table—hasn't dared to look up once.

She hasn't spoken a word since we walked through the

door. It's always that way under this roof, and I fucking hate it.

My little sister is so full of life and sass. Yet, everything changes the second she steps through the front door here. Years of being ignored, and abandoned by the one person she should be able to rely on has left her mute.

She learned long ago that he wasn't interested in anything she had to say, so she just... stopped.

Maria is great. She tries her best, but even she's stopped being able to get through to her. If Dad isn't here, they'll chat. But the second his presence is felt, Millie locks down.

We all wait with bated breaths as Dad stands there staring down at Maria. This isn't the first time this has happened, and I doubt it'll be the last.

The worst outcome would be flying fists, the best that he storms out.

Although I'm sure that while that might be the best for Millie and me. For Maria, we all know that his wrath will come later. When they don't have witnesses.

A shudder rips through me at the thought of what he does to her behind closed doors.

Dad's volatile anger means he's as quick with his vicious words as he is his fists. Something I know all too well firsthand.

"This is my only day off this week," he seethes. "All I wanted was to have a nice meal with my family. But you fucked it. Totally fucked it. This was all you had to do this week. Cook and look pretty. And you couldn't even manage that."

His chair topples back as he stands abruptly. A whimper comes from Maria before he picks up his plate and launches it toward the wall.

It shatters on contact as his roast dinner coats the cream and gold wallpaper.

Then with another barbed word in Maria's direction, he storms from the room.

The second the back door slams, alerting us to his departure, she lets out a cry before also running from the room.

"And that's our cue to leave. Grab your bag, Mills. We're done here."

Not needing to be told twice, Millie silently jumps up and all but runs out of the room and toward the front door.

There was a time that we'd hang around to make sure Maria was okay and to help clean up, but those times are long gone.

By the time I get to my car, she's already in the passenger seat sobbing into her hands.

It breaks my fucking heart, and only fuels my determination to ruin that fucking cunt for everything he's done to us.

27

RAINE

"Hold up, Teddy." I cut across the perfectly tended grass, making a beeline for the boy still holding my phone hostage. "We need to talk," I rasp, trying to catch my breath.

It's early Monday morning and I've been waiting for him to appear.

I want my phone back and I don't plan on letting up until he gives it to me.

"No, we really don't." He shoulders past me, physically shoving me out of the way with his annoyingly big body.

Shocked, I stare after him, rubbing the tender spot on my arm.

Okay, that didn't quite go as planned but maybe he's just got that Monday feeling.

"Theo, come on." I take off after him. "I need my phone—"

He whirls around on me, pinning me with a furious stare. I've seen all the rainbow of emotions painted on his pretty perfect face, but I don't think he's ever looked at me with such hatred.

Something curdles into my stomach, but I shake it off. "What's wrong?" I ask before I can stop myself.

"Like I'd tell you."

"I see." My teeth grind. "Good enough to fuck but not good enough to talk to. Got it."

I start to spin around. Fuck him and fuck his mood swings. I'll find another way to rescue my—

"Fuck, sunshine, I..."

"Yeah?" I turn back slowly, hating how relieved I am at the softness in voice.

"Nothing." His icy mask slams down again. "Forget it."

Disappointment wells in my chest. I shouldn't be surprised. We're not friends. I don't know what the hell we are, but clearly the fact he's been inside me, on his knees before me, means nothing.

"My phone," I snap. "I want it back."

"You should have thought of that before."

"Seriously, Theodore," I glower, "I. Want. It. Back."

"Yeah, well I want a lot of things but they're not going to happen anytime soon so you're shit out of luck, sunshine."

"What's your problem, you're not usually this—"

"Watch it." He practically growls the words, but then something catches his attention over my shoulder.

I glance back and my stomach sinks.

Keeley.

She spots Theo and her whole face lights up.

Damn, it stings. More than it should. He made no promises to me, and if this morning is anything to go on, the temporary truce between us is well and truly over.

But it doesn't stop the dejection spreading through me like barbed wire.

Because it's just another reminder that I'll never be the type of girl he chooses.

What the fuck am I saying?

I don't want Theo to pick me. But I can't deny this cat and mouse game we play is addictive. And somewhere over the last couple of weeks, I've come to look forward to our interactions. The banter.

The undeniable chemistry.

"Theo, can we just—"

He doesn't even acknowledge me as he stalks across the lawn toward a smug looking Keeley. She drapes herself over him like a cheap throw and I stand there, mouth agape, while he lets her practically dry fuck his leg.

"What are you— oh." Millie joins me, making a gagging noise. "They are so gross."

"Yeah."

"I don't know what my brother sees in her. She's so... vapid and fake. He needs a girl with a little more bite." Glancing at her sideways, I arch a brow and she grins back at me. "Know anyone who fits the description?"

"Ha ha." I laugh but it sounds brittle. "Never going to happen."

"It could. You'd be good for him. And unlike Keeley, I like you."

"I appreciate the shining endorsement. But your brother isn't my type."

"Who is your type then?"

"Aren't you a little young for this kind of talk?"

Millie shrugs, a shadow falling over her expression.

"What did you do with your weekend?" I ask, sensing her pulling away.

"Nothing worth mentioning." She barely meets my gaze.

"Millie?"

"You should ask Theo about it," she murmurs.

"Theo, why would I—"

It hits me.

Theo isn't angry at me—well, maybe I am a contributing factor—he's angry about something else and I got the brunt of his bad mood.

"He tries to hold it all together," Millie goes on. "But it's hard and I know he worries about leaving me to go off to uni."

"And what about you, do you worry about that?"

She meets my curious gaze and offers me a small smile. "It is what it is. At least I can board here until it's my turn."

I didn't want to get close to these people, to feel sympathy for them. But I can't help it.

Millie reminds me so much of myself.

And Theo...

I refuse to think about him.

Especially, while he's letting Keeley Davis paw all over him.

Maybe he's doing it to make me jealous or maybe he's doing it to prove he is the arrogant tosser I suspect him to be. Whatever his reasons, I don't want to play his game this morning. So I loop my arm through Millie's and drag her in the opposite direction.

"Come on," I say. "I'll walk you to your building."

All morning, I stew on my run-in with Theo, and Millie's words.

I should stay out of their business. It's nothing to do with me. I should avoid getting any more tangled up with them than I already am.

I tagged his car and ruined their party for God's sake. But what started as a quest to get one up on the Heir and his friends, and knock them down a peg or two, has become something else entirely.

I like getting a reaction from Theo. I want to see how far I can push him. To see what his reaction will be. Because somewhere under all the bravado and arrogance is a boy that understands me.

At least, I thought he did.

After this morning, I'm not sure anymore.

Great sex doesn't equal a basis for a friendship let alone a relationship.

Not that I want one of those with Theo or anyone else.

But the point is the same. Maybe all we share is a fiery attraction. He's the match and I'm the fuse, and I can't resist the urge to see how brightly we'll burn.

So I can only cuss myself out as I follow him out of the building after break time and around the back of the gym. I have no idea where he's going but I don't stop.

I can't.

And I guess that's the reason I'm really annoyed at myself. Because I do care.

Even when I don't want to.

Theo ducks into a small shed, the door rattling behind him. I don't think about it as I slip inside and after him. Until his angry gaze lands on me, sucking all the air from the small room.

"The fuck are you doing?"

"I—"

"I said"—he advances, backing me up against the wall, the air cracking and sparking between us—"the fuck are you doing?"

"You're angry."

"No shit." He cuts me with an icy glare. "You need to leave."

"No."

"No?" His brow lifts. "Who's the stalker now?" he snarls the words, but I've heard worse.

Theo doesn't scare me. But what me being here means does.

Crap. This was a bad idea.

When I don't reply, he adds, "If you've come to ask for your phone—"

"That's not why I'm here," I say. "Millie said something this morning and it got me thinking..."

"Millie? You're here because of my sister?" he asks, incredulous.

"What happened yesterday, Theo?"

"No." He steps back, putting some space between us. "You don't get to ask that. You don't get to fucking act like you care. And how many times have I told you. Stay the fuck away from my sister."

"And if I do care?"

He pauses, mistrust glittering in his eyes. "What game are you playing?"

"No game." I lift my hands in surrender. "I swear. I figured you might need to talk—"

"I don't."

"Well, I'm here anyway."

His eyes narrow as if he's trying to work out my angle. "I don't trust you," he murmurs.

"The feeling is mutual."

I don't add that I don't trust myself around him either. But I have a feeling that's just another thing we might have in common.

His gaze darkens, a smirk tipping the corner of his mouth. "You want to help me, sunshine? Want to let me work off some of this anger?" He stalks toward me, an apex predator about to devour his prey. But Theo doesn't hold all the power here.

I hold up my hand and he instantly stops, quirking a brow. "I'll make you a deal," I say.

"A deal." He snorts. "I'm not sure you're in any position to negotiate."

"Tell me something real and then I'll help you work off some of that anger."

"You seriously came here to talk?" His brows pinch with confusion.

"Actually, I came here to listen. You look like you could

use a friend, Theo. No ulterior motives. No games. Just a friend."

He wants to argue. To prove me wrong. It's right there in his eyes. But he doesn't.

Instead, he runs a hand through his hair and blows out a steady breath.

"You want to know something real, sunshine?" I nod, and his smirk creeps back into place. "I do this. I talk and you listen. And then, I get to do whatever I want to you."

Shit.

I hadn't anticipated this. But then Theo has a way of making it hard to think straight.

"Scared, sunshine?" He chuckles but I see the flash of vulnerability in his eyes.

He needs this.

He needs me.

And there's power in that. That's something I don't want to acknowledge.

I lift my chin in defiance, giving a little shake of my head. "I'm not scared of you, Theodore Ashworth."

He steps forward, erasing the space between us, sending my heart into a wild frenzy.

"Want to know a secret?" he asks, so close I can almost taste him. And then he utters three little words that make my head spin. "You should be."

28

THEO

Her scent makes my mouth water. My need for her makes every nerve ending in my body tingle with desire. But what she wants from me...

The truth.

How could I possibly trust her with something as ugly as my life?

She'd use it against me in a heartbeat.

From the second that Raine turned up here, all she's done is taunt me and strike out.

I might not have proof or have figured out how she made it happen. But deep down, I know it's her.

So giving her this kind of ammunition... bad fucking idea.

So why is it that a little bit of my truth is dancing on my tongue desperate to slip out.

"So?" she taunts, completely unfazed by me and my closeness. Well, in the way she should be at least. It's impossible to miss how dark her eyes are, how fast her breath is rushing past my face.

Unable to resist, I lift my hand and her lust-filled gasp rips around the small storage shed we're in as I squeeze her breast. A whimper rumbles in her throat, and fuck if it doesn't get my dick hard.

"You can have that one for free but that's all you're getting."

"It amuses me, sunshine, that you think you're in charge here."

Her smirk grows, silently telling me that that is exactly where she thinks the power lies. "You want me. You know what you've got to do."

"You think I'd let you out of here now without taking what I want? That's really fucking stupid of you."

"Maybe. Maybe not," she counters.

My nostrils flare at her attitude.

I could have any of the girls from All Hallows' in here with me and I guarantee they'd already be on their knees and sucking my dick.

Yet, here Raine fucking stands demanding to know who I really am.

Fuck that.

Fuck. That.

Not even my boys, Millie, know the whole truth behind my motivations. And after all these years, I'm not shattering everything I've been working toward by telling some misfit they allowed attend here to suck my secrets out of me, especially without actually sucking me.

"So, what's it going to be, Teddy?" she asks, tilting her head to the side.

Dammit. I want to refuse. I want to turn my back on her and walk right out that door as if this never happened.

My head screams for me to do it. But the rest of me... fuck, that really wants what she has to offer.

Leaning forward, I let my rough jaw graze her cheek before my breath tickles over her head.

"Theo." My name is barely a whisper on her breath.

But I hear it.

I hear it loud and fucking clear.

"I'm eighteen soon," I confess quietly. "I've been planning my eighteenth for years."

"O-okay," she stutters, confused as to why I'm talking about what she assumes will be a raging party.

"On my birthday, everything changes. And I'm worried about what that means for my future." For Millie's future. Although I keep that last bit back. She's already tangled up enough with my little sister. I don't need to add fuel to that fire. I'm already risking enough by telling her this much.

"I-I don't understand," Raine whispers, her voice cracked with need.

"You didn't ask for something that did. You asked for a truth. That's it."

"But—"

"No buts," I bark, glancing to the side, spotting something I can make very good use of. "You asked for something. Some might say you begged for it."

"No that's— What the hell are you doing?" she balks when I drag her arms behind her back and begin binding her wrists together with the rope.

"Doing exactly what I want with you now that I've given you my truth."

With nothing more than a gentle shove, I force her to the dirty floor. "Aw, now look who's on her knees bowing to the Heir."

"Fuck you," she hisses, staring up at me with nothing but unfiltered hate in her eyes.

There's a part of me, a really fucking big part, that wants to believe the words she came in her spewing. That she really just came here to listen, to help me work through the anger that's been festering inside me since I was forced to listen to the way Dad spoke to Maria, and all the unknowns that might have happened after we left.

I should have checked in. But Millie is my priority. She's

the child here. She's the one who needs protecting. Maria is a grown-arse woman who willingly—to a point—put herself in that position. It might be harsh, but I can only protect so many of us here. All I can hope is that everything I've been working toward comes fast enough.

"Yeah, sunshine. That's pretty much the plan. But first, I want to watch you down there with your lips wrapped around my cock."

Her eyes flare with heat.

"You like the sound of that, don't you?" Slowly she nods. "You didn't come in here to talk. You couldn't give a fuck what I have to say or what's bothering me. All you want is my dick. Isn't that right?"

She doesn't respond. Not that I need her to.

Her dark eyes, her parted lips, her heaving chest. They all tell me exactly what I need to know.

Raine's eyes remain locked on mine as I reach for my belt and rip my fly open.

"Your mouth is watering right now, isn't it?" I ask, shoving my hand into my trousers and squeezing my hard dick. "That's how badly you've missed my cock."

"Theo," she warns impatiently.

"You know, if you didn't try to fucking play me the other morning, you could have had so much more of it. But you had to go and fuck it up by trying to gain the upper hand. I'd have thought you'd have learned by now… I set the fucking rules, sunshine."

"You're sure wasting a lot of time for someone who apparently wants to get their dick sucked," she taunts.

Shoving my trousers and boxers down, I hold my length right in front of her. "You're a dirty, dirty girl, Raine."

Finally, her eyes drop from mine in favour of my dick, and it doesn't escape my notice that she doesn't even try to argue.

"Now, you're going to take my dick like a good girl. And if you blow me well enough, I might just reward you."

I tease her, rubbing the head of my cock over her lips, painting them with precum which she eagerly laps up. "You want that, sunshine?"

"Yes," she whimpers. "Use me."

"Fuuuuuck," I groan as I thrust forward, parting her lips with my thickness until I hit the back of her throat.

She gags in surprise, but she doesn't even attempt to pull back. Instead, her determined, fire-filled eyes hold mine.

Give it to me. All of it, she silently commands.

Sinking my fingers into her hair, I hold her in place as I do just that.

I fuck her mouth, using her to expel this anger, this uselessness, this hatred at the world for the cards Millie and I were dealt.

I'm not stupid. I know that a lot of what we've been given in life has its perks. We have money, enough that Millie is able to board here and be relatively safe. But money isn't everything.

"Fuck, Raine," I groan, staring down at her as I punish her for following me, for trying to get me to talk.

Tears streak down her cheeks, staining her skin black.

Her entire body trembles with need. And I know for a fact that if I were to drag her to her feet and push my hand between her thighs, I'd find her dripping for me.

"Your mouth is fucking sinful, sunshine," I groan as the first tell-tale signs of my release make themselves known.

I want it. I need it. But fuck, I could stand here and watch her like this forever.

"I'm going to fill your throat with cum," I tell her. "But you want that, don't you? You want to swallow me down like the good little whore you are."

Her eyes flare but she doesn't let up, she just keeps sucking me down until my cock jerks and my release slams into me.

"FUCK. RAINE. FUCK," I bellow as I spill my seed, filling both her mouth and her throat.

The second I'm done, I pull back, drag her from the floor with my hand around her throat and slam my lips down on hers.

I can taste myself on her tongue, but it does fuck all to lessen my need.

That was great. Fucking epic, if I'm being honest. But I need more. So much more. More than I think this filthy little rendezvous in the storage shed can deliver.

Spinning us around, I swipe my arm across the shit that's littered across a dirty, old, battered desktop sending plant pots and marker sticks everywhere before throwing her onto it, face down.

"Theo," she cries as I pin her there with a hand between her shoulder blades as I flip her school skirt up and find her bare arse staring back at me.

"Sexy," I mutter, training a finger over the thin strip of fabric that runs between her arse cheeks.

"Oh God," she whimpers when I drag it away from her body and continue lower, desperate to find out how wet she is.

And I am not disappointed.

"Oh, sunshine. You really fucking loved sucking my dick, didn't you?"

"Yes. Yes. Please," she begs, pushing up on her toes to offer herself up to me.

"Whore," I bark before cracking my palm across her arse.

My handprint instantly blooms on her pale skin and my chest puffs out in satisfaction.

Fuck yeah.

I land another before ripping her knickers from her body and stuffing them into my pocket.

"Oh God, yes," she cries when I drop to my knees—without instruction this time—spread her wide and lick up the length of her. Clit to arse. "THEO," she screams, ensuring that anyone who might be hanging around outside this very unsoundproofed wooden building knows exactly who is delivering this much pleasure.

I eat her like I haven't had a meal in a week, lapping at her and swallowing down her juices as if they're my own.

She cries out as I push her closer to her release. Her body trembles with her need to let go, but I hold it off. Punishing her. Testing her.

"NO," she screams when I finally convince myself to stop and get to my feet.

"Shut the fuck up, sunshine, or I'll have to gag you as well."

She does as she's told the second I step up behind her and run the head of my dick through her folds.

"Yes, please. Fuck me. Please."

"Couldn't say no even if I wanted to."

With my fingers twisted in her hair, holding her against the tabletop, I thrust into her.

She screams like a banshee, and I fucking love it.

Listen to that All Hallows'. This fucking girl is mine.

I fuck her like a savage. In only minutes, my shirt is sticking to my back, sweat beading my brow. But I won't stop. I can't. I am too fucking addicted.

Dragging her up, I change the angle, making her scream before I rip open her shirt, sending buttons pinging across the small space around us.

"Oh God."

The cups of her bra go next, giving me the access I need.

"Yes. Yes. Yes," she chants when I pinch her nipples.

"Your pussy squeezes me so fucking tight," I groan, barely holding it together. "Come for me. Let me feel how much you love my cock."

"Theo. Fuck. YESSSS."

"Good girl," I praise, making her gush before I fill her once again.

Our heaving breaths are the only thing that can be heard as we come down from our highs.

"Fuck. I needed that. Thanks."

A laugh of disbelief tumbles from Raine's lips as I lower her back to the desk and pull out. But it soon dies when she turns back to look at me and finds me fully dressed again and at the door ready to leave.

"Theo?" she warns.

"Thanks for the ride, Raine." And then I'm gone, leaving only the sound of her angry voice to follow me.

29

RAINE

I stare at the door in disbelief.

He didn't...

Except, he did.

Theo tied me up, fucked me six ways to Sunday, and then left me here as if it meant nothing.

Fuck.

Anger and shame swirl in my chest as I try desperately to loosen the rope binding my wrists. But Theo must have been a Boy Scout in a previous life because it doesn't give even a millimetre.

With a frustrated huff, I sink down to the cold floor and try to figure out my options. I could walk out of here with my head held high and find help. But there would be too many questions. Not to mention the fact he's completely ruined my uniform.

And the only people I could turn to are Millie or Tally and the girls.

Not happening.

Running my eyes around the place, I search for something that might help me. I spot some gardening shears and an idea springs to mind.

I won't be able to hold them properly, since my wrists are bound and all, but maybe I can wedge them open and slice the ropes apart.

It's risky but what other choice do I have?

Theo isn't coming back.

He got what he wanted. Epic sex and my humiliation.

A shiver goes through me as I remember how good it was. We might clash in every way possible but when we touch it's nothing but perfect chemistry.

Damn him.

I manage to clamber to my feet and go over to the counter. It's a bit tricky setting the shears in place but I manage to open them and anchor them apart. Carefully I align the rope between my wrists and start sawing it against the sharpened blade. My pulses thunders in my ears as I try to focus. One wrong move and—

"Fuck," I hiss as the shears slip, slicing into my skin. Blood wells, pain shoots through me.

Great. Now I'm restrained and bleeding with no way of helping myself.

The cut doesn't feel too deep, but the blood is everywhere, making me a little woozy.

"Think," I hiss. "Think."

My eyes land on the door again. I have no choice but to go for help. If I don't, I'll be stuck here until nightfall.

Sucking it up, I march toward the door only for it to swing open.

"I'm— shit, what happened?" Theo pales, his expression guttering.

"If you've come to gloat, you can fuck off."

"Raine, that's not... you need to get that looked at."

"It's fine. I just need to clean and dress it. Cut me loose and I'll sort it."

"Shit, yeah. Come here." He grabs a smaller pair of

gardening scissors off a shelf and takes my hands in his. "I didn't come to gloat."

"I don't believe you."

"You want the truth?" I press my lips together as he cuts me free. "You're under my skin, okay? I'm not used to... to feeling like this."

"You tied me up, fucked me senseless, and then left me here. Am I supposed to believe that was your attempt at wooing me."

"No, that's—" The muscle in his jaw tightens. "I came back."

"Yeah. Although the jury is out on why. I need to go." I snatch my hands away the second I'm free, cradling my injured arm to my chest. Blood coats my skin and my ruined school blouse.

"Wait, Raine." Theo grabs my arm, gently tugging me back to him. "I'm sorry, okay. I didn't know..." Our eyes clash and for the first time ever, I see a hint of regret in his eyes. "Just let me fix this, okay?"

"I... fine."

"Come on." He pulls off his blazer and wraps it around my shoulders, gently nudging me toward the door, and I hesitate. Something about this feels different.

I'd felt it earlier too, when he gave me a small, albeit vague piece of himself.

But I'm a fool if I let myself fall any deeper for him.

Because Theo's future is all mapped out for him, and my life will only truly start when I age out of the system and get as far away from here as possible.

A strange pang of sadness goes through me. But I shake it off. I don't belong here, with Theo and his friends, in a place like Saints Cross.

I can't ever forget that.

Even in the quiet moments, when it feels like the lines of

our hate for one another are blurring into something else, I can't forget it.

Theo Ashworth isn't mine.

He never will be.

"Seriously, you're bringing me to the Chapel?" I gawk at Theo as he pulls out his keys and unlocks the door.

"Got a better idea?" His brow lifts in that annoying smug way of his.

"Fine, but I'm leaving the second you patch me up."

"Yeah, yeah. Come on, sunshine. Let's get you cleaned up."

My shirt is ruined and my skin is sticky and wet with blood. I'm aware I probably look like something out of a horror show. But when Theo runs his dark eyes over me, I feel something else entirely.

"Don't tell me the blood turns you on," I quip, trying to lighten the mood, the intensity crackling between us.

"Only if I put it there." He flashes me a feral grin.

"You kind of did," I point out.

"Yeah, well, I didn't realise you'd go all Bear Grylls and try and hack yourself free."

"And if you hadn't have come back? What the hell did you think I was going to do?"

"I... I wasn't thinking, okay? Come on. I think there's a first aid kit in the kitchen cupboard."

Theo jams his fingers in his hair and stalks off.

I traipse after him, trying my best not to drip blood all over their immaculate fancy Heir-worthy floor. This place is... well, it's exactly what I expected.

Ostentatious. Fancy. Over the top. It's the epitome of posh boy domain and I can't deny I'm completely out of place here.

It's the kind of place I've only ever seen in films or on the TV.

Another world.

A sigh slips from my lips. What am I doing here? Pretending that Theo cares.

He might even think he does but we both know he's not really capable of those feelings. Because the world he lives in, tells him he doesn't have to care. People will always bend over backwards for him, cave to his will, because his name means something around here.

And I hate that. I hate that he'll never have to struggle or worry.

"You look ready to bolt." His voice startles me, and I slowly look over at him.

"I shouldn't be here."

"Relax, I invited you."

"This was a bad idea. I should—"

"Just let me get you cleaned up, okay? It would assuage my guilt."

"Guilt?" Laughter bubbles in my chest. "I didn't realise you were capable of such things."

"One thing."

"What?" My brows pinch.

"I gave you one real thing. Now it's your turn."

I scoff. "I think that negotiation was well and truly over the second you tied me up and left me in the abandoned shed."

"Come on, humour me." He stalks toward me again, his eyes burning into my own. Searching for answers I can't give him.

"Who are you, Raine? What are you running from?" He's on me now, so close I could reach out and touch him.

I don't though.

I can't.

"Theo." My breath catches. "What are you doing?"

I need him to stop. Because the urge to tell him something, to share my broken pieces is overwhelming.

But he's not my friend. I can't trust him.

"I don't know. I don't fucking know." He reaches for me, brushing the hair out of my eyes. "For what it's worth, I am sorry. I went too far."

"You only care because I got hurt."

"Truce?" he asks quietly.

"What—"

"Look, I don't know how you did it, but I know it was you who tagged our cars and ruined the party. And honestly, sunshine, I'm impressed. But if you keep on down this road, I won't be able to protect you."

"Funny, because I thought you said the person I should be scared of is you."

His lips quirk at that. "Yeah, I did say that."

"But?"

He stares down at me, making the butterflies in my stomach flap wildly. It's always the same with Theo, he reels me in, holds me captive until I can't think straight.

"Seems like I only want to hurt you now if it ends up with you screaming my name."

Fuck.

"Now let me clean you up and then we talk about how I'm going to make it up to you." Theo guides me over to the counter, his hand on the small of my back. Without warning, he lifts me up as if I weigh nothing and deposits me on the side.

"You're going to need to get out of that shirt." He's careful as he helps me out of it.

"Eyes up here." I snap my fingers, unable to hide my amusement at his obsession with my boobs.

"Stay put."

Theo is meticulous as he gathers all the supplies he needs

to clean and dress the cut. "It isn't too deep but it might need butterfly stitches."

"I'll be fine," I insist. "Just plaster me up and send me on my way."

"Raine, I—"

"Stop." I press my finger against his lips. "This isn't us, Theo. Let's not pretend it is."

"Have you always been this cynical?" he asks as he carefully applies a dressing to my arm.

"When you grow up in the system, you learn pretty quickly that there's very few people you can trust."

"Must be lonely."

"It's less complicated that way." I shrug.

"There, all done." He steps back, surveying his handiwork.

"You're pretty good at that."

"One of the downsides of playing rugby." He takes my hand and runs my pointer finger over a faded scar along his collarbone. "This bled like a bitch. I thought I was dying." I pull a bemused face and he chuckles. "I was only eight at the time."

"Poor baby." I run the pad of my thumb along the raised skin and his eyes shutter, the sound of his harsh swallow filling the space between us.

"That probably shouldn't feel so good," he admits.

"We're all a little scarred, Teddy." I smile.

"Yeah." He holds my gaze, a hint of a challenge there.

I should thank him and be on my way. Anything else is too dangerous. But I don't move, and he makes no attempt to encourage me.

Then out of the blue, he blurts, "Want a tour?"

"A tour?" I frown.

"It usually impresses girls." He gives me a sheepish shrug.

"I'm sure it does."

"It's your call," he says, giving me the choice.

I can leave or I can stay.

"Go on then, Theodore the Heir," I drawl. "Impress me."

30

THEO

Pinning her in place on the counter with my hips, I reach behind my head, and drag my shirt from my body.

"What are you—" she starts, her eyes locked on my chest the second I reveal the skin.

"Take your bra off," I demand.

"Theo," she whispers.

"You can't walk around like that. If the others come back and see you then..." I trail off scared of what saying the next few words of that sentence might mean.

But she's not going to give me the easy way out. Not that I really expected her to. That isn't how we roll.

"Then?" she prompts, her thighs clamping around my hips as if her body is desperate to drag me closer.

I hold her eyes, my heart thundering in my chest.

I want to lie. I want to spew some bullshit about Elliot losing his mind having a practically topless girl in his space when we should be in class but no doubt she'd call me out on it the second the words fell from my lips.

"Then... I might have to kill them."

I swear her gasp of shock sucks all the air from the vast room.

But she doesn't move.

Taking charge in the hope of distracting her from the truth in that confession, I reach behind her and unhook her bra, letting her already pretty exposed tits spill free.

Fuck me, they are insane.

Firm, round, and just the right size for my hands, with rosy, pink nipples that just beg to be sucked.

And right now, they're hard. Just like my dick.

What is it with this girl, and why can't I get enough of her?

"You're staring," she points out, resting back on one palm without a care in the world.

Her confidence is so fucking sexy.

My cock jerks, trying to convince me to just take her here on the kitchen counter, but then there's this other part of me, a part I don't think I've ever heard before telling me to treat her properly. Show her that I'm not exactly what she thinks I am. A sex-obsessed, elitist knobhead.

"Yeah, well. That's how good they are. Thank fuck I've got a couple of videos so I can watch them whenever I want. They're especially good when they're bouncing."

Her eyes darken, letting me know that if I were to try something right now then she'd be on board.

The memory of ripping her knickers off earlier slams into me.

If I were to lift her skirt...

Lock it down, Theo. Show her you're more.

Rearranging the shirt in my hand, I finally drag it over her head, for all the good it does. The top few buttons are undone showing me the valley between her tits and teasing me with the fullness of them, and her nipples press against the fabric.

"That looks a hell of a lot better on you than it does me, sunshine," I admit, finally stepping back, wrapping my hands around her waist and lifting her from the counter.

Her body slides down mine making my teeth grind.

If she wasn't aware of what her presence—her tits—were doing to me then there's no doubt she does now.

"So," I start, forcing myself to take a step back from her and wave my arm around the room. "Kitchen."

Her brows lift. "Yeah, I was wondering," she deadpans.

"Are you always this much of a smart-arse?"

"No," she states flatly. "Sometimes I'm worse."

Shaking my head, I reach for her hand and tug her into the living area, which admittedly she could see from the kitchen, but this is a tour after all.

"And you didn't want a bigger TV?" she asks, gazing at the massive screen on the wall.

"Yeah, we did but apparently it was too big and didn't align with something and it triggered Elliot's OCD so we had to downgrade a little.

"Elliot has OCD?"

"Nah, not diagnosed. He's just a fucking control freak in every sense of the word. Probably best not to tell him that you were just sitting on the kitchen counter without any knickers on while getting wet with the sight of my body."

She pauses and laughs. "Wait? You think that—" She points at my chest and makes a sweeping motion around my body. "Makes me wet. The girls around here really are desperate, huh?"

"You do know it would only take me a second to prove your bullshit." I turn into her body and stalk forward, giving her little choice but to reverse into the back of the sofa, pinning her against it with my hips.

"Even if you're not wet for me, which we both know you are. I fucked you bare an hour ago, I've no doubt that my cum is still running down your thighs."

Her breath catches at the truth in my words.

"How easy would it be to take you right here?" I ask before ripping my eyes from hers and jerking my chin in the direction of the sideboard. "Or there? Or back in the kitchen. Or on the dining room table?"

"Okay, you've made your point," she says, pressing against my chest to make me back up.

She doesn't mean it, not really. Her eyes tell me exactly what she wants, and it's not me farther away.

"Shall we continue?" she asks.

"Sure." Taking her hand again, I walk her through the rest of the ground floor before bringing her to a stop in front of a door.

"I don't need to see the cupboards," she teases when I reach for the handle.

"Oh, sunshine. This isn't a cupboard. Don't tell me you haven't heard rumours about our basement."

She chews on her lip for a second. "Of course I have. Every girl lacking a few brain cells dreams of spending their night's down here with one of you. Thought it was all lies and speculation though."

"Have you found anything about our reputation to be lies or speculation?"

She shrugs. "Can't say I've had enough experience to form judgement yet."

"If you say so. But I think I've proved at least one of my well-known skills pretty well."

"Are you calling yourself a whore, Teddy?"

"Practice makes perfect, sunshine. And right now, you seem to be the lucky girl reaping the benefits."

"Lucky... right. I'll try and remember that," she teases as I turn the light on, bringing the ancient hall lights to life.

"Well, this isn't creepy at all," Raine mutters as she follows me down the old stone steps, the temperature of the air around us cools.

"If you're really lucky, I'll tie you up and make you my sex slave."

"Can think of better ways of spending the rest of my day."

"Suuure," I mutter before pushing the key into the lock once we hit the bottom.

"Ready?"

"This had better be good, Teddy."

With a smirk, I shove the door open, revealing our playground inside.

"Umm... it's a bed. Not exactly creative," she points out, disappointment laced through her voice.

"Yes. This is just a bed. A four-poster bed," I agree, backing her against one of the posts, pinning her there with my hand around her throat. "But just think of all the fun that can happen when you're tied to it, and knowing I have a whole host of toys to play with."

Her breathing increases as she considers my words.

"Vibrators, nipple clamps, floggers, whips. You name it, we've got it. You like a little pain with your pleasure, don't you, sunshine?"

Her lips part to say something but my grip on her throat tightens, stopping her.

A smirk spreads across my mouth when her pupils dilate. Leaning forward, I let the tip of my nose trail across her cheek. "Filthy whore," I whisper in her ear, loving the way she shudders beneath my hold. "You'd let me do it all, wouldn't you?"

"Theo," she manages to gasp.

"Do you have any hard limits, sunshine?"

Her shriek of shock rips through the air when I bite her earlobe.

"N-not that I've found."

"Interesting," I muse, taking a step back. "Fuck, you look good."

Combing my fingers through my hair, I let my eyes eat her up.

Her nipples are so hard they're trying to cut through my

shirt, her chest is heaving with the erratic beat of her heart, and if she were to spread her thighs…

"Look around," I force out before I bend her over the bed and take what I need.

It takes her a hot second to register my words but the moment she does, she pushes from the post and begins exploring.

The minute her back is turned, I shove my hand into my boxers and squeeze the base of my needy dick.

Typically though, she looks back just as my eyes shutter.

"Problem, Teddy?" she asks, her eyes alight with amusement.

"Nothing you don't have the skills to fix."

She smiles innocently. "We'll see. So where is all the good stuff hidden?"

I point out the chest that holds most of our goodies before letting her explore the other rooms.

"Holy shit. Is that—"

"A St. Andrews Cross? Sure is, sunshine."

She stands in the doorway staring at it in amazement.

Stepping up behind her, I press the length of my body against her back before wrapping one hand around her hip, grinding her arse against my aching cock. "Can you see yourself tied up to that?"

"Theo," she whispers.

"You'd be totally at my mercy."

Dipping my head, I brush my lips against her shoulder where my shirt has fallen down.

A shiver rips through her as we connect.

"You'd have no control, Raine," I whisper when I get to the juncture between her shoulder and neck. "And I'd have it all." My other hand finds the bottom of my shirt and disappears inside. "Just think about all the things I could do to you up here. All the pleasure I could give you."

"Oh God," she moans when I cup one of her heavy breasts.

"I could run my lips and my hands over every inch of your body."

Her already increased breathing picks up.

"I could eat you until you're screaming with no way of getting away from my tongue."

"Fuck," she gasps when I pinch her nipple hard.

"I could make you come and come and come until you can't take anymore. Then, I could either let you down and take care of you, or I could leave you up there to think about all the trouble you've caused. Maybe, I could tell Elliot that you're guilty and let him play too." Over my fucking dead body, but she doesn't need to know that. "He's quite the dab hand at torture. I think you'd really enjoy it."

I suck on her neck making her entire body convulse. "I wonder if you'd bleed as prettily for him as you do me?"

Silence falls between us as the images I've just painted play out in my mind.

It would be so easy to make each of them come true.

So fucking easy.

But... not happening. Not today at least.

Taking a step back, I release her, leaving her to sag in disappointment.

"Want to see my bedroom?" I ask, forcing the desire out of my voice.

"Um..."

As we climb the stairs, I'm suddenly struck with a bolt of nerves.

Until Olivia and Reese started hooking up, no girls were allowed upstairs. They're still not unless they're a girlfriend. Elliot had no choice but to tweak that rule once Abi and Tally joined the group.

I shouldn't be taking Raine up there. She's not my girlfriend and is unlikely to ever be. But there's this weird need growing inside me that I want her in my space. I want to see how she looks, how she acts in my domain instead of hers.

Will she be as confident, or will she let her walls drop enough for me to get a few more glimpses of the real girl hiding behind the façade she shows the rest of the world?

"And this is where all the magic happens," I say, throwing my bedroom door open.

"I bet you say that to all the girls," she teases, stepping inside, and scanning the contents.

"No other girl has ever been up here," I blurt like a prick.

Shock rocks through her before she turns around, her eyes locking on mine. "So why am I?"

And well, if that isn't the million-dollar question.

31

RAINE

"So why am I?"

The words hang between us, heavy loaded. And Theo looks every bit as uncomfortable as I feel.

This wasn't supposed to happen.

I wasn't supposed to develop feelings for one of All Hallows' cocky, entitled Heirs.

Yet, here we are.

I'm in his room, in his domain, and despite the trickle of unease sliding down my spine, like this might all be part of some trick to get one over on me, I also feel an odd sense of relief.

Theo stares at me, lifting his shoulder in a small dismissive shrug. "Wish I knew the answer."

"If it makes you feel any better, I didn't expect to end up here either."

"Honestly, sunshine." He takes a step toward me. "I'm not sure that it does."

"I'll ask you again, Teddy." I crane my neck to look up at him as he towers over me. "Why am I here?"

"You know"—he reaches for a strand of my hair, toying

with it—"I don't think there's a single person I'd let get away with calling me that."

"Except me."

"Except you."

"Sounds dangerous."

"Oh, it is." His lips curve with wicked intent and he leans down to kiss me I assume. But I duck out of his way, putting some much-needed space between us.

He lets out a small, frustrated breath behind me but I don't turn around. If I do, I'll cave. I'll give into the undeniable chemistry between us, and I need to keep my wits about me.

I need to keep my walls intact before I figure out what I want from all this.

From him.

"Your room is exactly what I expected. I'm almost a little disappointed."

"Is that so?" There's a humorous edge to his voice as he watches me move around his room. The muted tones reflect his stormy personality. And the expensive sheets and furniture hint at his wealth. But it's the lack of personal effects that make my heart ache. No family photographs on the wall. No collection of childhood accolades. There's nothing that hints at the boy beneath the All Hallows' uniform.

"What?" he asks.

"It suits you." I finally look at him over my shoulder. "But it doesn't tell me anything about you, not really."

"Maybe I like it that way. Maybe I don't want to give away my secrets." He leans back on his desk, the corded muscles in his forearms drawing my attention.

Theo is beautiful. In a harsh, eat you alive kind of way. It isn't any wonder my traitorous body has taken a fancy to him.

"How about another trade? A secret for a secret?"

I arch a brow at that, trying to figure out what game he's playing. "Are you going to give me something real this time?" I ask.

"I will if you will." He folds his arms across his chest, his dark gaze daring me to play with him.

Damn him.

I can't resist.

I should, but I can't. He makes it too difficult to pull away. To protect myself.

"Fine. You first."

"When I was nine, my mother killed herself."

"I know," I whisper, pain clenching my heart.

"You do?" His brows furrowed. "How— Millie."

I nod. "We have therapy together, remember?"

"And here I thought I was giving you my darkest secret."

"For what it's worth, I'm sorry."

He gives me an imperceptible nod. "I found her."

"Theo." I inhale a sharp breath.

"I don't want your sympathy or pity, sunshine. It was a long time ago. But I've never forgotten... I'll never forget." Something ripples in his gaze—something that makes me think there's a lot more to the story.

Without thinking, without considering what it means, I go to him.

Reaching for his hand, I squeeze gently. "I really am sorry."

"Your turn, sunshine." A faint smile ghosts his lips, but it doesn't reach his eyes. "What are you running from?"

"I got into some trouble in my last foster home," I confess. "It was either come here and finish out my A Levels or spend a year in a young offenders' institute. My social worker and foster carer managed to convince the board to send me here."

His eyes narrow, harsh and assessing. "What kind of trouble?"

"The bad kind."

"Let me guess, tagging cars and tampering with electric supplies?"

"I already told you, I had nothing to do with that."

Theo's dark chuckle fills the room. "Such a good little liar." His hand curves around the side of my neck, his thumb stroking my thundering pulse point. But I'm not scared, his touch is almost reverent.

"What are you doing?" I breathe, my stomach knotted with desire.

"Making good on my promise to make it up to you."

"Theo, I—"

His mouth crashes down on mine, stealing my protests and all rational thoughts, as he pulls me into his body.

The kiss is hard and bruising as he lays claim to my sanity. But there's something different about it, something even more terrifying.

It's tender.

Theo isn't trying to dominate me, he's trying to apologise, and it completely throws me for a loop.

His hands slide down my waist and under my skirt and then he's hoisting me up and carrying me over to his bed.

"This is a bad idea," I murmur between kisses, my arms wrapped around his shoulders.

"Bad ideas are always the best kind."

"Your friends—"

"Aren't here. And honestly, I wouldn't give a fuck if they were. You're mine, sunshine." He lays me down and hovers over me. "Mine."

My head ratchets in my chest at his declaration, and my internal defences scream at me to make a run for it.

It's the only option that makes sense.

Theo and I have no future. We have no hopes at a normal relationship.

There's only one way this ends, in heartache and pain. I know that. He must too.

But it doesn't stop me from letting him strip me naked and trail kisses all over my skin. And it doesn't stop him from threading his fingers through mine, the most intimate gesture he's ever given me.

"Been dreaming about you in my bed," he admits, wrapping his tongue around my nipple and pulling it into his mouth.

I let out a breathy hiss, far too comfortable with the little bite of pain.

"My dirty girl likes it to hurt, doesn't she?"

His words echo through my mind.

My dirty girl.

My girl.

His girl.

It can never happen. So why does it light me up inside?

Vaughn really must have done a number on me, that I'm falling so easily for Theo's charm when I should be running for the hills.

But I know it's more than that. You can't help who you fall for. On paper we couldn't be more different. Broken foster kid with barely a penny to her name and the rich entitled kid from Saints Cross with his future mapped out before him.

It's as tragic as it is laughable.

So why does it feel so good?

"Ah," I cry out as he massages my boobs, trailing hot wet kisses down my stomach until he drops off the end of the bed.

Grabbing my ankles, he gives me a sharp tug and pulls me down the bed before burying his head between my thighs and working on his apology.

"Fuck, you taste good," he rasps, licking at me like a man starved.

I writhe beneath him, arching my hips and demanding more. My fingers slide into his short hair and hold him there.

"Such a greedy little thing." He chuckles, the blast of warm air skittering across my clit almost too much.

"Theo," I beg.

He answers my plea, pressing two fingers inside me and

curling them deep as he rolls his tongue over my clit in torturous circles.

"Yes... fuck, yes."

My fingers curl into Theo's expensive sheets as pleasure saturates every inch of me. He's so damn good at this, it's impossible to remember all the reasons why this is a really bad idea.

"I'm going to make you come on my tongue, then I'm going to fill you up with my cum."

"Yes... yes," I whimper.

"Jesus, sunshine. Keep up those sexy little noises and I'm pretty sure I'll blow."

Theo switches tactics, using his thumb on my clit and licking into me. Deep thorough licks that suck the air clean from my lungs.

He reaches up and squeezes my boob hard and I shatter, coming so intensely I see stars.

"Fuck yeah," he drawls, lapping at my release.

Slowly, he crawls over me, gazing down at me with utter arrogance.

Bastard.

But I'm too blissed out to care.

"Taste yourself," he orders, kissing me. Our tongues slide together and the sharp taste floods my mouth.

When he pulls away, there's a look of surprise in eyes.

"What?" I ask, feeling the subtle change in the air.

"Ready to get fucked?" He switches on the Heir mask, hiding whatever he'd almost revealed to me.

It makes my heart drop a little.

But of course that's how it will always be between us. We might offer up pieces of ourselves, flirt with the line that separates us, but we'll never truly be more than this.

And maybe, deep down, we both know that.

In a way, it makes it safe.

Acceptable.

Justifiable.

Theo will never give me his heart and I'm not sure I have one left to offer.

We have this though.

Stolen moments and hate-fuelled kisses.

It's easier this way.

Less messy and complicated.

It's why I don't put an end to it. Why I don't shove him off and make a run for it.

Because feeling something is better than feeling nothing.

He stares down at me, awaiting my answer. And I realise he's waiting for permission again.

I reach up and stroke his brow, smiling.

"Do your worst, Ashworth."

And part of me, means it.

32

THEO

This shouldn't feel so good.

I shouldn't have brought her up here.

I should have just fucked her in the basement and then sent her back to her dorm room happy that she was no longer leaving a trail of blood behind her because of me.

But I didn't.

I couldn't.

Having her here. In my space. In my bed.

Every single thing about it feels right.

It should also probably freak me out, but it doesn't.

I'm too content and sated to care.

Too blissed out on everything Raine has given me in the past few hours to remember reality even exists.

Is this why Reese and Oak fought as hard as they did? Because of moments like this.

My abs clench when Raine runs her hands down my stomach making my semi stir despite the fact I blew inside her again only a few minutes ago.

I've always been pretty insatiable. But this is on another level.

A growl rumbles deep in my throat as her hand continues

to run over my skin. My entire body is alert, my nerve endings sparking, begging for more, for anything she can offer.

But then with just a handful of words, she shatters the bubble.

"I should go before the others get back."

I still as ice washes through my veins.

"Don't give a fuck about the others, sunshine."

"Yeah, well. You're not the one who's going to have to do the walk of shame past them."

"They won't give a shit. I've done a hell of a lot worse."

She rears back, her eyes wide. "Oh yeah?"

Not taking the bait, I chuckle. "Yeah. And something tells me that you have too."

Her lips part to argue but she quickly finds that she has no argument.

"Exactly. Be bad with me, Raine. It's fun."

"I have been. We've missed classes. I've missed therapy. You've missed practice. We've already—"

"Nowhere near," I confess, rolling over her, pressing the length of my naked body against hers as I claim her lips in a filthy kiss that ensures I'm completely full mast and ready to go.

"Theo," she moans when I begin kissing down her already hickey-covered neck.

Hooking her leg around my waist, I grind against her. "You sore?" I whisper in her ear.

There's a question I've never bothered to ask before.

I hear the words echo back to me and shake my head lightly.

Since when have I fucking cared enough to even think about it, let alone ask?

What the fuck is wrong with me?

Or... what is so right with her?

"Nothing I can't handle. I like a bit of pain, remember."

"Fuck, you're perfect." Lining myself up, I slowly push

inside her. She tenses, letting me know that she's more than a little sore. But the second her eyes find mine, they fiercely and silently demand for me to continue. So I do. Slowly.

"One day," I tell her, letting my lips brush hers as my hips roll. "I'm going to take you downstairs, and I'm going to do all those filthy things I promised to you down there. You'll look so fucking beautiful at my mercy on that cross."

A groan spills from my lips as she gushes around me.

"You like that, don't you, sunshine?" She nods. Not that I need her to. Her body tells me everything I need to know. "You want to hand all control over. Let me do whatever I want. I'll hurt you, punish you, mark you. Maybe even make you bleed."

"Oh God, Theo," she gasps.

"Make." Thrust. "You." Thrust. "Mine." Thrust.

Despite our slow pace, her nails dig into my back, carving me up in the best possible way.

"I'll eat you until you're screaming for mercy and fuck this tight little pussy until the only name you remember is mine."

"Fuck," she pants.

Lifting my hand, I push a finger into her mouth. "Suck," I demand, loving that she instantly complies.

Her eyes hold mine as she wraps her tongue around my digit, predicting what I want.

The second she's done, I pull it free and slide my hand down her body. "And I'll take you here," I say, pressing my finger against her arsehole.

"Oh shit, Theo," she cries when I push it slightly inside.

"You want that, don't you, sunshine? You want me to own every inch of this sinful body."

"Yes. Please, Theo."

Fuck if the sound of her calling my name as she's about to come doesn't make me feel like a motherfucking king.

"Come for me, Raine. I want to feel your pussy milking my dick."

"Oh God, yes. Yes," she mutters as she falls.

She's not as loud as previous times, but holy shit is it just as beautiful to watch her fall.

She's almost done when she finally drags mine out of me.

But I don't get to enjoy it like I should because feet pound up the stairs on the other side of the door before it's thrown wide open.

"What the fuck, Ashworth? Coach is going to have your balls for th— oh shit," Elliot gasps, as Raine tucks herself into my body as if she's trying to hide.

More footsteps approach.

"What's going—"

"Theo has a girl in his room," Elliot announces haughtily, cutting off Reese's question.

"Fuck off, does he. Theo never brings anyone up he— fucking hell," Oak gasps.

"Will you fucking get out?" I bark.

"Who is she?" Reese asks.

I glance over my shoulder and find the three of them standing there with smug fucking smirks playing on their lips.

"Fuck. Off."

Looking back down, I find Raine with her eyes wide beneath me.

She didn't want to do this, she didn't want to get caught.

If I'd have let her go when she said then—

Fuck.

"Please," I say quieter. "Leave."

"Yeah, man," Oakley agrees before they all shuffle out and close the door.

They might be down for a laugh and to do anything to rile me up, but Reese and Oak have girls now. They get it.

Fuck. Does that mean I get it?

If it were Keeley or any of the other chasers in my bed right now—un-fucking-likely—I'd have kicked their arses out of my bed and I would have given zero shits about her being naked and forcing her to face them.

But there is no fucking chance of that happening with Raine.

I'm not sharing her with these motherfuckers. No fucking way.

"Shit. I'm sorry," I whisper, dropping my brow to hers.

"Not your fault," she replies quietly. "What are the chances they'll forget all about that and go out instead of waiting for us to come down?"

"Slim to fucking none."

"That's what I thought."

"We could just stay in here? I can think of plenty for us to do," I tease, rolling my hips, letting her know that I'm still inside her.

"You keeping him warm or something?" she asks with a smirk.

"Or something."

Before she can ask any more questions I'm not sure I want to answer, I steal her lips again.

"You're a little bit too distracting, you know that?"

"Been called worse, sunshine. Where are you going?" I pout when she ducks under my arm and rolls away from me.

"To clean up and attempt to sneak out."

She throws the covers back and confidently marches across my bedroom completely naked.

It is fucking everything.

Swinging my legs off the edge of the bed, I watch her arse and hips sway as she moves.

"There will be no sneaking. That implies that you're ashamed of this."

She pauses in the doorway. "You mean, you're not?" she asks without looking back.

Her question is like a knife straight through my chest.

I knew her confidence was all an act to cover up... well,

whatever she's covering up. But I wasn't expecting it to be that low when all the layers are peeled back.

Pushing to my feet, I close in on her.

Despite the fact that she must hear me coming, her entire body jolts when my hands land on her waist.

"Never," I promise before dropping a kiss on her shoulder. Stepping around her, I take her hand and look her dead in the eyes. "Let me clean you up. Then I'll walk you home."

She shakes her head. "No, you don't have—"

"You're right, I don't. I want to."

She swallows nervously as I tug her into my bathroom. I don't let her go as I lean into the shower and turn the water on, and the second it's warm, I pull her inside with me.

"Wherever you just went," I say, staring down into her eyes. "It's a place you don't need to be. I'm not ashamed of how many times I've made you come this afternoon. And neither should you be."

She sighs, her chest rising so high her nipples brush my chest temptingly, but she never says the words that are on the tip of her tongue.

I want to push her. But I'm also terrified about what she might say, so I take the pussy's way out and reach for my shampoo instead.

"Turn around, I want to take care of you."

Without words, she reaches up on her toes, and presses a kiss to the underside of my jaw before doing as she's told.

"Good girl," I praise with a light smack to her arse before getting to work.

The second our footsteps are heard as we descend the stairs, silence replaces the chatter and TV that previously filled the vast open space of the ground floor.

I keep my head high, wanting to prove to Raine that what I said upstairs was true. Also, I don't exactly think any of these lot will be overly shocked when her identity is revealed.

"Ready?" I whisper.

"Absolutely not," she snaps. But it's too late, we're here and—

"Raine?" they all parrot at once.

Okay so maybe they are a little shocked.

Lifting her hand, she waves somewhat nervously as the girls all hop up from their seats and come rushing over.

Leaving them to grill her, I make my way over to my boys.

"Thought you hated her?" Elliot asks, studying closely.

"Oakley thought the same about Tally and look where that got him," I counter.

"Not sure this is the same but okay. It was only a few hours ago you were convinced she tagged our cars and cut out power, now you're inviting her upstairs and letting her warm your dick?"

I lift one shoulder in a shrug. "She hurt herself. I was taking care of her."

"Oh well, that explains it," Reese teases. "Theo the good Samaritan, taking in all the criminals in their hour of need."

"Shut the fuck up. She was hurt because of me. I was just—"

"Giving her a pity fuck?" Oak asks.

"No. I just..." I run my fingers through my hair before scrubbing my face. "I don't know what the fuck I'm doing, okay?" I confess quietly before glancing back to make sure Raine's attention has been completely stolen by the girls. "It just... it felt right.

"Fucking hell," Elliot mutters, falling back on the sofa in disbelief.

"What?"

"You've fallen for her, haven't you?"

"What? No. She's just a good fuck and—"

"Sure, man. Keep lying to yourself. I can assure you, it totally makes the whole thing easier," Oakley says smugly.

"I don't like her, I just… she's a really good fuck, okay? And I needed that after Sunday."

"Sure. We totally get it," Reese says, elbowing Oakley while Elliot stares up at the ceiling. "She staying for dinner? We're ordering pizza."

"We are not. It's game week. Protein-rich meals all around."

"So," Reese says, ignoring Elliot as he pushes to his feet. "Pizza all around?"

33

RAINE

"Abi, please stop looking at me like that," I murmur as I sit with the girls while the boys inhale the pizza they ordered.

"I just... I envy you."

"What? Why?" I'm a little taken aback by the defeat in her voice.

"Because you've been here weeks and already got Theo wrapped around your little finger." She hesitates, glancing toward Liv and Tally but they're deep in conversation. "I'll never be that girl."

"What girl?"

"The girl who goes after what she wants. The girl who gets the boy." She lets out a soft sigh, her pained gaze moving around the room until it lands on Elliot.

"He likes you," I say. I've noticed the way he watches her and picked up on the fact everyone gives him shit about it.

"No, he doesn't. He feels sorry for me."

"Abi, I'm sure that's not—"

"It is." She lowers her face, letting her hair shield her scars. "I'm not like the girls he messes around with. Sexy. Confident... Experienced. Even if he did like me a little bit, he wouldn't act on it. He sees me as a little bird that needs sheltering. Protecting. It's sweet but it also hurts."

"Have you told him how you feel?"

"I've thought about it. But then I'd lose him completely. Having him care about me as a friend is better than not having him at all."

I'm not sure I agree but I don't argue. Because she has a point. Elliot would eat a girl like Abi alive. And I'd hate to see her get hurt.

"You could have told me, you know," she adds quietly.

"I didn't think there was anything to tell." I shrug.

"And now?"

I glance over at the boys, trying to tell myself that this doesn't change anything. That my plan is still the same. Turn eighteen and get the hell out of here.

I don't belong here, I never will, no matter how much I want to sit here and pretend.

"It's just a bit of fun." I meet her knowing gaze and force a smile.

"Does he know that?"

"I—"

"If you want pizza you'd better get in here before Reese eats it all," Oakley chimes.

"Fuck off, arsehole. I've had like four slices."

"And a whole box of dough balls."

"So, I'll work it off later when I'm balls deep in your sis—"

"Let's not do this again, shall we?" Liv gets up and goes over to them, perching on the arm of the sofa beside Reese. But he wraps an arm around her waist and drags her into his lap.

"Here, eat." He hand feeds her a slice of pepperoni much to Oakley's annoyance.

"You not going to feed your girl, Teddy?" Oak teases, and I glower at the lot of them.

"Leave it out." Theo leans over and whacks him upside the head. "If Raine wants to eat, she can feed herself."

"Spoken like a true gentleman," Tally snickers.

"Because Oak is such a nice guy," Elliot scoffs, and she frowns.

"Oh, I don't know. He sure knows how to treat me right."

"Damn straight, Prim. I'm all about the giving."

"Does every conversation you have turn into a sexual innuendo?" I ask, mildly amused.

"Pretty much," Elliot grumbles. "But you'll get used to it. So, Raine Storm—what kind of fucking name is Raine Storm anyway?"

Everyone looks at me and I want to shrink into the ridiculously comfy sofa. "My mum was a bit kooky."

"You don't say."

"Oh, I don't know, I kind of like it." Abi offers me a sympathetic smile. "Is that why you call her sunshine?" She turns her attention to Theo.

"I..." He gulps, running a hand over his head and down the back of his neck.

"Awkward." Oakley whistles, loving every second of the ripple of tension that goes through the room.

It's Tally who finally comes to our rescue. "Oakley tells me you have a big birthday on the horizon Theo."

"Beckworth needs to learn to keep his mouth shut."

"Just because you're the baby Heir." He grins, and Theo flips him off. "We need to start planning something epic."

"Is anything really ever epic now the two of you are wifed up?" Elliot asks, and it isn't lost on me how he leaves me and Theo out of the equation.

It shouldn't sting so much as it does, but I can't say I'm surprised.

I'm not one of them.

He knows that as well as I do.

"You sound a little jealous there, Eaton," Reese taunts. "You know I'm sure you could easily rectify—"

"Reese," Liv hisses, clapping her hand over his mouth.

Elliot's expression darkens as he shoves out the chair and stalks out of the room.

Abi lets out a heavy sigh. "Do you have to keep goading him like that?"

"What, Red? It's funny."

"We all know he's—"

"I need to go." Abi shoots up too, grabbing her bag and fidgeting with her hands. "I'll see you all tomorrow."

"Abs, wait. Fuck, I didn't mean..." But she's already gone, hurrying out of the Chapel like there's a monster on her tail.

"Well done, dickhead." Liv swats Reese's chest. "I thought we agreed no more poking the bear."

"Fuck that. The sooner he gets out of his head, the better. We can all see he wants her."

"Have you considered that maybe he's staying away because he cares?"

"Nah, he's a coward. If you want something, you should go after it." Oakley puffs out his chest, grinning at his sister. "Worked for you and Reese, and me and Prim."

"Because we can deal with your macho bullshit. Abi is different."

"You know, she's probably a lot stronger than you all give her credit for," I say.

Theo gets up and comes over, dropping down beside me. "Raine's got a point. Abi can handle her own. She's proved that more than once."

"Yeah, but can she handle Elliot?" Reese asks, and the mood turns sombre.

Theo moves closer, lifting his arm toward me but I stand. "I should probably go."

"Go?" he echoes.

"Yeah. I have some homework and stuff to do."

"Stuff..." He arches his brow. "Fine. I'll walk you out."

"No, don't do that. I'll be fine. I'll talk to you later."

I give the girls a small wave and hurry out of there. It's silly, I know. But it's too intimate, too much too soon.

I could too easily get used to it.

And that's a huge problem. Because this isn't my life. Here, with these people.

For a second, I think Theo might follow, but to my relief, he lets me leave.

And it isn't until I'm outside, treading the path back to my dorm, that I realise he still didn't give me back my phone.

So I can't text him later.

Even if I wanted to.

When I arrive back at the Bronte Building, Millie is just heading out. "Oh, hey," she says. "Where were you?"

"I... just with Abi." The lie sours on my tongue. But I'm not sure Theo will want her to know about us.

Not that there is an us to know about.

It was sex.

Really great sex with some unexpected pizza thrown in.

Hardly the beginnings of a beautiful relationship.

Ha. Not that I'm capable of that. Because to be capable of that, you have to be able to trust people. Something that I've learned over the years is not as easy as it sounds.

"Are you okay?" she asks, eyeing Theo's shirt. "Your neck—"

"I'm fine," I blurt, slapping a hand over my neck.

"I'm just heading to the centre. They're having a game night. Do you want to come?"

"I... can't tonight." The flash of dejection in her eyes is like a fist around my heart. But I'm a mess.

I'm not even wearing my own clothes for God's sake.

I need to go to my room, take a long hot shower, and forget all about the last couple of hours.

"Oh, okay. Maybe another time then."

"Definitely." I go to move past her, but she snags my arm.

"Oh, and Raine?"

"Yeah?"

"You're a terrible liar."

Millie stalks off, leaving me standing there in a puddle of guilt.

Shit. She knows.

Well, maybe she doesn't know, but she suspects something.

I make a beeline for my room and slam the door, frustrated with myself and this whole ridiculous situation.

I let my guard down.

I let my guard down and Theo made his move.

Damn him.

Surely he must know that nothing can ever come of this.

Who am I kidding? That's probably all part of the allure. His evil plan.

Get me to fall for him and then break my heart.

As if I'd ever give him the chance.

I strip out of his shirt and my school skirt and head into the shower. The water feels incredible, sluicing over my skin. My gaze snags on the fingerprints on my hips. The little hickeys littering my boobs and chest.

He marked me.

Theo marked me, and I hate to admit I like it.

I take my time, washing away the memories of his touch, his treacherous kisses. When I'm finally done, I turn off the water, grab a towel and step out of the cubicle.

The girl staring back at me in the mirror isn't me.

She looks... different.

Happier.

It's a strange feeling. And part of me is angry at myself for falling for the lie. The illusion.

For forgetting who I am and where I come from.

I towel off my hair before wrapping myself in a bath sheet.

When I go back into my room, I freeze, a small gasp slipping off my lips.

In the middle of the bed is a note with my phone.

Plucking it off the bed, my heart ratchets in my chest as I read the neat scrawl.

Don't run from me again.
T

He was here again.

In my room.

I want to be angry and maybe a little part of me is. But another emotion overrides the frustration I feel at his little drop and dash.

Excitement.

The threat is clear, but I can't deny a little thrill goes through me at his warning.

At the promise woven into every word.

34

THEO

"Okay, that's everything," Christian Beckworth says, stuffing the papers I just signed into a folder and then hiding them into his briefcase that sits between us on their dining table.

"And you're sure about this, Theo?" Fiona asks softly. Concern glitters in her eyes, but it's pointless.

"I've been planning this for too long to let it go now."

"We know sweetie. It's just... it's going to be huge."

"Nothing less than he deserves."

"Agreed," Christian growls fiercely, his fists curling on the tabletop. "Thank you for trusting us with this, Theo."

I nod, feeling all kinds of things about the fact my eighteenth birthday, the day my life changes for the better, is approaching. I've been waiting for this. Counting down the days. Praying it would come faster.

And it nearly is.

It's almost time for the world to know what a cunt Anthony Ashworth really is.

I've spent years documenting his indiscretions, collecting evidence to prove that almost every word that comes out of his mouth is a lie.

In only a few days, all that work is going to pay off, triggering a whole line of events that both Christian and Fiona have planned for.

We're going to be fine. Nothing really needs to change for us.

All of this is about justice and keeping Millie safe, and those are my biggest priorities.

Even if the thought of having to prepare her for what's about to come twists up a tight knot in my stomach.

It'll be worth it.

It has to be worth it.

No one needs a sick and twisted piece of shit like him in their lives, not after what he's done to us.

"Wouldn't have trusted anyone else," I say honestly. Not only is Christian a kick-arse lawyer, Fiona too, but seeing as they've both been in my life as far back as I can remember and hell, they've been better, kinder parents to me than my own father.

"Okay, well, if you're happy. I've got a few calls to make."

Christian pushes his chair back as the front door to the house slams closed.

"Dad?" Oakley calls, making my heart sink into my feet.

Fuck. My eyes collide with Christian's, but he's as cool as a cucumber, as always.

"Oh, hey," Oak says as he bursts into the room. "Have you seen— Theo?" he balks, not expecting to find me sitting in the middle of the kitchen with his dad and stepmum. "What are you doing here?"

"He was searching for you," Fiona says smoothly, also pushing her chair back. "Would you like a coffee?"

"Uh..." Oak rubs the back of his neck as his eyes dart suspiciously between us all. "I told you this morning I had a revision session after school."

He drills me with a look.

"Shit, yeah. I totally forgot. When you weren't at the

Chapel, I thought I'd try my luck here," I lie, hoping I sound as smooth as Christian and Fiona.

"What's so important you needed to hunt me down?"

Shit.

"Um... I wanted to... I wanted to talk about..." I swallow nervously, desperately trying to dig something believable up. "Raine."

A wide smile curls at Oakley's lips, and I breathe a sigh of relief.

"Oh, man. I've been waiting for this day," he states, placing his hand over his heart like a proud father. "Come on. I'll tell you everything I've learned."

"Oh Jesus," Fiona mutters while Christian watches us both with amusement.

"And then come find me again and I'll put you right."

"Tally has no complaints," Oak states proudly.

"Not what I overheard her saying to Liv," Fiona adds over her shoulder before disappearing from the room with her coffee.

"Oh burn," I laugh.

"She's lying. I know she's lying," Oak sulks.

"Maybe I should have gone after Reese for this. Get all his secrets about how he makes your sister—"

"Yeah, and we're done now," Christian says, following Fiona out.

"Dude, you really know how to clear a room," Oakley mutters as he pulls the fridge open and grabs a couple of cans.

"So what is it you need to know? Is it about periods?"

Fuck my life.

After having to spend longer than I ever wanted to listen to Oakley give me his wealth of advice when it came to having a girlfriend, we finally left his house and headed back to the Chapel.

Thankfully, he never questioned me again about why I was there in the first place when he had very clearly told me about the study session he was doing. I guess talk of Tally was enough to distract him. And the second we walk into the Chapel, the girl in question steps straight into his arms and he forgets I even exist.

"Where the hell have you two been?" Elliot asks, nosey motherfucker.

"Nowhere exciting. You untwisted your knickers at last?" I ask, remembering him storming off last night and his noticeable absence from the group all day.

He glares at me but says nothing.

"Dude, all I'm saying is if you want to talk, I'm all ears. You want her, you don't, what the fuck ever. But until you make a decision and stick with it, you're going to get ribbed about it."

"I don't," he mutters.

"Then maybe stop watching her like she's the only girl in the world," I suggest, clapping him on the back before I move toward the stairs.

There might be girls here, but it was abundantly clear from the moment I stepped through the door that she wasn't and my need to see her is too much to deny.

"I'm going for a shower," I announce to no one before taking the stairs two at a time.

The second I burst through my bedroom door, I pull my phone from my pocket and open up the app I installed last night.

Grabbing that camera alongside her phone was a spur of the moment thing. But once the thought had taken hold, I couldn't let it go. The prospect of watching her, learning more about the real her was too much to deny and I had it in my pocket long before I could even begin talking myself out of it.

It's an invasion of privacy, sure. I'm more than aware of that.

But she tagged our cars and ruined our party.

She might suck cock like no other and have a pussy I can't stop thinking about. But she still went after us in a way no one else would be brave enough to.

Just because we're fucking, it doesn't mean I've forgotten.

"Hurry," I snap at my phone when the app takes longer to open than I'd like.

The second the image of her room appears something settles inside me, but it's empty.

"Shit," I hiss. But my disappointment only lasts so long before there's movement on the other side of the room.

I lower my phone to the side as I strip out of my uniform, leaving it in a heap on the floor before climbing onto the bed in only my boxers.

"Oh hell, yeah," I groan when she does the same in only a small pair of shorts and a vest.

Thank fuck for the wealthy parents of this town who pay over the odds for education and heating to keep their precious little princes and princesses warm even on the coldest of days.

Folding her legs, Raine opens her laptop in front of her and starts typing.

For the longest time, I just watch her.

But eventually, and inevitably, I get a little bored.

Finding my iPad in my bedside table, I install the app on there as well, before getting myself comfortable with it in full view while I open my messages on my phone.

> Theo: What are you doing?

She pauses writing and reaches behind her.

I still when a wide smile curls at her lips.

Fuck. She's beautiful.

Sunshine: Homework.

> Theo: Sounds like fun.

Sunshine: Meh. I can think of better things to be doing. What about you?

> Theo: Oh, I can certainly think of better things to be doing.

Sunshine: So what are you doing?

A smirk kicks up the corner of my lips.

> Theo: Lying on my bed wishing you were in it with me.

The second she reads those words, she kicks her laptop away and stretches her legs out before her.

Sunshine: Theo…

Sunshine: You're bad.

> Theo: Down to the core, baby! Wanna be bad with me?

She stares at the screen for a few seconds, and I start to panic.

But then as she starts typing her smile grows and I know I've got her.

Sunshine: How do I know you're not out with the guys?

> Theo: Because I'd be wearing more clothes than this.

I snap a photo of myself from the neck down and send it over.

Her eyes widen when she receives it, giving me a nice ego boost. Not that I really need it.

> Sunshine: Someone looks like they're enjoying themselves a little too much seeing as they're alone…

> Theo: I'm thinking about you. What do you expect?

Reaching up, she tucks a lock of her hair behind her ear.

> Theo: You're thinking about me too, right? About how good it feels when I'm inside you.

Her lips move as she says something and I rush to turn the volume up on my iPad, although not before double-checking the microphone on my end is off.

That would be bad, and I have no intention of fucking this up before it starts.

> Sunshine: Not really, I'm thinking about my assignment.

> Theo: Liar. I bet your nipples are hard and your pussy is wet.

> Sunshine: Maybe you should show your face and find out.

> Theo: Or…

> Theo: You could test my theory out and let me know what you find.

> Sunshine: What am I going to get in return?

> Theo: Whatever you want.

I hesitate before sending that offer, but in the end, I figure it's true.

> Sunshine: Anything?

> Theo: Within reason, of course. Believe it or not, there are actually some things I'm not capable of.
>
> Theo: And I should point out that making you come from a distance isn't one of them. I have every intention of having you crying out my name within thirty minutes.

Sunshine: Thirty? You really are confident, huh?

> Theo: You think you can do the same for me?

Sunshine: I already am. You've confessed to thinking about my pussy. I bet you've already got your dick in your hand right now.

> Theo: Confidence is sexy on you.

Sunshine: Prove me wrong.

> Theo: Can't.

Sunshine: Prove. It.

Shoving my boxers down my legs, I kick them from my feet as I wrap my and around my shaft and take a photo.

> Theo: Been sitting in class like this today wishing we were back here. Addicted, sunshine.

Sunshine: I hate to admit this, but you have a really pretty cock.

> Theo: Pretty? Is that meant to be a compliment or an insult?

She barks out a laugh at my reply and I can't help but chuckle with her.

> Sunshine: I think the number of orgasms it gave me yesterday should answer your question.

> Theo: I guess it does. Are you touching yourself too?

She hesitates and I wait to see if she's going to lie to me or not.

> Sunshine: Not yet. What did you want me to do?

"Fuck me, you're perfect."

> Theo: Everything. But start with your tits. Slide your hand up whatever top you're wearing and pinch your nipples.

> Sunshine: Who says I'm wearing a top?

"Oh, you're good," I mutter watching in fascination as she does exactly what she's told.

> Theo: I like to think you aren't. But I guess I'll never know for sure.

> Theo: Imagine your hands are mine. Be rough.

The second she reads that demand, a loud moan falls from her lips as she follows orders.

Oh, fuck yeah, this is what I need tonight.

35

RAINE

A whimper spills from my lips as I do exactly what Theo ordered.

God, this boy.

He's so far under my skin I worry there might be no getting him out. Which means, when I leave, it's going to hurt.

And I'll only have myself to blame.

The vibration of my phone startles me and I hurriedly snatch it up, desperate for his next words.

His orders.

> Theo: Slide your fingers down your stomach and feel how wet you are.

> Raine: This isn't going to work. Call me?

The shrill of my phone fills the room, sending my heart into overdrive.

"Are you wet?" Theo rasps and I can imagine him with his hand wrapped around his perfect dick, stroking it hard and fast. "I bet you're soaked."

Slipping my hand down my stomach, I suck in a sharp breath as they dance over my knickers.

"Tell me," he demands.

"I'm wet."

"Yeah, you are." I hear the grin in his voice. "Push two fingers inside your pussy, imagine it's me."

"Okay."

"Good girl," he drawls as I hook my underwear aside and slowly press two fingers into myself.

"Fuck, yeah. Thumb on your clit, get yourself nice and worked up."

I barely hear his words as pleasure fires off around my body.

"It feels good," I murmur.

"It looks good too."

"W-what?"

"I've seen how good you look taking my fingers, my cock. Got those images imprinted on my mind." He grunts.

"Are you close?" I ask, eyes closed and head thrown back as I imagine him here, touching me.

"Yeah. I want to come all over your tits. Would you let me do that, sunshine? Would you let me use you in any way I wanted?

"Yes... yes," I pant, a wave building inside me.

I'm so close. My legs begin to tremble as I—

The frantic bang on the door perforates my pleasure bubble, replacing it with sheer frustration.

"I swear to God, Theo, if that's—"

"It isn't," he growls, clearly pissed. "Don't open it. We're not done."

"You're not the boss of me, Teddy." I fix my clothes and clamber off the bed.

"I swear to God. Raine. Do not open that—"

I hang up on him, the phone sex high falling away as the banging grows more insistent.

I grab my door handle and yank. "What the fuck is— Millie." Confusion washes over me as I take stock of her dishevelled appearance. The tender spot along her cheekbone.

"What the hell happened?"

"C-can I come in? Please..."

"Of course. Come on." I wrap an arm around her shoulder and pull her inside.

"Let me grab a hoodie," I say, giving her a gentle shove toward my bed while I make myself decent.

"What were you doing?" she asks innocently enough.

"Just chilling," I lie.

"I'm going to get a cold compress for your face, okay?"

My phone starts ringing and panic races through me. But Millie pays it no attention, staring at the carpet, her expression completely numb.

Shit.

I'm out of my league here.

Grabbing my phone on the way to the bathroom, I quickly text Theo.

> Raine: Sorry, dorm drama. Rain check?

> Theo: What's going on? Who was at the door?

I roll my eyes at his overbearing arse.

> Raine: Just one of the girls. It's all good. See you tomorrow?

He doesn't reply and I let out a little huff.

Boys.

They sulk worse than girls.

But that's not my problem right now. My problem is a twelve-year-old girl with a bruise on her face and tears in her eyes.

Wetting a small flannel, I fold it into a compression pad and return to Millie.

"Here." I offer it to her, and she presses it against her cheek, hissing with pain.

"What happened?"

"It was an accident. I... I walked into a door. I'm so clumsy."

"A door." I frown. "You walked into a door."

"So silly, right?" She won't meet my gaze, her whole demeanour closed off.

This isn't the Millie I'm used to. There's something so sad about her. So crushed.

"Millie, did somebody hurt you?"

"What? No!" Her head whips up, fear shining in her eyes. "I told you I walked into a door. Theo will..." She trails off, her worried gaze darting from mine.

"Theo will what, Mill?" I sit down next to her.

"When he sees the bruise, he'll think... he'll think the worst. And I don't want to make him angry. I don't want—"

"Hey." I take her hand in mine, coaxing her to look at me. "Theo loves you. I'm sure he'll understand it was an accident."

I don't for one second think it was an accident, but Millie doesn't need an interrogation right now, she needs reassurance.

"You could help me cover it up? Before class, you could use concealer or something and we could—"

"That's not a good idea," I say softly.

"B-but I thought we were friends. I thought you would help me."

"I will help you. But I won't help you lie to your brother. Nothing good can come from that."

"Because you've got a thing for him, right?"

"Millie, that's not—" The door flies open and Theo steps into the room.

"How did you—"

"What. Happened?"

"Hey." I bolt off the bed and put myself between him and his little sister. "You don't get to just barge in here and demand answers. When Millie is ready, she'll explain— wait, a second." My brows pinch. "How did you know she was here?"

Guilt flashes in his eyes but it's gone as quickly as it came.

"Theo," I demand when he says nothing. "Fine, it doesn't matter. You're here now. Millie had a little accident with a door, but she's worried you'll overreact. I'm beginning to realise she's right."

"A door. She walked into a door?" Disbelief coats his words.

"That's what she said." My eyes narrow at him.

Darkness bleeds into his expression and for a second, I think he might do something stupid. But then his angry mask falls away revealing nothing but pain.

"Hey, Mills," he says, stepping around me.

And this time, I let him.

"Hey." She sniffles.

"Want to tell me what really happened?"

"I... already told Raine." Her eyes flick to mine and I offer her a reassuring smile.

"Yeah, I know." He goes over to her and kneels down. "But I'm thinking there might be a little more to the story."

"Maybe I should go—"

"No," Millie blurts. "Please don't." Her eyes fix on her brother and the two of them seem to have a silent conversation.

Theo nods, and Millie lets loose a thin breath.

"It was Dad."

"What?" The sheer anger radiating from Theo takes my breath away and I'm beside them in an instance.

I sit beside Millie and try to catch Theo's eye. He finally senses me and slides his murderous gaze to mine.

"You good?" I ask.

"I... fuck. Yeah. Yeah, I'm good. Sorry, Mills. Go on."

"He didn't mean it. He just got so angry, Theo. I... I shouldn't have gone home. I didn't know. I didn't know he'd be drunk."

"It's okay," he soothes, wrapping his arms around her. "It's okay."

His eyes flash to mine again, and the utter hopelessness there stuns me.

I bring my arm around Millie, letting my fingers brush over Theo's.

There's so much more to this boy than meets the eye. I realise that now. He keeps people at arm's length to protect himself.

To protect Millie.

Pulling back, he inhales a sharp breath. "Can you tell me what happened, Mills?"

"I wanted to borrow some of Mum's old things. I'm doing a project with Miss Linley. But when I asked him where the boxes were he just lost it."

"He hit you?" Theo vibrates with pure anger.

Millie nods and the temperature in the room turns icy cold.

"I'll kill him." He staggers to his feet. "I'll fucking kill him."

"No, Theo. You can't... you can't. Please, this is why I didn't want to tell you. He was drunk. He didn't know... and I shouldn't have asked about Mum. I shouldn't."

"Theo isn't going anywhere," I reassure her. "Are you?"

He doesn't answer, but he doesn't move either.

Ignoring him for a second, I focus on the broken girl beside me. "Hey, Mills? Why don't you climb on up into my bed and I'll stick the TV on."

"I can stay here?"

"Of course you can. Come on." I help her get into my bed and dim the lights. "I'll be right back, okay?"

She nods, staring at the TV.

Grabbing Theo's hand, I yank him into my small bathroom and close the door.

"You need to calm the fuck down," I snap.

"Me? Me? You saw what that bastard did to her face. She's twelve, Raine. She's fucking twelve and he—"

Taking his face in my hands I get all up in his space. "I know, okay. I know. But anything you do now is only going to make it worse. You're angry, I—"

"Angry? I'm fucking livid. She shouldn't have been there without me."

"This has happened before?" I ask.

"With our mum."

"Oh."

"Yeah, oh. Anthony Ashworth is a piece of shit that I've spent my entire life trying to protect Millie from."

"You could tell somebody."

"No."

"No?" I frown. "But—"

"Just leave it, yeah. I appreciate you looking out for her, I do. But this is family business. I can handle it."

The coolness in his words hit me right in the chest. "Theo, come on that isn't—"

"I said leave it, Raine."

"I see." I step back, shoving my hands into my hoodie pockets. "Do you want to stay with her?"

"Yeah, but I'm not sure—"

"I'll take her room."

He runs a hand down his face, grimacing. "That's not what I meant."

"It's fine. You should stay with her." My heart squeezes. "Like you said, it's family business. I'll just grab a few things and I'll be out of your hair."

I hurry to the door, desperate to get away from him before he sees the cracks in my façade.

Part of me half-expects him to call me back. To try and fix the sudden gaping hole between us.

But he doesn't.

And I should be relieved. Because Theo just did us both a favour. He reminded us that I'm not one of them.

I never will be.

Millie is sleeping soundly when I slip back into my room. I linger for a second. She doesn't deserve any of this. But at least she has someone fighting in her corner.

I never had that growing up.

And I sure as hell don't have it now.

I'm all alone in the world.

I always will be.

36

THEO

My body vibrates with anger and my need to drive across town and put an end to our cunt of a father once and for all.

I always feared this would happen.

Millie is the spitting image of our mum. I've heard him comment on it a few times over the years, and every single time it's turned my blood to ice.

I promised myself a long time ago that I'd do whatever it takes to keep Millie safe.

I thought I'd achieved it. I've got everything ready to go. But he moved first.

I'm furious that she decided to take off and go back there without me. But I'm not about to wake her up and let her know.

She's already suffered the consequences of her decisions. The last thing she needs is me going off at her.

It's almost over.

In only days, that cunt is going to get everything he deserves.

I've just got to wait a few more days and everything I've been planning will come to fruition.

Millie's soft snores fill the room as I stare up at the ceiling.

As much as I try to ignore it, Raine's scent fills my nose, tempting me, taunting me.

I was mortified when she hung up, choosing whoever was on the other side of the door over me. But then I saw Millie's terrified face and the tears that were filling her eyes and I was dressed and running over here before I had a chance to think.

My little sister, her safety, her future mean everything to me. I will do anything, any-fucking-thing, to make her happy.

But right now, she's not the one who's up in my head.

That's the girl who should be in this room.

I shouldn't have let her go, but I was too fucking blinded by anger to stop her.

Such a fucking idiot, Theodore Ashworth.

Without waking Millie, I roll off the bed and grab my phone from the side.

Silently, I slip out of Raine's room and make my way down the silent hallway. I pause when I get to Millie's door, questioning my need to be here, my need to see the girl who's hiding inside to give the two of us some time.

I didn't want her to go. And not just because she knew the truth. Because I wanted her to be there with us.

Despite me warning her off, she's been there for Millie since the first day she arrived at All Hallows'. She deserves to have everyone in her corner right now.

Pressing my key card to the panel beside the door, I wait for the click of the locks disengaging before twisting the handle and pushing the door open.

The room is in darkness, only the light of the moon shining through the open curtains illuminates the room.

It's all I need though to see Raine curled up asleep in the middle of Millie's bed.

I stand there for a few minutes trying to talk myself out of it. But it's pointless. The pull toward her is too strong.

Millie is safe. She's locked up in Raine's room fast asleep. No one is going to know she's there let alone get to her.

I'm exactly where I need to be.

As quietly as I can, I pull my hoodie from my body and shove my jeans down my legs. Wearing just my boxers—I'm in my little sister's bedroom after all—I stalk toward her.

She moans softly as I lift the duvet and slip in behind her. The second the heat of her body hits mine something inside me falls back into place.

Wrapping my arm around her waist, I tug her back into my body, getting us as close as physically possible.

"Teddy," she moans, her voice raspy from sleep, making my cock jerk against her arse.

"Shh, sleep, sunshine," I whisper, pressing a kiss to her shoulder.

She doesn't reply and after long, silent minutes, I figure that she's done as she's told for once and fallen asleep.

"He's going to get everything he deserves," I promise darkly, needing to hear the words.

Seconds pass as my heart pounds in my chest, my need for vengeance burning through my veins like wildfire.

"Theo, what have you done?" Raine whispers, startling me.

My fingers twitch, slipping under her shirt to get closer. But I don't make a move.

"Exactly what needs to be done. I know all my father's dirty little secrets, sunshine. I'm going to ruin him."

"Don't do anything stupid."

"Why? Would you miss me?"

"Millie deserves better than someone who can't keep a cool head," she says, dodging the question.

"Something we agree on," I mutter, pressing my lips to her shoulder again.

"Theo," she warns, shifting a little, grinding her arse against me in the process.

"I'm not doing anything, sunshine. You're the one who's trying to get closer to my dick."

"Just getting comfortable," she hisses. "Someone intruded on my peace."

"I can leave again if you like," I offer insincerely as I nuzzle her neck.

I might have been surrounded by her scent in her room, but it wasn't enough.

Watching her through the camera as she followed orders earlier was almost good enough. But having her pinned against me. It's everything.

Without warning, she flips over and wraps her arm and leg around me.

"Fuck, Raine," I groan when the heat of her pussy burns through the fabric separating us.

I'm in my sister's bed.

I'm in my sister's fucking bed.

Do not do something you'll regret.

"What are you doing here, Theo? You're meant to be with—"

"She's passed out in your bed, she's okay."

"So you thought it would be a good idea to sneak in here and do what exactly?"

"Didn't have any plans," I confess.

"Liar," she warns.

"Been called worse, sunshine."

"Most recently by me." She smiles up at me, her eyes twinkling in the moonlight with mischief.

"Yeah, although I quite like your insults."

"Weirdo," she mutters with a smirk.

"That the best you can do, sunshine? You're losing your edge."

"I was asleep," she argues.

"You were, and now here you are wrapped around me like a blanket."

"Complaining?" she asks.

I roll my hips, making her gasp.

"I'm not fucking you in your sister's bed, Teddy. You can get that out of your head right now."

"I know," I say, moving close enough that our lips brush.

"What are you doing then?" she whispers, her brows pinched as she stares into my eyes.

"I don't know," I confess honestly. "I've no idea what I'm doing. All I know is that I don't want to stop."

Sliding my hand down her thigh, I grip her arse and drag her even closer. If it's even possible.

"Talk to me. I know it's killing you not to do anything."

"I can't, Raine. Everything I know, everything I've done. I can't tangle you up in it."

She nods, understanding. "Will you tell me about your mum?"

A pained sigh falls from my lips. "I don't think I ever got to discover the woman she really was. By the time I was old enough to remember anything, Dad had got his claws into her."

I swallow thickly, desperate to keep all this inside but also feeling this weird need to confide in her.

"I've no idea when she started taking antidepressants, but from as early as I can remember she had a cocktail of drugs.

"I thought she was sick. Someone at school lost their dad to cancer when we were in primary school, and I was convinced that was going to happen to me as well. I was terrified she was going to die and leave us alone with Dad.

"He was always so cold, so angry. Life was always better when he was gone, and the thought of him being our only parent was horrifying. Millie was so young. She needed Mum. I knew I was too young to give her what she needed.

"Every day I made sure Mum took those pills. I had no idea what was wrong with her, but I knew she needed them to keep her with us."

"Theo," she whispers, her grip on the back of my neck tightening.

But unlike what I was expecting, I don't see pity in her eyes.

Just understanding.

"What about your mum?" I ask, needing a reprieve from talking about ours.

A sad laugh spills from her lips. "My mum never had issues not taking pills. She was more than willing to swallow whatever she could get her hands on and chase them with vodka, or whisky, hell she'd probably even go for a glass of piss if it were the only thing on offer.

"I spent my life watching her get off her tits while men took their turn coming all over them."

"Jesus," I grunt at the brutality of the image she paints.

"Fuck knows how I stayed with her as long as I did. She was probably blowing the social worker who used to turn up to check on my well-being. He was a creep just like the rest of them."

"How old were you when they took you away?"

"Seven."

"Foster home?" I ask, desperate to uncover more about this mysterious girl who's wormed her way under my skin without permission.

"Yeah. Then another, then another, then a couple of group homes."

"Shit."

"Yeah. Apparently, I'm hard to deal with. Who knew."

I can't help but laugh. "They clearly all got you wrong, sunshine."

"My thoughts exactly."

"So what was it you did that almost landed you in juvie?" I ask. She shut it down so fast last time that really, I'm not expecting an answer. And she doesn't disappoint.

"What happened? How did she..."

"Kill herself?" I ask bluntly.

Raine nods.

"Overdose. Those pills I so diligently ensured she took thinking they'd keep her alive were what ended her."

"That's not your fault," she says, closing what little space there is between us.

"I know that. It's his," I growl dangerously.

"Did he—"

"Enough talking, sunshine." I steal her lips in a searing kiss before she gets a chance to argue with me.

Her hands push against my chest, trying to shove me away, but she doesn't stand a chance.

Not only am I stronger than her, I'm also determined.

I might be willing to do the right thing and not fuck her six ways from Sunday in my little sister's bed but that doesn't mean we're going to do nothing.

My sister got in the way earlier. I figure she owes us.

"Theo," Raine cries when I grind against her.

"How close were you to coming all over your fingers for me earlier?" I groan, kissing across her jaw before nipping her earlobe.

"Close," she gasps. "So close."

My hips continue as I roll her onto her back. My hands wander, gripping her arse before slipping under her shirt to grab handfuls of her tits.

"Theo, please. I need—"

"I know what you need, sunshine. You need my dick so deep inside you that you don't know where you end and I start."

"Yes. Yes."

Dragging her tank down, I suck one of her nipples into my mouth.

Her nails rake across my back as her release approaches.

"Come, Raine. Fucking come for me."

"Fuck. Fuck. THEO," she screams as her body locks up with pleasure.

"Beautiful. So fucking beautiful."

The second she's done, I fall behind her and drag her back into my body.

My blood runs red hot, my cock rock hard and my balls aching for release, but I ignore it all in favour of doing the right thing for once in my life.

"Theo, what are you—"

"Shh, Raine. Go back to sleep."

"But—"

"No buts. You can make it up to me tomorrow."

"Oh, I can, can I?"

37

RAINE

My eyes flutter open as I try to get my bearings.

Where am I?

I blink, noting the room similar to mine, but definitely not my room.

Millie's room.

I'm in Millie's room, in her bed with her brother.

Crap.

Theo stirs behind me, his hand brushing up my stomach, sending shivers skittering through me.

The memories trickle in. Being at the Chapel with Theo and his friends. Finding Millie hurt and upset. Theo turning up and shutting me out.

Theo sneaking into his sister's room to apologise.

God, I'm a mess.

This boy—this broken boy—has completely shattered my defences and got me wanting things I can never have.

"Morning, sunshine." He brushes his mouth over the curve of my shoulder, dragging me closer to his body. "Fucking love waking up—"

A throat clearing startles us both, and Theo shrieks, "Millie, what the fuck?"

"In case you've forgotten, big brother, this is *my* room."

Shit.

I peek out from behind him and give Millie a guilty smile. "Hi, Mills."

"Hi, Raine."

"It's not what you think," I start, but the low growl coming from Theo stops me in my tracks.

"You are so predictable, Theodore." Millie cuts him with a withering look, but I hear the amusement in her voice. "I wondered when I'd finally catch you two sneaking around. Would have preferred not to find you in my bed. You owe me clean sheets, by the way."

"Mills," Theo grumbles, flipping back against her pillows and pulling me with him.

"Theo." I smack his stomach. "We need to get up."

"Why? She's seen us now. We can all hang and—"

"I'll be in the kitchen. Finding something to eat that won't make a reappearance every time I think of my brother sexing up his girlfriend... In. My. Bed."

"Number one. Raine's not my girlfriend"—Theo finally extracts himself from the bed—"and two, I wasn't sexing her up. What the hell do you know about sex anyway?"

"I know that you're a terrible liar."

"I think I should go," I say, slipping out of the bed and pulling on my pyjamas.

"I'll be up in a minute," Theo says.

"Sorry, Millie. We didn't plan—"

"Sorry?" She smiles. "You don't need to be sorry. I knew there was something going on... and don't listen to my brother. He's never, ever brought a girl around me before. So the fact I caught him down here with you... it means something."

"Millie," he groans again, and I don't dare look at him. I don't want to see whatever's in his eyes.

He made it pretty clear just now that this doesn't mean anything.

"I'll see you soon, okay," I say, all but fleeing from her room.

Theo calls after me but I don't stop until I'm safely in my room, with the door closed behind me.

Last night was a mistake.

I shouldn't have let him apologise. Let him touch me.

It would have been easier that way.

A clean break.

I need to get ready for class but I'm not sure I have the energy, so instead, I go into the bathroom and strip off.

A hot shower will help.

And if it doesn't, at least I won't be wrapped in Theo's scent.

After stripping off, I enter the shower and step under the jet stream. I don't hear the door open or Theo step in behind me.

I don't realise he's there, until he slides his arms around me and buries his face in my neck.

"Sorry about that," he murmurs.

"Theo," I sigh, remaining tense in his arms. "You shouldn't be here."

"That's where you're wrong, sunshine. Me and you have unfinished business." His fingers glide lower, toying with the soft curls between my thighs.

"Theo, don't..."

He stills, turning me in his arms so that the water trails down my back.

"What's going on with you? I thought—"

"I'm leaving, Theo. As soon as I age out, I'm leaving. This... us, it's better to end now before..."

"Is this because I told Millie you're not my girlfriend?"

"No, that's not it. But we're getting too deep."

"You're scared." He smirks but I see the flash of fear in his eyes.

"I don't want to hurt you."

"You don't need to worry about me, sunshine. I'm a big boy, I can handle myself."

"Theo, come on, be serious."

"I am. This, us, I'm not ready to give it up. I'm leaving too, you know. After the summer, I'll be heading to uni. You're not the only one with plans, Raine."

"Just another reason this is a mistake."

He stares at me with a look that makes my stomach curl. "Millie was right, you know." He pushes the wet hair from my face. "I've never brought a girl around her before. Or the boys. And definitely not to the Chapel.

"I don't know how the fuck it happened, sunshine, but you mean something to me. And I'm not done with you."

"Theo." I run my hands up his chest, leaning closer.

He lowers his head to my ear, brushing the skin there with his lips. "Give me a chance to change your mind... A chance to give you a reason to stay."

"I—"

His mouth slams down on mine, stealing whatever words were on the top of my tongue. Maybe I was going to argue, to tell him it's a bad idea. Or maybe I was about to concede. To trust him with my heart.

But I can't, can I?

Because even if I stay?

Even if I let myself believe that maybe I've finally found my place in the world, Theo will be leaving in August, and I'll be all alone again.

Theo pushes me up against the wall, hooking my leg around his waist and grinding into me.

"Jesus, you get me so fucking hard, sunshine." His big hand collars my throat but it isn't forcefully. It's soft and tender, matching the emotion in his eyes.

"What have you done to me?" He smiles and it's so at odds

with his usual cold, brooding attitude that it completely undoes me.

"Theo," I whisper, reaching for him, needing him closer.

"Tell me you're mine," he breathes the words onto my damp skin. The demand rocking me to my core.

I can't say it.

I won't.

Even if I want to.

So I kiss him instead. Plunging my tongue deep into his mouth and shoving my fingers into his hair.

"Fuck, sunshine," he rasps. "I need to get inside you."

"Yes," I beg. "Yes."

Theo hauls me up against the wall, trapping my body between the tiles and his chest. He's so big and strong, I feel safe in his arms.

I shouldn't.

But I do.

He thrusts into me with one smooth glide, filling me to the hilt, our collective moans drowned out by the water.

"Never, not ever gonna get enough of this." Theo growls.

I won't ever admit it...

But I hope he doesn't.

We end up missing first period. But it's worth it.

Theo heads over to the gym to grovel to Coach Walker while I head to class. His words play on a loop in my head.

Tell me you're mine.

I didn't say the words, but I didn't exactly stop him from fucking me in the shower either.

Everything is such a mess.

But he's dangling the chance at something better in front of me. Even if it's crazy, even if we both know it can never work.

Jesus, Raine, you need to get a grip.

I avoid all the common areas between my classes, keeping a low profile for the day. Theo texts me a couple of times, demanding to know why I'm avoiding him but I make up some excuse about having an extra session with Miss Linley.

Surprisingly, he doesn't hunt me down and call my bluff.

By the time the final bell of the day goes, I'm a nervous ball of energy. But I can't see Theo yet. Not until I figure out what I'm going to say or do.

I can't stay here.

Can I?

I've made friends—albeit tenuously—with Tally, Abi, and Liv. Something tells me they'll accept me into the fold no questions asked if Theo declares me his.

The same with the other Heirs. Although, I'm not sure what Elliot might do once he discovers the truth about who tagged his beloved car.

I must really be broken because part of me almost wants to find out.

Thankfully, I have group straight after classes end, giving me a genuine reason to avoid Theo a little while longer.

Millie doesn't show though, and before I know what I'm doing, I pull out my phone and text Theo.

> Raine: Is Millie okay? She isn't at group?

> Theo: Yeah, she's with me. Thought we should spend some time together... since you're avoiding me.

> Raine: I'm not, it's just been a busy day.

> Theo: You're a terrible liar, sunshine. But I'll let you have the rest of the night. I know I said some pretty intense things...

> Raine: Do you regret saying them?

I bite down on my lip, unsure if I'm ready for his answer.

Theo: Is it going to scare you off if I say no?

Raine: Honestly, I'm not sure...

Theo: Sleep on it. We can pick this up tomorrow when I come pick you up and take you to breakfast.

Raine: Breakfast you say. I like breakfast.

Theo: Be ready for seven forty-five. I know a place.

Raine: Won't we get into trouble leaving campus before classes?

Theo: Since when do you care about getting into a little trouble? And besides, you'll be with an Heir. I'm untouchable, remember?

Raine: And so modest.

My lips curve.

"Okay, we're done for the day." Miss Linley ends the session, her gaze finding me across the circle. "Raine, a word please."

Shit.

Guess I wasn't being as discreet as I hoped.

Pocketing my phone, I linger while the other students leave.

"What's up?" I ask.

"You seem distracted today. Is everything okay?"

"Everything's fine." I smile, hoping it's genuine.

"Okay, well, if you do want to talk, I'm always here."

"Got it. See you tomorrow."

"Have a good evening. Stay out of trouble."

I barely refrain from rolling my eyes.

It's almost dark when I walk out of the centre, but I know the short walk back to the Bronte Building well enough now that it doesn't faze me.

Except as I cut across the path leading me around the side of one of the buildings, a trickle of awareness goes through me.

"Theo." I glance around my eyes lingering on the tree line. It's bloody freaky out here at night, my mind must be playing tricks on me.

I keep going, hugging myself tight but I can't shake the feeling that someone's out there.

"Theo, come on," I sigh. "Are you following me? Because it's not—"

A dark figure bursts from the shadows, grabbing me and pulling me until the darkness swallows us whole.

I scream, terror saturating every inch of me.

It's just Theo fucking with me.

It's Theo.

Just Theo.

"Hello, Raine, baby."

I go deathly still, the fight dying inside of me.

No.

No.

"Vaughn, what are you doing here?" Fear chokes my voice off, my heart lodged in my throat as he turns me to face him.

"Figured it was time to say hi." He crooks a wicked smile.

"But... how..."

My head spins as I try to make sense of what is happening.

I came here to escape that life.

To escape him.

Our secrets.

He steps forward and I step back, trying to keep some distance between us.

"Raine," he tsks, "did you really think you could hide from me?" Another step forward. Another step back. "Did you really think I wouldn't find you?"

"I..." I can't speak. Can't find the words to convey what I feel.

He can't be here.

He can't—

"Shh, my little storm." His hand snaps out and he roughly grabs my face, running his thumb across my lips. "I'm here now. And you've been a bad, bad girl."

BRUTAL CALLOUS HEIR: PART TWO

1

THEO

"I don't think I've ever seen you smile like that," Millie says, focusing on me instead of the giant piece of rainbow cake sitting on the plate in front of her.

"Shut up," I mutter, unable to wipe said smile off my face.

I can't help it. I've been in this annoyingly good mood since I woke this morning and discovered the hot little body snuggled next to mine, my morning wood happily resting against her perfect arse.

Of course, one cough from my sister killed it instantly, but it didn't matter. I was riding too high to care.

Especially when I found Raine hot and naked in her shower not long after that.

I knew I fucked up by saying she wasn't my girlfriend. But what the fuck was I meant to do? Agree that she was and terrify her even more.

Rock and hard place, anyone?

I'm pretty sure I pulled it back though.

The way her eyes widened in shock when I demanded for her to tell me that she's mine.

Fuck.

I want to see that every day.

Even if she never actually said the words.

I felt them in her kiss. Her touch. In everything.

"It's cute." My sister grins.

"I'm far from cute, Mills."

"So not true."

"Eat your cake," I demand, uncomfortable with this level of teasing, especially coming from her.

"You know, I never thought I'd see you this lost and yet found at the same time."

"What the fuck does that even mean?" I mutter, cutting off a massive forkful of chocolate cake and shoving it into my mouth, praying that she does the same and shuts the hell up.

"I think it means you've found the one."

How I don't spray her with half-chewed cake, I don't know.

"I'm sorry, what?" I balk.

"Raine. She's it for you. Just like Liv is it for Reese, and Tally is it for Oak."

"What the hell are they putting in the cake here these days?" I ask, desperate to divert this conversation.

"You're not honestly going to sit there and argue with me, are you?"

"She's hot." I shrug. "We have fun together."

"In my bed," she mutters to herself.

"Nothing happened in your bed."

She glares at me. "I can see through your lies, *Teddy*," she teases.

"Fine. I didn't have sex in your bed, Millie. Not that you should even know what that is."

"I'm twelve, Theo. I'm more than aware."

"Just tell me you haven't—"

"I said I'm twelve, not a whore. Christ. All the boys in my year are idiots anyway. The girls too, to be fair."

My mouth opens and closes but I can't find any words to

respond to that comment. I finally settle on a muted groan of, "Good. Th-that's good."

"Doesn't mean you're getting away with not changing the sheets."

"Already done." I smirk. "I had new Egyptian cotton ones delivered and put on this morning."

"And they say money doesn't buy happiness," Millie deadpans.

"Nope, just a comfortable bed." Pulling my phone from my pocket, I scan through my notifications, looking for one from Raine.

"A watched kettle never boils."

"Will you please stop being such a bloody smart-arse? I'm just reading messages from the guys."

"No, you're not. You're hoping for a message from Raine. Did something happen?"

"No. Yes. I don't know."

"But you're so happy." Her brows furrow. "What did you do?"

"Why do you automatically assume I did something?"

"Because you're a boy."

"Brilliant," I mutter while having another mouthful of cake while Millie's eyes drill into me. "She told me that she was leaving."

I regret the words the second they fall from my lips.

"What? When?" Millie's expression falls. "She can't leave. She belongs here with us."

"She told me that once she's eighteen and out of the system she's going to disappear."

"She can't," my sister repeats. "You need to do something. Give her a reason to stay."

"That's exactly what I told her I would do."

"When's her birthday? How long do you have to prove to her that she's fallen in love with you and can't live without you?"

There's a light-heartedness to my sister's words but it doesn't stop something squeezing inside my chest.

"Millie," I say, trying to disguise my panic, "are you a little bit of a romantic?"

"What? No. I hate people and love is for idiots," she argues.

"Are you trying to say I'm an idiot?"

"Are you trying to say you're in love with Raine?"

My chin drops and I trip over any answer I might have to that question. "Stop putting words in my mouth."

"Stop trying to run away from everything."

"I'm not. I'm trying to—" Both our phones buzz on the table.

Looking over, my heart sinks and Millie groans at the email.

From: Maria Ashworth
Subject: Plans for Theodore's 18th Birthday

"What's wrong?" Millie asks mockingly when I don't open it. "Don't you want to know what caterers Dad insisted you have? Or what band? Or what the dress code is?"

"No. I really fucking don't."

There's only one reason I'm going to be turning up to that party and it's not going to have anything to do with the food or the entertainment.

Well, actually, that's a lie. It just won't be for the entertainment Maria has been instructed to book.

I'm bringing a whole heap of my own that night.

My eighteenth birthday. A day I've been planning for longer than anyone—besides Christian and Fiona—know about. A day that can't come fucking soon enough.

"Why can't they just piss off to the South of France or something?" Millie muses.

"I won't let him get away with hurting you, Mills. You know that right?"

"Of course I do." She shrinks into herself, and I hate it. I hate that my ballsy sister is a shell of herself whenever *his* name comes up in conversation. "It was my fault anyway. I shouldn't have just turned up."

"No," I bark, forcing more than a few sets of eyes to turn our way. "That's bullshit and you know it," I say a little quieter. "Nothing about what happened is your fault. You should be able to go home whenever you like and not have to worry about the mood of the monster inside."

"It's not our reality though, is it?" she says sadly.

I shake my head, hating that this is her life.

"It's going to get better," I promise her.

"How? Do you have plans to kill him?" she jokes lightly.

I have no idea what she reads on my face, but her expression instantly drops. "No, Theo. Please don't do anything crazy. I need you. If I lose you too I don't know what I'd—"

Reaching across the table, I take her hand in mine. "I'm not going anywhere. You have nothing to worry about."

She narrows her eyes at me, studying me as if she can read every one of my thoughts. "What are you planning, Theodore Ashworth?"

"Nothing you need to lose any sleep over. Just know that our lives are going to turn around soon."

"That doesn't exactly reassure me," she mutters, eating another forkful of cake.

"So what should I do about Raine then?" I ask.

I hate turning this back on me and my potential love life—fucking hell, I have a love life. But it's the lesser of two evils right now.

"You need to make a grand gesture. Show her that all the crap you threw at her before was a load of rubbish. Prove to her how you really feel. Ooh, you should do it after a rugby game in front of the whole school."

"No. I really shouldn't," I hiss.

"But it's not a grand gesture if no one sees it," she points out.

"I don't need the world to see it, Mills. Raine is the only one who needs the reason to stay, not anyone else."

"Okay, so... you need to do something that she'll appreciate, that proves you know her. So no fancy meals at the golf club or pretentious days out to the races."

"Can't say either of those options had entered my mind," I mutter honestly.

"She loves art. What about a day in London visiting the galleries? Has she been?"

I shrug, hating how little I know about her.

Raine has confessed to living in multiple foster homes, she could have lived in and experienced almost every corner of the country for all I know.

"Okay, I'll find out her birthday and you figure out the plans. If it's soon then you could do a weekend. If we've got a little more time, then half-term is only just around the corner. You could take her away for the whole week. Pretty sure she'd be up for that. No expensive hotels though. That'll make her run."

"Got it. Find the worst hotel I can," I joke.

"Not the worst," Millie chastises. "Just not The Ritz or something stupid. Make her feel comfortable, not like she doesn't belong. She has enough of that here."

We both manage to force a second slice of cake down before leaving Dessert Island. I take Millie back to her dorm, and despite desperately wanting to go and check in on Raine, I force myself to walk back out of the building.

I said that I'd give her the night to think about everything I said, and for once, I'm going to do the right thing and give her the space I promised.

"Look out, lover boy returns," Oakley sings like the wankstain that he is when I walk into the Chapel.

"Fuck off. Where are the girls?" I ask, noting their absence. The days of it just being the boys here seem like a distant memory now.

"Doing homework, or yoga or some shit," Reese mutters before Oak throws the remote at his head. "Ow, fuck. What was that for?"

"When my sister talks, you listen, bellend."

"I listened," he argues. "But I also forgot."

"Where have you been?" Elliot asks, ignoring the bickering idiots.

"Took Millie for cake."

"Nice. She doing okay?"

I tell the three of them what happened yesterday during lunch seeing as I couldn't track Raine down.

"Yeah," I add. "She's fucking blaming herself though."

"That's bullshit," he snaps fiercely. "It's not her fault your father is a cunt."

"Exactly what I told her. I fucking hate it. I just know that he looks at her and sees Mum."

"I wish there were more we could do." Pure hatred burns in his eyes, and I know he's not just talking about our sick prick of a father, but his own too.

Johnathon Eaton might not be beating little girls, but he's just as big a monster as Anthony Ashworth. And irritatingly, just as untouchable.

I know what Elliot has told us about his life barely scratches the surface of what he's suffered through. I'm pretty sure he's going to take the depth of what he's endured to his grave. It's going to take someone pretty fucking incredible to dig under the layers of armour he's built up around himself and find the man who lives beneath.

Out of all of us, Elliot is the one who needs the façade of the Heirs the most.

Reese, Oak, and I love the status that comes with the title, but Elliot needs it. He needs the identity, the power it gives him in a totally different way to us.

"Their time will come," I say.

I hate lying to my best friends. I wish I could tell them everything I know, everything I've been planning. It's not that I don't trust them.

I do.

With my life.

But I can't risk any part of this going wrong for any reason.

Anthony Ashworth's reign of terror in our family is almost over and I'm not risking anything. I've promised Millie that things are going to get better.

And I will fucking deliver.

2

RAINE

Vaughn is here.

  In Saints Cross.

  On the grounds of All Hallows'.

It's the only thought that has consumed my mind ever since I stumbled back to my room in a daze, after he threatened me.

After he ruined my life.

Again.

I should have known that things were too good to be true. That the second I let my guard down something would happen.

Only, I expected Theo to be the one who shattered the fragile little life I've built here.

Not Vaughn Ronson.

God, just his name sends a violent shudder through me.

He's here.

It's the worst possible thing that could ever have happened and yet, in a strange way, part of me isn't surprised he found me. He always said that he'd never let me run.

My phone vibrates and fear paralyses me.

When we parted ways, he said he'd be watching. I didn't expect him to contact me so soon.

But it isn't Vaughn.

It's Theo.

With shaky hands, I unlock my screen and open the message.

> Theo: If you're trying to blow me off, it won't work. I meant every word I said, Raine. You're mine.

"Fuck."

Fuck.

I squeeze my eyes shut wishing I could wake up from this nightmare.

> Theo: I know I said I'd give you space, but your radio silence is kind of denting my ego, sunshine...

> Raine: Sorry. Therapy was intense.

> Theo: Shit. Do you need me to come over? I bet I can think of a few ways to help you get out of your head.

> Raine: Not tonight. But I'll see you tomorrow.

> Theo: Yeah, okay. Tomorrow it is.

I wince at his short reply, and even though you can't deduce somebody's tone from a text message, I know Theo well enough to know he's pissed.

Or maybe even a little hurt.

But I don't know what to do.

Vaughn is dangerous. And although the Heirs hold a lot of power and status in Saints Cross, I'm not sure they could go up against someone like Vaughn and come out unscathed.

Not that I'd ever expect Theo to go head-to-head with him for me.

Why would he?

It's one thing to say I'm his but he doesn't mean it, not really. He doesn't know the things I've done. The secrets I keep.

Inhaling a sharp breath, I check my windows and door. Locking it won't keep Theo out, not if he's dead set on seeing me, but hopefully it will keep Vaughn out.

Who am I kidding?

Locks and bolts won't keep Vaughn away.

My gaze lands on my backpack and for a second, I consider it.

I consider shoving whatever belongings I can in there and taking off tonight. Hoping to outrun him. But he warned me not to do anything stupid. And I know all too well what he's capable of.

Leaving would be the sensible thing. The only shot I have at escaping him. But what if he hurts Theo? Millie or the girls? Because that's the kind of man Vaughn is.

Part of me hopes Theo will text again and give me a small sign that we're okay. It's more than I deserve. But I want to cling on to the fantasy that we could have had something, that maybe we could have made it work.

Once he finds out the truth, he'll never look at me the same again.

By the time morning rolls around, I'm a mess.

I barely slept, constantly tossing and turning, dreaming of Vaughn's face. The wicked glint in his eyes as he stepped out of the shadows.

I go through the motions of getting ready for class but I'm hardly present, lost in a life I thought I'd left behind.

When you find yourself lost and alone in the world, it's easy to latch onto the first good thing that comes along. And after a string of bad foster placements, Vaughn had been that for me.

He'd protected me, showered me with gifts and attention. He'd made me feel safe. And then when my guard was down, he'd lured me into his web and before I knew it, he owned me.

My phone taunts me as I grab it off my desk. I could text Theo. Confide in him and—

It doesn't matter.

He'll never want me once the truth comes out, and it will. Vaughn likes to play games. It's what he's best at.

Before fear gets the better of me, I grab my bag and make my way downstairs. Of course, Millie appears right on cue. As if she's been waiting for me.

"Morning." She smiles, quickly pocketing her phone.

"Hi." I frown, unable to disguise the suspicion in my voice. "Who was that?"

"No one."

"Did Theo ask you to wait for me?"

"Nope. I was just heading to school."

I don't believe her, but I don't argue.

"So you and my brother... I didn't see that coming at all." She grins.

"Millie..."

"Oh, come on. I found you in my bed and—"

"Please, stop."

"What, why? I thought..." Her brows furrow as she studies me. "What's wrong? What happened?"

"Nothing." I force a smile. "I'm just tired."

"Did Theo sneak over? Because he didn't say—"

"No, I didn't sleep well is all."

"Oh. Are you sure you're okay? Because he did mention that you were avoiding him."

"It's... complicated and I really don't feel like talking with you about it."

"Just because I'm only twelve doesn't mean—"

"It has nothing to do with your age, Millie." A frustrated sigh rolls through me. "But what's between me and your brother is between me and your brother."

Her expression falls flat, and I feel like a total bitch. But I can't drag her into this anymore than I already have.

Especially not now that Vaughn is here.

I glance around, half expecting to see him hiding in the tree line.

I barely feel even a lick of relief when he isn't. Because he's out there somewhere. Watching.

Waiting.

"I really need to get to class," I say.

"You mean you need to get away from me."

"Millie, that's not—"

"Yeah, whatever Raine. I guess I'll see you around." She takes off toward the main building, and I let out a heavy sigh.

This is going to be harder than I thought.

But I don't know what to do.

I manage to get into the sixth form building without anyone spotting me. But when I turn the corner and head down the corridor, Theo lifts his head, dark circles under his eyes.

Everything slows down around me until I can hear nothing but the blood racing in my ears. I knew I'd have to see him eventually, but I didn't know I'd feel so... so desperate.

"Hi." He pushes off the wall and approaches me.

"Hi."

"Millie, said—"

"Making your little sister spy on me, that's a bit weird, even for you, Ashworth."

"Yeah, well, desperate times call for desperate measures."

He advances and I retreat backward until my bag collides with the wall and I have nowhere else to go. "You're avoiding me." He looms over me, his eyes simmering with hurt. "Listen, the stuff I said—"

"Theo, can we not do this now. I have class."

"Afraid that's not going to work for me, sunshine." He lowers his head a little, carving out a private little bubble as the last few stragglers hurry to class.

I feel their stares, their curiosity. But Theo doesn't seem to care that he's basically got me pinned to the wall in public.

"Theo," his name is a soft desperate plea.

I don't want to do this.

I don't want to see the disdain in his eyes when he discovers the kind of girl I really am.

Because the truth is, I have fallen for him. This arrogant, entitled, gorgeous boy has stolen my heart even though I swore to myself I wouldn't give it to him.

"Let's go somewhere, right now. Just you and me." He brushes his knuckles down my cheek. "I missed you yesterday."

"I... we can't." My heart crashes against my chest.

"I came on a little strong, I get that. But it doesn't change anything. It's still just you and me, sunshine."

Oh, Theo.

It changes everything.

And even if it didn't, nothing will be the same now Vaughn is here.

Emotion rushes up my throat and I swallow it down.

"What's wrong?" Concern etches into his expression. "Raine? You're starting to freak me out a little."

"I... I can't—" The words get stuck.

Theo's brows draw tighter as he glances down the hall before grabbing my hand. "Come on," he says, dragging me into an empty classroom. He engages the lock and stalks toward me. I drop onto the edge of a desk, craning my neck to look at him.

"Tell me we're okay," he says. "Because you look like a cornered animal about to dart."

"You know it isn't that straightforward, Theo."

"Because you're leaving."

"I... yeah."

God why do the words hurt so much.

That was the plan.

Turn eighteen then leave.

"Fuck that. We have something, you can't tell me you don't feel it."

"You know I do," I admit quietly, unable to look at him.

He slides his fingers under my jaw and lifts my face. "Raine, don't shut me out. I'm fucking begging you. I know I'm a lot to handle—"

"It's not you, it's me."

"Seriously?" He jerks back like I've slapped him. "You're going to stand there and give me that line. You think I want to feel like this?" He grits out. "You think I like not being able to get you out of my fucking head? It wasn't supposed to happen like this."

"See, we're a disaster waiting to happen." I offer him a weak smile, but it does little to soothe his anger. "Maybe it's better this way," I add.

"No. Fuck that. And fuck you." His eyes narrow with anger, but I see a flicker of fear there too.

And I hate myself for it.

"You don't get to decide that we're done, just like that, just because you're scared. I shared things with you, things I've never shared with anyone. I fucking trusted you."

The words hang between us, the air thick with tension.

He isn't saying anything I don't already know but I can't fix this.

"Say something," he seethes.

"I... I'm sorry."

He blinks. Once. Twice. As if he's seeing me for the first time.

"Yeah, whatever." He almost rips the door off its hinges as he blows from the room.

A single tear slips down my cheeks as my heart cracks and I whisper the words I know mean nothing now. "I'm sorry."

3

THEO

"We wondered where the fuck you were," Elliot booms as he walks into the Chapel a few hours later to find me sprawled out on the sofa with a bottle of his fancy vodka hanging from my fingers. "Shit. What happened?"

"Nothing," I grunt, lifting the bottle to my lips and swallowing down a couple of shots.

"Sure. Because skipping class and day drinking just screams 'I'm okay'," he taunts.

"Fuck off."

"Not gonna happen. The others are already on their way."

"Not the girls," I say, hating how pathetic I sound.

"I guess that explains the issue," he says, carrying over a bottle of water from the fridge and dropping onto the opposite sofa. "What did you do?"

"Why the fuck does everyone always assume it had to be me that fucked anything up?" I bark.

He shrugs. "History states that it's usually the man that fucks shit up."

"Well, not this time," I scoff. "I didn't do anything wrong. I thought I was doing everything right."

"Okay, where is he?" Reese shouts a second after the front door crashes open.

"We swung by the cafeteria and got—" Oakley takes one look at the state of me and trips over his words. "You in the fucking doghouse already, man?"

My irritation with the world explodes like a fucking firework inside me and I pull my arm back and throw the almost empty bottle against the old stone wall of our living room.

The thing shatters into a million pieces before raining down on the flagstone floor.

"Was that fucking necessary?" Elliot snaps, slamming his bottle down on the coffee table and jumping to his feet so he can clean it up.

"Nice work, bellend," Reese mutters as we all watch Elliot go to find his beloved dustpan and brush.

"So?" Oakley demands. "What did you do?"

"I haven't done anything," I repeat, hating that my friends immediately assume that I must have done something wrong.

I know I'm a bit of a fuck up. That's not exactly news. But their lack of faith in me pisses me the fuck off.

"I was honest about what I wanted, and she threw it back in my face."

There's a beat of silence before Reese asks, "Can you blame her?"

I stare at him in disbelief. "What?"

"He's right," Oakley agrees.

"But... isn't that what all girls want? I told her I wanted her. I forgot about everything I've said I've ever wanted. The free and easy, single life I've fucking loved for so long and told her I wanted her. That she was mine."

"Correct me if I'm wrong," Elliot says. "I'm not exactly the expert here. But I'm pretty sure girls want to hear that from guys who haven't treated them like shit, embarrassed them in front of the entire sixth form, and shamed them every chance they got."

"We've moved on from that," I mutter.

"You might have. But has she?" Reese asks.

"I'd be inclined to say not," Oakley adds with a shit-eating grin.

"Do you need to look so fucking smug?"

"Bro, come on, how many times have you adamantly told us that you'll never lose your head to a girl?"

"Once or twice," I whisper, aware that it's total bullshit.

"Yeah, something like that."

"Taking the piss out of our heartbroken Casanova isn't going to help," Elliot points out.

"Alright, agony uncle. What do you suggest we do instead?" Oakley asks.

"Personally, not a lot because I clearly have the least experience here. But you both have girls now. And you fuck up, often might I add. You should have some solid ideas for how to fix this," Elliot points out.

"Grovel," Reese states as if it's that fucking simple. "On your knees for as long as it takes until she's trying to rip your hair out and is screaming your name."

"You're a fucking cunt," Oakley grumbles.

"What? It works and you know it."

"My fucking sister," Oakley mutters under his breath.

"Whatever," Reese says, caring about as much as he always has. "Best way to fix this is to prove to her you're serious. Every single person at All Hallows' knows you as the opposite of a guy who professes his love for a girl and wants to settle down."

"I never said anything about love."

"Then maybe you need to stop lying to yourself." Oakley smirks.

"Fucking hell." I drag a hand down my face, so done with these idiots.

"Look, it's simple," Reese says, sitting forward and resting his elbows on his knees. "You want her?"

Silence ripples through the room.

"Well, do you?"

"Yeah," I confess, feeling like a pussy for doing so.

"Then go and take her. Show her how you feel. Make her feel the same."

"So romantic," Elliot murmurs as if we've all lost our minds. And maybe we have.

"Do you have a better suggestion, Mr. I Can't Admit How I Feel About A Certain Redhead?"

"This isn't about me," Elliot scoffs.

"No, but we can turn it to you next if you like," Oakley offers. "You need a serious talking to as well. Maybe we could just slam your heads together and be done with it."

"I need more alcohol for this," I groan.

"It's the middle of the day. You've got class and training later."

"Don't give a fuck."

"Getting wasted and giving up on life will definitely help her come around. Great idea, mate," Reese deadpans.

"Eat this," Elliot says, throwing a packet of something into my lap. "And sober up. You're attending class *and* training this afternoon."

"Fuck off."

"No. I'm serious. If your old man finds out there are issues, then you're going to be in even bigger shit than you are now. But after training, you go after her and prove to her why she's wrong."

I'm silent for a moment, my biggest fear balancing on the tip of my tongue.

I fight it. I really do. But in the end, it comes spilling out anyway.

"But what if she's not."

Nothing but stunned silence follows my words.

"Theo," Reese says while the other two look at me with sympathetic expressions on their faces. "She is. You're fucking epic, she'd be lucky to have you, mate."

"So what if you had a rocky start?" Oak adds. "We did with Liv and Tally and look at us now."

"It's different."

"How?"

"I don't know because somehow, she outsmarted us and tagged our cars. Ruined our fucking party."

Elliot tenses at the mention of his beloved Aston. But the others let it go.

"We don't know that for sure," Oak says.

"She never confessed," I admit. "But it was her. I'd put good money on it."

"I can't speak for all of us," Oakley says. "But you at least deserved it."

"She's not like us. Everything about her life is—"

"So fucking what?" Elliot barks. "Just because she isn't one of us, it doesn't mean you can't care."

"Is that right?" Reese muses, while getting flipped off by Elliot.

"Eat and get your shit together. This sulking shit isn't you."

I did as I was told and turned up to my afternoon lessons half-cut. As far as I was aware, my teachers didn't notice. Not that they'd be brave enough to say anything if they did.

Coach on the other hand, saw it the second I walked into the locker room, and he fucking punished me for it from that moment on.

He worked my arse harder than anyone else's out on that field. Had me running drills until my legs felt like they were going to fall off and had me on the receiving end of plays until my arm cooperated with my brain and I actually started catching shit and scoring tries.

By the time he let me go, I was fucking dead, and there were three things I wanted more than anything.

A shower. A joint. And my girl.

Two of them I could make happen without much effort. The third, probably not so much.

The second I got back into the locker room, I dug my phone from my pocket and sent off a text to my new dealer. With any luck, he'd be local enough to hand over exactly what I needed. Sure enough, by the time the four of us had finished our showers and let the rest of the team take theirs, I had a message waiting for me letting me know that he'd be waiting in my usual meeting spot.

"You're late," he complains as I emerge through the trees to find the hooded figure waiting for me.

I haven't been in contact since he turned up to our party on Saturday night and scored a whole new list of names to sell his gear to.

He was grateful. Probably why he dropped whatever he was doing this evening to be standing here in the rain with me.

"Got held up," I mutter, not willing to give this guy any intel other than the fact I like his best weed. "You got what I need?"

"Of course, man."

Slipping him some money, I wrap my hand around the second thing I'm craving and immediately turn around to take off.

"Theo?" he calls.

"Yeah?" I say over my shoulder.

"You partying again this weekend?"

"You fucking know it. Saturday night. You in?"

"Yeah, man. Your fucking girls are wild." He grins. "Wouldn't miss it for anything."

With a nod, I take off into the night.

Pulling out the bottle of vodka I stashed in my bag before we left the Chapel to go back to class earlier, I twist the top off and throw it into the undergrowth. Something tells me that I'm not going to put the lid back on tonight.

There is a group of girls sitting outside the dorm under the canopy. Almost all of them look up at me but unlike what usually happens, no one makes a move to approach me.

It makes me wonder what they can read on my face.

Lifting the bottle, I take a large swig of the vodka and push forward. My hands tremble and my heart pounds. But it's not with nerves. I don't think so, anyway.

It's determination.

Or at least that's what I tell myself.

After that pep talk from the guys earlier, I'm ready to try and prove myself. To show Raine that she's wrong. That she's running scared, but she doesn't need to. I'm here. I want to be here. And I really want to wrap my arms around her and hold her tight, keep her together.

I've told her things. Things I haven't even told the guys. And I almost gave her so much more.

If Millie hadn't turned up yesterday morning, then I probably would have told her everything. All the plans I've put into place with Christian and Fiona. All the ways I plan on ruining my father for everything he's done. How I plan to care for and protect Millie when our life implodes in only a few days' time.

There's no way I'm letting her run away from what we've found. It's too good. Too strong.

Too... big.

When Reese got with Liv, and then Oak with Tally, I thought they were crazy.

But I get it now.

This need to be with Raine, to tell her all my secrets, to be my true self. It's all-consuming. It's addictive. It's... every-fucking-thing.

Ignoring everyone who's loitering in the hallways, I make my way to her room. And without wasting any more time, I press my key card to the lock and throw her door open. I haven't put much thought into what I'd find when I got there. I was just too determined to stand in front of her and tell her once and for all what I want that I didn't even consider what she wants.

But the second I step into the room and find her sitting in the middle of her bed sobbing into her hands, I swear something inside me shatters.

"Sunshine," I breathe, abandoning the bottle of vodka and my bag, and rush toward her.

It doesn't even enter my head that she might push me away. Hell, she might try but I'll refuse to allow it. Instead, I pull her trembling body into my arms and hold her tight.

Just like I told myself I would only a few minutes ago.

4

RAINE

"Fuck, what's wrong?" Theo falls to his knees in front of me and gently pries my hands away.

"N-nothing." I try to pull away. "I'm fine."

Desperately swiping at my cheeks, I try to erase the evidence of my tears.

"Raine, look at me." He captures my chin and gently pulls my face around to his. "What's going on?"

"N-nothing. I'm just pissed off."

"With me?" His jaw clenches.

Crap. What am I supposed to do?

Tell him the truth?

I can't do that.

Not until I know what Vaughn really wants—until I know he isn't going to go after the people I care about.

A violent shudder goes through me, and Theo wraps me in his arms. It's such an intimate move that I sob against him, letting out all the frustration and anger and helplessness I feel.

"Sunshine." One of his hands runs down my spine. "Tell me what to do here."

"I..." The words teeter on the tip of my tongue, but I

swallow them down. "It's nothing." I pull away again, swiping at my eyes. "I'm just overwhelmed."

"You sure?" His eyes narrow as he searches my face for answers I can't give him.

I nod. "I'm good. But why are you here?"

Hurt flashes across his expression but he locks it down. "Raine, I—"

His warm breath skitters over my face and I frown. "Are you drunk?"

"I'm not fucking drunk." He climbs to his feet and rakes a hand through his hair.

I stand, studying him. He doesn't seem drunk, but I definitely smelled alcohol on his breath just now.

"But you have been drinking."

"I didn't realise there was a law against that, sunshine," he drawls. A little too smoothly.

"Theo," I sigh, really not ready to do this with him.

I knew I couldn't avoid him forever, but I thought I'd have more time to get my story straight.

"What, sunshine? Do I make you uncomfortable?" He stalks toward me. Although prowling seems like a better word to describe the way he tracks me with every step.

"Theo," I repeat, a little harsher this time. I can't let my guard down. But he's looking at me like he's starving and I'm the only thing on the menu.

"Fuck, I want you," he says thickly. He reaches me, curving his hand around my neck, sliding his fingers into my hair.

"You shouldn't be here," I force the words out over the lump in my throat.

"Don't shut me out again." He whispers into my hair. "I can't fucking stand it."

"Theo..."

"No, Raine." He tilts my face up to his. His dark eyes pinning me to the spot. "I need this. I need... you."

His mouth captures mine and I'm powerless to stop him. I should shove him away, tell him that this can't happen. But if it's the last time I get to be with him before the truth comes out, then I'm going to take it.

I press closer to him, needing to feel him.

"Fuck, sunshine. Need you." His hands start to roam, mapping my curves. Digging into my hips. "Need you so fucking much."

Theo trails hot wet kisses over my jaw and down my neck, his fingers ripping at my pyjamas.

"Slow down," I breathe, suddenly unsure I want to do this.

I mean, I do. I want him so fucking much it hurts. But it's only going to hurt so much more after.

"No, no," he murmurs, licking and sucking the sensitive skin beneath my ear. Shivers run down my spine, making me whimper. "That's it, baby. Moan for me."

Lost in the sweet sensations he is wreaking on me, I don't realise he's got me half-naked until his fingers dance over my underwear.

"Wet for me already?" he croons, cupping my pussy like he owns it.

"You wish, Teddy." I tease even though we both know he's right.

"The things I want to do to you."

"Yes, yes," the words tumble out before I can stop them.

"My fucking pleasure." He grabs the back of my legs and lifts me, carrying me and shoving me roughly against the wall.

But my cry of pain is drowned out by his tongue in my mouth and his fingers on my clit. "Oh God," I whimper, climbing his body, needing more.

"That's it, ride my hand, my dirty girl." He scissors two fingers inside me, stretching me. Curling them so deep, my eyes roll.

I can't think.

Can't breathe.

I can't do anything except ride the wave of intense pleasure building inside me.

"Never going to get enough of this," he groans, licking into my mouth.

"More," I pant. "I need more."

"You want my cock, sunshine?"

I nod, licking my lips. Trying to catch my breath.

"It's yours. All you gotta do is take it."

I dip my hand between us and start tugging at his waistband. Theo chuckles darkly, the sound doing things to me as he shoves my hand away and pushes his sweats down over his hips.

"You want it? Take it," he orders. I fist his shaft and notch him against my entrance, sinking down as slowly as I can go.

"Fuuuuck," he chokes out.

"Oh my God." My entire body trembles as my orgasm hits, crashing over me with such intensity that all I can do is hold on.

"Fuck, you feel incredible." Theo's big hand curves around my hip as he drives forward.

"Yes," I cry out. "Fuck, yes. You feel so good."

He feels... right.

I lock those feelings down.

But then he groans the worst possible word he could.

"Mine," rumbles in his chest, tethering something inside me.

The tension between us snaps and Theo fucks into me like a man possessed. It's dirty and rough and a little bit wild but nothing, not a single thing, feels wrong about it.

"I need to get deeper." Theo grunts, pushing my thighs wider. Pressing in so close I feel him everywhere. "You don't have to say it, not yet," he breathes, punctuating his words with a bruising thrust. "But I know you feel it. I know you're mine."

"Theo," I cry, another wave building.

"Fuck, *fuck*..." He grits out. "You are amazing, sunshine. Fucking love this pussy."

Theo slams into me once more and I shatter, crying out his name as he fills me with his cum. He buries his face in my shoulder, riding out his orgasm until his dick softens and he pulls out of me.

I practically wilt against the wall but then he's scooping me up again and carrying me into my bathroom.

"Theo," I complain at the way he manhandles me.

But secretly, I love it.

I love how small and dainty he makes me feel when I've spent my whole life having to act tough.

But as he lowers me to the floor and turns on the shower, the bubble bursts and the illusion drifts away.

Because this might feel good now, but it won't last.

Vaughn will make sure of that.

There is no scenario here that ends with me and Theo finding our happily ever after.

So as he pulls me into the shower with him, I decide that I'm going savour every second we have.

Because losing Theo—losing the way he makes me feel—is going to hurt far more than Vaughn betraying me ever did.

"Go, you've got to go." I try to push Theo away, but he won't listen, peppering my face with tiny kisses.

Laughter spills out of me, and I want nothing more than to freeze-frame this moment.

"Let me stay," he groans. "We can wake up tomorrow and have lazy morning sex."

"We can't. I promised Millie I'd meet her for breakfast. And she can't see you leaving. No one can."

"But—"

"Theo." I give him a little shove and he pouts. Jesus, he's too cute like this. Playful and teasing. "You need to go."

"Fine. Fine." He lets out an irritated sigh. "I'll go. But after you get done with Millie, your arse is mine, sunshine." He slaps it for good measure.

"Bye," I say, locking down the hurt swelling inside me. This could be the last time he's here, in my room.

The last time I ever get to kiss him.

Throwing myself at him, I kiss him desperately. He pulls me into his arms, chuckling. "You're the one sending me away and now you're acting like you don't want me to go."

Because I don't, I swallow the words.

"Okay, go. Go." I shove him again and he gives me a strange look.

"I'll see you tomorrow, yeah?"

"Yeah." I nod, swallowing down the lump in my throat.

"I won't let you run again," he says.

"I'm not running."

It's not a lie, not really. I'm not running. But it won't matter once he learns the truth.

"Night, sunshine."

"Night, Teddy." I smile, hoping he can't see the sadness in my eyes.

I don't ask how he intends on getting out of the dorms without being noticed. As I've learned by now, he seems to have no problem coming and going as he pleases.

"Tomorrow," he adds before slipping out of my room.

I drop onto the edge of my bed, letting out an exasperated breath. There are so many emotions coursing through me I don't know which one to latch onto first.

Instead, I replay every second of the last two hours. Every touch and kiss and whispered word. All the things we didn't say but felt anyway.

If I wasn't head over heels for Theo Ashworth before, tonight has sealed the deal.

Not that it matters anymore.

Sadness envelops me, and I wish more than anything that it didn't have to be this way.

Knowing it will be a while before I can sleep, I decide to go and raid the kitchen. It's empty so I grab a handful of snacks to take back to my room. Movement behind me catches my attention and I smile to myself.

Sneaky boy.

"Theo, you can't—"

"Sorry to disappoint." Vaughn's voice turns my blood to ice as he steps into the kitchen and closes the door behind him.

"W-what are you doing here?" I choke out.

"I would have come sooner if it wasn't for your boyfriend. Really, babe. A jumped-up little rugby player who thinks he's God's gift to women just because he has a few quid in the bank and drives a nice car."

I don't argue. There's no point. Vaughn Ronson only believes his own bullshit.

"What do you want, Vaughn?" I clip out, my eyes darting to the door behind him.

I could scream, try and alert somebody. But who knows what he might do, and Millie is in this building.

"I want to discuss the terms of our arrangement."

"We don't have an arrangement," I say, trying to keep the tremor out of my voice.

"Now, now, don't play dumb with me." He steps closer and I dart back. But he's quicker and before I know it, his hand shoots out, grabbing me around the neck. His eyes drop to the love bites along my collarbone, his expression turning murderous. "We both know you're going to do exactly what I say."

"I'll leave," I rush out in pure desperation. "I'll go with you. Just... just leave them out of it. Please."

"Now why would I do that?" He leans in, kissing the corner of my mouth. "When the fun is just getting started."

5

THEO

I'm dressed and ready for school long before the others wake up and emerge from their pits.

There's only two days until the insanity of my birthday hits, and when it does, I want to know that Raine is going to be standing by my side.

It might be selfish to want to drag her into it. But I know the scandal I'm about to cause, the upheaval, and I need her beside me.

Something tells me that Millie is going to need her as well.

With my coat on and my hood up, I step out into the bitterly cold, wet morning. The sun—if there actually was any—has barely risen, casting All Hallows' in eerie dark shadows, making it look even more sinister than it does on a normal day.

With my head down and the rain quickly soaking me, I make a beeline toward the cafeteria. A place we never used to step foot in, since we're Heirs and have access to a private chef. But everything is different since Reese and Liv got together. Now, more often than not, we eat with the masses.

Fucking hell, I can understand why Raine had the opinion of us she did at the beginning. We really are entitled dickheads. Wouldn't change it for the world though, and I'm really fucking hoping that now she knows the man I am, she wouldn't want to change me either.

Raine kicked me out last night because of a breakfast date with my sister. I may not have been invited by either of them, but I sure as shit invited myself.

These two girls are the most important people in my life right now, as well as my boys of course. And just like they all said, I need to do everything I can to prove to Raine that I want her.

Last night was pretty incredible. But I'm not stupid—or arrogant—enough to think that a handful of orgasms and a roll around in her bed is going to fix everything that happened yesterday.

I freaked Raine out, I know that. But she's going to have to get used to the fact that when I decide I want something, I jump in with both feet until I've made it mine.

My tenacity has done me well so far. It's going to get me the result we both desperately need when it comes to our father, and I can only hope it'll serve me well in my quest to make Raine mine.

The cafeteria is a hive of activity when I step inside. Students from every year group in the school are in here filling their bellies. The salty scent of bacon and the sweetness of pancakes fill the air.

Knocking my hood off, I unzip my drenched coat and walk deeper into the vast space, searching for the two girls I've turned up here for. To begin with no one notices, but as soon as one person does, they elbow their mates and before long, almost all of the students in here are watching me with intrigued eyes as I move through the room.

There might have been a time I'd have given them something to really stare at, but right now, I have no interest. So what if it's unheard of for an Heir to turn up here alone for breakfast? I rule this school, I can do what the fuck I like.

With the volume of the chatter reduced, and everyone's

intrigued stares burning into me I finally find who I'm looking for.

I shouldn't be surprised that they've chosen a table tucked right back in the corner of the room. Millie has always tried to hide and blend into the background.

My status makes her a target. Although anyone stupid enough to go after her would pay for it. And Raine has caused a stir from her first day, and it's obvious that that hasn't been limited to the sixth form. Her whole demeanour screams 'I don't belong here'. She wears it like a badge of honour and allows anyone who might be interested to see it.

Unlike everyone else in here, both of them have their heads down, uninterested in anything but the conversation they're engaged in.

Well, that's about to change.

I step up to their table, engulfing them both in my shadow.

"We're not interested. Fuck off," Raine barks without so much as a glance up.

Her ballsy attitude makes me smile. It also makes me want to drag her off her chair and shove her to her knees in front of the entire school.

When I don't move, Millie is the first one to look up. She gasps when her eyes meet mine before looking back at Raine who's poking some food around her plate. Her hackles are up as if she's waiting for a hit.

"Raine," Millie hisses, giving her little choice but to glance up at my sister. Millie jerks her chin in my direction. It takes Raine a second but after a sigh, letting everyone know she's not really interested, she looks up.

The second my identity registers, her eyes widen and her chin drops.

"Hey, sunshine. Room for one more?" I ask when she just stares at me utterly dumbfounded.

Well, there goes any hope I might have had about her being pleased to see me and jumping into my arms.

"Theo?" she asks as if I'm not actually standing right here in front of her.

I study her quickly. Her eyes are dark, and her make-up isn't as perfect as normal.

She's had a really bad night.

But why?

She was fine when I left.

Reaching out, I thread my fingers through her hair and give her little choice but to stand up.

"Theo," Millie hisses in horror, but Raine doesn't fight me.

The chatter in the room dies out even more as they wait to see what I'm going to do. They probably all think that I'm here to punish her.

"What are you doing?" she whispers, her eyes bouncing between mine as if she's searching for the answer.

I lean in, and she gasps as she understands my intentions. Her hands lift to press against my chest to stop me, but she has no chance. I'll overpower her any day.

My lips meet hers as a loud gasp sounds out around us. When she doesn't move, my fingers tighten in her hair and my other hand finds her hip, dragging her tiny body into my much bigger one and pinning her to me.

"Be a good girl, sunshine," I tease. "You're mine now, remember."

She whimpers at my words and the second I push my thigh between hers, she caves. Her lips move against mine as the gossiping around us begins.

Let them have at it. I want the world to know this girl is mine.

"Okay, that's probably enough now," Millie mutters as I lick deep into Raine's mouth, claiming her for every motherfucker in this school to see.

Raine's hands slide from my chest in favour of threading into my hair, holding me closer.

"Seriously. Guys. Stop," Millie barks. "People are filming."

"So?" I mutter into our kiss. "Let them."

Coming back down quicker than me, Raine pulls away and lets her arms drop. She glances to the side and startles when she sees that Millie is right. People are probably already uploading photos and videos of this little announcement as we speak.

"What are you doing here?" she hisses.

"You said you were having breakfast with Mills. So I thought I'd come and spend some time with my two favourite girls."

"So you didn't just turn up to ensure I don't corrupt your little sister then?" Raine asks as she retakes her seat.

"Get up," I bark at a little kid at the next table when I realise there isn't a spare chair.

The kid jumps up like he just shit his pants and I steal his seat, spinning it backward so I can straddle it.

"Really?" Raine deadpans.

"What?" My shoulders lift in a half-shrug. "And no. I know I've said some shit about you two spending time together but I'm over it."

"You're over it?" Raine asks as if it's just as easy as that.

Reaching out, I snatch her hand that's resting on the table and twist our fingers together. The second I do, her eyes dart around the room.

I know everyone is still looking, I can feel it. But I don't care. I meant what I said in Raine's shower the other morning and again last night.

She's mine.

And every motherfucker in this town had better get used to it.

"I meant it, Raine. Every single word." Reaching out with my other hand, I steal a rasher of bacon from her plate and bite the end off. "Now are you going to eat up? Something tells me you're going to need your strength later."

"Ew, gross," Millie whines. "If you two are going to get all lovey-dovey, I'm gonna find somewhere else to sit."

"Nope. You are staying right there. I need to talk to you about something." Millie studies me suspiciously as I go on, "Tonight, I'm taking Raine out on a date."

"Excuse me?" Raine coughs having just swallowed some eggs. "A date? Oh no, I don't go on—"

"You do now. We're going out. End of argument."

"Oh God, it's going to be some pretentious, stuck-up fancy restaurant where I'm going to stand out like a sore thumb."

"You really don't trust me, do you?"

"Have you given me a reason to?" she counters.

"Touché," Millie chuckles, doing very little to help my cause here.

"You know I can get your pocket money cut off, right?" I snap.

"As if you would. You're all talk no action, big brother."

"Oh, I'm not sure Raine would agree. She loves my mouth and my ac—" Raine's hand claps across my face, cutting my words off as Millie makes a gagging sound.

"I take back what I said the other night, you're not cute when you're happy. You're disgusting."

I poke my tongue out at her the second Raine's hand slips from my face.

"What do you need me to do?" she concedes, too interested to find out what I'm up to.

"Tomorrow, I want you to take Raine out shopping for dresses for the weekend."

"For Friday night?" she asks hesitantly.

"Yep," I agree, dragging Raine's chair closer to me so I can wrap my hand around her thigh as she gawps at me.

"What's Friday night?" She glances between the two of us.

"Theo's birthday party at the golf club," Millie answers for me.

"Uh... no. I don't think—"

"I want you there," I say before leaning in so I can whisper in her ear. "I need you there, sunshine."

"Theo," she warns. "I don't belong at some fancy party at a golf club."

"You're mine, Raine. That means you belong everywhere and anywhere I am."

"Theo."

"Raine," I growl. "You can fight me all you like, but you're going out with Millie tomorrow and buying two dresses. One for the club Friday night and a second for the party at the Chapel on Saturday."

"I don't wear dresses," she sulks.

"Are you always going to make life this hard?" I ask, making her face twist in irritation. Lifting my arse from the chair, I pull my wallet out and pass my credit card over. "No limit. I want dresses, shoes, and sexy lingerie. Get your hair and nails done as well. Whatever you want."

"Oh no. No. Nope." She tries passing my card back but I refuse to take it.

"Take it or I'll make Millie buy it all."

"You're a dickhead."

"Loud and proud, sunshine. Now eat up, then I'm walking you to class." I smirk. "And if you're really lucky, I won't be very gentlemanly about it."

6

RAINE

Theo Ashworth is a force to be reckoned with.

He's cocky, brash, and he doesn't stop until he gets what he wants.

And he wants me.

I should be elated.

In any other circumstances, I would be. But Vaughn's words—his warning—circle in my mind over and over.

If I don't play his stupid game, he's going to make waves at All Hallows', waves that will hurt Theo. Waves that could hurt Millie.

He knows. That piece of shit knows that I care. And he's using it against me.

It's history repeating itself, except the last time he manipulated me, he used my feelings for him as the weapon.

A violent shudder goes through me as I sit in English, trying to pay attention.

When I first entered the room, everyone stared. Most of the girls whispered. Because Theo claimed me. He claimed me in front of the entire school, and I let him.

Then I let him walk me to class, push me up against the wall and do it all over again.

Part of me hates myself for it. But the other part... is going to cling onto every second I have with him. To live in the fantasy for as long as possible.

My life has never truly been my own. I've been abandoned. Bounced from foster home to foster home. Used. Berated. Hurt. Betrayed.

But Theo is different.

He's the first person to ever look at me and see past all that. Past the girl with the bad attitude and impenetrable walls.

And he's going to hate me more than anything when the truth comes out. But I don't know how else to protect him.

I don't—

I force the thoughts out of my head, inhaling a deep, calming breath.

Vaughn won't stop until he gets what he wants. He won't stop until he ruins everything I care about.

But if I follow his instructions, if I do as he says, maybe I can limit the fallout.

"Don't know what he possibly sees in her, she's... trash."

I glance over my shoulder, pinning the two girls with a hard look. One cowers, but the other holds her ground. Glaring at me with utter disdain.

Flashing her a bright smile, I whisper, "Did you say something?"

"I..." Her eyes dart past me to the front of the classroom. "N-no."

"Didn't think so," I mutter.

Thankfully, the bell rings not long after that, and I'm first up and out of my seat. Only to walk straight into Tally.

"Hey," she says.

"Uh, hi. Are you waiting for me?"

"Yes. We need to talk."

"We do?" I frown.

"I heard about what happened this morning in the cafeteria." She laces her arms through mine as we walk down the corridor. "I can't believe Theo claimed you like that."

Tell me about it, I trap the words behind my lips.

"The sixth form is rife with rumours," she adds.

"Lovely." I grimace.

"I already gave Keeley and her little bitch brigade a mouthful earlier."

"You did?"

"Of course. You're one of us now." She offers me a conspiratorial smile. "We've got to stick together." She leads me toward the cafeteria, and my stomach grumbles as if on cue. "You good sitting with us?" she asks, and I appreciate the choice.

Theo would *make* me sit with them.

My lips twitch, and I'm surprised how easy it is to fall into the trap of forgetting that everything between us is a lie now.

The second he spots me across the room, his eyes darken, running over my body, sending a shiver down my spine.

Okay, so maybe not everything is a lie.

"God, he looks at you like he wants to devour you."

"He's very... intense."

"They all are." Tally releases me as we reach their table, and Theo gets up, coming to me.

"Hi." He gazes down at me, the air crackling between us.

"Hi."

"Sit." A deep voice commands. "Both of you."

"Fuck," Theo murmurs, and I study his expression, ignoring Elliot's eyes burning holes in the side of my face.

"What's wrong?"

"I..."

"I said, sit."

"Who the fuck made you boss?" I spit at Elliot, not appreciating his tone. Or the way he's looking at me.

A flash of annoyance sparks in his eyes. "Figured it was time we talked about your little stunt."

Shit.

Oh shit.

I glance up at Theo and the muscle in his jaw tics.

"I may have told him."

"You... I see."

"Look," I say, pre-empting Elliot's tirade. "It was nothing personal."

"He knows that," Theo mumbles from beside me. "You really have to do this now?"

"Sit. The. Fuck. Down."

Like naughty children, we both take a seat. Tension ripples between us as Elliot watches me. "Do you have any idea how much damage you caused?"

"I heard paint jobs can be pretty expensive. Nothing you can't afford though."

Tally gasps but I see the twinkle of amusement in her eyes.

"And what about you?" He throws back. "Can you afford it?"

Something curdles inside me as I whisper, "You know I can't."

Elliot stares and stares. He stares so hard I want the ground to open up and swallow me whole.

I see it now; why everyone is so wary of him. There's a darkness in him, just under the surface of his cool, collected façade.

"So," he drawls. "I guess what we need to figure out is how you can repay me."

"Whoa, Eaton. That's not—"

"Theo," I sigh. "It's fine. He's right, I owe him."

I have no idea how I'll ever repay them for the damage I caused. But I won't cower either.

"What do you have in mind?" I ask.

"Sunshine..." Theo warns from beside me, throwing daggers at Elliot.

Elliot considers my words, his eyes darting between me and Theo before settling on me again. His icy cold composure slips a fraction, revealing a thin smile.

"I like you, Raine."

"What the fuck—"

"You're not afraid of us, are you?"

"I've met worse boys than you in my life."

"You're off the hook," he says.

"Just like that?" My brow arches. "I don't buy it."

"I said *you're* off the hook. But lover boy here"—his eyes slide to Theo—"can reimburse us all for any damages."

"No, that's not—"

"I'll do it." Theo doesn't miss a beat.

"Thought so." Elliot smirks. "I'll send you the invoice."

The two of them share a long look full of tension. But I'm still gawking at Elliot. He's letting me off the hook because of Theo.

"But no more games," Elliot says to me, and I don't miss the warning laced through his voice.

I nod, not trusting myself to speak.

Theo wraps his arm around me and drops a kiss on my head. "Could have been worse," he mutters.

Reese and Oakley choose that moment to arrive, breaking the lingering tension between us. Oakley dives for Tally, the two of them kissing loud enough to earn them a few disgruntled looks.

"Seriously," Liv tsks when she reaches the table. "Can't you do that in private somewhere?"

"Jealous, babe?" Reese tugs her down on his lap. "What did we miss?"

"Theo is paying for Raine's handiwork."

"Oh shit." He laughs, slamming his hand down on the table. "So it was you."

"Surprise." I force a smile.

"Shit, Ashworth, what did you do to her if she had to go after our cars like that?"

"I..." Theo stutters over his words.

"Let's move on, yeah," I suggest.

"The important thing is they figured out their differences." Tally beams, far too invested in the whole thing. "And in time for Theo's birthday party."

"Don't remind me," he grumbles.

"Do you have something to wear?" she asks. "Something to impress Theo's dad?"

"She doesn't have to worry about impressing anyone but me." He wraps a possessive arm around my waist, tugging me closer.

"I'm not using your credit card to buy a dress," I whisper, twisting around a little to look him in the eye.

"You'll buy a dress."

"Are you always this cocky?"

"Sunshine, I'm an Heir. It's what we do best." He steals a kiss and steals my heart right along with it.

Damn him.

I don't want to feed into this fantasy but it's hard not to.

"Don't look so pissed, Eaton," Reese chuckles. "You know Abi would be—"

"Don't," he grits out and I glance over at him.

Oh yeah, big bad Elliot Eaton has it bad. And the object of his desire just walked into the cafeteria.

"Oh look, Red is here," Oakley teases.

"Seriously, can you not?" Elliot hisses.

"Hi guys." Abi smiles, lingering on Elliot a little too long. He pushes a chair out with his foot, and she drops into it. "I'm so tired."

Abi folds her arms on the desk and lays her head there.

"Uh, everything okay, Abs?" Tally asks.

"Long night."

"Long night doing what exactly?" Reese jokes.

"My dad... bad night."

"Do you need anything?" Elliot says.

"I'll be okay." She turns her head to the side, looking at him. "But thanks."

He doesn't reply, but he doesn't take his eyes off her either.

"You're coming to the party still, right?" Tally offers her a sympathetic smile.

"I don't know. Maybe. He's not had a good week."

"You've got to be there, Red," Oakley adds. "If you don't come, our fearless leader will be all alone now Theo is wifed up."

Theo tenses but he doesn't deny it.

Another stab of guilt goes through me.

The boys spend the rest of lunch giving each other shit while the girls discuss dress options. But I can barely focus on what they're saying.

"Hey, you okay?" Theo asks me, his lips brushing the side of my neck.

"Yeah, I'm fine."

"You're unusually quiet. If it's about the Elliot thing—"

"It's not."

"Good because I have the money and it's partly my fault anyway."

God, why does he have to be like this?

Why can't he be more like the Theo I met when I first arrived here?

It would make what I have to do so much easier.

"I know you're not feeling the party," he goes on. "But I need you there, Raine. I need—"

"Shh." I twist again, touching my head to his. "It'll be okay, Theo," I whisper, the lie coiling around my heart like thorns.

"I just want it to be over," he admits. "I want him out of our lives for good."

"I know."

My heart breaks for him. For Millie. And part of me wishes I could be around to help them pick up the pieces.

But by the time Vaughn is done with me, I won't be welcome in Saints Cross ever again.

7

THEO

A weird nervousness zips around my body as I walk through the girls' dorms toward Raine's room. All eyes are on me. It's been the same all day since I claimed Raine in front of the entire school.

It was something I never thought I would do. Willingly hand my balls over to a girl.

But fuck, did it feel good.

And right now, with the weekend and everything I've been planning looming, I need the distraction of her more than ever.

Smoothing my shirt down, I step up to Raine's door and for once, I actually knock. It only takes her a couple of seconds to answer, and when she does I immediately discover that she's nowhere near ready.

Although, I can't exactly argue with her outfit of choice either.

"You knocked," she points out as if it's the most bizarre thing she's ever experienced.

"I was being a gentleman and picking you up for our date," I say, letting my eyes drop to the thin vest and tiny pair of knickers she's wearing. "But you don't seem to be ready."

"Theo," she breathes, taking a step back into her room when I move forward, desperate to get closer.

The second we're clear of the door, I kick it closed and continue backing her up until her calves hit the bed. She stares up at me with her wide violet eyes that I swear see deeper inside me than any other.

Fuck. This girl.

"Missed you," I murmur before slamming my lips down on hers and thrusting my tongue into her mouth.

It takes her a couple of seconds, but the second I slide my other hand around to her arse and squeeze, she melts against me.

I lick deep into her mouth, taking everything I need.

Well, almost everything.

Before I hit the point of no return which will result in me eating her pussy for dinner and nothing else, I release my hold on her and take a step back. "You need to get dressed," I say as I reach down to rearrange myself.

She watches me with heat burning bright in her eyes. "We could just stay in," she offers coyly.

"Nope. I'm taking you out. I want to show you off."

The second those words roll off my tongue, she recoils.

"What's wrong, sunshine?"

"I... I don't—" She cuts herself off, swallowing roughly as she averts her gaze from me.

"Raine," I prompt.

With a pained sigh, she huffs. "I don't have anything to wear, okay?" She looks down at my body. "You look like..." She gestures to me. "And I'm..." She points at herself.

"Beautiful? Sexy? Incredible?"

"Teddy," she sighs again.

"I'm going to find you something," I state, turning my back on her and marching toward her wardrobe.

I pull the doors open with a flourish of energy and

enthusiasm but the second the inside is revealed, my chin drops in shock.

"See," she says from behind me.

I don't need to look back to know she's got her arms crossed under her tits, her hip popped and her standard scowl playing on her lips.

"I don't have anything to wear out for whatever fancy-pants meal you have planned. I'm not one of you, Theo. I don't have Gucci dresses, Louboutin heels, and Chanel bags in my wardrobe that I'll only wear once so I don't get spotted in the same outfit twice.

"I have one pair of jeans, an old hoodie, some t-shirts with holes in them, and some shorts that show off most of my arse because I cut them wrong. I'm not sure any of those are suitable for where you had planned to take me tonight. I'm not that girl."

I take a second to let her words settle before I spin around.

The hunger that was burning in her eyes has turned to fury and her chest is heaving from a whole new reason too.

"Where do you think I'm taking you?"

"Well, based on your designer cargo pants and shirt, I'm guessing it's a place I don't belong."

"That's bullshit, and you know it, Raine."

"No, Theo. It's not. Our worlds, they're completely different. You're Ralph Lauren, and I'm charity shop. This... this isn't—" Her words are cut off when she collides with the wall. "Theo," she gasps.

"No," I argue, glaring down at her as my hand settles around her throat. Her pulse thunders beneath my fingertips, her body trembling with rage. "I don't give a fuck about what you do or do not have, sunshine. I'm not standing here right now because you have a wardrobe full of designer labels. I don't give a shit if everything you own is old and has holes in it.

"I'm here for you. For your smart mouth, your quick wit,

and your sinful body. You could be walking around wearing a bin bag and I wouldn't blink. I want you, Raine. Nothing else. Just you."

Her eyes fill with tears and her bottom lip trembles in a show of vulnerability I'm not used to from her.

She hates it. I know she does.

But she also can't help it.

I lean closer and she can't stop herself from searching out my lips. But this time, I don't give in to the chemistry crackling between us. Instead, I give her a chaste kiss before taking a huge step back.

"What are you doing?" she asks when I drag my shirt from my body and shove my trousers down my legs.

Ignoring her, I march back to her wardrobe in just my boxers and socks before pulling out her shorts, a t-shirt, and a zip-up hoodie.

"Put this on," I demand, holding it out in front of her.

"Theo?" she sighs, not moving an inch.

"Be a good girl, sunshine, and I might just reward you for it later."

She thinks about it for a moment before huffing a 'fine' and snatching the clothes from my outstretched hand.

I watch as she pulls her clothes on, my eyes locked on her ass as she tugs her shirt over her head.

"I don't know why you're so harsh on the shorts. They look pretty fucking awesome to me," I confess.

"What about you?" she asks, standing with her hands on her hips and a fierce don't fuck with me expression on her face.

"What about me?"

"You're in your boxers. And they don't exactly hide much."

I smirk as I glance down at my semi pressing against the fabric. "I think you like it," I taunt.

"Did I say I didn't?"

"So what's the issue then?"

She grinds her teeth as I close the space between us.

"Ooh, I see," I tease, leaning in close enough that my lips brush her ear. "You don't want other girls to see what they're missing out on."

"Because the entire female population of All Hallows' hasn't already had up close and personal experience?" she deadpans with a hint of disgust. "Pretty hard to be jealous when they've already been there, done that, don't you think?"

"I'm sure there are a few that haven't got this close," I point out.

"A few? That isn't exactly reassuring."

"Can't take back the past, sunshine."

Sadness washes over her face. "No, I guess not."

"Turn that frown upside down, my little Raine Storm. Date night isn't meant to be sad." With my arm around her shoulder, I lead her toward the door.

"You're seriously going to walk out there like that?"

"Yep," I confirm before pulling her door open and tugging her out with my head held high.

No one dares to say a thing as we leave the building. Safe to say that all eyes are on us, though.

The bitterly cold January air rushes over my exposed skin the second we step outside, and I instantly regret stripping down to my underwear.

"Aren't you going back to the Chapel for clothes?" Raine asks when I head toward the car park instead.

"Nah, might just go like this."

"Sure, if you were planning on taking me to a sex club. But for some reason, I thought we were going for dinner."

"Sex club," I mutter, images of her tied up and at my mercy fill my head again. "Why would we go to one of those when we have our own in the basement?"

"So..."

We come to a stop at the boot of my car, and I press the

button on my key to pop it open. Inside, I have a couple of sets of clean clothes.

Grabbing a pair of jeans, I drag them up my legs before tugging on a hoodie and shoving my feet into a pair of trainers. "How's this?" I ask, aware that Raine watched my every move.

"Think I preferred you almost naked. But I am hungry, and it would be nice to be fed so..."

"What my girl wants, my girl gets."

"So you haven't booked a fancy table somewhere then?" she asks once we're in the car and heading off campus.

"I know you better than that, sunshine."

"So where are we going?"

"You'll have to wait and find out."

Leaving All Hallows' behind, I head toward Oxford and a place I know she's going to love.

"Okay, maybe I should have given you more credit," Raine announces as we walk through the entrance of the old barn and into the rustic burger joint the boys and I found last year.

It's a vast space with an open kitchen at one end, where you can see your burgers cooking over a huge barbecue, and a live band playing in the opposite corner. All the furniture is upcycled, and nothing matches but it's a whole vibe. And outdoor heaters throw out enough heat to keep everyone toasty even on the most bitter of winter evenings all while the scent of the flame-grilled meat floats around them.

"This place is insane."

"And no pretentious waiter, or tiny portions in sight," I say a little smug.

Her hand squeezes mine as we wait behind another couple to be seated. "Thank you," she whispers, gazing up at me with her huge violet eyes.

"You're more than welcome, sunshine. You can thank me later."

"Table for two," a young emo guy asks as he grabs us two menus.

"Thanks, man," I say, wrapping my arm around my girl and following the guy toward a secluded table in the back corner of the barn.

"Oh my God, I'm so hungry," Raine murmurs as she stares at the menu.

It's nothing fancy.

Just really fucking good food.

"Order whatever you like," I say, not wanting her to feel like she needs to hold back, despite the fact that I know she will.

She shakes her head as she studies what's on offer before looking up at me.

"What?" I ask.

"Just... you. You're... nothing like I first expected."

"Never judge a book by its cover, sunshine."

"Just like you did me?" she snarks.

"I guess we're as guilty as each other."

"I guess so," she mutters, returning her attention to the menu.

After we've ordered our drinks. A cocktail for Raine and a beer for me, thanks to my very convincing fake ID, I sit back and study her as I think over the day.

"How did you do it?"

"Do what?" she asks after sipping her bright pink drink. It's way girlier than what I was expecting her to choose but it suits her.

"Get out of the dorm without getting caught to tag our cars?"

She smirks, the naughty glint in her eyes making my cock swell beneath the table. "There's a dead spot in the CCTV outside my window. It was really pretty easy."

I shake my head. "Of course," I mutter, irritated that I didn't figure it out before.

"I'm sorry. I know I shouldn't have but you were such a dickhead and—"

"It's okay, sunshine. If anything, I'm impressed. There aren't many people who'd have the balls to go up against us like that. I love that you're not like any of them. You test me, challenge me. Drive me fucking crazy."

She smirks, dipping her head low as she gazes at me from beneath her lashes.

"The feeling is mutual, Teddy."

8

RAINE

Theo watches me. No, that doesn't do justice to the way he looks at me.

Hungry and possessive, he's the predator and I'm the prey.

"Stop looking at me like that," I whisper.

"I'm afraid I can't." He moves closer, dropping his arm over my shoulder and tucking his body in close. "You look fucking edible, sunshine." Dipping his mouth to the skin right beneath my ear, he grazes his teeth at my pulse point, kicking my heart into overdrive.

"Teddy," I whimper, curling my fingers into his t-shirt.

"Just relax." His hand lands on my knee, sliding along my thigh.

Our table is pretty private, but anyone could walk by and see what he's doing to me.

"God," he breathes all husky and needy. "What I wouldn't give to drop my knees right here and taste your perfect fucking pussy."

Oh God.

My stomach clenches with desire.

"I thought you brought me here to prove you don't have a one-track mind."

"Huh, did I say that?" His lips curve into a knowing smirk as he grinds the heel of his palm right against me. Adding more pressure until I can't help but seek more.

"Ahh." My breath catches as I press my lips together, desperately trying to trap the moan building in my throat.

But he doesn't let up, rubbing me through my shorts. I melt into him, unable to do anything but ride the wave as he whispers dirty things in my ear.

"So fucking beautiful," he murmurs. "I want to watch you come, sunshine. Think you can do that for me? Think you can come all over—"

"Hello and welcome to The Barn," a new server says.

Everything inside me goes still as Theo casually removes his hand and sits straight. "Nice place," he says calmly.

Too fucking calmly.

All while I sit there a breathless, irritated mess.

I was so close.

So damn close.

"Do you know what you both would like to eat?"

"Oh, I know what I'd like to eat." Theo glances down at me with a subtle smile.

I narrow my eyes, hardly able to believe him.

Cocky arsehole.

"What's good?" he adds, breaking some of the tension swirling around us.

The waiter clears his throat, and I wonder if he knows exactly what he walked up on. "The steak and caramelised onion ciabatta is one of our more popular dishes."

"I'll take that please," Theo says with an air of confidence that only an Heir can pull off. "With an extra portion of skin-on fries and the house mac and cheese. "

"And for you?" The waiter turns his attention on me, and I inhale a sharp breath, trying to compose myself.

"I'll have the chicken Caesar salad please with a portion of garlic bread."

"Great. I'll get those out as soon as possible. If you need anything else just give me a wave."

He disappears and I sag against the back of the bench, shooting Theo an irritated glare.

"You look annoyed, sunshine." His eyes glint with mischief. "We could always sneak into the bathroom and—"

"No."

"No?" His brow arches.

"You had your fun," I purr. "You don't get to touch me again until we leave."

"Is that so?"

"Yep." I grab my cocktail and take a large sip.

For as much as I like being with Theo, he unnerves me. It's very distracting. And although I have no choice but to go along with things, I have to try and keep a level head.

I drop my gaze, needing a second.

It's so easy to forget that this isn't real.

"Hey." His fingers slide under my jaw so he can coax my face to his. "What's wrong?"

"N-nothing." I force a smile. "It's really nice here."

"Wait a second. Does the mighty Raine Storm actually sound impressed."

"Don't push your luck." I chuckle.

"Seriously, though." Theo's expression sobers. "You really like it? I didn't—"

"Theo"—I grab his hand and entwine our fingers, unable to fight the pull between us—"it's perfect."

And it is.

It's just a shame it's tainted by the dark Vaughn-shaped shadow hanging over me.

"Are you nervous about the party Friday?" I ask.

"No, it's long overdue."

"What are—"

"I can't wait to see your dress," he cuts me off. "Don't wear any underwear, I want full access to you all night."

"Theo, you can't say stuff like that when we're in public."

"Sunshine, I think we both know you're not in charge here." He winks at me, taking a long pull on his beer. "I wasn't lying earlier when I said that I know what I want to eat, Raine."

"Oh yeah?" I play along.

"Dinner might be the steak ciabatta. But for dessert there's only one thing I want." He leans back in, running his nose along my jaw.

"You."

Dinner is incredible. Somewhere between the first bite of chicken and the last bite of garlic bread, I might have died and gone to food heaven.

"You know you make sex noises when you eat, right?"

"I do not." I fume, unable to hide my smile.

It's been fun hanging out with Theo, away from prying eyes and our classmates' constant judgement. He's smart and quick-witted and so bloody gorgeous I find myself constantly checking him out.

The cocky prick knows it too.

If life was simpler, if I didn't have a monster in my past determined to ruin everything, I could easily fall in love with Theodore Ashworth.

I don't know when I realised that but now the thought is there, I can't unthink it.

He's everything I want in a partner. An equal. He wouldn't fight my battles for me, he'd stand by my side and cheer me on while I slay my own demons. And then fuck me senseless as a reward.

That's not to say he isn't all the things I first thought when I arrived at All Hallows'.

He is.

Entitled. Arrogant. Manipulative and cocksure. But he's all so much more than that. I see the way he tries to protect his sister. How loyal he is to his friends.

Theo loves as deeply as he hates, and I don't doubt he would give me the world if only I'd let him.

"Oh, you do, sunshine." He smirks. "I've been sitting here rock hard for the last forty minutes."

"You are such an idiot."

"But I'm your idiot, right?"

"Yeah." I drop my gaze, trying to keep composure.

He's so intense like this, always pushing my boundaries. Making me say things I shouldn't say. Want things I shouldn't want.

Things I will never get to have.

"You ready to get out of here?" he asks, and I nod. "Good because I'm so fucking ready for dessert."

The playful smile he gives me is like a bolt to the heart.

Theo flags down the waiter and settles our bill, then pulls me out of our booth and toward the car park.

His hand rests possessively on the small of my back as he opens the passenger door of his car. But before I can slip inside, he spins me around and kisses me hard. All tongue and teeth and sweet desperation.

"Theo," I gasp as he licks into my mouth.

"Fucking love your body, sunshine."

When he finally lets me come up for air, I'm breathless and aching.

"Ready to get dirty with me?" My brows crinkle and he chuckles. "Don't look so worried. The night is still young and I want to show you something."

"What is this place?" I ask Theo as he turns down a dark track off the main road back toward Saints Cross.

"I like to come here sometimes." He shrugs, keeping one hand on the steering wheel and one hand on my knee as he guides the car toward what appears to be a vast lake.

"It's beautiful," I whisper as my eyes drink in the shimmering body of water flanked by big sprawling trees.

"Yeah. I don't get out here as much as I used to. But when I still lived at home it was kind of my place."

"Theo Ashworth," I feign surprise. "Who knew you were such a romantic?"

"Nothing romantic about escaping another one of your old man's drunken tirades, sunshine."

"I'm sorry."

"Don't." He gives me a defeated smile. "We've all got baggage."

Theo drives the car down to the water's edge and parks. "Once I turn eighteen, things will be different," he says.

"Tell me about it," I reply, as he casts me a strange look. "What?"

"Sometimes it feels like you're going to slip through my fingers."

"Theo, I—"

"Don't." He shakes his head. "I don't want to talk about the heavy stuff, not tonight."

He seems so sad, so lost and vulnerable, it breaks my heart a little.

"What do you want to do then?" I ask coyly. Knowing full well what he brought me out here for. But the build-up is half the fun with Theo.

The heart-racing anticipation.

My boy is dirty and wild and a little bit dangerous, and I love it.

Except, he isn't your boy. I ignore the little voice of warning. Out here, we can pretend. Out here, we're just Theo and Raine, two lost souls looking for someone to guide them home.

"Come here." He crooks his finger at me, the intensity in his eyes sending shivers down my spine.

"Theo, there's barely room—"

"I said, come"—he reaches over and grabs me, dragging me across the centre console and into his lap—"here."

My knees fall open as I straddle him, wrapping my arms around his neck. "Hi." I smile at him.

"Hi."

"This is... cosy." My mouth twitches.

"I happen to like you on top of me. Under me. Anyway I can get you to be honest."

Soft laughter spills from my lips. "Such a sweet talker."

"You'd be surprised at the things I'd become for you."

Sweeping the hair off his brow, I press a kiss to his lips. "You mentioned something about dessert earlier."

"That I did. Not sure what I had planned is going to work in here though." He cracks the door open.

"I'm not skinny dipping in the lake." My brows furrow. "It's freezing out there."

"Don't worry, sunshine." His eyes bore into mine full of wicked promises. "I'll keep you warm."

9

THEO

With Raine's legs around my waist and my hands firmly gripping her arse, I climb out of the car.

"Theo," she gasps when I narrowly miss bashing her head on the door frame in my impatience to get between her thighs.

I could have just fucked her right there in my driver's seat. But as much as I need to sink deep inside her perfect pussy. I need my dessert more.

My mouth is watering for it. I'm like a fucking junkie who's about to die without his next fix.

The ice-cold winter air rushes over both of us, but it does very little to dampen the fire racing through my veins.

Marching around the front of the car, I lean forward, laying her out on my bonnet.

"Theo," she gasps as she loses the heat of my body.

It's pitch black out here, only allowing me to see the outline of her body. It's the only regret I have.

We'll do this again in the spring, I tell myself. When it's warmer and I can see her laid out like a prize before me.

If she's still here...

That thought hits me like a fucking truck.

I have never, ever been this attached to anyone else. Millie and my boys, sure. But never a girl.

"Theo," she says, reaching up and cupping my cheek with her warm hand.

It's not until we touch that I realise my eyes are closed.

"You look fucking perfect," I tell her, my voice rough with need and some unexpected emotion that's blocking my throat.

Don't be such a fucking pussy, Ashworth. Just eat her like you want and man the fuck up.

"Much better than that stupid caricature."

"Hey," she argues, pretending to be offended. "I think the likeness was uncanny."

"If that's how you really see me then fuck knows why you're here right now."

"Your shining personality and talented tongue," she quips.

"And you thought I was only here for one thing," I tease as my hands slide to the button at the front of her shorts. She lifts her hips to help me out and I groan as she grinds against my aching dick. "Such a dirty whore. You want my mouth on you, sunshine?"

"You know I do," she pants as I drag her shorts from her legs, somehow managing to tug them over her boots.

Pressing my hands against her inner thighs, I spread her wide for me. Even in the darkness, I can see what I want perfectly clearly.

I slide my hands down her legs, making her whimper with need. "Are you wet for me, Raine?" I ask, already knowing the answer.

She was right on the cusp of release when our server came over to take our order earlier. I bet her clit has been pulsating with need ever since.

"What do you think?" she snaps, her desperate feisty side coming through.

"I think these pretty lace knickers are fucking dripping. I

think your pussy is swollen, needy, and more than ready for me to push my cock inside."

She rolls her hips as if it'll be enough to convince me to do just that.

Not yet, sunshine. But soon. Very fucking soon.

"I think you've been fantasising about wanting me with my face between your thighs since I mentioned having you for my dessert. You want it, sunshine?"

"Yes. Teddy. God, yes."

Tucking my finger beneath the fabric of her underwear, I pull the lace from her body, barely touching her. "Oh, sunshine," I groan as her juices cover my fingers. "You're not just wet, you're fucking drenched for me."

"Please," she whimpers, shimmying about on the bonnet in an attempt to find some friction.

"Such a greedy little whore," I muse before my need for her overtakes my self-control.

Twisting my fingers in the delicate lace, I rip it easily and pull the fabric from her body. She shudders as the cold winter air rushes over her heated skin.

"Teddy, please. I need—"

"This," I bark before dropping my mouth to her pussy and sucking on her clit until she screams.

Her fingers sink into my hair as she holds me in place. It's not necessary at all. There's no fucking way I'm going anywhere until she's come all over my face.

I lick, nip, and suck until she's trembling beneath me, begging for relief.

But I don't give it to her.

Not yet, anyway.

"Theodore," she screams, pulling my hair until I swear she's close to ripping it clean from my head.

Releasing her thigh, I push two fingers inside her pussy. Her muscles immediately try to suck me deeper, to take what she needs. But she's not the one in control here. I am.

"Oh God, please," she moans, her head thrashing from side to side as I find her G-spot but continue to hold her off. "I'm going to kill you," she screams when I pull back again before she's able to fall.

"I'm banking on it, sunshine. And you know I'll give it right back."

Her heels dig into my back as she tries to force my hand. Slipping another finger inside her, she howls as I stretch her open, coating my digits with her sweet juices. But again, when she gets close, I pull one finger free and drop it lower, teasing her puckered hole.

"Theo," she cries when I put pressure against her tight ring of muscles.

"Relax, sunshine. Be a good girl and let me in."

She does as she's told and then gasps loudly when I push into her body. "Oh shit."

"I'm going to take you here one day soon, Raine. I'm going to make every inch of your body mine."

She gushes around my fingers showing me how much she likes the image I paint with my words.

"You want that don't you, dirty girl? You want me to own you."

"Yes, yes. Please," she begs.

Taking pity on her, and aware that I also want to come sometime soon, I up the ante on her clit and send her crashing into an intense release that has her screaming into the night, her entire body convulsing on the bonnet of my car as she rides it out.

The second she's done, I drag her down the bonnet and flip her over. She squeals as her front presses against the cold car before I grab the back of her neck and hold her down, just in case she was getting crazy ideas like trying to escape.

Kicking her legs wider, I rip my jeans open and shove them and my boxers over my ass, letting my dick spring free.

"Theo, what are you—"

Her words are cut off when I rub myself through her wetness. The second I push the tip in, she tries sucking me deeper.

"Desperate for my dick, sunshine?" I growl, slowly pushing deeper inside her, making my eyes roll back and my jaw clench.

So fucking good.

I don't think it's ever been this good.

"Fuck, Raine. Your pussy is fucking insane."

"You're insane," she gasps out as I fuck her harder. Each thrust of my hips makes her feet leave the ground.

"Your fault," I grunt. "I wasn't this fucking crazy before you showed your pretty face in All Hallows'."

"Don't believe you. THEO," she screams when I bring my palm down on her arse.

Her pussy practically strangles my dick as she embraces the pain.

I do it again. And again. Trying to imagine just how bright my handprint is glowing on her pale skin. I want it to last forever. In the back of my mind, I know that every time I fuck her, I'm one more thrust closer to her leaving.

And I don't fucking want her to leave.

But I fear I'm not going to be enough to keep her here.

My hand slips around the front of her neck and I drag her up from the bonnet, so her back is to my front. "Addicted to this pussy, Raine."

"Theo," she gasps when my grip on her throat tightens, cutting off her air.

"Right here, sunshine. Are you going to come all over my dick?"

She nods, her body trembles as she balances right on the edge of the cliff, ready to go flying over.

Slipping my hand around her hip, I find her clit and give her the nudge she needs to freefall into her release. The second her pussy contracts, she drags me right over the edge with her.

My cock jerks violently as I fill her with cum, marking her as mine in the most primal way.

When I come back to, I'm laying over her petite body, crushing her against my car. Our breaths rush out in white clouds, and despite being covered by my body, her smaller one shivers with the cold beneath me.

"I should get you back. Wouldn't want you getting in trouble for being out past curfew," I say with a dark chuckle, pushing from her and reluctantly pulling out of her warmth. "What are you looking for?" I ask after tucking myself away and finding her looking at her feet.

"My knickers."

I chuckle again. "Even if I didn't rip them. You wouldn't be getting them back. They're going straight into my private collection for when I don't have you next to me."

"Seriously?" She snorts.

"I don't joke about your underwear, Raine."

With a huff, she tugs her shorts on, groaning once they're in place.

"What?"

"Do you have any idea how gross this feels?" She complains as she drops into the passenger seat.

"My cum dripping out of your pussy? That's not gross, sunshine. That's hot as fuck."

"I beg to differ."

"I'll put my foot down, that way I can take them off you again."

"Staying the night, are you?"

"Too fucking right. I've got to share you with my sister tomorrow, I'll take whatever I can get."

My mention of tomorrow night makes her tense beside me.

"What's wrong?"

"Do you really need me there this weekend? I'm not sure your parents will—"

I can't stop the bitter laugh that escapes me. "Sunshine, at what point did I give you the impression I give one single fuck about what my dad thinks?"

"You didn't. I just... I don't belong at the golf club. I'll stand out like a sore thumb."

"You won't after Millie has had her way with you tomorrow. That girl is a shopping pro. You'll look like a million dollars."

"I'm not taking your money, Theo. I'm not with you because of that."

"I know. I'm not suggesting you are. But I want you there with me Friday night. And I want you to look all hot and shit in a pretty dress."

"I don't do dresses."

I turn to smile at her as I pull into the car park. She's illuminated by the campus lights, they give her skin a soft glow and make her violet eyes even more mesmerising than normal.

"You will Friday night. I promise to make it worth your while," I say with a wide grin. "Come on, I'm not finished with you tonight."

Killing the engine, I throw the door open before she has a chance to say anything. By the time I'm at the bonnet, staring down at where I took her not so long ago, she's already out as well.

"That was hot," she confesses with a wicked smirk playing on her lips.

"It was. But I couldn't see you. And I'm more than ready to strip you bare and trace every inch of you with my lips."

She swallows roughly.

"You want that, sunshine?"

"Sure, I was thinking of starting with you though."

"You want to suck my dick, sunshine? All you've got to do is ask," I tease.

10

RAINE

I wake to a wall of heat, Theo's body wrapped around me like a blanket.

"Can't breathe," I chuckle, trying to extricate myself from his hold.

"Mmm, come back," he murmurs.

"We have to get up. We have class."

"Fuck class. I have all I need right here." Theo wins, hooking his arm around my waist and dragging me back into his chest. His hand cups my boob as he tucks his face into the crook of my neck.

God, he's so adorable like this. Like a little puppy dog who needs lots of snuggles.

"Theo," I say. "We really need to get up. If Mrs. Danvers catches you in here—"

"Danvers won't do shit, she loves me."

"You're insufferable."

"I think you'll find I'm insatiable." He grinds his morning wood against my arse.

"Oh no, not happening." I twist out of his hold and come face to face with him. "She needs a rest."

"*She?*" His brow lifts.

"Yep. My pussy. She's broken." Somewhere around the third time he'd slid inside me last night.

"You loved every second." He flashes me a lazy grin.

"I did. But my answer is still no."

Theo pouts and I can't help but laugh at him. "You're no fun."

"You need to leave. Now."

"Fuck that." He pushes up on his elbow. "I want to walk you to class."

"Well, you can sneak out and come back for me then."

"Embarrassed to be seen with me, sunshine?"

Pressing a chaste kiss to his lips, I slip out of bed and pull on a t-shirt.

Last night was... a lot.

I shouldn't have let it get that far. Shouldn't have indulged so much. But Theo makes it impossible to resist, and the selfish part of me wants him.

I want him so much.

But Vaughn will never let me be happy.

A sinking feeling goes through me, but I try my best to shake it off.

Not good enough though.

Theo frowns. "What's wrong?"

"Nothing. Just tired because somebody kept me up half the night."

"Stamina, baby." He winks, tucking an arm behind his head.

"You look awfully comfortable for someone who's supposed to be leaving my room."

"Just enjoying the view." He smirks.

Bastard.

"Well, *the view* needs a shower. Please don't be here when I come out."

"I could always give you a helping hand."

"Don't even think about it. I'll see you in a bit. Outside of the building. Acting like you didn't spend the night here." I pin him with a stern look, trying to hammer home my point. Knowing he'll probably choose to ignore me.

Theo—all the Heirs, really—are a law unto themselves.

I take my time in the shower, making sure to lock the door, so Theo hopefully gets bored and takes off.

But I also need a second to catch my breath. To push down all the fear swimming in my veins. It's been three days since I last saw Vaughn, but I don't for one second think he's gone.

He's simply biding his time, letting the fear get to me. The threats.

I hate him.

I hate him so fucking much but I don't know how else to break free from his hold on me.

If I do this one last thing for him, I'll finally be free to move on with my life.

I don't even realise I'm crying until the tears drip off my chin.

"Get a grip," I hiss at myself. I didn't come to All Hallows' to put down roots. I'm supposed to be passing through. Doing my time until I age out.

No one should matter to me here.

Except, they do.

Theo matters. Millie and the girls too.

For the first time in my life, I feel like I have a place in the world.

But it's nothing more than a fantasy.

One that will never come true.

Thankfully, when I pluck up the courage to go back into my room, Theo is gone.

But there's a note on my dresser.

Four little words that crush my heart.

You own me, sunshine.
See you outside.

T

"I can't wear that," I say, staring at the dress Millie is holding up.

"What? Why?"

"It's so... bright."

"I thought it would bring out your eyes." She grins, clearly loving every second of this.

"If I've really got to do this, I think black is more my colour."

"Noooo, you can't go with black. You need to make a statement."

"I really don't." Walking into Theo's party on his arm is going to be a statement enough.

I can already imagine people's surprise—and horror—when they realise the girl from out of town is his date.

I can hardly wait.

Shoving down the bitter taste on my tongue, I walk over to another rack and thumb through the dresses, but nothing stands out to me.

I'm not this girl. I don't play dress up for my boyfriend and his rich family.

"I'm sorry if I touched a nerve." Millie comes up beside me.

"It's fine. I just... I don't exactly feel comfortable in a place like this."

"I don't like playing dress up either." She nudges my arm. "But it's Theo's birthday, he needs us."

"Yeah..."

Guilt snakes through me but I shove it down. Even if Vaughn wasn't holding me over a barrel, I'd want to be there for Theo tomorrow night.

He trusted me enough to open up to me about his dad. The least I can do is be there for him.

Even if he'll hate me for it one day.

"Okay so colours are out. What about monotones?" Millie asks, steering me toward a rack of sparkly glittery dresses.

"No bling," I state with a shudder.

"Okay, how about"—she scans the boutique, her eyes landing on a smaller rack in the corner—"yes, I think that could work." She tugs me toward it, reaching for one of the dresses. "What about something like this?"

I stare at the black bodycon dress with lace collar and cap sleeves.

"I..."

"Pretty, right?" Her mouth twitches and I roll my eyes because damn her, she's right.

It is pretty.

And if I've got to wear a dress to the party, I want it to be something as kick-arse and gorgeous as this one.

"Try it on."

"What? No, I can't—"

"Try. It. On." She thrusts it at me.

"It's probably not my size."

"It's your size. Now, go."

"Fine." I snatch it from her and hook the hanger over my finger, heading for the dressing room with Millie's laughter following me the whole way.

She's such a little know-it-all but as I slip the dress on, I can't help thinking that Theo knew what he was talking about when he said Millie would help me find the perfect dress.

Because it is perfect.

The soft material fits me like a glove, accentuating my curves and drawing attention to my collarbone. The lace is sexy and playful and gives the whole look a dark edge.

It screams Raine Storm, and I love it.

I do.

But when my eyes snag on the price tag, I almost fall over.

"Come on, the suspense is killing me," Millie calls from beyond the changing room.

"I don't think it's the right one," I say, barely hiding my disappointment.

"What? Why?" The curtain is ripped open, and Millie stands there gawking at me.

"Do you mind?" I spit but her face splits into a wide grin. "What?"

"You look... holy crap, my brother is going to die."

"I can't buy this dress Millie. It's three hundred and fifty pounds."

"So? Theo told you to get whatever—"

"Exactly. It's too much. Let's go to another shop."

"No. This is the one, Raine. This is the dress. He won't be able to look away."

"I..." I turn around and stare at myself in the mirror again. It really does look like it was made for me. "Yeah, okay," I breathe, hardly able to believe it.

But I've never had this before, and I'll probably never have it again.

"Right choice, Raine." Millie giggles. "I can't wait to see his reaction. Do you have shoes? Oh, we need to get you a bag too."

"Millie, I don't want to go crazy."

She whips out Theo's credit card and grins. "We're girls. My brother will expect nothing less."

"I am so stuffed." Millie slumps back in the booth and rubs her stomach.

"I said you wouldn't need the extra portion of fries."

"But they're so good." She grins, and I shake my head at her.

After Millie loaded me up with a matching clutch bag and shoes, we headed to a local restaurant for something to eat.

It's been nice, hanging out with her. Spending some time away from All Hallows'. She seems like herself again. The shadows of her father's recent abuse are long gone. But I know that kind of hurt doesn't disappear. You just get really good at burying it.

"How do you feel about the party?" I ease into it.

She shrugs, focusing on her Coke. "It is what it is. It's Theo's eighteenth. It's not like I can't not go."

"You could—"

"I know what you're doing." She glances up at me.

"Oh yeah?"

"I've been in therapy for a long time, Raine."

"Fine, okay. Maybe that wasn't the most subtle lead in. But I want you to know you can talk to me about this."

"There's nothing to say. My father is... he's not a good person."

"At least you'll have me tomorrow night. We can stick together." Something tells me I'll need a friend too.

"One look at you in that dress and Theo won't let you out of his sight."

"We'll see." I wink at her. "I had fun today."

"Me too." She smiles, before shuffling out of the booth. "I need to pee. I'll be right back."

Millie weaves her way across the restaurant, and I take a moment to check my phone, smiling at the two messages from Theo.

> Theo: Can I at least get a sneak peek later?
>
> Theo: Come on, sunshine, you're killing me here. Mills said I'm going to owe her big time when I see it, which has me all kinds of intrigued.

I text him back.

> Raine: Nope. No seeing the goods until tomorrow night.

> Theo: Spoilsport.

> Raine: I'm sure you can handle it.

Another text comes through, but it isn't from Theo. With shaky fingers, I open the message.

> Vaughn: You look beautiful tonight.

Icy cold fear races down my spine as I glance at the glass windows overlooking the street.

Vaughn stands there, watching.

> Raine: What do you want?

> Vaughn: Just checking in on my investment. Time's a ticking baby.

Inhaling a shaky breath, I text him back.

> Raine: You shouldn't be here.

> Vaughn: How is the sister? Millie, is it?

> Raine: I swear to God, Vaughn…

I glance up again, but he's gone. I don't feel even an ounce of relief though.

My phone dings again, and my heart sinks.

> Vaughn: I'll see you soon, baby. I'll see you real soon.

11

THEO

I'm early.

Stupidly fucking early. But I can't wait any longer.

I've been pacing back and forth in my room since the moment I got back from practice. Wishing that I could hit fast forward on the clock and wake up tomorrow morning with my girl in my arms and our father exactly where he should be.

For years, I've been dreaming about this night. About finally proving who our father really is and committing him to a life of punishment for everything he's forced on us over the years.

I should be excited. I guess a part of me is, but really, I just want it over.

I'm exhausted. I've barely slept all week, just tossing and turning as different scenarios for tonight play out in my mind. Some scenarios where the plan goes off without a hitch, and others where it goes disastrously wrong.

I might be confident in everything Christian and Fiona have done but there's still a tiny part of me that fears Dad knows. That while I've been busting my arse to bring him down, he's on the other end of this case getting all of his evidence in place to prove his innocence.

I wouldn't put it past him. He's a sneaky bastard. And if he is aware, then there's no way I'll win against him, even with Christian and Fiona on my side.

And my life won't be worth living.

Fear rips down my spine as I consider where that will leave Millie. I've done all of this to protect her. To put an end to Dad's reign of terror over her. Over Maria.

Over me.

All our lives have been beyond tainted by that cunt, and it's time we found our freedom.

With my hands trembling and my palms sweating in an unusual show of nerves, I let myself into the girls' dorms and I take the stairs two at a time. There's only one person who can distract me from what's to come, and she's hopefully busy getting ready in her room.

I don't bother knocking, I wouldn't be able to cope if she refused to let me in right now, so I just unlock the door and storm inside.

Only, it's empty.

All the air rushes from my lungs as I spin around in the spot as if she's going to appear in front of me magically.

"Fuck," I hiss, pulling my phone from my pocket to check the time.

We need to leave in an hour. Where the fuck is she?

Tapping out a message, my pacing starts up again as I wait for her to read it and then reply. But she does neither. My heart races as thoughts I really don't fucking need begin flickering through my mind.

She didn't want to come tonight. What if she's bolted to get out of it?

Raine isn't a pussy. In most circumstances, she's happy to throw her shoulders back and stand up for herself. But a golf club full of rich socialites isn't exactly her norm. I'm more than aware of that. I'm also aware that I was selfish to ask her to attend tonight. But I need her there.

Fuck. I need her like I've never needed anyone else before and I'm not entirely sure how I feel about that.

When it feels like an hour has passed, I hit call and lift my phone to my ear. It rings and rings, but she never answers. Instead, when her voice fills the line, it's her voicemail message.

"Hi, you've reached Raine. Sorry I can't take your call right now, I'm too busy being fucking awesome. Laters."

My teeth grind.

"Where the fuck are you?" I growl, cutting the call before the beep.

My pacing starts up again and I only get more and more antsy as the minutes pass. I'm about to give up and go to Millie's room to see if they're getting ready together when her door finally opens and a harassed-looking Raine steps inside wearing only a hoodie I left here one night this week.

It hangs around her thighs, leaving the rest of her insane legs on show. Her hair is curled and her make-up is flawless but there's something in her eyes that makes my stomach clench painfully.

"Where have you been?" I demand, my voice sounding way more frantic than I was hoping for.

Her lips open and close a couple of times before she finds some words. "I... uh..." She looks back over her shoulder nervously. "Millie needed help with her make-up."

Narrowing my eyes, I take a step forward. "I need you more," I whisper, hating how vulnerable I feel but unable to do anything else.

Her eyes flash with something. Surprise, I think before her brows dip low. "What's wrong?" she asks, having to tip her head back to keep eye contact with me.

"I need you."

If we weren't so close, she'd have no chance of hearing me. But she does, and she also knows exactly what I need. Her fingers lift to the zip running down the front of my hoodie and she drags it down. My heart thuds against my ribs with every passing second and every inch of skin she reveals. All the air leaves my lungs in a rush when the fabric parts and I find that she's bare beneath bar a tiny G-string.

"Fuck, sunshine. You really know how to distract a guy, huh?"

Pressing her palm in the centre of my chest, she shoves until I take a step back. I'm so entranced by her incredible body that I let her push me across her room until my legs hit her bed. "Talk to me," she demands, her eyes continuing to hold mine captive.

"T-tonight," I stutter like a fucking moron as she reaches for the belt around my waist and begins tugging it free.

"Go on," she encourages, unhooking my trousers and shoving them down my legs.

"Oh fuck," I groan, my head falling back as she grabs my dick, rubbing it through my boxers. "I've done something," I confess.

"What have you done, Theo?"

"Our dad. H-he... fuck," I gasp when she shoves her hand under the waistband, the heat of her skin against mine searing me to the bone.

"He what, Teddy?" she rasps, her voice giving away how horny she is right now.

"Gonna... gonna get payback."

My boxers are ripped down my thighs a beat before her palms crash against my chest, and I fall back on the bed.

"Keep talking." Her knees hit the thick carpet beneath our feet and her fingers wrap around my cock, slowly stroking me making precum leak from the slit.

"Jesus, you're hot," I murmur barely able to focus.

"Keep. Talking," she demands harshly.

"He's done some shit. Worse than hitting Millie. And I've — RAINE," I bellow as she licks around the head of my dick like I'm her personal lollipop.

"More," she mumbles around my shaft.

"Christ, sunshine. You're making it really fucking hard here."

She smirks up at me, her eyes flashing with accomplishment.

"I really fucking needed this," I say, resting back on one hand while the other sinks into her hair, guiding her as she sinks down on my length. "FUCK."

Thankfully, she forgets about making me talk and instead continues to suck me off like a pro.

"Fuck. Your mouth is fucking sinful, sunshine," I groan again as she takes me back into her throat, making my balls draw up all too fucking soon.

Her eyes stay locked on mine, making this even more intense. My heart swells as I watch her worshipping me. It aches in a way I've never felt before. It's as exhilarating as it is terrifying.

She takes me all the way again and just before I hit the point of no return, my fingers grip her hair tighter, and I pull her off.

"What are you—"

"As much as I want to come down your throat, I want you walking into that party tonight with my cum running down your thighs."

"Theo," she gasps, her eyes dilating even more with my dirty words.

I reach for her, tucking my hands under her arms and haul her from the floor. Falling back on the bed, I settle her over my lap. Slipping my fingers under her underwear, I drag them to the side, my eyes feasting on her glistening, swollen pussy.

"Sucking my dick get you hot, sunshine?"

"Theo," she moans as I run my fingers through her folds, collecting up her wetness.

Lifting my hand, I suck those two fingers into my mouth, craving the taste of my girl. She watches with wide dark eyes.

Her nipples are hard and her chest heaving. She needs me just as badly as I do her right now.

"Not enough," I mutter even as her taste floods my mouth. "Get up here."

She hesitates, but there's nothing she can say right now that will stop me from getting a proper taste of her.

Wrapping my hands around her waist, I drag her up my body, setting her knees on either side of my head. Exposing her again, I lift my head from the bed and lick up the length of her. But it's not enough. I'm pretty sure it never will be.

"Sit on my face. I want to eat you until you're screaming my name."

"Theo," she whispers, but I'm over her hesitation. Wrapping my hands around her thighs, I drag her lower until the only thing I can taste, the only thing I can smell is her.

"Mine," I growl into her pussy before plunging my tongue inside her.

"Theo," she cries, her hands reaching up to cup her breasts and pluck her nipples as I fuck her. "Yes. Yes. Fuck."

She's so worked up from just sucking my dick that I have her screaming and coming over my face in a matter of minutes.

The second she's down, I lift her to my lap again, sitting her over my aching dick. "Ride me. Let me see those tits bounce while you sink down on my fat cock."

In a rush, she reaches for my length as I continue to pull her ruined underwear to the side. "Good girl," I force out between gritted teeth when she does exactly what she's told, taking me inside her hot, wet body. "Jesus. I'll never get enough of this. Your pussy was made for me."

She cries out as she rolls her hips, using me to find another release.

"That's it, sunshine. Take what you need."

I watch her losing herself in this connection between us

and the pleasure that is shooting around our bodies, but before long, it's not enough.

Nothing ever is when it comes to her.

Sitting up, I slide my hand into her pretty curled hair and crash her mouth to mine, claiming her in a wet and filthy kiss, letting her taste herself on my tongue.

With her arms over my shoulders, she uses me to help her move, continuing to fuck me until she's squeezing me so tight, I can barely hold off my release.

Slipping one hand between us, I find her clit and pinch it.

"THEO," she screams as she falls headfirst into another orgasm. Her pussy clenches and ripples around me, milking my dick and sending me crashing over the edge. And just like I promised, I fill her up, smirking as I do, knowing that she's going to be walking around for hours, feeling me leaking from her.

Wrapping my arms around her sweaty body, I tuck my face into the crook of her neck, stealing her strength and warmth. Something tells me that I'm going to need it tonight and in the coming weeks.

"Theo," she whispers. "You're scaring me. What's going on? What have you done?"

I suck in another deep Raine-scented breath before pulling back from my hiding space and finding her eyes.

"Theo?" Her voice quivers.

I stare at her, the girl who holds my heart in a vice. "I've done what I need to do to make our lives better. And I need you right there as it all plays out. I need you, sunshine, and Millie is going to need you too."

12

RAINE

Nervous energy vibrates under my skin as we arrive at the exclusive golf club on the outskirts of Saints Cross. It's exactly the kind of place I'd expect Theo and his friends' families to hang out. A huge ostentatious building with perfectly tended lawns and polished windows. It reeks of money. And despite the overpriced dress I'm wearing, the clutch bag and heels, I still feel extremely out of place.

"Just breathe," Abi says quietly as we follow the girls and their dates for the evening toward the double doors.

The place is lit up against the dark moody sky, but I can see the greens in the distance.

It isn't the grounds that draw my eye though, it's the cars. Expensive sleek cars that look like they belong in a James Bond movie or something.

Of course, there's valet parking. Because that's all par for the course at a place like this.

A place where people have more money than sense.

Lock it down, Raine.

Tally and Liv look every bit the part tonight. Hanging off their boyfriend's arms with poise and beauty. When I first saw them all, waiting for me and Abi, I couldn't deny the stab of jealousy I felt.

I thought I'd get to arrive with Theo. But his father demanded he and Millie arrive with him and Maria. So after taking what he'd needed, Theo had kissed me and left.

I didn't blame him. But it still felt like he'd left me to the wolves.

"This place is insane," I whisper.

"It's not that bad," Abi replies. "But then, I've been here a lot over the years. My dad has a membership. Well, he used to, before..."

Taking her hand, I squeeze it gently, flicking my gaze to where Elliot walks on ahead. Abi's gaze follows and I notice the slight blush staining her cheeks.

She's so obvious. They both are. And there's a new strain between them tonight. As if the tether between them is ready to snap at any moment.

"He looks good, huh?" I ask, and she gives me an imperceptible nod. "He couldn't take his eyes off you when we arrived."

"It doesn't matter."

"I think it does."

"Raine... don't. Please."

"Why do you do that?"

"Do what?"

"Act like he couldn't possibly want a girl like you. You're one of the best people I know, Abi."

She gives me a sad, resigned smile and says, "You'll see."

I'm about to ask what she means when the door swings open, and we file into the building. People mill about, sipping glasses of champagne. Adults. Kids I recognise from school. Some I don't.

But I see what Abi means. The second people notice the Heirs—notice Elliot—the mood shifts, a ripple going through the air. Girls start to whisper and point. Their attention is mostly fixed on the last available Heir.

"Wow, and I thought things were bad at All Hallows'."

"Yep." Her voice is right as we cling to each other.

I realise then, that she's not wholly comfortable amongst these people either.

"Do you see Theo?" I ask her.

He wouldn't tell me what he meant earlier but I can't help thinking he's done something stupid.

I get he's angry about his dad, that he wants to protect Millie. But there was something vulnerable in his gaze, it scared me.

The depth of my feelings for him scares me.

God, I'm a mess.

"I need to go to the bathroom," I say to Abi. "Come with—"

"Red, get over her," Reese calls and I spot him standing with a murderous looking Elliot.

She glances between us, her expression telling.

"Go," I say. "I'll be fine."

"The bathroom is down the corridor on the left. You can't miss it."

With a small nod, I take off, weaving my way through the crowd. A few people stare, clearly unimpressed that I'm here. A couple of girls go as far to make sure I hear their snide comments. But I keep my head held high as I make a beeline for the bathroom.

Inside, I check my reflection and reapply my lip gloss. I don't like being so dolled up, but the girls all reassured me that Theo's reaction will be worth it.

When he finally appears.

A couple of girls enter the bathroom, sneering when they notice me.

"Keeley said he'd bring you, but I didn't believe it," one says, her lip curling with disgust.

"Am I supposed to give a shit what you think about me?" I retort, fluffing my hair for effect.

I won't give them the satisfaction of thinking their words matter, even if they reinforce all my insecurities about being here.

"Do you really think Mr. Ashworth will accept you? He expects Theo to marry someone from a wealthy family. Someone with... potential."

"I—"

"You really messed up coming tonight." Their laughter grates on me, making me wince. "He's going to take one look at you and tear you apart and we're all going to be right here to witness it."

"What's going on?" Millie appears, glowering at the girls.

"Oh, Millie, hi. We were just telling Raine how pretty her dress is."

"I bet you were," she murmurs. "I've been looking for you." Her gaze lands on me and relief skitters down my spine. "Theo is waiting to introduce you to our dad. He can't wait to meet you." Millie gives them a saccharine sweet smile before grabbing my hand and pulling me out of there.

"Rule number one. Don't go off on your own. There are vipers waiting to strike around every corner." Her mouth twitches. "You look amazing, by the way."

"Thanks. And thanks for the save back there. They kind of caught me off guard."

"You're nervous."

It's not a question and I don't dignify her with an answer.

She knows I didn't want to come tonight.

"Where are they?"

"Who?"

"Theo and your dad." I frown.

"Oh, they're not really waiting to meet you. I just said that to shut those bitches up."

"Oh." My heart sinks. Because of course Mr. Ashworth wouldn't want to meet me.

He probably doesn't even know about me.

And it occurs to me then...

I have no idea what I'm about to walk in on.

There's no sign of Theo or his dad when we move into the main hall. It's a vast room with a glass dome ceiling and a huge crystal chandelier hanging in the centre.

If I felt out of place before, I feel completely lost as everyone begins to take their seats.

There's a seating plan and Theo didn't tell me, he didn't—

He enters the room and finds me in an instant. His gaze darkens as he lets his eyes fall down my body and back up again. I'm paralysed. Completely and utterly frozen to the spot as he drinks his fill, his lips curling with approval.

I'm about to go to him when another man enters the room behind him. A carbon copy of the boy I'm falling for.

Older, sure. But with those same dark eyes and chiselled features. He notices his son looking at me, but one cursory glance and Mr. Ashworth deems me unimportant as he places a hand on Theo's shoulders and steers him away and toward one of the tables.

"You're sitting with us," Abi says, startling me.

"There's a seating plan."

"Theo didn't tell you?"

"No, he didn't." I grimace, my stomach churning with apprehension. "What if I don't have a seat?"

"You do. With us. Come on.

But when we arrive at our table—or what's clearly the Heirs table—I realise my name card is Elliot's plus one.

"Surprise," he says coolly.

"You knew about this?"

"Just trust him, okay."

"So what? I'm supposed to be your date?"

His heavy stare flicks past me to Abi and his jaw clenches. "It's only for theatrics."

"Theatrics, right."

"It's just a name card," Abi points out. As if it matters. As if I shouldn't care that I'm here as a nobody.

What did I expect though?

Theo to introduce me as his girlfriend? To a father he hates.

A father he's plotting against.

"He's not going to do anything stupid, is he?" I ask Elliot quietly while everyone chats around us.

"What do you mean?" His brows furrow.

Then it hits me. What if I'm the weapon?

What if Theo is planning to use me to get back at his father?

No, he wouldn't do that.

He wouldn't—

"You're freaking out," Elliot notes.

"I don't know what to think."

"I've known Theo a long time, Raine. And I've never seen him care like he does about you. Just trust him. Yeah."

Theo takes his seat at another table with his father, Millie, and a woman I assume is Maria. There are also three other adults sitting with them.

"Oakley and Liv's dad Christian and Reese's mum Fiona," Abi says. "And the other man is Elliot's dad Johnathon Eaton."

"I feel sick."

It's too much. The lies. The games.

The fact I'm pretty sure I'm falling in love with a boy I can never have.

I shouldn't be here.

I should have run and never looked back the second Vaughn showed his face.

But there's no running now, it's too late. I have no choice but to do what he wants.

It's the only way to buy my freedom and protect the friends I've made here.

My bag vibrates in my lap, and I dig out my phone.

> Theo: You look sensational. I almost walked over to you and kissed the fuck out of you in front of all these people.

I want to ask why he didn't. But I don't.

> Raine: I should given the price tag.

> Theo: Best five hundred quid I've ever spent. I can't wait to fuck you in it.

> Raine: You didn't say we wouldn't be sitting together.

But Mr. Ashworth commands his son's attention, barking at him to put his phone away before he can read my reply.

"I hope they bring the food soon, I'm fucking starving," Oakley complains.

"You're always hungry." Tally rolls her eyes, and everyone laughs.

Everyone except me.

I'm too nervous. Too confused and worried.

It feels like everything is spinning out of control and this is only the beginning.

"Raine." Abi touches my arm and I blink over at her.

"Yeah?"

"I asked if you want some champagne."

"Oh, no I'm okay thanks."

The last thing I need right now is to get drunk.

I need to keep my wits about me because this room is full of sharks and at the first scent of blood, they'll attack.

13

THEO

The TAG Heuer watch Dad and Maria gifted me for my birthday feels like a lead weight on my wrist as I follow the two of them into the function hall for tonight's dinner.

I purposefully kept myself out of all the planning for this event. I don't want to be here, so I certainly didn't need to know every single detail about it. As the room reveals itself, I shake my head. If you didn't know better, you'd think we were all here celebrating a wedding. It's... ridiculous.

What eighteen-year-old wants to have a sit-down fucking meal with the elite of the town and all his father's dickhead friends?

Me, apparently.

There's even a fucking string quartet up on a stage at the other end of the room. If I ever needed any more evidence that my father has no clue who I am or what I like, then here it is.

The second I slip around Dad, who's stopped to talk to a colleague in the entrance, I scan the room. There is only one person here I'm looking forward to seeing. I just wish she were the only one in the room.

It's been over an hour since I had little choice but to leave her in her dorm room to finish getting ready earlier. And I'm dying without having her by my side.

But I couldn't do it to her.

When Maria rang me the other evening to ask if I was bringing a plus one to sit at our table, I said no. The guilt from that blatant lie threatened to swallow me whole. But there was no fucking way I was forcing her to sit and endure what Millie and I will have to when she could be with her friends.

Why should she have to suffer just because I've made her mine?

I'm pretty sure it's the most selfless I've ever been. I'm not sure if Raine will see it that way when she discovers what I've done but I figure I've got a few ways I can make it up to her later.

The second my eyes land on her, they widen to the point I'm surprised they don't pop out of my head.

She looks…

She looks fucking incredible.

Sure, she still oozes that dangerous edge that lets everyone know she's not to be messed with that I love, but she looks… beautiful and elegant.

She looks like one of us for the first time since she arrived in Saints Cross.

Unlike the last time I saw her, her hair is sleek and curled around her shoulders. Her make-up is dark and flawless and her dress…

Fuck me, the dress.

I owe Millie fucking big for this.

My eyes drop from Raine's and take in every single inch of her body that's wrapped in that sinful dress. And the shoes… there is no fucking way she's taking those off later.

My cock swells and my temperature spikes despite the fact I only had her recently. That release is long forgotten though as I lick my bottom lip in the hope her taste still lingers.

My fingers curl into fists, my heart pounding against my chest as she takes a step toward me. I do the same, drawn together like two magnets. But then her eyes lift from me and focus on someone behind me.

A hand lands on my shoulder and I startle but the second he speaks, I know the exact reason Raine faltered, and I don't blame her one bit. With one final glance and what I hope is an apologetic smile, I allow Dad to lead me away. Thankfully, Raine's attention is quickly stolen by Abi, who guides her toward the table I wish I was sitting at.

Millie aside, that table seats my family, not the one my father is leading me to. Although, I can't deny the reassuring smiles both Christian and Fiona give me, settles something inside me.

Nerves riot within me as I greet everyone else at the table and lower myself into my seat, more than ready for this whole night to speed the fuck up so I can take my girl home.

Ignoring the conversation going on around me, my eyes linger on the other side of the room. They're in the opposite corner, as far away from Dad and his acquaintances as possible. If he had his way, they wouldn't even be here. Thankfully, that was one thing he conceded on. It helps of course that all their parents are here. But if he knew the truth about Raine and her lack of social standing in this town then there would be no way on Earth he'd have allowed her inside the building, let alone to sit down and eat the meal he's spent fuck knows how much on in a lame attempt to impress everyone.

He probably thinks the ridiculously pretentious food is what everyone is going to remember about tonight. Little does he know that I've got something much more elaborate and much more memorable up my sleeve.

My skin burns with attention, and I finally rip my eyes away from my girl to find Fiona studying me.

"You okay?" she mouths while Dad is preoccupied by someone who's walked over to say hello.

I nod, wishing we could hurry it up.

Why did we plan to do it after dinner exactly?

The conversation continues to flow around me, but my focus is across the room. Everyone else at Raine's table is talking and laughing. I even see them try to engage her, but she isn't having any of it.

I know she's uncomfortable here. This isn't her scene. I know it was selfish of me to even ask. But just being able to see her, it settles something inside me.

"You're really gone for her, aren't you?" Millie asks quietly, too terrified to speak too loudly in case she pisses Dad off.

He's on his best behaviour tonight. And will continue to be. But that doesn't mean he won't ensure we'll be fully aware of any misdemeanours after the event.

Thankfully, the starters and mains come and go without too much fuss or drama. Both Millie and I mostly poke at our meals. It's not unusual for her, but it is for me.

"Is everything okay, Theo?" Maria asks me, noticing my barely touched plate.

Out of the corner of my eye, I spot movement on the other side of the room. My heart lurches when I spot my girl slipping out through a set of double doors with Abi hot on her tail.

"I'm not feeling great. Probably the excitement," I lie. "Excuse me," I say before pushing my chair out and walking away.

I spot Abi slipping into the ladies' bathroom at the other end of the hallway, and after a quick glance around to see if anyone is watching, I take off after them.

I catch the door just before it closes.

"I hate this," Raine complains.

"Trust me, it's not my idea of a fun night either. But he needs you. He needs his boys," Abi reasons, proving once

BRUTAL CALLOUS HEIR: PART TWO

again that she's more aware of what's happening around her than we often give her credit for.

"I know. I know. I just... something bad is going to happen, Abs. I can't stand it. I just wish I could talk to him, be close to him. I—"

Stepping out of the entrance to the bathroom, I silently announce my presence.

"Ask and you shall receive," Abi jokes.

"Theo," Raine gasps. "What are you—" Her words are cut off as I wrap my hands around her waist and force her backward until she collides with the tiled wall.

The second we stop, I dip down and claim her lips in a wet and filthy kiss that will probably result in me being the one wearing her crimson lipstick. But fuck it. There are worse problems to have.

"Oh my God," Abi gasps, her eyes fixed on us. "I... uh... I'll leave you to it."

I don't hear her go, I'm too lost in the taste of my girl's kiss and the warmth of her curves under my hands. "Fuck, Raine," I groan, ripping my lips from hers and kissing down her neck.

But while she might have kissed me just as passionately and desperately as I did her, she's not so willing now, her body tenses beneath my touch.

"What's wrong, sunshine?"

Stupid question really.

It's fucking obvious.

"Why am I sitting on the other side of the room to you?" She half chastises, half moans when I suck on the skin beneath her ear.

"I did it for you, Raine," I tell her honestly. "You're better off with our friends."

"I came to be with you, Theo. I came because *you* needed me."

"I do."

"On the other side of the room?" she asks suspiciously.

"Trust me." I breathe, hitching up the bottom of her dress and rubbing my fingers over the lace of her knickers. "Fuck, Raine. You're soaked."

"We're going to get caught," she says.

"So?" Resting my brow against hers, I stare down into her eyes. "Since when do you care about getting into a little trouble?"

"We're in the golf club. I'm sure getting fingered in the bathroom is frowned upon by all the stuck-up—" She abruptly swallows her words and averts her gaze.

"Go on," I encourage, an amused lilt to my voice as I continue teasing her.

I may be one of the stuck-up golf club members, but I'm fully aware of the kinds of people who hang out here. If it weren't for being forced by my father, I'm not sure I'd be spending my days chasing a little white ball around a field. I much prefer a bigger leather one.

"I'm just saying, it's not exactly the kind of place to—Theo," she cries when I tug her knickers aside and drag my fingers through her folds. "What if your stepmum walks in?"

"Then I'm pretty sure she'd walk back out fast."

"Millie?"

"Isn't as naïve as she looks." I hate to admit it, but it's true. She's growing up faster than I can cope with.

"Jesus. Fuck. We can't—"

"Too late," I say, pushing two fingers deeper into her. "It's already happening. And I'm not going back out there until you've come all over my fingers and I've got your taste on my lips."

"Fuck. You're filthy," she gasps.

"You love it," I say with a smirk before latching onto the addictive skin of her neck and sucking until I'm confident that she'll walk out of here with a bright red love bite on her neck.

Her moans and cries for more soon get louder, and only

seconds after I add another finger, stretching her wide open as she finally falls for me.

Her body tenses and her eyes fall shut, her mouth open as she whimpers my name.

"Look at me," I demand, giving her little choice but to find my eyes. "I want to watch you as you fall, and I want you to know exactly who's doing it."

"Theo," she cries, her pussy sucking my fingers deeper as she rides out the waves of pleasure.

"So beautiful," I muse, loving the way her cheeks redden.

Pulling my fingers from inside her, I lift them up before pushing them into my mouth, licking her juices from my skin.

My cock aches, desperately trying to burst its way out of my trousers.

She knows it too.

"Raine," I warn as she drops her hand to rub me.

"What's wrong? Don't you want me to return the favour?"

"Like you wouldn't believe. But I need to get back."

Her eyes darken with disappointment.

"I promise you, as soon as this is done, we can leave. I'm taking you back to the Chapel and I'm going to spend all night making you come."

"What is all of this, Theo? What have you done?" She searches my eyes, desperate to find the truth within them.

"It'll be over soon," I say cryptically. "I just need you to trust me a little while longer."

She nods slowly.

"And, when it happens, I need you to get Millie, okay?"

"Theo."

"It's all going to be fine. I just need to know she's safe. If you need to take her to the Chapel, then do it." Silence fills the space between us. "Promise me, Raine. I need you. We need you."

She sighs, her eyes softening. "I promise."

And with that, I give her one more knee-weakening kiss

and stalk out of the bathroom, taking my raging boner with me.

The second I step into the room though and spot Dad searching for me, it sinks faster than I thought possible.

Just get through dessert and then the show can commence...

14

RAINE

"Is everything okay?" Abi asks me with a small, knowing smile as I take my seat back at our table.

"Fine." I give her a curt nod, aware that I'm still flushed and a little breathless.

"Is Theo—"

"He's fine," I snap, harsher than I intend. But I'm on edge.

Something is about to go down and my gut tells me it isn't anything good.

I search out Millie seated at her father's table, and my heart aches when I spot her crestfallen expression. She isn't the feisty, funny girl I know. She's a timid little mouse sitting there.

And I know exactly why.

Fear.

She's scared of her father, a man who is supposed to protect her, not hurt her.

Anger bubbles beneath my skin as I curl a fist against my thigh.

"Hey." I startle at Abi laying her hand on my arm. "Are you sure everything is okay?"

"Sorry, I'm just a little on edge."

"Theo didn't help with that?" Her lips twist with amusement.

"Not really," I murmur.

"Your neck would suggest otherwise."

I try to pull a few strands of hair free to cover the love bite Theo took pleasure in branding on my skin.

I wish I could say I hate it—I don't.

I don't hate anything about the boy with the weight of the world on his shoulders.

My phone vibrates in my clutch bag, and I dig it out, an icy trickle of fear sliding down my spine as I read the message.

"Raine?" Abi asks.

"It's just my social worker, checking in," I lie, grateful when the waiters start bringing our dessert.

Tally and Abi discuss the strange looking concoction on the plate, both of them groaning and giggling when they take a bite.

"Seriously, watching you eat dessert is like foreplay," Oak says, his hungry gaze fixed on Tally as she devours her pudding.

"Want mine?" I ask them, my stomach too unsettled to eat anything else.

"Are you sure?" Tally asks, a slight blush to her cheeks.

"Go for it. I couldn't eat another thing."

Lie.

Lie.

Lie.

My whole life feels like a lie sitting here, playing dress up with my friends. Friends who wouldn't look twice at me if they knew the truth.

A truth I can't seem to outrun.

While they're all distracted with dessert and each other, I check my phone again, carefully reading every word of Vaughn's message.

> Vaughn: This is the target. You know what to do.

The next message is an image. A man's face. I study the grainy photo before closing the message thread and shoving it back in my bag.

I inhale a shuddering breath as I reach for my glass of champagne and take a big sip.

As if tonight isn't tense enough, now Vaughn is on my case.

My gaze flicks over to where Theo and Millie sit with their father and his friends, a sense of dread curling in my stomach.

I shouldn't have come tonight.

I should have stayed away.

But how could I when Theo and Millie needed me?

Even if they'll end up hating me one day, it doesn't change the fact I care about them.

A part of me always will.

When dessert is over, there's a small break before what I can only assume will be a speech.

People mill about near the bar, talking and laughing. Theo excuses himself from his table and makes his way toward us. He talks to Elliot first, the two of them in a tense, hushed conversation. Both their dark gazes snap over to mine, and I drop my eyes, embarrassed that they caught me watching.

I'm so out of my depth here, I feel like I'm drowning.

I'm about to excuse myself when Theo moves around the table to talk to Oak and Tally. He leans over her, resting his other hand along the back of my chair, his fingers brushing my shoulder.

My breath catches as I glance around, worried someone might see. I wouldn't be surprised if Mr. Ashworth has heard rumours about the girl from out of town his son has taken a shine to, but everyone knows the Heirs reputation as playboys. He probably thinks I'm nothing more than a desperate Heir chaser willing to spread my legs for a boost up the social ladder.

He hasn't so much as looked twice in my direction so I'm obviously of no concern to him.

The thought bothers me more than it should.

"When's the actual party starting?" Reese grumbles. "This is as dull as shit."

"Won't be long now," Theo says but I don't miss the strain in his voice. "I should get back to Millie."

"How's she holding up?" Elliot asks.

"She's okay. At least, she will be soon." His fingers graze my shoulder again and then he's gone, strolling across the room like he owns it.

"Excuse me," I say to no one in particular. "I'm going to the toilet again."

I grab my clutch and hurry to the ladies' bathroom. A couple of girls shoot me a derisive look but I ignore them. I've got bigger things to worry about besides whether or not the spoiled rich bitches of All Hallows' approve of my outfit.

When I'm done, I wash my hands and take a deep calming breath. But the second I slip back into the hall, my heart catapults into my throat.

"I don't think we've met," Mr. Ashworth says coolly.

But it isn't Theo's dad I'm surprised to see. It's the man standing beside him. The man from Vaughn's photo.

"You're Elliot's plus one?"

"I... that's correct." I purse my lips, trying to steady my racing heart.

"Pretty little thing," the other man says. "What did you say your name was again?" He laughs and it's so full of arrogance and entitlement that I vomit in my mouth a little.

"I didn't."

"Raine Storm, I believe."

So he has heard of me.

I school my expression, refusing to back down.

"Quite the name," he adds with mild distaste.

This man oozes self-importance, the smug glint in his eyes telling me all I need to know about Theo and Millie's father.

"For quite the girl, so it appears," the other man says.

"Stan, let's not scare the poor thing. From what I've heard she's had quite the upbringing."

My stomach curls with uneasiness as the two men openly leer at me. Mr. Ashworth's glare seems full of disdain like he thinks I'm beneath him. Beneath Theo and his friends. I can feel his judgement permeating the air around us.

But his friend—Vaughn's target—looks at me with a kind of longing that makes my stomach churn.

"If you don't mind," I say as politely as I can manage. "I should probably get back to my friends."

Without giving them a chance to reply, I slip past them. But Mr. Ashworth grabs me, his grip a little too hard. My eyes flash to his, narrowing slightly.

"Is there a problem?" I ask.

"I don't know, you tell me."

"What—"

"Dad," Theo's voice cuts through the tension, and his father drops his hand.

"Theo, Son. I was just saying hello to Elliot's date."

I glance over at Theo as his jaw tics. "I think he's looking for you. You should probably get back to your table."

With a small appreciative nod, I hurry past him. But I can't stop myself from looking back at the three of them. Theo says something to his father, the two of them in a clear battle of the wills, while Stan stares brazenly in my direction.

Creep.

I hurry back to my table and say a silent prayer for this night to be over sooner rather than later.

"What did he want?" Elliot asks me the second I sit down.

"To introduce himself, I guess."

"Stay away from him, Raine."

"I didn't, that's—"

"Relax, Elliot didn't mean it like that, did you?" Olivia scolds.

"Shit, no." He lets out a weary sigh. "I just... don't let him corner you again. Not unless you want Theo to lose his shit."

"Will everyone just relax," Oakley drawls, draining his beer. "This is supposed to be a celebration."

"Beckworth has a point," Reese says. "When can we ditch the dinner party and get the real party started."

"I thought you were having a party at the Chapel tomorrow," Abi says.

"We are." He grins. "And it's going to be fucking epic. Theo's new dealer— Ow, fuck, Prim. What the hell was that for?"

"Because you're being inappropriate." She glowers at him. "Some of these people know my parents."

"Worried what Mummy and Daddy will say if they find out you're with a bad boy? Maybe we should give them something to really talk about." He smirks and grabs the back of her neck, crashing his mouth down on hers.

"Fuck's sake," Elliot groans, running a hand down his face.

They start bickering but I'm too distracted, my heart and head pulled in two directions.

Vaughn's threat hangs over me like a dark cloud but right now, Vaughn isn't here. Theo is. And something is about to go down.

I sense the shift in the air. The foreboding. He might not have told me what's going to happen, but he told me to be ready. To get to Millie when it does happen.

People begin to take their seats again as Mr. Ashworth hovers by the stage, talking to the manager. It's a pitiful exchange, the manager practically falling over himself with niceties.

God, I hate this place, these people.

Well, not all of them.

My gaze flickers to Theo and Millie. He's whispering something to her. She gives a little nod, the pain in her eyes dissipating a little.

Then the object of her fear steps onto the stage and the room ushers into silence.

"Good evening, everyone. I'd like to thank you all for joining us tonight to celebrate my son's eighteenth birthday." He lifts his glass toward Theo's table. "Theodore. You're officially a man. The hard work starts now, Son."

Laughter ripples around the room. But I don't laugh. I can't. Too fixated on the silent exchange between father and son as Mr. Ashworth waxes lyrical about Theo. About his achievements and accomplishments. But I realise that tonight isn't about Theo at all. It's about him. About presenting the right image.

"Theo and his sister haven't always had an easy time. After their mother, God rest her soul, left us, things were hard for a while. But Theo has grown into a determined and focused young man, and I don't doubt he'll go far. Now, let's welcome the birthday boy up here to say a few words. Theo…"

Theo stands, his expression giving nothing away as he rakes a hand through his hair.

But I'm hit with the sudden urge to rush over to him, to stop whatever is about to happen. I want to protect him. To shield from anything that might hurt him or Millie.

The intensity of the emotion makes me suck in a sharp breath, and Abi lays her hand on my arm.

"Are you okay?"

"I… I don't know." I watch as Theo steps onto the stage to

join his father. Mr. Ashworth grips him on the shoulder and smiles. A predatory smile that makes my chest tighten.

"Elliot," I breathe, unsure of what I'm asking.

"It's okay," he says calmly. "He's got this."

His words offer little reassurance as Theo takes the mic from his father, and I realise it's too late to stop him.

15

THEO

It takes every ounce of strength I have to hold my hand steady and not show the entire room that I'm trembling. That the prospect of what's about to happen isn't rocking my entire foundation until it barely holds me up.

I'm doing the right thing, I know I am. But it's still fucking terrifying.

His hand squeezes my shoulder a little too tightly. I know why. It's because of that exchange with Raine in the hallway.

He fucking went after her.

I suspected he would, that her cover as Elliot's date wouldn't work. Anthony Ashworth sees and hears everything. There isn't anything I've ever done he hasn't known about and then ripped me a new one for. But I was also confident that Raine would be able to hold her own. She's proven time and time again that she can go up against all of us, I had no doubt that would extend to my cunt of a father.

Power and position in this town means nothing to her. And I know that after seeing the evidence of him raising a hand to Millie, he really means nothing to her.

Lifting the mic to my lips, I inhale a deep breath and find her in the crowd. The second our eyes connect, something settles inside me. It doesn't matter that her face is wrought with worry over what's about to happen. She's here. She's with me and I know she'll follow through on her promise of picking Millie up when the shit hits the fan.

"Thanks, Dad, for that glowing reference. And for this," I say, gesturing to the room. "I'm so grateful that you managed to squeeze in a table at the back for my friends while the rest of the room is full of yours."

An awkward chuckle fills the air while Dad bristles beside me.

Almost every other day of my life, I've pandered to his needs. Done anything I can so as not to light the very short fuse he walks around with.

But not today.

Today I'm going to light that motherfucker up and watch him implode.

"And you're right," I continue, my eyes shifting to Millie. "Mills and I have had it hard. Losing Mum at such a young age greatly impacted our lives. I'm sure it's something we'll never forget.

"I guess we should be grateful we were left with our one remaining parent, right?"

Maria's spine straightens, her eyes narrowing on me. Nervous energy and fear radiate from her. I give her a very slight nod, letting her know that I know what I'm doing, that everything is going to be okay, before continuing.

"But I can speak for both of us when I honestly say that we're not."

The gasp that comes from the crowd, as I say that is large enough to suck all the air out of the room.

"Theodore," Dad hisses angrily, but I ignore him. The time for abiding by his rules is over.

"Because the man we were left with hasn't been the kind of father I would wish on anyone." Dad lunges at me, attempting to steal the mic, but I'm faster. "I won't go into all the reasons right now. There is just one I want to share with you all."

A door at the back of the room is cracked open, letting me know that everyone is in place. Thank fuck because if they weren't, this entire room might be witness to something they really never would forget.

"All of you know Anthony Ashworth as a distinguished lawyer, an upstanding citizen, and a generous philanthropist."

Suddenly, a whole host of police officers surge into the room and my heart pounds faster than I swear it ever has in my life. I find Raine. Her face is pale, her eyes wide in shock as she shifts to the edge of her seat, ready to run. But her eyes aren't on me.

They're on Millie, just as I knew they would be.

"But it's all a cover," I state firmly. "Anthony Ashworth is nothing but an abusive, corrupt murderer."

There is a beat of pure silence before the entire room erupts in chaos.

I catch sight of Raine darting toward Millie before my father grabs me and hauls me across the stage.

"What the hell is this?" he barks, fury etched into his features.

He shakes me, his grip tightening but I don't fight. I let my body go limp and allow him to do whatever he wants. It's just more evidence for the coppers closing in on us.

"The truth," I spit. "I know you did it. I know you killed her," I seethe.

"Anthony Ashworth, we're arresting you on suspicion of murder," one of them starts while they try to drag him off me.

"Get your hands off me," he demands, trying to shake them off. But he stands no chance. He's more than outnumbered.

"You do not have to say anything. But it may harm your defence if you do not mention when questioned something which you later rely on in court. Anything you do say may be given in evidence."

"You're a disgrace," he sneers, glaring down at me, his grip on my shirt iron-clad as the officers overpower him.

He finally releases me, leaving me to crash to the floor as more policemen surround him.

"What are you talking about? Murder? Have you lost your goddamn minds?" he seethes as one of the officer's cuffs his wrists in front of him. "I haven't done anything. My son is a liar. He hates me and he's making shit up.

"Tell them, Theo. Tell them what a liar you are."

None of them say a word, and it's more than noticeable that no one in the crowd does either.

I don't fight for him.

And nor does anyone else.

Not his wife. His daughter. Or any of his so-called friends.

It's everything and more than I could have asked for.

"You can't do this. Do you know who I am?" he bellows, continuing to fight against his restraints.

I stay where I am for a few more seconds, unable to look away as I feel my boys step up behind me. I need to see this; I need him to know that it was all me. That I'm the reason his world has been upended.

"You won't get away with this," he spits, pure rage etched into his expression.

I step closer, aware of everyone ready to jump in case I do something I'll regret. "I hope you rot in hell you piece of shit."

Before he can reply, Dad is dragged off the stage and my friends descend on me.

"What the fuck was that?" Elliot says, his eyes on the officers leading my father from the room.

"That was a long time coming."

"He killed your mum?" Oak asks, ignoring the show and keeping his eyes on me.

"Yeah. The suicide story was all a cover."

"Shit," Reese says, scrubbing his rough jaw.

A shadow falls over us as Christian and Fiona appear.

Christian holds his hand out, a determined and accomplished expression on his face. Sliding my hand into his, silence falls around us as my friends learn who I had on my side throughout all of this. I know it'll hurt that I didn't confide in any of them about it. But I couldn't. I couldn't tempt fate or risk anything going wrong tonight.

"Job well done, I'd say," Christian finally says as our hands part.

Fiona isn't so formal with her celebration, and steps forward, pulling me in for a hug. "We're so proud of you, Theo. If you or Millie need anything, you know where we are."

"Thank you," I force out through the lump in my throat. "For everything."

"You're family, Theo. All of you," she says, glancing around our huddle. "Where's Millie?"

As I scan the room, the softest of smiles pulls at my lips. "She's with my girl."

"Your girl?" Oak teases, elbowing me in the ribs.

"Hell yeah," I say with a grin. "You fuckers coming or what?" I ask, pushing through all of them.

I'm fucking done with this place and bullshit party.

There's only one more person I need to see before I can put all of this behind me.

"Maria," I say softly as I approach where she's still seated, staring at the stage where her abusive husband was arrested not so long ago. "Maria?" I try again when she continues to stare through me.

Dropping to my haunches, I cover her fidgeting hands with my own and wait. It takes a couple of seconds for her to see me, and when she does, tears flood her wide eyes, and her body visibly trembles.

"It's over, Maria," I promise her. "He's never going to hurt you again."

She shakes her head, and my stomach knots. "N-no, I-I…

He'll come back," she whispers, sounding as terrified as she does when he flies off the handle at her.

"He won't. You're free."

"B-but the house... Millie..."

"I have everything in hand. You have nothing to worry about." I have so much more that I need to explain to her, but I hold it back for now. I doubt she'd hear me or understand even if I tried.

She holds my eyes for a long time. I have no idea what's going on around us. I'm too concerned about her falling apart in front of me. But as her first tear falls, I see a shift in her. It's subtle, but the scared woman Dad has turned her into begins to fade away, and I start to see the fun-loving woman who's been the best mother she can be to Millie and me over the past few years.

"Thank you," she whispers, switching our hand's position and squeezing mine. "Thank you, Theo."

It's my turn to shake my head. "You deserve it. So does Millie. We're all free now."

The breath she releases is so huge, I wonder just how long she's been holding it for.

"Go home, Maria. Figure out what your future looks like. Millie and I will come and see you tomorrow, okay?"

I push to stand and find Fiona watching us from a few feet away.

"We'll take her," she says. "Go find your sister. Give her a big hug from us."

I nod and take a step back as my boys surround me.

"Come on. Your girl and sister are at the Chapel," Elliot says, throwing his arm around my shoulders.

"Whoa, you allowed them in unattended?" Oak balks.

"Fuck off," Elliot barks, leading me toward the exit.

Some people have already left, but others linger, waiting to see if the show is over, no doubt. This town is nothing if not gossip-hungry. While I might have more than a few sets of intrigued eyes on me, no one dares speak to me.

I follow Elliot and Abi toward his car while the others make a beeline for Oak's.

"You can go with them if you want," Elliot offers when he notices her following us.

"And spend the journey in the middle of their weird sex games? No, thank you."

I snort a laugh as I think about Reese and Oak playing a game of *who can make their girl scream first* for bragging rights when we get back.

"Fair enough. And because my night just went fucking spectacularly, I'll even let you ride shotgun so you can sit next to my boy," I say, winking at her, loving how her cheeks bloom bright red.

"N-no. It's okay, I can sit in the—"

"Nope. In you get," I say, holding the door open for her like a gentleman. "Put your foot on it, Eaton. I need my girl."

"Fucking whipped motherfuckers," he mutters as he jabs the start button bringing the engine to life.

"Ah, just wait, my friend. Your time is coming."

Slamming his foot down on the accelerator, he sends me flying back into the seat with a dark chuckle as he speeds out of the car park and toward home.

Pulling my phone from my pocket, I find a screen full of notifications but there is only one I'm interested in.

> Raine: I have Millie. We're at the Chapel. She needs you.

I lift my thumb to reply but Elliot makes me pause.

"How fucking long have you been planning that?" he barks.

"Too fucking long."

"It feel good?"

I pause for a minute, giving myself a moment to actually

think about how I feel. A smile spreads across my lips as I think back to the moment Anthony Ashworth was marched through the event room in handcuffs ready to spend the rest of his miserable life in jail.

Oh, how the mighty fall.

"Fuck, man. It feels so fucking good."

His eyes meet mine in the rear-view mirror and I see his own need for revenge on his father burning in their depths. "Enjoy it. You deserve it."

The second he pulls into the car park closest to the Chapel, I throw the door open and run, leaving both of them in my dust in my need for my girl and my sister.

16

RAINE

"What the hell was that?" Millie rushes out as I usher her out of the cab.

My hands shake as I grab her slim fingers and tug her toward the Chapel. "You're safe now," I say, a slight quiver to my voice.

Thanks to Theo's cryptic warnings, I knew something was going down tonight but I still can't get my head around what happened back there.

Mr. Ashworth was arrested. Carted away in handcuffs in front of the elite of Saints Cross. Because he murdered their mum.

A shiver runs down my spine as Millie burrows into my side.

"Come on," I whisper, wrapping an arm around her. "Let's get you inside."

She shouldn't have had to witness that. But I get why Theo did it.

God, no wonder he's been carrying all this anger around with him.

We reach the ornate doors, and I dig the key Elliot gave me earlier out of my clutch.

"Who gave you that?" Millie asks.

"Elliot."

"Did he know?"

"I don't think so, but he knew something was going down. We both did."

"Theo told you to get me out of there, didn't he?"

"I..." I hesitate for a second and then nod. "He did."

She doesn't reply, just stares at me as I unlock and push open the door, stepping aside to let her enter first.

"I'm not usually allowed in here." Her voice sounds so small. Nothing like the girl who enjoys giving me shit about her brother.

"I guess they're making an exception. But we should probably go up to your brother's room."

"Lead the way."

We walk upstairs in silence. When Theo's bedroom door creaks open, Millie walks ahead of me. Making a beeline for the bed.

Kicking off her shoes, she sits on the edge and lets out a weary sigh. "Is it true? What the police said about my dad?"

"I... I don't know. But if Theo and the police say it is, then..."

"He killed her. He killed our mum. And he... he—" The words get caught in the sob that rips from her throat.

I sit beside her and pull her into my arms. "Shh, I'm here. I'm right here."

Violent sobs wrack Millie's body as she clings to me. I don't know how long we sit there for but eventually, the tears recede to a gentle sob.

"It's getting late," I point out. "Why don't you get into bed."

"You'll stay?"

She's nothing more than a frightened little girl, but her vulnerability speaks to me, and I find myself nodding.

Not that I'd ever leave her alone like this.

"Come on." I pat the bed. "I'm sure Theo has an old t-shirt you can wear."

I stand and go over to his dresser, rooting around in the drawers. My eyes snag on a small tin tucked away under all his socks but I don't linger, grabbing Millie a t-shirt from the next drawer.

"Here." She's already half undressed, sniffling through each motion as tears streak down her cheeks.

"Do you think Theo will be back soon?" she asks, pulling on the t-shirt before scooching into bed.

"I'm sure he will be." I dig out my phone, surprised to see no text yet. But I guess he might need to speak to the police before he comes here.

Part of me—the part falling for Theo—is a little hurt that he didn't tell me the plan. But the other part, gets it. What we have is still new. He doesn't know if he can trust me yet.

He trusted me to get to Millie and get her out of her though.

"He might be annoying, but Theo would do anything for you, you know that, right?" I ask, pushing the tear-soaked hair from her eyes. "He's a good big brother."

"The best." Millie yawns, drying her eyes on the sheet. "You'll definitely stay?"

"I said I will."

"You're good for him, you know. For each other."

Guilt snakes through me, fisting my heart.

I can't think about that—about what's to come—right now though. So I kick my shoes off and shuffle up the bed so I'm sitting beside Millie.

"Get some rest," I say.

She gives me a little nod, her eyes shuttering as she snuggles a pillow into her chest.

I hate that she's going to end up in the crossfire, caught in the middle between me and Theo. But she's tough. If anyone can get over it, it's her.

Still, it doesn't stop me from wishing that things could be different. From wishing that my life was my own and that I could choose Theo and Millie and their friends.

I guess it's karma. Vaughn might have pulled my strings for the last few years, but I was complicit. I went along with him.

Now I only have to do one last job for him, and I'll be free.

Leaning my head back against the wall, I watch Millie sleep. She's so lucky to have Theo. He'll never let her stray onto the wrong path. Maybe if I'd have had someone looking out for me, I wouldn't be here now, and things would be different.

But if I'd never have come to All Hallows', I would never have met Theo.

And I can't regret that.

Not ever for a second.

Sometime later, I hear them arrive back at the Chapel.

After checking on Millie, I slip out of the room, and go in search of Theo. Nervous energy thrums inside of me, my heart crashing against my chest.

"You want a drink?" someone asks—Reese maybe.

Their voices grow louder as I reach the staircase.

"You should go to them." That's Elliot. "Mills will be—"

"She's fine," I say, descending the stairs. "I left her sleeping."

Theo's eyes immediately find mine, a violent shiver running down my spine at the darkness there. The void.

"You good?" I ask, keeping my head held high.

He gives me a small imperceptible nod.

The air crackles between us and I'm aware of the rest of them watching us. Something has changed, and it isn't me.

Theo stands, stalking toward me like a predator. Long, angry strides until he's right in front of me.

For a second, I don't move. I can't breathe as he stares at me, his anguish a living, breathing thing between us. But then he throws his arms around me and pulls me against his chest, and I realise he isn't angry. He's barely holding on.

He trembles as I wrap my arms around him and hug him tightly. "It's over," I whisper, my heart cracking.

"She's okay?"

"She's confused and upset but she's okay. She's asleep in your bed."

He nods again, giving me his eyes. "Thank you for getting to her."

"Of course."

Tension radiates off him and I want nothing more than to help him relax. But not with an audience. Not while Millie is asleep upstairs, her heart breaking.

"You want to go see her?" I ask, stepping back a fraction. Trying to keep a level head.

His eyes flash with something and I know he's thinking the same thing.

He wants me.

He wants to bury himself inside me and use me to erase the events of the night.

"Later," I whisper, taking his hand. "She needs you."

That seems to snap him out of it.

"We'll be in my room," he says to no one in particular.

"If you need anything..." Elliot lets the words hang.

"Thanks." Theo moves ahead of me and tugs me toward the staircase.

We make our way to his room in silence. But he doesn't let go of my hand, gripping it like I'm his life raft and without it, he might slip under and lose his fight.

When we reach his bedroom door, he pauses, inhaling a sharp breath. "What if she hates me for it?" he asks.

"Not possible. Millie loves you, and she knows why you

did it." His eyes search mine and I force a smile. "You're not a bad person, Theo."

He looks like he wants to argue but he gives me another curt nod, before pushing his door open and going inside.

Millie is exactly where I left her, curled up in a ball on her brother's bed.

Theo falters, taking in the sight of his sister. "Fuck, she looks so small," he breathes, running a hand down his face.

"She's tougher than you think." I nudge him into the room so I can close the door behind me.

"I keep thinking, did I do the right thing? Now she has nobody except me."

Moving around him, I cup his face in my hands, staring up at him with every ounce of emotion I feel. "As someone who grew up with nobody to count on, I can tell you that you're wrong. You are enough, Theo. More than enough."

He leans down, touching his head to mine. "I'm so fucking glad you're here." His lips brush my skin, sending my heart into a tailspin.

It hits me like a bolt of lightning right in my chest.

I love him.

I'm falling in love with Theo Ashworth and I'm going to break his heart.

Not as much as I'll break my own though.

Emotion wells inside me, rising to the surface like a tidal wave.

"Th-Theo?" Millie's voice startles us both, cutting through the moment like ice.

He releases me and turns to his sister. "Hey, Mills."

"Theo," she whimpers, sobbing in her hand. He rushes to her side and gets up on the bed, pulling her into his arms.

"I'll leave you two—"

"No, stay." His expression softens as he pats the space beside him. When I hesitate, he mouths, "Please."

"Okay." I go to him, unable to resist.

I must be a glutton for punishment, but I can't resist him. Especially knowing that this will all be over soon, and I'll be nothing more than his biggest regret.

A choked sob claws its way up my throat but I swallow it down, burying my face into his side and the three of us lie there.

Millie's breathing evens out again signifying she's asleep, but I know Theo is wide awake, his fingers brushing circles down my spine.

"So long as I've got the two of you, I have all I need," he says quietly.

"Theo, I—" I trap the words. Too cowardly to confess.

"Get some sleep, sunshine," he adds. "We can talk in the morning."

He's right, we can.

Only, I'm not sure what the hell I'm going to say.

17

THEO

I lie still with Raine's head on my chest and her leg entwined with mine. Her warm breath rushes over my skin every few seconds while Millie snores lightly on my other side.

I meant what I said, as long as I have both of them, I know everything will be okay.

Tonight, well, last night now, went off without a hitch. It was everything I could have hoped for. Watching our father get frog-marched out by police was the vindication I needed.

The pure disbelief on his face was just more proof of his guilt. His guilt and his total disregard for my tenacity.

He had no idea that I was on to him. That over the past few years, I've been digging deeper and deeper into his corrupt dealings. I scrutinised everything he said, every move he made. And then once I was confident in my suspicions and I enlisted Christian to the cause, he dug even deeper.

I thought that once he was arrested, I'd relax. The hard part has been done. But as I lie here now with both mine and Millie's futures resting on my shoulders, I realise it was only the beginning.

Barely eighteen years old and responsible for a minor. It's a relief that Christian and Fiona are so good at their jobs because I'm not sure many other people would be able to convince the authorities that I'm the best person to take care of my kid sister.

They managed it, though, and despite being fucking terrified, I know it's the right thing.

It's going to be hard. Exams, uni, parenthood in a sense, but I'm confident that we'll smash it. Anything has to be better than what we've lived through thus far.

It really can't get any worse.

I startle when Raine's hand twitches against my stomach, and I glance down just as she lifts her head, her sleepy violet eyes finding mine. "Have you slept at all?" she whispers.

"A little," I lie.

With a soft sigh, she stretches up, letting her lips brush against mine in the sweetest kiss.

A moan rumbles deep in my throat. I needed her so badly by the time I got back last night. I was desperate to lose myself in her and forget everything for a few hours. But I couldn't, not with Millie sleeping in my bed.

She has to be my priority now, even more than she always has been. I'm solely responsible for her. Not that she knows that yet, of course.

"Everything is going to be okay, you know?" Raine whispers.

"Yeah, I do. I wouldn't have done all this otherwi—"

My words are cut off when Millie lets out a loud snore making both of us chuckle.

"She's cute," Raine says, making me smile.

Reaching down, I grab her arse and squeeze until she yelps quietly. "You're not," I growl.

"Theo," she gasps, although it's more breathy and needy than I'm sure she means for it to be.

"What, sunshine? I'm being good."

"And it had better stay that way," a rough, sleepy voice comes from the other side of the bed.

"Morning, Mills," I sing, my heart aching with the prospect of all the things we need to discuss today.

"I swear to God, if the bed starts rocking, I'm leaving town and never coming back," she warns.

"I'd chase you down and drag you home before you left town," I chuckle.

"Don't I know it," she mutters.

Keeping her safe is my biggest concern going forward, right now, I'm not sure I'll let her out of my sight, let alone Saints Cross.

"I'm going to the bathroom, you have ten minutes to do whatever you need to do in here." Without looking back for fear of seeing something she shouldn't, Millie clambers out of bed and stumbles sleepily toward the bathroom.

"Stop worrying about her, she's going to be fine," Raine muses as I stare at the closed bathroom door.

"I hope so. What if I fuck all this up?" I ask, hating the vulnerability in my voice.

"You won't," she promises me, her stare burning into the side of my face.

Ripping my gaze from the door, I look down at her. "Fuck, Raine. You're everything," I blurt before claiming her lips in a filthy kiss, making the most of these few minutes of alone time Millie has allowed us before the serious shit starts.

I don't hear the bathroom door open but I sure as shit hear my sister clearing her throat.

"Should I go or..."

"No," I blurt, missing the softness of Raine's lips instantly. "We're good." Pushing myself up against the headboard, I keep the covers over my bottom half as my boner sinks.

An awkward silence falls over the three of us.

I hate it.

"I'm just going to..." Raine trails off as she hops out of the bed and makes a beeline for the bathroom. She squeezes Millie's hand in support as she goes but she doesn't say anything.

"Do you want a coffee?" I ask. "Hungry? I should feed you. I should—"

"Theo," Millie says softly, halting my verbal diarrhoea. "Stop. I'm okay."

"Right now, you are. But what about tomorrow? What about next week, next month, next year? All of that, it's—"

"Theo," she says, again crawling onto the bed beside me and slipping her hand into mine. The warmth of her touch calms me, and when I look into her eyes, my panic ebbs away. "Did he really do that?" she asks quietly. "Did he really kill M—" She swallows, cutting herself off.

Millie barely remembers Mum, but that doesn't mean this revelation doesn't hurt her as much as it has me.

"Yeah, Mills. He did," I say, pain slicing through my chest as tears fill her eyes.

She nods, accepting my words as the truth. "I don't want the details. Not yet," she says thoughtfully. "I want to process this before I have anything else to think about."

I squeeze her hand, accepting her request.

"What happens now?" she asks quietly as the sound of the shower turning on in my bathroom fills the air.

I get what Raine is doing, she's giving us some time to find our feet with our new reality. I understand why she might feel she needs to leave us, but honestly, I want her to be a part of this.

She is a part of this.

"I waited until yesterday so I could officially be your guardian," I confess.

Her eyes drop from mine in favour of the bed. "No," she whispers. "You can't do that."

If I weren't so close, I wouldn't hear her words.

"Yes, Millie." Reaching out, I tuck my fingers under her

chin and force her to meet my eyes again. "I've done all of this for us. For you. To enable us to have the future we want. One without fear, without worrying about him making demands of us or his actions when we disobey him. It's just us now. Us and whatever we want."

"But you're eighteen, Theo. You're about to do your exams, go to uni. You don't need to be dealing with me."

"I won't be *dealing with you*, Millie. You don't need dealing with. You are a bright, headstrong young woman. You've lived without a real parent almost all your life. He might have been in the background, pulling our puppet strings, but it's been me and you all this time."

She stares at me, absorbing my words. "What about Maria?"

"I've already put everything in place to ensure she's going to be okay. She can stay in our lives if she wishes, but I'm not tying her to us. She's been under Dad's control for long enough, don't you think?"

"I guess." She swallows, absorbing everything I'm saying. "Did she know about any of this?"

I shake my head. "Only Christian Beckworth and Fiona Brown knew. I couldn't risk getting anyone else involved. If it went wrong, then…" I trail off. The words don't need saying.

Her sad, tired eyes hold mine, making guilt tug at my insides.

"I'm sorry I didn't tell you or give you any kind of warning. I wanted to, I really did but—"

"I get it, Theo. Last night was a shock, I'm not going to lie. But I understand why you did it the way you did. He needed the entire town to witness that. His shame is probably worse than anything else right now. And it might be wrong, but that makes me weirdly happy. I just wish they could see everything else he did to us."

"Me too, Mills. Me too," I say as I wrap my arms around her shoulders and pull her in for a hug. "We've got this. We're going to be so much stronger from here on out, I promise you that."

She sniffles into the crook of my neck, but I quickly discover that she's not the only one getting emotional because when I look up, I find Raine standing in the doorway to my bathroom with a towel wrapped around her and tears clinging to her lashes.

"Come here, sunshine," I command, holding one arm out to bring her into the embrace.

She hesitates but after a couple of seconds, she moves closer. Her clean scent fills my nose and I instantly feel more settled knowing that she's close.

Her arms wrap around both of us, and we fall into a comfortable silence. It's exactly what I need to confirm that I've done the right thing.

Our embrace is only broken when someone's stomach growls loudly.

I chuckle. "I guess I should feed my girls, huh?"

"I've got it," Raine says, standing from the bed and walking over to my dresser to find one of my t-shirts.

Seeing her here in my space is so right. I've never wanted a girl up here before, but suddenly, I don't want her to be anywhere else.

"You've got that look in your eyes again," Millie warns.

"What look?" I stupidly ask, my eyes locked on Raine while Millie averts her gaze when the towel drops.

She leans closer so only I can hear her response. "You're in love, Theo."

I cough, choking on my own saliva. But I don't argue.

How can I?

Instead, I watch Raine as she pulls my t-shirt over her head, hiding her curves from me.

"It suits you," Millie muses, sounding happier than she probably should given the situation. "And I think she'll make an epic sister."

All the air rushes from my lungs as images I really shouldn't be seeing appear all too vividly in my head.

"Come on, Mills. Let's go and see what we can find to eat.

"Okay," she hops up and rushes over to Raine as if her world hasn't just been flipped upside down around her. "Can we make pancakes?"

"You think Elliot keeps flour and eggs in his kitchen?" Raine asks in amusement.

"He'd better or we can make him go out to get them for us. Chocolate chips too."

"Jesus," I mutter, more than aware that given a chance, Millie will wrap my boys around her little finger even more than she already has.

"No wonder Theo has kept you away from this place," Raine laughs, pulling the door open and gesturing for Millie to go first. "I bet you'll have Elliot making those pancakes for you within the hour."

She giggles as she goes, and I can't help but smile at the sound of her joy.

"Raine," I call my girl before she disappears from my sight.

She pauses and looks over her shoulder, her eyes locking on mine.

"Thank you," I say, my sincerity clear in my tone.

Slowly, her smile grows. It's not as fast as I'd like but I'm aware that she still has a lot of questions about all of this.

"Take your time," she says after a few seconds. "I'll make sure Millie doesn't cause too much trouble."

"Sure you will," I call with a laugh as she finally slips down the hall. I think we both know that if there's trouble to be had, Raine will be the first one to find it.

18

RAINE

"Who knew he could cook." My gaze flicks to Elliot who glowers at me as I lower my knife and fork.

"Oh, Eaton is full of surprises, isn't that right?" Reese grins, and Elliot shakes his head. "Good, Mills?"

"So freaking good." She rubs her stomach. "But I think I ate too much."

"You want anything else?" Theo asks her.

He's sat between us, his arm around the back of my chair, fingers toying with my hair. There's an energy between us, lingering from last night. But I'm not sure we'll get any time alone now that Millie is here.

And maybe it's better that way.

"What will happen?" Millie asks, and everyone goes quiet. "To the house? Where will I stay? Will we have to live together?"

Theo runs a hand down his face, and I slip my hand under the table to squeeze his knee.

"You don't have to go back to the house," he says. "Not if you don't want to."

"I can stay here?"

"For a few nights. Until things calm down. Then you'll have your room in the dorms, and we'll figure out what to do with the house."

"Can we get our own place?" Her face lights up at the idea.

"I... we'll figure it out. This is all new to me too, Mills."

"I know."

He ruffles her hair. "Why don't you finish up here and go get a shower. Then we'll do whatever you to."

"Can I go to the party tonight?"

"No," Theo says at the same time as Elliot says, "We'll see."

"The fuck?" Theo barks at him.

"She's here now. You can't lock her up in your room."

"Watch me. She's twelve, asshole."

"I won't cause any trouble."

"No." Theo pins her with a dark look. "No parties."

"Fine." Millie stands, the chair legs scraping across the tile. "I'm going for a shower."

"You need me to show you where everything is?"

"No, I got it."

"I'm heading upstairs," Tally says. "I'll show you where the fresh towels are."

Millie nods, following Tally toward the stairs.

"Fuck," Theo breathes, rubbing his hand down the back of his neck.

"She's okay," I whisper. "She's going to be okay."

"Raine is right, man." Oakley pipes up. "Little sis is going to be fine with you in her corner. I still can't believe your old man— Ow, what the fuck was that for?" He rubs his arm and Reese chuckles.

"This is an Anthony Ashworth free zone, remember?" Reese offers Theo a small nod. "But if you ever want to talk about it, we're here."

"It's done. He got what he deserved, and Millie and I can

move on with our lives now. I've got all I need right here." Theo squeezes the back of my neck and guilt bubbles inside of me.

"I still can't believe Dad was in on—"

"Oak!" Liv snaps. "Can you shut up for a second?"

"What? I'm just saying—"

"Okay, Beckworth, let's go." Reese nudges his chair.

"Go, go where?"

"Let's hit the gym. You still haven't managed to beat me on the free weights."

"Because you're a fucking savage," Oakley mumbles, dragging himself up.

"Maybe you need a little motivation. Liv let me fuck her—"

"Reese, oh my God." She gives him an indignant glare.

His laughter fills the room but I'm not focusing on their little spat. I'm too focused on the quiet boy beside me.

"You okay?" I ask Theo. His eyes darken as he stares at me.

"That's my cue," Elliot says, and I'm vaguely aware of him leaving the table too.

Their voices get quieter as they leave the room, leaving us alone.

"Come here." Theo pushes his chair back slightly and tugs on my hand. I stand and go to him, letting him pull me down on his lap so that I'm straddling his thighs.

He studies me for a second, staring at me like he can't believe this is real.

Can't believe that I'm real.

It's such a heady feeling, one I want to treasure. To feel every time he looks at me.

"Are you okay, really?"

"I am now." He collars my throat gently, stroking his thumb over my thundering pulse.

"Theo..."

"What?"

"We can't, not here. Not with Millie upstairs."

"I know," he sighs, pulling me closer. "I just want to feel you for a second. Have you close. Maybe get a kiss." He flashes me a crooked smile, one that has my insides curling.

"You are such a bad influence," I whisper.

"Yeah, but you love it, sunshine."

"Yeah, I do."

Too much.

Theo closes the distance between us, hovering his mouth right over mine. The air crackles between us, charged with electricity.

"I want you so fucking badly," he murmurs. "I want to take you down to the basement and tie you up and show you just how fucking grateful I am that you're here."

"Theo..." My breath catches as he bands his arm around my lower back and forces me to grind onto his thick length.

"You were made for me, sunshine. And I'm fucking gone for you." He stares into my eyes, trying to get past all my defences.

This broken beautiful boy disarms me in the best kind of way.

And I wish things were different.

I wish I wasn't the girl dragged up in care, forced to do things no girl ever should be.

I wish I was the girl who got to have her happily ever after.

But that's not my story.

So I'll take these pieces—these scraps—until Vaughn swoops in and destroys everything.

Because he will.

This is all a game to him.

Foreplay.

A violent shiver goes through me and Theo frowns. "What's wrong?"

"Nothing." I smile, hoping he can't see the shadows in my eyes. "You said something about a kiss?"

The distraction works and he attacks my mouth with slow, drugging kisses. Our tongues tangle as I press closer, the friction between our bodies so fucking good that I'm sure I could get off like this if he just—

"No fucking at the breakfast table," Oakley's voice cuts through the air and Theo murmurs something under his breath, burying his face in my neck.

I glance over my shoulder at Oakley and he grins. "Sorry, lovers. Just grabbing some water and then you can continue."

"Tosser," Theo spits, earning him a deep chuckle from his friend.

Oakley saunters out of the room, leaving us alone once more.

"Now, where were we?" Theo flashes me a wicked grin but I gently press my hand against his chest.

"Ease up, stud. Millie is upstairs and she's been through enough without walking in on doing something we don't want her to see."

He pouts, and I can't suppress the laughter bubbling in my chest.

"Fuck, I love that sound." He brushes his mouth over mine, stealing a chaste kiss. "And for as much as I want to lay you out on the table and eat your pussy until you're screaming my name, you're right. She's been through enough."

He gets a faraway look, but I gently scrape my nails over his jaw, coaxing him back to me. "Millie's your sister, she'll be fine."

He gives me an imperceptible nod. "I hope so."

"She knows that you'd do anything to protect her, that means something Theo. Why don't you go work off some steam with the boys and I'll go check on her."

"Fine. But later, I'm cashing in on this." He grabs my arse and thrusts upwards a little, making us both moan.

"Tease." I chuckle.

"Damn right." He slaps my arse as I clamber off his lap.

God, I'm going to miss this. For the first time in my life, I feel like I belong.

He did that—Theo gave me that.

But it's all going to come crashing down when he finds out the truth.

I don't think I've ever hated myself more than I do in this moment.

Swallowing down the wave of emotion rising inside of me, I inhale a small breath and give him my best smile. "See you in a bit?"

"You know it." He smiles back and I see it, right there in his eyes.

Theo loves me.

He's in love with me.

And I'm going to break his heart.

Me and Millie spend the morning hanging out in Theo's room while the boys do whatever boys with more money than sense do.

When he finally appears, he's sweaty and flushed but has a twinkle in his eye that wasn't there earlier.

"What are my girls up to?" he asks.

"Playing Monopoly," Millie says, moving her little Scottie dog piece around the board. "It's kind of our thing."

"And can I get in on this thing?" He comes over to get a closer look.

"You hate board games."

"True. But it looks kind of fun."

"You'll cheat and ruin the game," she snickers. "Besides, you're all gross and sweaty. Go take a shower."

"Is this how's it going to be now? You bossing me around?"

"Yup." She pops the P, grinning at me as if we're sharing a secret joke.

Truth is, Millie is handling everything well.

Almost a little too well.

Theo laughs, his gaze finding mine. He crooks a smile at me, and I smile back, trying to ignore the flutter in my chest.

Vaughn has been quiet since last night. But I know he'll pop up when I least expect it now that he's revealed his target to me.

I wish I could tell Theo. Take my chances and come clean. But I could never do that to him and Millie. I don't want Vaughn Ronson anywhere near them.

I'll do this one last job for him and then disappear.

For good.

"Oh, and Mills?"

"Yeah?"

"I talked to the boys, and we all agreed you can come to the party for the first hour. But you stay with Raine or one of the girls the whole time. And no make-up."

"Seriously? I can come."

"Yeah. You're my sister. You should be there for a little bit."

"Thank you. Thank you, thank you, thank you." She beams.

He gives her a little nod before disappearing into the bathroom.

"Oh my God," she shrieks. "I can't believe he agreed."

"Okay there, party girl. Calm down."

"Crap, sorry. It's just he's never treated me like this before. I've always been his annoying little sister."

"Theo loves you very much Millie. He just wants you to be safe and happy."

"I know. But it's an Heir party." Her eyes dance with wonder.

"I thought you didn't buy into the whole Heir tradition?"

"Oh, I don't. But still, I'm intrigued."

"Of course you are." I roll my eyes. "Just make sure you

don't do anything stupid. You wouldn't want Theo losing his shit."

"He could try." She sits a little straighter, grinning.

"Seriously, Millie. You have to behave."

"I will."

Something tells me Theo is going to have his hands full with his sister.

And it guts me that I won't be around long enough to watch him try and manage being her guardian.

19

THEO

"I thought I said no make-up," I bark when I walk into my bedroom to find it's been invaded by girls and more make-up and hair products than I think I've ever seen in my life.

"Relax, Teddy," Raine says with a smirk. "We're not going crazy. Just accentuating what she's already got."

"Millie is beautiful. Nothing needs accentuating," I mutter, staring at my sister and seeing her in a whole new light.

Her hair has been curled and is hanging around her shoulders in loose waves. She's got smoky eye make-up which makes her already large almond-shaped eyes seem massive and all-seeing. And her lips.

Oh, hell fucking no.

"The lipstick has to go," I demand. "I refuse to allow her to go downstairs with it on where any horny teenager can look at her lips and imagine—" I swallow down the bile that rushes up my throat. "No. Just fucking no."

Millie stares at me with tears glistening in her eyes.

"Mills, come on. Don't give me that look," I beg.

"Maybe we just go for this pink instead of the red?" Abi

suggests, trying to diffuse the situation. "It'll look cute as hell with the beading of your dress."

Millie looks down at herself before reaching for a face wipe and scrubbing at her lips.

"Drink this," Raine says, pushing from the bed and thrusting a small bottle of vodka at me.

"Do not tell me that you've let her—"

"Teddy," she sighs, sounding utterly exasperated by me. But the way her palms slide up my chest before her hands lock behind my head suggest otherwise. She looks up at me through her lashes and my dick jerks excitedly in my boxers. "I'm not always a bad influence. Tally, Liv, Abs and I just had a shot with our Coke." She leans in, letting her lips brush my ear as she whispers. "I'm not getting your kid sister drunk. Trust me, yeah?"

The length of her body presses against mine and I'm powerless but to grab her arse and pull her even closer, grinding my growing hardness into her stomach.

"Miss you, sunshine. Do you have any idea how hard it's been to—"

My words are cut off as she slips her hand between us, squeezing me tight. "I have a pretty good idea, yeah," she confesses, her lips against my throat before she sucks on the skin beneath my ear.

"I think that might be our cue to head downstairs to help the boys set up," Tally announces as the four of them get to their feet.

"Just keep an eye on—"

"Dude, Millie is in more than capable hands. Trust us. Trust her," Liv says. "We were all twelve once. We know what she's up against."

Raine's palms press against my chest, and she shoves me backward toward my bathroom as the girls usher my sister to the door.

"Millie?" I say before she disappears.

"What, Theo?" she snaps, clearly pissed off over the lipstick debacle.

"I do trust you. It's the boys I don't."

"I can handle stupid boys, Theo. Plus, I've got some pretty fierce wing-women to help."

There's a round of agreement as they all leave, letting the door fall closed behind them.

"Alone at last," Raine muses as she continues forcing me backward. Not that it's taking all that much effort on her part.

Unlike all the others, she's not ready for the party. Instead of a sexy dress, she's still wearing a pair of leggings and one of my hoodies. Her face is clear of make-up and her hair is piled on top of her head in a messy bun.

I can only hope that means what I think it means.

"You're dirty, Theodore Ashworth," she mutters, her hands slipping under my shirt before pushing it up my body.

"Filthy," I agree. "Just like you."

"Mm-hmm," she agrees, reaching up to drag my shirt from my head. I duck down to help her out, and the second the fabric passes my lips, I steal hers in a filthy kiss.

My shirt hits the floor, and she immediately starts working on my jeans. In seconds, she has the fly open and she's shoving both them and my boxers down my thighs. My hard cock springs free, the tip already coated with precum.

I needed this last night, but with Millie needing me, I knew I didn't stand a chance in hell of getting any action.

"Raine," I moan, ripping my hoodie from her body and finding her deliciously bare beneath.

My hands cup her heavy breasts as I demand, "Get rid of your leggings. I want you naked." She does as she's told and the second she's bare, I grip her thighs and wrap them around my waist, walking her backward into the shower stall.

She screams bloody murder when I turn it on, letting ice-cold water rain down over both of us. But I quickly cut it off by slamming my lips down on hers and plunging my tongue into her mouth, searching her eager one out.

She groans into our kiss, her hips rolling.

"Needy little whore," I moan into our kiss.

"Please," she whimpers.

"Fuck. You don't need to ask me twice, sunshine."

Pressing her back against the wall, I shift out our position a little and take myself in hand, rubbing the head of my cock through her wetness. "You're soaked," I groan, pushing the tip in enough to have her crying out.

"Theo," she begs, clawing at my back to force me into action.

"Fucking love your pussy, Raine," I tell her honestly. It barely scratches the surface of how I really feel about her, but it's all I'm willing to admit right now.

"Please," she pleads before sinking her teeth into my bottom lip hard enough to draw blood.

"Fuck. Yeah. Anything you want."

My hips jerk forward, thrusting my cock deep inside her in one swift move.

"YES," she screams, her nails digging deeper into my back.

"This isn't going to be slow and gentle, sunshine," I warn, barely able to hold back enough to say the words.

"Do your worst, Teddy," she groans.

So I do.

"You look so fucking hot in this dress," I moan in Raine's ear as my hands slide up her thighs. "Last night you were stunning. But tonight. Fuck. I need to get inside you," I confess. "Let me take you downstairs. I'll peel this dress from your body, unwrap your underwear like a gift and then I'll tie you up and give you everything you've ever fantasised about."

"As tempting as that is," she says, placing her hands over mine, stopping me from exposing her to almost the entire school who've turned up to celebrate my birthday. "I don't think Millie would appreciate it."

"Fuck. Is she still down here?" I gasp. I've been so focused on Raine and chasing the high the vodka and weed are providing I forgot all about the fact my little sister is somewhere in the chaos.

Guilt hits me square in the chest.

It's day fucking one and I'm screwing this up already.

"She's with Abi. She's fine."

I scan the crowd, desperately searching for her among the masses.

Eventually, I find her, huddled over laughing at something Abi said.

"She looks exhausted," Raine points out.

"She's going to fight me when I tell her to leave."

"Maybe. But you had an agreement and she's a good kid. She'll stand by it, I bet." Stepping back from me, she takes my hand and leads me over to put an end to my little sister's first Heirs party.

The second we approach, her eyes shutter and her smile falters.

She knows what's coming.

"It's time, Mills," I say. My voice sounds perfect to me, but the buzzing in my veins and the look I get from Abi tells me that I'm probably not coming across all that sober right now.

So what? It's my fucking birthday, and I just pulled off the impossible.

"Y-yeah, okay," Millie agrees just like Raine said she would.

"I'll come up with you for a bit. I could use some quiet time," Abi offers.

"Sure. But I draw the line at a bedtime story," my sister grins. "Theo might think I'm a child but—"

"I don't, Millie," I say, interrupting her and pulling her small frame into my arms. "I fucking love you, Sis."

She fights against me. "Yeah, Bro. I love you too. Enjoy the rest of your night. Try and..." She trails off, shaking her head. "Try and behave."

"Don't worry," Raine assures her. "I won't let him get into much trouble."

After allowing me another hug, I watch the two of them ascend the stairs.

When I spin away, ready to focus on my girl again, it's impossible to miss that someone else is watching Mills and Abi leave. "Love sick fool," I mutter, jerking my chin in Elliot's direction.

"Aw, I think it's cute," Raine says. "They'll figure it out eventually."

"Don't want to talk about them right now, sunshine. I want to go back to that idea I had about the basement."

"I think I need another drink for that."

Movement over her shoulder catches my eye, and when I look up, I find the guy who can help with more than just a drink for me and my girl.

"How about something even better?"

His eyes meet mine and I nod in greeting.

It takes him a few seconds to cut through the crowd, long enough for me to lose myself in my girl again. I can't help it, she looks so fucking delicious in this tight black dress.

I squeeze her arse hard enough to make her squeak. "Fuck, you're everything, Raine. Everything I didn't know I wanted but everything I can't live without."

"You're drunk and high. You have no idea what you're saying," she half whispers, half giggles as I nibble down her throat.

"Doesn't mean it isn't true though." A shadow falls over us and I lift my head. "Ah, here he is. Come on, man. I want you to meet my girl. Raine, this is the man who provides me with a whole different kind of high than you can give me. Vaughn, this is Raine, my incredibly beautiful girlfriend."

Girlfriend...

Did I really just use those words seriously?

Fuck me, what the hell has happened to my life.

I'm so lost in my own head that I totally miss the two of them introducing themselves to each other.

"So what do you fancy then, sunshine? My boy here can get you anything you need." Wrapping my arm around her waist, I tug her suddenly tense body into the curve of mine. "What's wrong?" I whisper, dropping my lips to her ear.

"N-nothing. Can you excuse me, I just need to go to the bathroom?"

She ducks from under my arm before I can do or say anything and I'm forced to watch her go, already hating the distance between us.

"So that's your girl?" Vaughn asks. "She's hot. Wouldn't have pegged her for an All Hallows' girl though."

"Nah, that's half the beauty. She isn't anything like these stuck-up bitches." I snort.

I can't keep the smile off my face as I watch her go. Just before she gets to the corner, she looks back, our eyes connecting for the briefest of moments before she disappears.

"So what have you got for the birthday boy then? You better have brought your best shit with you tonight. I'm in need of the best fucking high you can provide."

"Don't worry, man. I came prepared. You're going to have a night you'll never forget, I can assure you of that."

"Fuck, yeah. I knew I fucking liked you." I gesture toward a door that'll lead us outside to talk business. "Shall we?"

20

RAINE

I rush into the bathroom and lock the door, pacing back and forth as I try to calm my racing heart.

Vaughn is here.

At the party.

And Theo knows him.

He doesn't just know him—he gets his gear from him.

How is this happening?

Pausing at the sink, I curl my fingers over the edge of the basin, inhaling ragged breaths as the room closes in around me.

Vaughn is here.

He's here.

He's—

"Yo, hurry the fuck up," someone bellows, hammering on the door. "I need to piss."

Shit.

Shit.

The banging continues, only making my heart rate ratchet even more.

Desperately trying to compose myself, I inhale another deep breath before yanking the door open and coming face to face with a boy I vaguely recognise.

His glazed eyes study me and then widen a fraction. "Oh shit, aren't you—"

I barge past him and make my way down the hall. I don't know where I'm going or what I'm doing but all I know is, I can't go back in there.

I should have suspected Vaughn would do something like this. It isn't his style to stay in the shadows. But I hoped...

Foolish girl.

I shake my head, frustration rippling through me.

I want to run. To walk out of the Chapel and never look back. But I can't do it, even now, even when Vaughn has shown his hand, I can't abandon Theo and Millie.

God, Millie.

My heart aches for the girl upstairs.

Tears brim in my eyes as I hurry toward the front door. I need fresh air, I need to catch my breath and figure out what the hell I'm going to do.

But a voice calls after me.

"Raine, where are—"

I pretend I don't hear her and spill out of the door, sucking in a greedy lungful of air.

But of course, Olivia follows me.

"Will you just stop?" She grabs my arm and I whirl to face her.

"What's wrong?"

"I— Nothing." I force a smile onto my lips. "I just needed some air."

Her eyes narrow, looking too closely. "Where's Theo?"

"Busy getting high I imagine."

Her mouth twists. "I wish they wouldn't do that shit."

"He's celebrating."

"And hurting." She points out and I don't deny it. "What's really going on, Raine? You look like you're either about to bolt or puke all over yourself."

"I... It's just a lot, you know."

"You're in love with him."

I nod, a tear slipping free. Because I wish that things were different.

For the first time in my life, I wish I was the kind of girl good enough for someone like Theo Ashworth.

Someone like Olivia or Tally or even Abi.

But I'm not that girl, and it was foolish to think I could outrun my past.

"Isn't that a good thing? He obviously feels the same."

"I—"

"There you are." Reese staggers over to us, a wicked glint in his eyes. "I've been looking everywhere for you, sweet cheeks." He hooks an arm around Liv's shoulder, nuzzling her neck.

"I was just checking on Raine," she says.

"Everything good?" His glassy gaze slides to me, one of his brows lifting with concern.

"I'm fine." I manage a small smile.

"Where's Theo at?"

"Inside somewhere."

"And you're out here because..."

"Reese, leave it," Liv grips his jaw and coaxes his attention back to her.

"I'm going to head back inside," I say but they barely hear me, too lost in each other.

I don't want to go back in, but what choice do I have?

If I don't, Theo will only come looking for me.

Even worse, Vaughn might too.

So I hold my head high, take a deep breath, walk into the Chapel telling myself that I can do this.

"There she is, my only sunshine." Theo grins as I approach

him and our friends. Vaughn is nowhere to be seen but I don't doubt for a second that he's close by.

Watching.

Waiting.

The hair on the back of my neck prickles with awareness but as I discreetly scan the room, I don't see him.

"What's wrong?" Theo asks, his pupils blown. "You seem tense."

"I'm fine. What did you take?"

"Just a little X. Feel like I'm fucking flying." He leans in, ghosting his lips over mine. "You want some, baby?"

"No. One of us needs to stay clear-headed. Millie is upstairs."

Guilt sparks in his eyes. "Shit, I—"

"Relax," Elliot says in his usual commanding tone, and I'm hardly surprised he seems sober. He's careful about when he lets his guard down. "We've got her."

Theo nods, his hands roaming over my body. "Fuck, I'm horny," he whispers, pressing sloppy kisses along my jaw.

"Theo, not here." I press a hand against his chest. "Later."

"Now." He groans. "Let me take you down to the basement and—"

"Later," I say more firmly.

"Jesus, sunshine. You're killing my mood." He pouts. "You need to lighten up. It's a party, we're celebrating."

"I think I'm going to go and check on Millie," I say, trying to extract myself from his hold.

"Seriously? You'd rather hang out with my sister than me? What the fuck is your problem?"

"Theo," Elliot warns.

"You're drunk and high and I'm going to walk away before we both do or say something we'll regret."

"I might be drunk and high but at least I'm not being a fucking miserable bitch."

Everything inside me goes still, pain radiating through my chest.

"Enjoy your party." I blink back the tears as I walk away from him.

"Trouble in paradise?" Keeley smirks as I pass her and her friends.

But I ignore her, too on edge to get pulled into some mean girl drama.

Part of me is surprised she had the balls to show but then, she's probably waiting in the wings for when things between me and Theo go wrong.

My stomach dips as it hits me that will be sooner rather than later.

I make a beeline for the staircase, but another trickle of awareness goes through me and this time when I scan the room, I spot him.

Vaughn.

Anger flares inside me and before I know what I'm doing I storm over to him.

"What the hell are you doing here?" I spit.

"Nice to see you too, baby."

Checking the coast is clear, I grab his arm and yank him out of the room and into the bathroom. "You can't be here," I seethe.

"But I'm having so much fun. These rich kids have more money than sense." He lets out a dark chuckle.

"What do you want, Vaughn?" I sigh.

"I thought that was obvious. I need your help. One last job."

"It's not that simple."

"Seems perfectly simple to me. You do this final job for me and then we're even."

"Even?"

"Even?" A bitter laugh rumbles through me. "You sold me out, remember?"

"It wasn't even like that." He tsks. "You knew the risks. You knew—"

"I LOVED YOU," I shriek, shaking with rage. "I loved you and you left me there to take the fall."

"Raine, baby." He reaches for a strand of my hair, but I swat his hand away.

"Don't. Touch. Me."

"You know, it's funny. That you think you have any choice in this," he sneers. "What, you think just because you're fucking some rich prick from Saints Cross that you're suddenly better than me? I know where you came from, Raine. I know who you are. And if your boy out there knew half the things you've done for me, he'd throw you out of here quicker than you could blink.

"You're not one of them, baby. You're like me." He grabs a fistful of my hair, yanking my face to his.

Pain explodes along my scalp, but I bite back the scream building in my throat as fear saturates every cell in my body.

"You talk about me letting you take the fall but the first opportunity you had to screw me over, you took it. You caused a lot of problems for me, baby.

"Does he know? Does lover boy know you let old men fuck you for money? That you let them do dirty depraved things to your bod—"

"Stop," I plead. "Just. Stop."

Vaughn releases me with a hard shove, and I stumble backward, clutching a hand to my throat. "Why are you doing this?"

"Because I can. Because you need to remember who you belong to. And because I want to see you hurt, the way you hurt me." He grabs my face and squeezes my cheeks.

"Here's what's going to happen. You're going to end it with Ashworth. Then tomorrow night you're going to check in at The Grand Hotel. I'll text you the details. Wear something sexy. I've heard Mr. Stanley Harris likes his girls docile. Make sure to give him what he wants."

Tears drip down my cheeks as the final walls of my resolve crumble.

"Oh, and Raine. Make sure you break his heart. The last thing we need is Ashworth to come looking for you. It's time to come home, baby. Back where you belong."

I stare at him, tears dripping down my face.

I would rather die than ever be his puppet again. But I have no choice.

One last time, then I can make a break for it.

I should have run the second I knew he'd found me, but I stayed, telling myself I didn't have a choice.

But I realise now, I stayed for Theo. For Millie. To steal every second of time with them before this moment.

"What's it going to be, Raine?"

I nod. Just once.

Just enough to let him know I'm on side.

He steps forward and cups my face in his big traitorous hand. "Tomorrow then. Don't screw me over again, baby. You won't like the consequences if you do. Ashworth's sister sure is a pretty little thing."

"Stay away from Millie," I snap.

His mouth curves into a wicked smile. "You know what to do."

He slips out of the bathroom, and I sag against the wall, trying desperately to compose myself.

This is it. The moment I've been dreading.

Drying my eyes, I walk out of there on shaky legs.

"Raine?" A soft voice calls out before I reach the stairs and I turn to find Abi frowning at me.

"What's going on?"

"N-nothing." I desperately try and compose myself. "Me and Theo had an argument, so I'm going to call it a night and go check on Millie."

"Are you sure—"

"I'm fine, I promise. Enjoy the rest of the party," I rush out, before heading upstairs to Theo's room.

Knocking gently, I wait.

"Raine." Millie's face lights up as the door swings open. "Oh no, what's wrong?"

"Nothing." I smile weakly. "I'm over the party."

"My brother upset you, didn't he?"

"It doesn't matter." I slip past her.

"But—"

"Want to watch a film?" I ask, my eyes flitting to the bottom drawer of Theo's dresser.

"Sure, I'll warn you though. I'll probably fall asleep."

"That's okay. I'm tired too." I make quick work of stripping out of my clothes and into one of Theo's rugby shirts.

We climb into bed and Millie turns the light off.

"How long do you think the party will go on for?" she asks.

"Too long," I murmur, wondering if Theo's even noticed I'm gone.

Not that it matters now.

"Yeah, I figured as much. I'm glad you're here though." Millie moves a little closer, tucking herself into my side.

Me too, the words get stuck over the giant lump in my throat.

Then she says the worst thing she possibly can to me.

"I'm glad my brother has you, Raine."

21

THEO

With every shot I do with the team, the more my surroundings blur.

This is what I needed after the stress of last night and the impending future where I'm responsible for a twelve-year-old. One night of mayhem before reality hits and I need to start being the adult I apparently turned into yesterday.

"Go. Go. Go. Go," the guys chant around me as the year twelves reach for their shots.

They're off their faces too.

As I watch them force down another mouthful of vodka, it occurs to me that they haven't been set any tasks recently. Flickers of ideas flash behind my eyes, but I'm unable to grab onto any of them.

"Okay, I think you might have had enough," a familiar voice says when two strong hands land on my shoulders.

Glancing over, I find a bright-eyed Elliot studying me closely. "Initiation," I slur.

"Yeah, I'm cutting you off."

"Fuck that, man. It's my birthday."

"Yeah, and I'd like for you to see another, not die of alcohol poisoning on this one."

"You're no fun," I complain as he physically steers me away from the team.

On the makeshift dance floor, I spot Reese and Liv, and Oak and Tally grinding it up.

"Where's my girl?" I ask, my eyes scanning the Chapel for her dark hair and sinful curves. "Fuck. She looked so fucking hot tonight. Wanted to take her down to the basement but she wasn't up for it."

"Probably because she knew you were too wasted to get it up for her," Elliot quips.

"Nah, fuck that, bro. One look at her in that dress and I was hard as fucking nails. Feel," I say, reaching for his hand to prove my worth.

"Hell fucking no." Disgust falls over his expression. "I love you but not that much."

"Aw, Elliot Eaton loves me," I sing, the room spinning around me. "Where is she?" I ask again, my focus on my girl. "I want her."

"Then maybe you shouldn't have pissed her off.'

"I didn't. I—" I try arguing but honestly, I don't remember what I did. But it certainly sounds like something I'd do.

"Eaton, get your arse over here," someone calls.

Finally, he releases me. "You good, yeah?" he asks, but I'm already waving him off and stumbling away in search of my girl.

She's got to be here somewhere. I just need to find her.

"Sunshine," I sing. "Where are you?"

I search every inch of the Chapel but come up empty-handed. Well, not actually empty-handed. I get more than a few drinks shoved in my direction, and every single one I throw back without thought.

I catch sight of Vaughn lingering around, selling his gear to anyone who's interested.

He nods at me. As he fucking should. He's making a mint because of me tonight. Most dealers would give their left testicle to get this opportunity.

"Here's the birthday boy," an irritatingly high-pitched voice screeches.

Keeley.

Even wasted she's fucking annoying.

Hands land on my arm, spinning me around. I want to fight it, but I'm too fucking drunk to take control.

"Happy birthday," she sings, sliding her hands up my chest.

My skin prickles, my body instinctively knowing her touch is wrong. Her scent is wrong. Everything is fucking wrong.

"What?" I bark, already bored of her.

It's just a shame she doesn't have the same opinion of me.

"You look lonely. Told you Raine didn't have what it took to take care of you."

"Have you seen her?"

"Yeah, Theo," she says, the warmth of her palm burning against the side of my face when she cups my jaw and turns my attention back to her.

She's dressed to the nines. Her outfit is beyond slutty. Her tits are practically touching her chin and if she were to bend over, everyone in the room would get to find out if she's wearing knickers—which I suspect she isn't. But none of it interests me. I want my girl with the violet eyes and the smart mouth, my girl who doesn't put up with my shit. Not this cookie-cutter Heir chaser.

"I saw her leading a guy into the bathroom not so long ago. I hate to tell you this, but they looked pretty cosy."

Her words hit me like a truck. I blink at her, watching the accomplishment flash in her eyes. "You're lying."

She bats her lashes. "I'm not. Why would I?"

"Because you miss my dick."

"Aw, babe," she says, tapping my cheek patronisingly. "It's

good. But I've had better. And so has your precious Raine Storm if she's willingly dragging guys into the bathroom at her boyfriend's birthday party."

"No, she wouldn't... You're wrong."

"Here," she says, pulling a bottle of whisky from fuck knows where. "This will help." Twisting the top off, she thrusts it at me. "Then tomorrow, you can face her and ask her yourself. Just remember to grovel when you turn up at my door heartbroken and desperate."

Without another word, she spins on her heels and saunters away, her arse swaying, forcing a few sets of eyes to follow her departure.

Not mine though.

I don't want her.

I want my girl, not a lying whore like Keeley.

If only I could find her...

I'm dying.

Actually fucking dying.

I've no idea where I am or what happened. All I know is that it hurts.

It hurts so fucking bad.

There's a vague flicker of a memory of Elliot telling me to slow down, that I'd regret it. Fucking know-it-all asshole.

Refusing to open my eyes, I suck in a deep lungful of air through my nose and then back out through my mouth in the hope it helps.

My stomach rolls and my head pounds like a fucking bass drum.

Vodka.

Whisky.

Pills.

Fuck me, I was flying. I was flying so fucking high.

But the crash.

What a motherfucker.

Images begin coming back to me. The team. Our friends. My heart thumps harder as I remember Millie being here.

She was at an Heirs party. I let her—

Raine.

Panic surges through me.

She vanished. She vanished and—

Reaching out, I search for her, but I quickly discover that it's pointless because it seems I'm on the sofa.

Finally, I force my eyes open.

Holy motherfucker.

I've no idea what time it is but the winter sun is streaming through the stained-glass windows threatening to singe my eyeballs straight from my sockets.

But I don't let it stop me. With a deep, stealing breath, I jump to my feet. The entire building spins around me and I have little choice but to reach out, using the wall to stop me from falling.

Pathetic, Ashworth. Fucking pathetic.

But my need for her knows no bounds and in only seconds, I'm standing at the bottom of Mount Everest—aka: the stairs—trying to convince myself that I'm prepared for the climb.

My legs barely follow orders and my stomach protests the entire way. But my heart. My heart knows exactly what it wants even when it pumps what I can only assume is pure alcohol around my veins.

When I get to the top, I discover that the house isn't as silent as I first thought. There are voices and a not so discreet steady banging that comes from Oak and Tally's room.

Heat stirs in the pit of my stomach.

Oh, what I wouldn't give to lie back and watch my girl bouncing on my dick right about now.

My mouth waters as I think about finding her sleeping in

my bed, diving under the duvet, spreading her legs and eating her until she wakes up screaming my name.

Fuck, yeah. Is there any better way to wake up?

With a new sense of purpose, I rush toward my room and throw the door open.

I was expecting it to be in darkness, so the fact there are lights on throws me, so does the girl sitting in my bed.

"Oh my God, Theo," Millie cries, clapping her hand over her eyes. "You're naked."

I am?

My chin drops and I stare down at myself.

Huh. Would you look at that? Got a nice little semi on too from thinking about eating Raine's—

"Theo," she cries again when I don't move fast enough. "Are you trying to ruin the rest of my life?"

"Nah, just making sure you have standards, Millie. Any guy you—"

"Shut the hell up. Shut up. Shut. Up."

"Where's Raine?" I demand, cupping my junk to protect my sister's innocent eyes.

"I don't know. I woke up alone and assumed she was with you."

"Nope. I woke up alone too," I confess before my knees give out and I fall onto my own bed face down.

I land right on the pillow she slept on. It smells like her. And like the sad fucking bastard I am, I hug it to me, breathing her in deep.

"Theo?"

"Sorry, Mills," I mumble. "I think I'm dying. Elliot will be good to you."

"He just collapsed and passed out like that," a familiar voice says sometime later. "He's not dead though. He's been snoring like a beast," Millie explains. "Well, in between calling out for Raine."

"Fucking pussy," Elliot mutters.

"Where is she?" Abi asks, concern evident in her voice.

"I don't know. I've messaged her but it hasn't been read."

I don't need to open my eyes to see the look that passes between them. I feel it crackle in the air.

I did something stupid last night.

The reason Raine isn't here is because of me.

"I saw her leading a guy into the bathroom not so long ago."

The words slam into my brain without invitation making my brow wrinkle and my fists curl.

"He's waking up," Abi points out.

"Then that's my cue to leave. I'm not being forced to look at his tiny dick again," Millie says, almost sounding disgusted.

"Did someone just say that Theo had a small dick?" another voice asks, clearly coming to join the party.

"I'm going to go back to the dorms, see if I can find her."

"She's probably sleeping off last night," Tally offers. "You want me to walk with you."

"Yes," I manage to force out, my concern for my sister's safety trumping everything else.

Footsteps move closer before Oak announces, "Oh look, the beast is alive," before his palm cracks across my bare arse, shooting pain in every direction.

"You motherfucker," I roar, launching myself off the bed and straight at him.

"Oh, naked wrestling," Tally says teasingly. "On second thought, maybe I'll stay."

"I'm not rubbing my dick up against this arsehole, Prim. If you want naked wrestling, then we can schedule it for later."

"Gross," Millie mutters before disappearing.

"Millie," I call. "I'm sorry."

Honestly, I've no idea what for, but the words seem appropriate right now.

"Will you two stop fucking about," Elliot demands standing in the doorway with his thick arms crossed over his chest.

The girls leave, escorting Millie downstairs. It's probably a good idea. Fuck knows what state downstairs is in. Looking at my semi might not be the only thing that gives my sister nightmares.

"Good to know you didn't get laid again," Oak says, getting to his feet and pinning our leader with a loaded look. "You're tense as fuck. It was a party, man. You were meant to let off steam."

Elliot clearly has nothing to say in response to that when all he does is glare. "Theo, sort your-fucking-self out. Your sister needs you, and so does your girl, wherever she is.

"I saw her leading a guy into the bathroom not so long ago. I hate to tell you this, but they looked pretty cosy."

I squeeze my eyes closed, trying to push the nagging voice from my head.

Keeley Davis always has been a fucking irritant.

"But maybe shower before you go searching. You fucking stink, man," Oak adds before the two of them disappear.

Leaving me sprawled out like a loser on my bedroom floor.

22

RAINE

I should have left sooner.

That's the only thought running through my head as I sit on the edge of the bed watching the minutes tick by painfully slow.

When I left the Chapel this morning, everyone had been sleeping. I hadn't expected to see Theo passed out on the sofa half-naked, and for a second, I'd wanted to come clean.

To tell him the truth.

But I couldn't do it—I couldn't bear the thought of how he would look at me once he knew.

So I'd tiptoed out of there and headed back to my dorm room, where I've holed up for the last few hours.

At some point earlier, Millie came to check on me, but I feigned a headache, and she left me alone.

Part of me was hardly surprised I hadn't heard from Theo yet. He is probably still sleeping off a hangover from hell.

My stomach churns with what was to come. But in some ways, I am relieved.

Relieved it's almost over.

It was foolish to think I could ever move on while Vaughn was out there, looking for me.

Saints Cross might be miles away from Brewton, but it isn't far enough.

I won't make that mistake again.

When I leave this time, I will put enough distance between us that he will never find me.

My phone vibrates and everything inside me goes still. Inhaling a deep breath, I lean over and pluck it from the bedside table.

> Trudy: Just checking in. How are things? If you need me, you know where I am.

A shudder goes through me. It would be so easy to tell her the truth. To beg her to help make me disappear. But Trudy has her hands tied, I know that. If I tell her about Vaughn, she'll have to go to the police, and that is not an option. I can't trust them.

I can't trust anybody.

> Raine: Everything's fine.

> Trudy: Glad to hear it. I hope you're staying out of trouble? I heard a little rumour you met a boy?

A pang of something goes through me. Guilt. Sadness. Hopelessness.

I wasn't supposed to fall for Theo. He's everything I should have stayed away from. But I can't find it in myself to regret even a second of our time together. Even when we were at each other's throats, trying to tear the other apart.

Theo Ashworth gave me something I'll forever cherish.

He made me feel alive.

For the first time in my life, he made me feel like things could be different.

And that's worth something.

It's worth more than I ever realised.

Tears prick the corners of my eyes as I quickly text Trudy back, hoping my reply will satisfy her curiosity.

Not that it'll matter soon.

My gaze flicks to my backpack. The one now full of my meagre belongings.

I check the time, but it's only two-thirty. I still have hours until I need to be at the hotel.

But I can't go, not yet.

Not until I sever things between me and Theo, I at least owe him that much.

A clean break.

The thought fills me with a nauseating sense of dread.

I don't want to cause him any pain.

But Vaughn is right, I need Theo to believe I'm leaving of my own free will. I need him to believe that we're over.

Done.

That it was never anything more than a bit of fun.

My fingers curl into the mattress as anguish builds inside me. I wish it didn't have to be this way.

I wish—

A knock at the door startles me and I call out, "Who is it?"

"It's me." The crack in Theo's voice sends my heart into overdrive.

I knew he would come eventually but I'm not ready.

I don't think I'll ever be ready.

But then, something strikes me as odd. Usually, Theo would let himself in. But he knocked.

On shaky legs, I get up and go to the door, opening it.

"Fuck. sunshine," he rasps.

"You look like shit," I remark, wanting nothing more than to wrap him into my arms and make it all better.

But I don't.

I can't.

"I may have gone a little too hard last night. Can I come in?"

"Since when do you ask for permission?" My brow lifts as I step aside, granting him entrance.

"Since I woke up and you were gone."

"It's taken all day for you to decide to come over here?"

"It's taken me all day to drag my arse off the bed. I don't know what the fuck Vaughn put in those pills, but it was some good fucking shit." A faint smile traces his lips but I'm not smiling.

In fact, I feel sick.

"I missed you this morning," he admits. "Why did you leave?"

"I..." My gaze drops to the floor.

"You disappeared last night too." There's an edge in his tone. "Where did you go?"

"I hung out with Millie."

"Hey, look at me." He's in front of me in a second, sliding his fingers under my chin and tipping my face up. "What's going on?"

"N-nothing. I'm just tired and I have a ton of homework to do."

"Don't fucking lie to me." His eyes darken. "I needed you last night and you... you weren't there."

"You didn't need me, Theo." I gave him a small, sad smile.

"You're pissed at me for cutting loose and having some fun, after everything..."

"I'm not pissed at you. I just didn't want to be around you when you were out of control."

"Come on, sunshine. I wasn't out of control. I was having fun. I was celebrating." His fingers slide into my belt loops, tugging me closer. "I wanted to celebrate... with you."

"Pretty sure you wouldn't have even recognised me by the end of the night."

"Not possible." He grabs the back of my neck and pulls me even closer, burying his face in my shoulder. "Fuck, I missed you."

I go deathly still, trying to keep the tears threatening to fall at bay.

"Theo, we can't..." My hands go to his chest, pushing slightly.

"Can't?" He lifts his head, his hooded eyes meeting mine. "Of course we fucking can. I need you, sunshine. I always fucking need you."

The air crackles and shifts, a heavy weight crushing my chest. He isn't going to make this easy. But then, nothing with Theo has been easy.

No, that isn't true.

In some ways, things with Theo have been too easy.

"I'm sorry," I whisper.

"Sorry? What the fuck are you— No." He staggers back like I've physically hurt him. "Keeley. She said she saw you..."

"What?"

"You were with someone at the party?"

"No, Theo, that's not—"

"Fuck. *Fuck*." He grabs the ends of his hair, tugging. "She told me you'd do this. She told me—"

Panic rises inside me like a tidal wave. I need to end it, I need to let him go. But not like this.

I didn't want it to be like this.

"Who was it?" He turns on me, pure anger burning in his eyes. "Who the fuck was it? I'll kill him. I'll fucking kill him for—"

"It doesn't matter." I manage to find my voice, locking away every ounce of hesitation I feel. Ignoring the pit in my stomach screaming at me that this is wrong.

"No." He stares at me—through me. "You wouldn't... It's me and you, sunshine. You promised. You fucking promised."

The devastation in his eyes guts me but I shove it down.

"I'm leaving, Theo. You knew that. You knew this was only temporary."

"You're..." He takes a hand down his face, letting out a

heavy sigh. When he looks at me again, what I see there makes me shudder.

This isn't my Theo.

It's the boy I met all those weeks ago.

Bitter laughter spills out of him. "Yeah, whatever," he says, moving to the door as if I didn't just break his heart.

"Theo, wait," I cry, wanting to take it back.

Wanting nothing more than for him to look at me like he used to.

"Nah, sunshine," he spits the word, something severing between us. "I should have listened to her."

"To... her?"

"Yeah, Keeley. You're not one of us, you'll never be one of us. And I was a fucking idiot for ever dipping my dick in your charity case pussy."

Pain explodes in my chest as I fight back the tears burning the backs of my eyes.

But Theo isn't done.

Of course he isn't.

"Stay away from me and stay the fuck away from Millie. You're dead to me, Raine. And if you have any fucking sense, you'll leave sooner rather than later. Because when everyone finds out what you did, that you're nothing more than some poor, desperate skank, after all, your life won't be worth living at All Hallows'."

I suck in a sharp breath, his words landing like bullets.

"Theo, I—"

But he's gone, blowing out of my room like a violent storm. The door slams behind him and I flinch, my heart stuttering in my chest.

I drop to the edge of the bed, letting the tears fall.

I couldn't stop them if I tried.

No one else visits, not that I expect them to.

By now, my name is probably mud among the Heirs and their inner circle.

I broke Theo.

I broke his heart and, in the process, I shattered my own.

But maybe it's better this way.

Better that he hates me than spends his days wondering why I left.

Why I ran.

I finish writing the note to Millie and tuck it into the envelope. It's too risky to go and see her, to say all the things I want to say.

But I can't leave without saying *something*.

Grabbing my bag, I throw it over my shoulder and glance around the room one last time.

When I first arrived at All Hallows', I thought it would become just another cage. But it wasn't that at all. Meeting Theo—meeting the girls and even the other Heirs—showed me that life can be better. It can be filled with fun and laughter... and love.

My heart squeezes but I shut it down.

I shut it all down, pushing my time here, my memories, into a little box and closing the lid.

I can't be this girl anymore.

Not for what I'm about to do.

But maybe, one day, I can find her again.

Maybe when this is all over, I can let the memories out and remember the boy who taught me how to love without limits.

23

THEO

The front door crashes back against the ancient brickwork of the Chapel as I storm inside.

Everything hurts. Worse than when I woke up with a raging hangover. Now it's not just my head and my limbs, it's carved deep into my chest. The kind of unbearable pain you hear about in songs and watch on awful sappy rom-coms where people try to make you believe that a broken heart is a real thing.

I thought it was bullshit.

No one has the power to shatter the most powerful organ in our bodies.

Turns out, I was wrong.

It's not fucking bullshit.

It's real. And even more painful than the lyrics lead you to believe.

I woke up this morning thinking I was dying.

But I was wrong.

Now. Right fucking now, I am dying. Metaphorically bleeding out all over the old flagstone floor.

"What's wrong?" Reese asks, looking back at me from over his shoulder from where he's sitting at the dining table.

My lips part and my chin drops, but no words come out.

I can't...

I can't tell them what she's done.

I let her in. Despite what everyone else in this school thought—*knew*—I let Raine into my life, into our lives. Into my little sister's inner circle and this is what she does.

I was right about her in those first few days.

She never belonged here.

"Theo?" he says, pushing the chair out and getting to his feet. "What's going on, you look like—"

"I can't," I force out, my eyes dropping to the floor so he can't see the pain and utter devastation in my eyes.

"You can't what? What's happened?" He's trying to stay calm, but the panic is starting to edge into his voice. "The girls just left to take Millie for milkshakes to cheer her up. They're okay, right?"

I nod, suddenly understanding his panic.

He's got a girl who hasn't ripped his heart into a million and one tiny shards.

A girl he loves.

A girl who loves him back just as hard.

Voices filter through the Chapel behind me. Laughter. Fucking laughter as if everything is okay. As if my world isn't falling apart.

I guess that's it, though. It's my world. No one else's. As far as they are concerned, everything is cushty.

"Shit. What happened?" Elliot asks, the first to notice me standing here looking like I no longer have a place.

"I don't know, he won't say anything," Reese says, a deep crease between his brows.

"Bro, you good?" Oak says, clamping his hand over my shoulder. "Shit," he breathes when he ducks down and meets my eyes. "What the fuck was in that shit your dealer gave you? This is some fucking come down."

"It's not a fucking come down. It's the fucking end. It's

over," I shout, suddenly unable to stay quiet. "After everything. Everything I've done. Everything we've done. It's fucking over."

"Okay, man. Let's go and sit down, yeah. Reese, coffee. And make it fucking strong."

"I don't need fucking coffee."

"Didn't say it was for you," he mutters. "And text the girls, find out what the fuck has gone down."

"This was Raine?" Oak asks, looking shocked and he looks between the three of us like the answer is just going to appear out of thin air.

"Of course it's Raine. What else would make him this unhinged?" Elliot says, gesturing to the mess of a person she's turned me into.

"I'm sitting right fucking here," I grunt.

"Yeah, we can see you. Wanna tell us what happened?"

"Not really," I scoff. "Get me alcohol. And those pills from last night. There are some left, right?"

"No," Elliot barks. "You're not getting fucking wasted to deal with this. Talk." He lowers his arse to the coffee table in front of me and just stares.

"Fucking prick," I mutter.

The scent of coffee gets stronger and only a few seconds later, Reese and Oak drop down on either side of me. If I weren't so fucking broken I might appreciate their friendship right now. But as it is, I'm just fucking numb.

Silence falls around us seeing as I refuse to talk and all they want to do is listen.

Whoever said that guys don't talk about the hard shit are fucking liars. Or at least, they don't have knobhead friends like mine to force you to do exactly what you don't want to do.

"Fuck this shit," I grunt, pushing to my feet, ready to bolt. But hands grab my forearms, stopping me from going anywhere.

Fucking dickheads.

"Sit your arse down and talk," Elliot warns. "What the fuck happened?"

"We're done," I say simply.

"Done? Why?"

"Because she—" All the air in my lungs comes rushing out as I bite back my next words.

Because she fucking cheated on me. At my own birthday party. In my fucking bathroom.

I shake my head. Mortified that she could play me so well.

Everything I've told her, the things we did, the promises we made, and all of it was bullshit.

"What did she do, Theo?" Oak asks as footsteps get closer before the girls all spill into the living room.

"She fucking cheated, okay?" I roar, finally getting to my feet successfully, and storm off.

Only, I only make it a few feet before I come face to face with my sister's utterly devastated face.

"What did you just say?" she whispers so quietly that if I weren't so close and the Chapel wasn't so silent, I wouldn't stand a chance of hearing her.

"No, don't look at me like that. Keeley said—"

"Keeley?" Millie screeches in disbelief. "You're throwing Raine away because of some bullshit that Keeley Davis has told you. You're smarter than this, Theo," she seethes before reaching out and smacking me upside the head. "Use your brain."

I suck in a deep breath through my nose, trying to talk myself down from throttling her.

You're not your father, get a fucking grip.

"Raine confirmed it. Last night she went into the bathroom with a guy and she... she— FUCK," I roar, threading my fingers into my hair and pulling until it hurts.

But I'm pretty sure I could rip it clean from my scalp and it still wouldn't hurt as much as my heart.

"No," Millie states, tears quickly filling her eyes. "No, she wouldn't do that."

"It's cute that you think so highly of her, Mills. It really is. But she did. She told me. I just went to her dorm, and she told me that we were over. That everything we had was bullshit. All the promises she made to me were fake. She's leaving, and we're done."

The sight of Millie's tears cascading down her cheeks rips me in two. She looks even more devastated by this than she was finding out the truth about our father on Friday night.

"NO," she cries, refusing to believe what I'm saying as Tally and Liv gather her into their arms.

"Accept it. She fucked us over just like I'm sure she did to the people who cared about her wherever she came from. I never should have let her into our lives. It's the biggest mistake I've ever made."

Having said everything I've got to say, I sidestep Millie and march through the living area, more than ready to find some stashed pills in my room and drink myself into oblivion.

I'm almost at the stairs when Millie's emotional voice cuts through the air. "She wouldn't have done that to you, Theo. She loves you. She fucking loves you," she sobs.

Without instruction from my brain, my legs stop. I suck in a deep breath and turn around. Millie has broken free from her embrace and rushed after me.

She stands in the middle of the room, her eyes wide as she begs me to reconsider. "She loves you, Theo. She didn't want to, she wanted to hate you, but she doesn't. Whatever this is, it's not what you think. She wouldn't hurt you, hurt me, hurt everyone," she says, gesturing at our audience surrounding us, "Like that."

"She's right," a distant yet familiar voice says as our missing piece walks through the front door, quickly assessing the situation she's walked into. "Raine wouldn't hurt you on purpose."

"Abi, you don't even know what's going on."

"Maybe not. But just like everyone here, I'm not blind, Theo."

If I weren't so lost in my own relationship drama, I might scoff at that. Out of everyone in this room, her and Elliot are the blindest of the lot.

"That girl is gone for you. This is something bigger than she's letting us see."

"Jesus, she really has got you all wrapped around her little finger, hasn't she? She's leaving. Her bag was packed, and her leaving present was fucking someone else right under my nose." I throw my arm out pointing in the direction of the bathroom. Abi's eyes follow it before she frowns, her lips parting to say something.

But I'm done.

So fucking done.

Unwilling to listen to anymore, I turn my back on all of them and run up the stairs taking three at a time in my need for solitude.

"I saw Raine come out of the bathroom last night," Abi confesses, forcing me to slow down halfway up. She's not talking to me, has no idea I'm listening, but I'm powerless to keep moving. "But she didn't look like she was hooking up with anyone. She looked… she looked scared."

I shake my head, refusing to believe this is any more than her trying to get one over on me.

It's how our relationship started, so why should I expect the end to be any different?

Slower than before, I continue to drag my exhausted body up the stairs. Abi continues but her words barely register as I shut down faster than I can control.

All my life all I've wanted was to be an adult and to make my own decisions. Turns out, it's fucking bullshit.

Being an adult sucks.

"Who was she with?" Elliot asks as I get to my door.

"I think... I think it was the guy Theo was buying his gear from." Her words float around my ears, but I don't allow them to settle.

So what? She was with Vaughn, she was probably buying shit. Everyone on campus knows I get the best gear, that's no fucking secret.

I bet she fucking stole from me to buy it too. That really would complete the picture of the poor girl who turned up from the wrong side of the tracks and set about trying to bring us down.

Hell, maybe that's why those pills hit so hard. Maybe she made sure they were spiked. Maybe she was trying to kill me.

The laugh that spills from my lips sounds manic, even to my own ears.

And to think, yesterday morning, I woke up thinking I had it all. Our piece of shit father was behind bars, I was confident that Millie would be looked after, and I thought I had the most incredible woman by my side.

If only I knew...

I could have made the move first.

Pulling my phone from my pocket, I open my messages and find my last chat with Keeley.

If you can't beat them, join them, right?

Fuck you, Raine Storm.

Fuck. You.

24

RAINE

I sit quietly, tapping my finger against the bar. The bartender, a gorgeous dark-haired man with twinkling blue eyes catches my attention and offers me a flirty smile.

For a second, I pretend that I'm here to meet someone like him. Young. Handsome. Respectable.

The kind of man who will show me a good time.

Not the kind of man currently heading toward me with a wicked glint in his eyes.

"Drinking alone?" Stanley Harris asks as I swirl the stirrer in my cocktail.

"My date stood me up." I bat my lashes, offering him a sad smile.

"Your date must be an idiot. Pretty young girl like you"—his eyes rake over me, lingering and leering, but I block it all out—"I'd empty my whole damn schedule for a date with a girl like you."

"That's very kind of you to say." I chuckle softly, taking a sip of my drink.

My almost empty drink.

"Can I get you another one?"

"I'd like that." I flip my hair off my shoulder, drawing his eye to my neckline.

It's nothing I haven't done twenty times before. But this time feels different.

Because this time, I'm in love with somebody.

A deep sense of grief fills my chest.

It's been hours since I left All Hallows'.

Millie would have found my note by now. Theo will know that I'm gone for good.

His expression still haunts me, the shock and disbelief in his eyes, the utter devastation.

He never said the words, but I'd felt them.

And now I'll never hear them.

I'll never know what it feels like to be someone's person.

The centre of somebody's universe.

I shove the crushing sense of hopelessness down, focusing on the task at hand.

Just a few more hours and then I'll be free…

If everything goes to plan.

"Have we met?" He studies me, his interested gaze brushing up my body like a thousand tiny spiders crawling over my skin.

I always hated this part the most.

"I don't know, have we?" I flash him a coy smile, dipping my eyes.

"The party." He snaps his fingers. "You're friends with Theo Ashworth."

"We go to school together, that's all."

The weight of the words crush me.

"School?"

"College," I correct him. Not that I'm sure it would matter if I was still in school.

Men like Stanley Harris don't tend to have a moral compass when it comes to seducing young girls.

Relief coasts over his expressions and I have to bite back a dry laugh. He might be relieved, but I would put money on him sticking around regardless.

"I'd remember those eyes anywhere," he croons, leaning in a little closer.

Biles rises up my throat, the realisation that this is it—that if I do this, there's no going back.

I knew that the second I lied to Theo. The second I punched through his chest and ripped out his heart. But this is different. That was just words, this will be...

I lock it down.

Forcing myself to a place of isolation.

Complete and utter numbness.

My time in Saints Cross was always finite.

Nothing more than a brief moment in time.

It's my own fault for getting tangled up with Theo. For letting my guard down and letting myself believe that maybe things could be different, that maybe I could have had the happily ever after I've never dared to dream of.

But that wasn't my destiny.

And he'll get over me.

He'll meet some rich beautiful girl who he can be proud to call his. Someone who knows how to live in his world.

Someone deserving of his love, his affection.

A true equal.

Mr. Harris watches me, his intense stare making it hard to breathe. I suck in a shaky breath, and he crooks a smile. "Don't be nervous." He slides a fresh drink towards me.

Hollow laughter crawls up my throat, but I trap it behind a thin smile.

I'm not nervous.

I'm broken.

And after tonight, I'll never be the same again.

Brittle laughter spills out of me as I laugh at Stanley's lame attempt at a joke.

We're on our third drink of the evening and he's done most of the talking.

He's not as obvious as some of the men I've lured. His hand rests precariously on my knee, occasionally stroking back and forth, but he's kept it respectful for the most part.

I don't doubt that'll all change once we're behind closed doors.

It always does.

Some men are too good at hiding behind a mask of civility and honour.

"Forgive me for being presumptuous," he says. "But I feel like I've known you for a lifetime."

And here it comes.

The compliments and platitudes.

The clichés.

My eyes drop to his hand, the wedding ring still resting on his finger and heat creeps into his cheeks.

"Yes, well..." He coughs, a weak attempt to disguise his sudden nerves. "Marriage can be a complicated thing."

"I'm sure it is." My lips twist as I fight the disgust churning in my stomach.

"I've offended you," he says quietly, his hand dropping away from my knee.

It would be so easy to use this moment to my advantage. To get up and wish him a good night and walk out of here. But I don't doubt Vaughn is close by. Watching from the shadows, making sure I don't do anything stupid.

"No," I force out. "I just... I don't do this often."

"Do what?" His brows furrow.

"Drink with strange men in bars."

"I'd like to think I am no longer a stranger." His slightly glassy gaze lingers on the low-cut neckline of my dress. "We could get another drink? Maybe something to eat? I'd love to hear about your plans for after college."

Because he thinks I'm in second year.

He thinks I'm eighteen.

"It would be nice to talk somewhere quieter," I reply. "A booth, maybe?"

His eyes light up at my suggestion. "Of course." He stands, offering me his hand as I slip off the stool. It feels all wrong wrapped around my slim fingers, but I ignore the alarm bells in my head, the utter repulsion spiking through me.

This is a means to an end.

My way out.

I glance at the door, wanting nothing more than to see Theo storming through it. Here to rescue me. But it's a hopeless fantasy. A distant dream.

If Theo knew...

A violent shiver rolls through me.

"Raine?" His big hand presses against the small of my back and I blink up at him. "Shall we?"

I nod, letting him steer me over to one of the more private booths. It feels different here, the shadows and low lighting swallowing us as he slips in beside me.

"You are so beautiful," he rasps, stroking a hand along my neck, pushing my hair off my face, clearly feeling bolder now that we're secreted away.

"Oh, to be young again." Laughter crinkles his eyes. "You know I used to be quite the catch in college."

"I'm sure you were." I sip my cocktail, forcing myself to stay in the moment. To play the game.

Before, back in Brewton, it had been second nature. Vaughn had manipulated me and moulded me into the perfect trap. And part of me—the part desperate to be loved—craved his approval, his satisfaction.

I knew it was wrong, the things he made me do. But I told

myself that it was a way to show him I was loyal and that I loved him.

Vaughn didn't love me though, he exploited me. He used me. And then he hung me out to dry.

In some ways, I guess he did me a favour leaving me to take the fall that night everything went to shit. Because if he hadn't, I would have had no bargaining chip with the police and things could have ended very definitely for me.

"Had all the girls clamouring to date me." Stanley goes on. "I played for the Saints rugby team. I was one of their best players."

"Amazing." I flash him a bright smile, draining the rest of my drink.

"Another?" he asks.

"I should probably switch to water."

"How about I order you another cocktail and a water?"

"Okay."

He flags the waiter down and gives him our order.

"Would you like any to eat?" the waiter asks.

"Not for me, thank you."

"Just the drinks please," Stanley says.

"I might get room service later," I add.

"Room service?"

"Oh, I'm staying here for the night."

"You are?" His eyes widen.

"Once I realised I'd been stood up, I booked myself a room for the night. I figured I could get room service and treat myself."

"I see. Well, at least you have company now."

"I do." I smile.

Something simmers in his eyes. A subtle hunger. It's the same way he'd looked at me at the party. But I was nothing more than a fleeting notion then.

Now, I'm a possibility.

A dream that might come true.

God, men are such fickle creatures.

Not all men. But the ones I've had the pleasure of knowing all my life. Men so eager and willing to defile young girls. To bury their sense of right and wrong for a chance to fuck a teenager.

"Raine?" Concern coats his voice as I fight the urge to vomit.

I don't want to do this.

I don't want—

"You feel a little warm." He presses the back of his hand to my forehead. "Maybe you should get some fresh air."

"No," I rush out. "I think I just need to lie down."

"I can walk you back to your room?"

"I'd like that, thank you."

He helps me out of the booth, wrapping his arm around my waist.

It feels all wrong still. A heavy weight I feel everywhere, crushing the air from my lungs.

No one bats an eye as we walk out of the bar area and into the hotel foyer.

But why would they?

They only see a beautiful young woman being wined and dined by a handsome older gentleman. It's nothing they haven't seen hundreds of times before.

"I'm on the second floor," I say, retrieving my key card from my wrist bag. He plucks it from my fingers, ushering me into the lift and tucking me against his side.

"I think it was the last cocktail," I lie. "It went straight to my head."

"We'll get some water inside you and something to soak up the alcohol." His fingers brush down my waist and my eyelids flutter closed.

I imagine it's Theo next to me. His arm around me, his aftershave permeating the air. But when the lift doors ping open and I force myself to open my eyes, reality comes crashing down around me.

Theo isn't here.

And he isn't coming to save me.

Not this time.

25

THEO

"What the fuck are you doing?" Oak barks when I stalk through the kitchen a few hours later, with my sights set on the front door.

My anger from before has waned, leaving behind nothing but devastation and a whole heap of embarrassment.

She played me.

Me.

An Heir.

How fucking stupid is she?

It's a good thing she's leaving because there's no way in hell she'll be able to show her face at school again. If she thought shit was bad when she first arrived, it will be nothing compared to the onslaught if she dares turn up for class tomorrow.

You don't treat us like that and get away with it.

No one does. Her pussy might be good, but it isn't that fucking good.

Okay, so maybe it is, but I'm not admitting that to anyone including myself right now.

"Out," I bark, unwilling to discuss my plans with him.

But before I get even halfway across the room, Oak is on his feet, and then footsteps thud my way as Reese joins us.

"Where are you going?"

"Out apparently," Oak mutters like an arsehole.

"What the fuck is this? You two trying to replace my father or some shit?" I bark.

"Fuck, no," Reese grunts. "But you've just had your heart brok—"

"I'm not fucking heartbroken. I'm pissed off my regular access to decent pussy has fucked off."

They both glare at me, seeing straight through my lie.

"I don't want or need your fucking pity," I sulk, spinning around and giving them my back.

"Good because you're not getting it. We will stop you from going out there and doing something stupid though," Oakley argues.

"Whatever," I scoff, more than ready to leave this bullshit behind. But being the pain in the arse friends that they are, they dart around me, blocking my exit. "Do you fucking mind?" I growl, losing my grip on my patience.

My phone buzzes and I stupidly lift it to read the message. Only, Reese is faster, and he has it out of my hand before my hungover brain has even noticed.

"Jesus, Theo. You really are dumber than you fucking look," he chastises before passing my phone to Oak.

The second he sees who I'm talking to, his eyes narrow and his lips purse. "You're not fucking doing this, man."

"She cheated on me," I blurt before I can catch the words.

"You don't know that for a fact."

"She told me," I argue. "Right to my face."

"Did she really?"

"Look, we might be wrong here," Reese placates. "But Raine doesn't seem like the kind of girl who'd do that."

"How the fuck do you know that? We don't even know her."

"You do," Oak argues.

"Yeah, and I'm telling you that she's a cheating fucking whore. Now get out of my way."

"You'll regret it," Reese warns.

"Doubt it. You've fucked Keeley," I spit. "You know she's good for it."

"Oh yeah, I'm sure it'll be great for the few minutes you're inside her. Then what? You're pissed, we fucking get it. But there will be no coming back from this if you do it."

"Worth it," I bark, snatching my phone back and dropping it into my pocket.

I step forward, waiting for them to move but the stubborn tossers just fold their arms across their chest and glare at me.

"Move," I demand.

They glance at each other, having a silent conversation that I'm not privy to.

"Fuck's sake," I mutter, taking matters into my own hands and physically shoving them away.

"Don't come crying to us when this all blows up in your face. We tried to warn you," Oak states as I reach for the front door.

But as I go to pull on the handle, it swings open, almost breaking my nose in the process. "The hell are you do—Mills?"

The sight of my sister with tears and make-up staining her cheeks makes my heart clench and my stomach knot.

"What's happened? What's wrong?"

In a split second, her emotions flip, and the sadness is engulfed by pure fury.

"You fucking dickhead," she screams, taking me by surprise before her palms land forcefully on my chest, making me stumble back.

"Millie," somebody warns a second before Liv and Tally emerge behind her.

"This is all your fault," Millie continues to wail, her arms moving so fast as she pounds on me that I've no chance of catching them. "You did this. You did all of this. How c-could y-you?" Her voice cracks and so does my heart.

I love my little sister to death, and seeing her hurting wrecks me. But I need her to stop fucking hitting me.

"Mills, you need to calm down," I soothe, still attempting to capture her wild arms.

For such a small person, I must admit, her tiny fists actually hurt a little.

"Okay, baby Ashworth. Shall we calm down?" Oak says, somehow managing to wrangle the uncontrollable octopus, pinning her crazy arms to her sides.

"I hate you," she seethes, really driving a knife through my heart.

"I think we all need to calm down," Reese says, throwing his arm around Liv's shoulders and dropping a kiss on her temple.

The sweet move makes my breath catch.

This time yesterday, I could do that.

"What's happened, sweet cheeks?" he asks quietly as Oak leads my sobbing sister deeper into the Chapel.

Liv shakes her head before nodding toward Millie.

"Well?" I ask, lifting my arms from my sides impatiently when Oak risks releasing her.

"She's gone," she states flatly, lifting her hands to wipe her eyes.

My stomach immediately drops into my feet, replaced by an unforgiving lump of dread. "Gone?" I ask simply, desperately trying to cover how those two words make me feel.

I was just on the way out of the door to go and fuck Keeley. I shouldn't care.

"There was a note under my door, Theo. It was a goodbye. She's gone for good. And it's all your fault."

"I wasn't the one who—"

"Stop it. Just stop it. She didn't cheat on you. She wouldn't. She—"

"Millie, stop. She—"

"She loves you, Theo. Do you know what her note said?" she asks, her brows shooting up.

"How the hell would I know?" I seethe.

"She said she's sorry."

"Right? She should be. I knew from the very beginning that she'd—"

"Oh, just shut up you big idiot," Millie snaps. "She isn't sorry because she did something wrong. She's sorry because she doesn't think she's good enough for us, for you... for this." She throws her arms out wide, gesturing to the extravagance around us. "Do you even know her, Theo? Really know her. Where she came from, what her life was like before here? Why she was in therapy?"

I swallow thickly because no, I don't know any of that. Not really.

"You're the one who should be apologising."

"I haven't done anything wrong."

A bitter laugh spills from Millie's lips. "You're an idiot. She loves you and look what you've done."

"Me? Millie, I haven't—"

"Find her," she demands, placing her hands on her hips while giving me the full weight of her stare. "Find her and bring her back. She belongs here with us, Theo. You know I'm right."

The Chapel turns deadly silent as we continue to glare at each other. My friends are watching, waiting for one of us to cave or blow.

But that never happens because footsteps and voices approach before the final two of our group emerges.

Together.

Interesting.

"What's going on?" Elliot barks after quickly assessing the situation.

"Raine has left," Millie states at the same time Reese supplies, "Theo was going to fuck Keeley."

"You were what?" Millie screeches in such a high-pitched voice I'm pretty sure only dogs should be able to hear it.

"I didn't do it, clearly," I mutter.

"Yeah, because I stopped you on your way out. Jesus, Theo. Could you fuck this up anymore?"

My teeth grind so hard I'm surprised one of them doesn't crack as I glare at my little sister.

When I started putting everything into place to get Dad locked up for crimes he thought he'd gotten away with, I expected to be the one taking over the parenting, not the other way around.

"She might have a point, Theo," Abi says, walking farther into the room with a folder in her hand. "You need to read this," she says, smacking it none too gently against my chest.

"What is it?" I ask, peeling it away and finding Raine's name printed on the sticker in the top corner.

"Her file. Transfer documents. Medical reports. Her past, it's all there," Elliot says.

"And you just picked these up from where, exactly?"

"The admin office, obviously," he deadpans.

"Right? Just hand these over willy-nilly, do they?"

"Obviously not. But how we got our hands on it doesn't matter. It's what's inside that does."

"Well, go on then," Millie encourages.

Turning my back on all of them, I take the folder to the sofa and fall back into it. Flipping to the first page, I scan through her information. Full name, date of birth, address, social worker...

"Keep going," Abi encourages, coming to sit next to me.

The list of her previous address makes my head spin. She told me she's been pushed around a lot, but hearing those words and seeing the list of addresses is an entirely different thing.

"Fucking hell," I mutter.

"I'm going to make coffee," Liv announces. "Some help, please," she says firmly, ensuring the others follow her to the kitchen to give me some space.

Millie doesn't go though. She sits her butt on the coffee table in front of me and waits patiently with her arms wrapped around herself.

"Court case?" I whisper, flicking to an official looking letter.

"Keep reading."

"What is— Vaughn Ronson, oh fuck," I gasp, my hands trembling as reality dawns on what I'm reading.

"I told you it was him," Abi states.

"When the fuck did you say that?" I demand as Elliot comes rushing back over.

"Don't fucking talk to her like that," he seethes, looking ready to jump to Abi's defense.

"Y-yesterday," she stutters, curling in on herself. "I was sure it was him. She looked terrified, Theo."

"See, I told you," Millie says with a huff. "She hasn't done anything wrong."

"Okay, so… what does all this mean?" My mind is working overtime as I try to piece together everything we've learned.

"It means that prick you've been buying gear off is a bigger scumbag than meets the eyes. When did he show up exactly?"

"Umm…" I think, trying to cast my mind back.

"Before Raine started here, or after?"

"After," I confess, remembering the first time I met him. "Definitely after. Motherfucker," I seethe. "I'll kill him. If he's laid a finger on her, I'll fucking kill him."

"Who is he? What has he done?" Millie asks, but thankfully, neither Elliot nor Abi answer her.

I know she's not a naïve child, but she doesn't need to know all this right now.

It's not important.

"We need to find her," I state.

"I agree, but where do we even start?" Elliot asks.

"Where did they meet? Would he take her back there?"

"Assuming he has her," Abi offers. "What if she's running from him?"

"Jesus Christ."

"My dad could track her phone," Oak suggests, clearly listening to everything despite being on the other side of the room.

"No, he can't," Millie says quietly. "It's in her room. She left it."

"Fuck. FUCK," I bark, shoving my fingers into my hair and pulling until it hurts.

"We'll find her, man," Elliot assures me. "We'll find her."

26

RAINE

"Jesus, you're so beautiful." Stanley runs his hands down my waist, nuzzling my neck from behind.

It took him precisely seven seconds to drop his nice guy routine. I'm not surprised but the crushing realisation of what I'm about to do, sits heavy in my chest.

All the other times, I'd been too eager to please Vaughn, desperate for the praise he gave me after.

Deep down, I knew it was messed up. But when you've been dragged up, bounced from foster home to foster home, forced to survive neglect and abuse and utter loneliness, you crave attention. And when you get it, you hold onto it so tightly the lines between right and wrong, and good and bad blur until you could no longer see the edges.

This time, it is different.

This time, I don't want to please Vaughn. But I need to convince him that I'm willing to play his game. Just long enough for me to make a run for it.

I glance at my backpack on the floor by the desk. My worldly possessions reduced to one bag. How pathetic.

But another emotion trickles through me.

Guilt.

I shut it down though. It doesn't matter now. I made my choice—I chose to give Vaughn what he wants in order to get him out of Theo and Millie's life.

And yeah, maybe part of me did it to protect myself, to prevent Theo from ever finding out the truth. But what's done is done.

There's no going back now.

"Let me make you feel good."

His words yank me back into the moment.

"Let's have a drink." I wiggle out of his hold, rushing over to the mini bar.

"A drink, of course." He loosens his tie, his eyes fixed on my body.

The hotel room is lush. Far nicer than the places Vaughn used in Brewton.

I pour us both a vodka and tonic and offer him the glass.

"To new friends." A faint smirk traces his mouth.

"New friends." I'm hardly surprised when he drains his glass in one.

He's nervous.

Probably hasn't ever cheated on his wife before. And if he has, probably wasn't with a girl young enough to be his daughter.

"Drink up," he encourages, growing bolder by the minute.

My palms sweat as I bring the glass to my lips, knowing that the vodka will numb me to whatever happens next. But I also know I can't afford to let him get me too drunk. Not if I want to make a break for it.

I need to keep my wits about me. Which means I'll have to find another way to escape the inevitable disgust and despair I'll feel when he's no longer content with just talking.

"You seem nervous," he remarks. "You don't need to be. We don't have to do anything you don't want to."

"I'm fine." I force my lips into a convincing smile, batting my eyelashes to soften the slight edge to my words.

"We talked a lot about me," I say. "But you didn't tell me anything about yourself."

Much to Stanley's disappointment, I sit in the small tub chair, and he perches on the end of the bed instead of taking a seat on the sofa.

"Oh, I'm not sure you'd find my story interesting." He chuckles.

"What do you do for work?"

"I'm a freelance consultant. Systems management and IT."

"Sounds fancy."

"It isn't, not really. But it pays well. Allows me to enjoy the finer things in life. Spoil the people I care about." He gets up and stalks toward me. My breath hitches, and not in a good way.

Taking the glass from my hand, he gently tugs me to my feet. "I'd love to spoil you." His hand brushes over my shoulder, pushing my hair back. I peer up at him, trying to hide my nerves.

"From what Anthony said, you're new in town," he says it like it matters. "I could show you around. Give you the Stanley Harris tour."

"Your wife," I blurt, and his brows furrow.

"Not a problem." He leans in, letting his lips feather across my cheek. "She's married to her job almost as much as I am. Besides, I'm pretty sure she's been fucking her personal trainer for the last five years."

"Oh."

"Don't worry about any of that," his voice dips lower. "This is our night. Nothing outside that door matters." His lips linger against my neck, and I have to resist the urge to shove him away and scream at him never to lay his hands on me again.

I'm Theo's.

My heart knows it.

But my head...

My head knows it doesn't matter.

After what I've done, Theo will probably be balls deep inside of an Heir chaser by now. Fucking away his sorrows.

Fucking me out of his system.

Pain radiates through me, coiling around my heart and making it hard to breathe.

I can't do this.

I can't—

"Raine," he breathes, cupping my face. Staring down at me like I'm all his fantasies come true. "I'm going to make you feel so good, beautiful girl."

Bile churns in my stomach, silent tears rolling down my cheeks as he begins to strip me, his hands and mouth trailing over my skin hungrily.

"God I'm going to fuck you so good, show you what a real man can do."

I press my lips together, trapping the scream there. The utter disgust and repulsion crawling up my throat.

The air shifts, the change in him, almost violent. He shoves me toward the bed, pushing me down on my hands. The air leaves my lungs on a sharp breath. This can't be happening.

It can't—

But I hear the snap of his belt. The rustle of material. Feel his hand grabbing at the skirt of my dress, cool air hitting the back of my thighs.

"Please," I cry, choking on the fear swarming me.

This wasn't supposed to happen again.

Vaughn wasn't supposed to find me.

He wasn't supposed to be here. Ruining everything. Destroying the only good thing I've ever had.

For a second, I pretend that Theo is here. Bursting through the door to save me.

To tell me how much he loves me and that he'll never let me go.

But I stare at the door, willing it to open, and nothing happens.

There's no rescue party.

No Heir in shining armour.

Because Theo isn't coming. I made damn sure of that when I ripped out his heart and stomped all over it.

"Don't flake out on me now," he chuckles darkly. "You were begging for this downstairs in the bar. Fluttering those long lashes at me, giving me all the right signs."

He's right, I was.

Luring him in, making him think I want this.

I don't.

God, I don't want to be anywhere near him. But what choice do I have?

It's my only shot at freedom. At walking—running—away from Vaughn forever.

With a renewed sense of determination, I manage to push up to my feet and take control of the situation. "Let me take care of you," I drawl, running my hands up his chest, slowly unbuttoning his shirt.

Stanley lets me turn him and push him down on the bed, his movements a little jerky, probably from all the vodka. His glazed eyes track my movements, his hands gripping my waist. Fingers digging into my skin with desperation.

"I'm all yours, beautiful girl."

Swallowing over the giant lump in my throat, I hitch my dress up, allowing me to straddle his thighs as I push him down on the bed. His rough laughter makes the fine hairs along the back of my neck stand to attention.

I hate this.

I hate myself.

Hate that my mum didn't love me enough to protect me from this cruel world full of men like Vaughn, men like Theo's dad, and Stanley Harris. Men who are all too willing to prey on women. To take what they want because they can. Without little thought to the consequences.

Vaughn played on my weaknesses, exploited by my vulnerability—my desperation to be loved.

And I paid dearly.

I'm still paying.

His hands clamp down around my hips as he grinds into me from below. "Fuck," he groans. "I'm going to need a little more than that."

"Patience," I giggle, trailing my fingers over his bare chest, trying to avoid the inevitable.

But he's done waiting.

Taking control again, he sits up abruptly, managing to flip me underneath him, his heavy weight pinning me to the luxury mattress.

There's no more compliments or sweet talk. He doesn't check in with me for my permission. He claws at my dress, my body, my soul like a man possessed. Licking and sucking my neck. Biting.

"Ouch," I cry, and he chuckles into my shoulder, his hand firmly gripping my throat.

"What? You don't like a little pain with your pleasure? I thought all you young girls liked it rough?"

Tears sting my eyes but we're past the point of niceties.

"I'm going to fuck you so hard you'll be feeling me for days." He shoves a hand between us, yanking and clawing at my underwear. I tamp down the urge to scream, forcing myself into that place inside my head where I'm numb.

There, but not.

This is no doubt all part of Vaughn's plan to punish me. To show me that he still holds all the power.

Sometimes, he would let his target fuck me. Beat and berate me. Other times, he'd intervene before things got out of control. But it was always on his terms.

Part of me had hoped he wouldn't let it get too far tonight.

Stanley chokes me harder, lost in the fantasy of having a young beautiful girl at his disposal. My vision blurs slightly as I vaguely feel him touch me. Defile me.

But I burrow deeper into my mind. My safe place. Pretending I'm still in All Hallows' with Theo and Millie and our friends.

A bite of pain lances through me as he tries to drag pleasure from my body. But I'm broken. Ruined by Vaughn's final act of deceit.

He didn't have to do this.

He could have let me go.

He could have let—

The door swings open and Stanley staggers back, yanking up his trousers. "Who the hell are you?" he stammers.

I shouldn't be relieved to see Vaughn standing there. But I can't deny I am.

Shoving my dress down, I sit and straighten my hair, sucking in deep breaths as I watch the familiar scene play out before me.

"You good?" Vaughn asks me, and I nod.

"W-what is this?" Stanley glances between us, his eyes full of panic.

"This is the part where you and I have a little chat. Sit." Vaughn points to a chair, so calm and collected, even I shudder at the authority in his voice.

"I will not. You can't just barge in here and—"

"I said sit the fuck down." He manhandles him into a chair and goes to the dresser, pulling out the small camera there.

"W-what is that?" Vaughn rounds the table and I use the moment to slip around him.

"Where the fuck are you going?" he barks, and I flinch.

"The bathroom."

He nods and I grab my backpack and slip into the bathroom.

This is my chance. My one and only shot to escape. But I have to time it just right.

Vaughn enjoys this part. Presenting his targets with the proof of their indiscretions. Threatening to make it public, to unravel their perfect lives if they don't give him whatever it is he's after. Usually money.

Lots and lots of money.

His voice rumbles through the room as I quickly change into the spare clothes shoved into my bag earlier. I drag my hair into a ponytail, ignoring the finger and bite marks littering my skin. Double checking the envelope of money, I slip the backpack over my shoulders and take a deep breath.

"I will not!" Stanley bellows.

"I don't think you understand, I will send this video to your wife. Your business associates. Your children..."

Vaughn's voice is cut off by the blood roaring in my ears.

It's now or never.

I grip the door handle, quietly opening it. I don't glance back, don't stop for a second as I make a beeline for the door and make a run for the hallway.

"Shit. Fuck," Vaughn says but the door clicks shut behind me and I take off down the hall.

Away from Vaughn.

And toward my freedom.

27

THEO

"He's at a function in London," Oak says, holding the phone away from his ear for a beat.

"Then get him back here. We need him. Raine needs him," I beg.

"They're trying to get hold of their IT guy. We don't actually need him. Just his tech people."

"Right, brilliant," I mutter, continuing with the pacing I started when Oak first pulled his phone out to call his dad.

My heart pounds, my hands tremble and fear knots up my insides.

The things I read in Raine's file...

Fuck.

The things she's been through, the shit she's been silently dealing with.

I wish she'd told me.

If she had then I never, ever would have allowed Vaughn to be in her life.

No wonder she acted so fucking odd when I introduced them.

I knew life in the system could be shit. It's the exact reason I waited until my birthday to bring our father down. There was no fucking way I was ever risking that happening to me or Millie.

"Theo, you need to stop," the girl in question says, stepping right in front of me, her tiny hands gripping my upper arms.

"Mills," I sigh.

She blinks up at me, desperately trying to fight back her tears. "We'll find her. We'll bring her back. We have to. She… she belongs here."

"I know," I say softly. It's at total odds with the oppressive need for violence that's pulsating through my veins. Pulling her into my arms, I drop my nose into her hair and breathe her in, hoping her presence will calm the wildfire roaring inside me.

"Yeah, okay," Oak says down the line, making my head pop back up. "Number. We need his number."

"Shit, yeah." Releasing Millie, I dig my phone out and find Vaughn's contact.

Just the sight of his name makes something hot and dangerous explode within me. My lips part to relay the number, but I quickly find my voice doesn't work.

Sensing my struggle, Oak steps over and reads it straight from my screen. "Yeah, okay. We'll be waiting." He hangs up, making the lump in my throat grow larger.

"If they can track it, they'll get back in touch," he explains.

"And what if they can't?" Millie asks hesitantly.

"We'll worry about that if it happens. Dad's guy is solid. He'll make it work."

"And if they're not together?" Abi asks.

"Can we just try to be a little positive here?" Liv suggests. "We'll get the location and then we'll go get her. Easy."

"Nothing is ever that easy," I force out.

"No, well… maybe today is our lucky day," Liv muses.

No one agrees, in fact, the only response she's met with is silence and desperation.

If Raine ever needed proof that she belonged here, then this is it. Eight people all desperate to know where she is and to bring her back safe.

She has no idea. No fucking idea what kind of impact she's had on the lives of the people under this roof. She's been a friend to Liv, Tally, and Abi. A big sister to Millie. And everything to me.

Turning my back on them, I march toward the sofa and drop onto it, my head falling into my hands. I sense their concerned stares as they all join me, but no one says anything as the tension in the room continues to build.

"Why did she run?" I whisper. It's more to myself than the others but it doesn't stop Abi from trying to make it better.

"Maybe she felt like she didn't have a choice." She hesitantly shuffles closer, before a cautious hand reaches for my knee.

Her touch burns, not as much as Elliot's glare from the opposite couch.

But fuck him.

"She could have told me. I could have helped. I could have... I could have done anything she needed."

"Has she talked to you much about her past?" Liv asks.

"She's alluded to stuff. None of it good. I should have made her tell me more. Maybe we wouldn't be here then."

"It's too late for that now," Reese points out.

"You think?" I sneer.

Silence falls once more.

"Maybe we should search her dorm room. See if we can find any clues about where she might go," Tally suggests.

"Raine isn't that stupid. If she's run, she won't leave anything behind."

"But if he has her... What if she left something behind so we could find her?"

"This isn't some bloody soap opera," I snap, making Oak's chest puff out ready to protect his girl. "She could b-be—"

"Let's go and check it out," Abi says, pushing to her feet. "It can't hurt. All we're doing right now is sitting here wasting time waiting for the phone to ring."

"Fine, let's go."

Because if I sit here a minute longer, there's every chance I might explode.

"There's nothing here," I complain after tearing her room apart like a tornado. "She's packed almost everything she owns." Which wasn't a lot in the first place.

There are no hidden notes, no clues, no nothing.

I fall back in her bed, letting her scent surround me as my desperation hits a whole new level.

"There's got to be something," Millie urges, desperate to find something.

"There isn't. It's point—"

Oak's ringing phone cuts off my whining and I immediately sit up, my feet firmly on the floor and ready to run.

"It's Dad," he confirms, swiping the screen and putting it on speaker.

"We've got him," Christian confirms.

"Where?" I bark, already halfway to the door.

"Sending you the link now."

My phone buzzes in my pocket right on cue.

"But we don't know if she's with him," someone says.

"It's a start," I call over my shoulder as I begin running down the hall, the location of Vaughn's phone loading before my eyes.

Eventually, it settles on a position.

"Got you, motherfucker," I grunt as footsteps pound behind me. "They're in Oxford."

"I'll drive," Elliot confirms. "Direct me."

"What about us?" Abi calls.

"Look after Millie. We've got this."

"This is bullshit," my sister spits, making my teeth grind. "I want to come get her. If it weren't for me then—"

Spinning around, I grab my sister by the upper arms and stare into her watery eyes. "She's going to need you, Mills. When we bring her back, she's going to need you. Let us do this, then you can take care of her."

I'm pretty sure I'm lying. Something tells me that the second she's back in my arms, I'm not letting her go for anything. Not even my little sister.

"We can tidy her room up," she suggests, nodding.

"She's not going back to her room," I state. "She's coming home with me."

"Bro," Elliot starts.

"Don't," I spit, holding my hand up. "Just don't. If you want to make anything nice for her then do it to my room. Cover it in flowers and fucking glitter if you think it'll make her happy, I don't care."

"Not sure that's—"

"We gotta go," I say, my heart sinking when I realise the dot on my screen is moving.

Of fucking course, he's not going to make this easy for us.

"Let's go. This motherfucker is moving."

"You got it," Reese agrees as the four of us run toward the exit and then make a beeline for Elliot's car.

"We're on our way now," Oak says, still on the phone to Christian, although I notice he's taken it off speaker. "No, it's fine. We'll just—"

"What's going on?" I ask, twisting around in my seat as Elliot takes the road out of Saints Cross at double the speed limit.

"We're not going to need—" Oak lets out a heavy sigh. "Fine. Fine, okay. Yes. Okay, bye."

"What's going on?" I repeat.

"He's sending some guys to follow Vaughn and help us out."

"Not necessary," I spit.

"Exactly what I said."

"That motherfucker is mine. I'm not ending tonight without him knowing he's been fucking with the wrong people."

"Just get your girl. Let Christian sort out the rest," Reese says, sitting forward and clamping his hand over my shoulder in support.

"He's not just some guy from her past. He's inserted himself into our lives. Into my life in order to get to her. This is personal." Anger courses through my veins like acid. "I fucking trusted him with my life. He could have been selling me all kinds of shit these past few weeks."

"Then maybe you should think yourself lucky and step away while you can."

"Fuck that," I scoff. "Is that what you wanted to do when that cunt took Tally? Step back and let it happen?"

"I didn't have a fucking choice."

"Yeah, well. I do. And I want to watch him fucking bleed for this. I don't care if he knew her first, if he had her first. She's mine now, and no one fucking touches what's mine."

"Let Dad handle him," Oak tries to reason with me, but I'm past all rational thought.

"Not happening," I state. "They're still moving. You need to put your foot down," I bark at Elliot.

He shoots me a glare, holding his speed where it is.

"If this were Abi you'd be going faster," I mutter under my breath, although loud enough for him to hear.

His fingers tighten on the wheel until his knuckles are practically translucent, but he doesn't respond.

He doesn't need to.

We all know the truth.

"We're ten minutes out," I say as Elliot is forced to slow down when we hit the edge of Oxford city centre.

The dot hasn't moved for a while and a quick Google search tells us that they're at The Grand Hotel. That knowledge should reassure me. At least it's not some abandoned building in the middle of nowhere he hopes he'll never be found.

But here, he's hiding in plain sight.

"Remember that this might not be leading us to her, just him," Reese says.

"I know," I growl, my grip on my phone so tight I wonder how the screen hasn't cracked already. "Shit," I gasp when I look down again. "He's moving again."

"We're five minutes away," Elliot states.

I keep my eyes glued to the screen. "He's left the hotel."

"Shit," Elliot hisses, doing what is probably the most reckless overtake I've ever witnessed him do.

"Fuck. Even Elliot is panicking," Reese points out, clearly thinking the same as me.

"I'm not panicking. Just getting us there as fast as possible," he states calmly.

"Sure thing," Oak teases.

"He's behind the hotel. I think he's going down the backroads."

"Can I get the car down there?" Elliot asks.

"I don't fucking know," I snap.

"There's the hotel," Oak points.

I watch as our location aligns with Vaughn's, my heart jumps into my throat as I stare at the building separating us.

"Those are Dad's guys," he says. "In the blacked-out SUVs."

But I don't look. I can't. I'm too busy searching for any

sight of him or my girl. Reese is right. She might not be here with him. But my gut tells me that she is.

She's close and she needs me.

"Pull up down there. We'll go on foot," I demand when there seem to be no roads to take us behind the building.

"Are you sure that's—"

"Just fucking do it," I bark, my fingers already around the handle, ready to shove the door open and run.

"Fuck. Yeah, okay."

I check the tracker one more time, and the second the car comes to a stop, I take off.

"Theo, wait," Oak calls after me as footsteps pound behind me.

I don't need to turn to know that all four of them are following. They might not agree with this plan, but that doesn't mean they don't have my back.

It takes us no more than twenty seconds to fly around the back of the building.

"Fuck, it's dark," I hiss, my legs pumping as we leave the illuminated street behind us.

"Up there," Reese says, pointing ahead. "There's a car."

"You think it's them?" I ask.

"Let's go and fucking find out."

28

RAINE

My heart races as I hurry out of the hotel and slip down the street.

I need to put as much distance between me and Vaughn as possible.

Shit.

Shit.

I did it.

I escaped.

Part of me almost feels bad for Stanley. Vaughn doesn't like being outmanoeuvred, and losing me...

I shut down that line of thought.

I'm free.

All I need to do is get to the train station and get a ticket out of here.

The bruises forming around my throat, my hips, and inside of my thighs are tender. A reminder of what almost happened, but I push down the pain and keep walking.

I'm close, so freaking—

Someone grabs me from behind, yanking me into a narrow alley between two buildings.

A scream tears from my throat but a tattooed hand forced

it back in, clamping over my mouth. Panic saturates every cell in my body as defeat rolls through me.

"You've been a very bad girl," Vaughn breathes in my ear as he drags me backward, the shadows swallowing us whole.

It's late, the streets of Oxford deserted.

I claw at his hand, desperately trying to pry his fingers away but he's stronger, easily overpowering me.

"You really fucked things up for me back there, baby," he spits the words. "Now if I let you go, are you going to behave?"

I nod, aware that I need to play this right if I'm ever going to get away from him again.

He slowly unfurls his fingers, in favour of grabbing me around the neck and holding me at arm's length.

"V-Vaughn," I choke out. "Let me just—"

"Uh-uh, your privileges are revoked. Clearly, I can't fucking trust you." His wild gaze darts back and forth. If I didn't know better, I'd say he's high on something.

Which means I have to tread carefully.

"What did you do with him?" I ask, and a wicked smile curls at his lips.

"Don't tell me you've suddenly grown a conscience?" He chuckles darkly. "A few weeks with your posh little boyfriend and you've forgotten where you came from, is that it?"

"No, I..."

"What? You what, huh?" He gets right in my face, anger rippling off him.

I blink away the tears, hating that he still holds so much power over me.

I don't love him anymore, I'm not sure I ever did. But there was a time I was infatuated with him. The fact that he picked me. I was desperate and lonely and so broken that the second he offered me a scrap of attention, I wanted more.

It became my drug.

My addiction.

But it gradually turned into something twisted. Something

dark and insidious. Deep down, I knew he was using me. Manipulating and exploiting me. But it was easier to pretend than admit the truth.

"I should have known you'd screw me over again. You're nothing more than a selfish whore." Vaughn backhands me so hard my head snaps to the side making me cry out in agony as pain floods my cheek and neck.

"I should have let him fuck you up. But I couldn't do it. I couldn't fucking do it. Fuck, fuck—" He hits me again, and this time I think I blackout for a second.

It isn't the first time he's hurt me. But this feels different. Our mutual betrayal hanging between us, poisoning the air.

"What am I going to do with you, baby?" He smooths his thumb over my tender cheek, forcing me to look at him. "Why do you have to make everything so fucking difficult?"

He pulls me down the alley like a rag doll, my head spinning so fast I see stars.

I try to take in our surroundings, not that I think it will do me any favours. Still, the shred of fight left inside me refuses to wink out.

It's a narrow alley beside the hotel, a row of dumpster bins lining the wall. Vaughn pulls me around the corner and my resolve crumbles. It's nothing but another long dark alley.

His grip on me is ironclad as he mutters to himself. I don't know what he's saying but he sounds unhinged, only confirming my fears. He's either high or experiencing some kind of mental breakdown.

Either way, it's not a good sign.

Not when he's already so pissed at me.

I spot a car up ahead. His car. And the fear multiplies.

This is it.

The end of the road.

If I let him force me inside his car, who knows where I'll end up.

Nowhere good, I silence the little voice. Refusing to accept that I came all this way just to end up right back at square one.

Blood roars in my ears, my pulse a wild thing in my chest. "Where are you taking me?"

He doesn't answer, just rips the door open and shoves me inside. My head smacks off the centre dash and I groan, slipping further under.

I'm aware of a door slamming, the car rocking beneath me. My heavy eyelids try and open so I can look out of the window but pain sears me to the bone.

God, that hurt.

I can barely open my eyes, everything drifting away as I fight to stay conscious.

"Raine," I hear someone yell. "RAINE?"

"Th-Theo?" I murmur, certain I'm hearing things.

Maybe I'm dreaming and he's here to rescue me. To take me back to All Hallows' and never let me go.

But the door opens and my fantasy bursts. Of course, Theo isn't here.

I barely make out Vaughn getting in, his form shimmering like a mirage. "Fucking prick..." he mutters, firing up the car and revving the engine.

Something slams into the back of us, and I try to glance over my shoulder but he presses the accelerator and the car takes off.

"What's go—"

"Shut the fuck up," he barks, shoving me back into the seat. "This is all your fault. Stupid fucking bitch."

My focus slowly returns, and I notice him checking the rear-view mirror. Twisting around I gasp when I spot Elliot's car tailing us.

He came.

Theo came.

I can't order my thoughts quick enough before Vaughn barks, "Did you warn him, huh? Did you—"

"N-no, no I didn't, I swear."

Theo isn't supposed to be here.

He isn't supposed—

Vaughn floors the gas and the car takes off like a rocket.

"You're going to kill us," I shriek, holding on for dear life. But he doesn't hear me, lost in his anger, his warped sense of reality.

I can barely see the buildings as everything rushes past in a blur.

Elliot's headlights stay on us, but it only makes Vaughn zig and zag, taking a sharp turn down a street that has me flinging against the door.

"Fuck," he grunts.

"Vaughn, this is crazy." Fear saturates my voice. "You need to—"

"Shut the fuck up, Raine. I can't think with you nagging me. I can't fucking think."

One of his hands thrusts in his hair, tugging the ends, as volatile energy swirls around him.

Tears cascade down my cheeks, my head pounding and heart galloping in my chest. I've been in some precarious situations in my life—most thanks to this man—but this feels different.

It feels... deadly.

"Shit, I can't fucking lose them." His eyes cut to me, pinning me to the spot as a lick of terror zips down my spine.

He looks feral.

Eyes blown and sweat beading along his forehead.

He's one step away from losing it.

"Vaughn, the road," I scream as headlights come toward us.

He manages to swerve, a loud horn cutting through the night.

I can hardly breathe, my heart lodged in my throat as he floors the gas again. "Vaughn, please..."

"Maybe it's better this way," he murmurs.

"What? What's better?"

Police sirens whir in the distance only feeding into his mania.

I realise then, we're not going to walk out of this alive. This is it; this is how I die.

At the hands of the man who broke me.

I squeeze my eyes shut, trying to calm down. Trying to shove down the fear I'm drowning in. But I can feel it, flooding my chest, my lungs, crawling up my throat.

I shouldn't have run. I should have waited, bided my time, tried to escape—

"Fuck," he roars, slamming his hand down on the steering wheel. "You really fucked things up this time. One job... one more fucking job..."

But it wouldn't have been one job. I realised that the second I saw Vaughn at the party. He infiltrated my life. Watched from the shadows as I fell in love with Theo.

Theo...

My heart twists.

He would never let me walk away from that.

I suck in a desperate breath, my gaze fixing on the road ahead of us.

I scream but he doesn't see the oncoming truck until it's too late.

The impact tears through me, flinging me forward. Metal on metal screams in my ears, the overpowering of smoke and rubber filling my nose. My head hits something, pain ricocheting down my spine as I crumple.

"Raine, shit, Raine," a voice calls but it's like being under water. Everything distant and distorted.

Warm liquid trickles down my forehead, pain spreading into every crevice of my body. God, it hurts.

It hurts so much.

I cry out but the darkness envelops me as I hear my name.

Raine.
Raine.
RAINE.
But it's too much. I can't fight the heaviness taking over my body.

Voices hover on the outskirts of my consciousness.

"Oh fuck, what do we do?"

"Raine, Raine, sunshine, fuck... somebody help, somebody..."

They disappear again as heat licks my skin, pressing down on me like a suffocating blanket. The acrid smoke filling my lungs until I can't breathe.

Until I can't fight it a second longer.

I begin to slip... to drift... falling into the abyss.

And all I can think is, I wish I got to tell him goodbye.

29

THEO

I'm pretty sure the moment I watched the truck plough head first into Vaughn's car will be something I never forget.

It doesn't matter what the outcome of this is. It is going to haunt me for the rest of my days, I know it. So will the sound of my own scream as I watched it play out from the passenger seat of Elliot's car.

The moment we realised that Vaughn had her in that car, we had hightailed it back to Elliot's car and took off after them. If we didn't already know it from the little we'd learned about Vaughn Ronson, then watching him drive confirmed that he was a fucking psychopath.

"Raine, baby. Stay with me. Please," I beg as I stand over her slumped, bloody body in the front seat of his mangled car. "I need to get her out."

"No," Elliot barks, grabbing my arm and wrenching me back before I even get a chance to touch her. "Don't. You might make things worse."

"Worse?" I shout. "Make it fucking worse? You are seeing the same thing I am, right?"

Smoke bellows from the crumpled bonnet, the car barely recognisable anymore.

"I know, Theo. I know," he says, his eyes alternating between staring at me and my broken girl.

"I need to do something. I need to help. I need to... I need to fix her."

Pain like I've never felt before rips through my chest. My nose itches and my eyes burn with tears as I study her.

She's covered in blood. There is so much that I don't even know where it's coming from. All I can hope is that it's not hers, but I think that might be wishful thinking.

We all saw the force of the collision, and she's not wearing a seat belt.

She's been thrown around like a rag doll.

My eyes drop from her face, focusing on her chest. As I wait for movement, I swear my own heart stops beating.

She's breathing.

She has to be breathing.

"I can't lose her, Elliot." My voice cracks. "I just can't. Not like this. Not—"

"You're not going to lose her. Come on, get out of the way." He physically shoves me, forcing me to back up.

"The fuck are you doing? I'm not leaving her." I fight him, shoving him back twice as hard. But he's expecting it.

"Bro, you need to back and let them help her," Reese says, gripping my upper arm in an unforgiving hold and yanking me away from the car.

"Raine," I cry. "I need to be with her."

"She needs the paramedics," Oak says, stepping up to my other side. "Let them do their job. Let them take care of her."

Every single muscle is locked up with my need to fight them off and go to her. But I don't. As much as it might hurt. I know they're right.

She needs them more than she needs me right now.

It fucking rips me apart.

The paramedics, the police, and the firefighters everything blurs to nothing but colours and flashes of light. The sirens, people shouting, it all morphs into white noise as time seems to stand still.

But my eyes never leave her.

Even when I can only see a sliver of her bloodstained skin, I keep my focus on her. Silently begging for her to come back to me. To fight.

To fight for me.

For us.

For the future.

But unable to hear anything, any diagnosis, or updates, I have no idea how hopeful those wishes are.

At some point, the dark, heavy clouds above us can't contain their misery any longer and the rain starts falling, soaking us through in only minutes.

"Come on. We can sit in the car," Elliot says, trying to encourage me to move.

"No," I state. "I'm not moving until she does."

"You're soaked through, Theo. We all are. She doesn't need you getting sick. She's going to need—"

"She needs me right here," I snap. "I'm not fucking moving." When he looks like he's about to argue again, I go for the low blow. "Imagine if that were Abi. Would you willingly fucking move then, ay?" I glance over just in time to see all the blood drain from his face. "No. Exactly. If you want to fuck off and get dry, be my guest. But I am not fucking moving until she does."

It doesn't escape my notice that neither Reese nor Oak say anything or even attempt to move. They get it. They understand.

A warm hand lands on my shoulder. "We got you, man. Whatever you need," Reese assures me.

Together, side by side, in the rain we stand there and watch as the roof of Vaughn's car is cut off and the two of them are gently lifted out and placed onto gurneys.

"She's going to get through this," Oak whispers as we all watch the paramedic's check the oxygen mask they've placed over her mouth as well as the IV they've put into the back of her hand.

"And what about him," I spit, hating that I spare a second of my time to look at Vaughn. "He doesn't deserve to walk away from this."

"Then let's hope he doesn't," Reese mutters.

"And if he does," Elliot adds, "we'll make sure what's left of his life isn't worth living."

It's not until Raine is in the back of the ambulance and the paramedics who have been working on her hop into the back that I force my legs to move.

"I'm coming with you," I demand, racing toward them.

"Oh, I'm sorry, sir. There isn't—"

"Tough," I grunt, hauling myself into the back of the vehicle. "She doesn't have anyone else. I'm not leaving."

I don't need to look at either of them to know they're having a silent conversation over my head as I drop down beside Raine and rest my hand over her cold, bloody one.

"It's going to be okay, sunshine. I'm here. I'm right fucking here."

"Sir, she needs—"

"Her name is Raine. Raine Storm." I glance out of the doors as the wind blows spray from the rain inside. "She's been in the system all her life. She doesn't have any family. Please," I beg. "I'm all she's got. And... and I l-love her."

It's pathetic. I am pathetic. But I don't care. There's no fucking way I'm letting her do this alone.

"Theo, we'll follow, okay? We're right behind you," Elliot shouts as the three of them race toward his car.

The paramedic's eyes land on me and I swallow thickly. "You had better not get in the way," she warns.

"You won't even know I'm here," I promise before turning

back to Raine. "Everything is going to be okay, baby. You'll be partying at the Chapel with us again before you know it."

"Take a seat over there," the paramedic says, pointing to a small fold-down seat.

Reluctantly, I release my hold on Raine and do as I'm told.

I might not like it, but fuck if I'm getting my arse kicked to the curb when my girl needs me most.

"It's been hours," I complain, pacing back and forth through the waiting room.

By the time I was shoved out here by the paramedic whose patience with my interfering had run out, the girls had arrived.

Millie ran full speed, launching herself into my arms before sobbing into the crook of my neck. The others all huddled around, forming a massive group hug which allowed me to cry with my sister without feeling like a zoo exhibit.

"It's barely been an hour," Millie points out, sounding exhausted despite the fact she's right about how much time has passed. "They said it could take a while."

"We're still mostly in the dark about what's wrong with Raine. All we know is that she's okay, but she needed emergency surgery. They won't give us any details. The only person they're willing to talk to is her social worker and she's not here yet. Nor is Christian, who I hope will be able to better convince them that I'm the one they need to talk to.

Fuck the social worker.

Fuck the rules.

Raine is my girl and I'm the one who's going to be there putting her back together.

It's another ten minutes of pacing before familiar faces walk through the doors.

"Dad," Liv cries.

"Christian, please." I rush over to him. "They won't talk to me. I have no idea what's going on. She's in surgery and—"

"Theo, it's going to be okay," Fiona says softly, placing a hand on my upper arm and squeezing gently as Christian makes a beeline for the reception desk.

A handful of terse words are exchanged before Christian nods and turns back to us. "Raine is currently in recovery, you'll be able to go and see her in a few minutes," he says to me.

"Thank you," I breathe, barely holding myself back from throwing my arms around him much like Millie did to me.

"Did you get details of what's wrong?" Fiona asks.

"She's sustained some internal bleeding and a lot of superficial injuries. She was very, very lucky."

"And Vaughn?" Oakley spits, pure venom dripping from him.

"Let's just worry about Raine right now," he suggests, making it clear that he doesn't know.

The next ten minutes pass by in a blur.

Raine's social worker finally shows her face and gets the full rundown of Raine's condition, which although sounds utterly terrifying is mostly cuts, bruises and a concussion. The internal bleeding they took her into surgery for was thankfully nowhere near as bad as they were expecting and they predict she'll make a full recovery after a couple weeks of rest.

Finally, after what feels like forever, I get the nod to go and see her. Well, me and the social worker.

Trudy is nice enough, but something tells me that her and Raine don't exactly see eye to eye. She's all sunshine and roses and my girl, well... she's more of a rainstorm.

The second the nurse opens the door to the private room Christian ensures Raine is placed in, I'm at her side and gently taking her hand in mine. "Sunshine," I whisper, my eyes burning again. "Fuck. That was the most terrifying thing I've ever experienced."

Trudy hovers at the end of the bed, watching us closely.

She's silent for so long as I study every inch of my girl, making note of every single one of her visible wounds, that she startles me when she does finally speak.

"You know, you're exactly the kind of bad influence I warned Raine to stay away from when she started at All Hallows'."

My shoulders tighten and my lips press into a thin line. "Lovely," I grit out. "Well as you can see, she heeded your advice."

"I'm glad she didn't," she confesses. "Raine doesn't tell me much. Or at least, she doesn't think she does. But I knew the moment something changed. There was a lightness in her voice."

Finally, I lift my eyes to the only parent figure Raine has in her life and find them just as glassy as mine must be.

"You probably don't need me to tell you that she's had a rough start in life, Theo. People she should have trusted have let her down time and time again. But you... there's something different about you."

"I love her," I blurt for the second time in a few hours. Spilling my guts to everyone bar the one person who should be hearing the words.

"I can see that. And I think the feeling is mutual." She falls silent despite the fact she clearly wants to say more.

"Go on," I encourage, desperate to hear what she has to say.

"It's not going to be easy. She'll make sure of that." Her lips twist as she glances at Raine again. "But if you fight hard enough, something tells me that it will be more than worth your while."

I nod at her, unable to speak past the huge, messy lump of emotion her words have caused.

But I know. And I totally agree.

Things with Raine might be wild. But I already know it's

going to be worth every second. And anyway, the fighting is often the best part.

"I'm going to give you some space. Here's my number," she says, placing her card on the side. "Call me if you need anything. I'll be back tomorrow to check in on her."

"What about him?" I ask, unable to say his name.

"If he comes through this, he'll be dealt with by the police. But rest assured, Vaughn Ronson will spend a long time behind bars."

I want to tell her that it's not enough, that he should never have gotten close enough to hurt her this time, but I bite back the words. Vaughn isn't my concern right now, Raine is.

"Thank you," I say, forcing the words out.

Thank you for dropping her right into the middle of my fucked-up life.

I had no idea how much I needed her.

30

RAINE

My eyelids flutter open, pain swarming every inch of my body.

God, it hurts.

The dim lighting makes it easier on my eyes. My lips part to speak, to say something but my throat is dry and scratchy and nothing but a weak croak comes out.

"Raine? Fuck, sunshine, are you okay?" Theo grabs my hand, his touch startling me.

I meet his concerned gaze, confusion swimming in my head.

What happened?

Where am I?

Why is he here?

"Can you speak?" he asks.

"W-water," I manage to get out.

"Shit, yeah, of course." He scrambles out of the chair and pours me a cup of water. "Want me to sit you up a little?"

I nod, and he uses the remote to raise the back of my bed. The sudden movement jolts me, sending a fresh wave of pain through me and I gasp.

"Do you need a nurse?"

"N-no. Not yet," I whisper, taking the cup of water from him.

"You have no idea how good it is to see your eyes."

I don't know what to say to that.

He's here...

And I'm—

"Vaughn, is he here?"

Theo's whole demeanour changes, his expression darkening. "Raine, I—"

The door opens and Millie sticks her head inside. "Is she— Raine." Tears pool in her eyes. "You're awake. Thank God, you're—"

"Mills," Theo warns but I wave him off.

"It's okay."

I beckon her over and she takes up position on the opposite side of the bed to her brother.

"Are you okay?"

"I... I don't know," I admit.

I can hardly remember what happened, pieces of it flashing through my mind.

Leaving Theo. Going to the hotel. Stanley Harris. Running. Vaughn. A car chase... tyres screeching, metal grating... Pain, so much pain.

"Raine?" Millie's voice pulls me from the distorted memories. "You're okay now," she says softly. "You're going to be okay."

"I... I don't understand."

"What do you mean?" Millie frowns.

"Why are you here?"

"Because we care about you. Because Theo lo—"

"Why don't you go and let the nurse know she's awake," he suggests.

"Fine. But I'm coming straight back. You can't keep her all to yourself, Theo. I care too."

"I know you do, Mills."

Millie leaves and the air turns thick. Theo watches me, and a trickle of unease goes through me.

"You left," he says quietly.

"I did."

The silence stretches on between us. I can sense he wants to ask me more questions, but I appreciate his restraint. I'm not ready to talk. I still can't get over the fact he's here.

He's not supposed to be here.

I glance away, too overwhelmed at the intensity in his eyes. All the things he's saying without uttering a word.

"Raine, I—"

The door bursts open and a nurse comes inside. "Raine, sweetheart, how are we feeling?"

"Everything hurts."

"That's to be expected. You're one tough cookie."

"I don't feel very tough." I rub my head, wincing at the scratch of the IV disappearing into the back of my hand.

"Well, your boyfriend here hasn't left your side since we brought you up to your room." She gives Theo a bright smile, but it does little to tamp down some of the tension radiating off him.

Boyfriend.

He told them he's my *boyfriend*?

"I had to tell them something to get the paramedics to let me ride in with you," he explains.

I guess that makes sense.

But I still don't understand why he's here.

Why he cares at all after what I did.

The nurse checks my SATS and makes a note on my chart before dropping it back in its holster. "The doctor will be around shortly. If you need more pain relief just shout, okay?"

"Thank you."

"You're in good hands, Raine." She gives me a warm smile before her gaze flicks to Theo.

"Thanks," he says, and she leaves us alone.

"Raine, I—"

"I'm tired," I blurt. "I think I'm going to rest."

"Uh, sure. I'll be right here."

"You don't have to stay. I'm sure you have more important things to be doing."

His eyes narrow. "If that's what you think, you clearly don't know me at all." Anger simmers in his expression but he doesn't let it rip. And it occurs to me, I don't think I've ever seen him so composed.

But I see the cracks.

He wants to give me a piece of his mind. But he won't. Not yet. Not while I'm lying in the hospital broken and bruised.

Unable to bear the tension for a second longer, I close my eyes, hardly surprised when exhaustion sweeps in.

I'm almost asleep when I hear him move. His fingers dance along my forehead, his lips touching my skin there. "I'll be back," he whispers.

The last thought I have is that when he discovers the truth about me, he won't feel the same.

When I wake again, Theo isn't in the room with me, it's Millie. She's curled up on the chair, clutching my hand as if she's scared I'm going to disappear.

"Raine?" she murmurs, sitting up. "You're awake."

"Hi." I force a smile, confusion still blanketing my mind.

"I'll get Theo—"

"No, don't." I rush out. "Not yet."

Her brows furrow. "What's wrong?"

"I don't understand... Why are you here?"

"Oh." She slumps back in the chair and tucks her hair behind her ear. "You didn't think he'd come."

"He wasn't supposed to," I whisper, the words hurting more than I'm willing to acknowledge.

"What? Why would you think that? My brother is—" She stops herself. "Why did you run, Raine? I mean, I know why. Because of him, right? Vaughn."

I nod, refusing to meet her stare.

"Were you worried we'd find out... about your past? About what he did?"

They know.

Of course they do.

I'd known it the second I woke up and realised hearing Theo's voice wasn't a dream.

"How did you..." I trail off, finally lifting my eyes to hers.

"They pulled your file."

"My file..."

Icy cold dread goes through me.

Theo knows.

He knows the deepest darkest corners of my soul. The things I did. The thing I let Vaughn do...

God.

"It doesn't matter, Raine." She squeezes my hand again. "All that matters is that you're here and you're safe now."

I wish I could believe her.

But once this gets out. Once everyone finds out... Theo won't want to be anywhere near me.

"I wish you could see how much my brother—"

The door opens and he appears. He looks as bad as I feel. Hair dishevelled and dark rings circling his eyes.

"I'll give the two of you some space." Millie gets up and lets go of my hand. I want to tell her to stay. To beg her not to leave me alone with him. But the words get stuck because Theo's looking at me and I can't breathe.

I can't...

"How are you feeling?" He comes to the side of the bed.

"Like I barely survived the end of the world."

Something flashes in his eyes, but he shoves it away. "Fuck, sunshine. You really had me scared there for a minute."

"I... I'm sorry."

The unspoken words hang between us.

"You left me." Hurt coats his voice. "You ran."

"I had no choice."

"There's always a choice, Raine."

"Not in my world."

Silence hangs between us. Thick and heavy. I don't know what to say to fix this. I ran and he wasn't supposed to come after me.

"You stole money from me."

"I did." Shame crushes my chest as I glance away, breaking the tether between us.

I'd taken the stash in his bottom drawer. "I needed a way to put as much space between me and—"

I can't say his name.

I won't.

"You could have told me."

The words land like a blow to my chest.

How?

How could I ever tell him the truth?

"We both know I couldn't," I say.

"Because you think I care about where you came from, what you survived?"

My eyes lift to his, the emotion I see in his expression sucking the air clean from my lungs. "Don't you?"

"Fuck, sunshine, when I realised you'd left... I didn't handle it well." He drags a hand down his face, exhaling a steady breath.

"I'm sorry. I never wanted to hurt you. But I couldn't stay, I couldn't—" The words die on my tongue as my eyelashes flutter.

Everything hurts.

My body. My head... My heart.

So much pain and betrayal.

"It doesn't matter." Theo takes my hand in his. "I've never felt this way before Raine, and I wasn't lying when I said you were mine."

"Theo," I sigh. "The things I've done... the things I've let—"

"I. Don't. Care." He leans in, forcing himself into my space. "Seeing the truck hit you, knowing I might lose you... I never want to experience that again. It's you and me sunshine, you and me against the world."

If only it was that easy.

I manage a weak smile, unsure of what else to say.

He's saying all the right things, but our relationship won't weather this storm.

My history.

He thinks it doesn't matter now, but it will.

It will eat away at him, driving a wedge between us, deeper and deeper.

Theo is destined for greatness. A life of the rich and privileged. I'll be nothing more than his dirty little secret.

People will always wonder why he chose me. What I did to trap him.

I don't want that for him.

I don't want that for me.

"Tell me what you're thinking," he whispers, brushing his thumb over the back of my hand.

"I..." My voice fails me.

Where do I even begin?

"I want you to come home with me. When you're better and they let you out of here, I want—"

"Theo, we need to talk about this. About us. I'm not sure—"

"No, sunshine. No." A flash of irritation passes over him, but he composes himself.

"I need you to hear me, right now, okay." He grips my hand tighter, staring at me with wonder. "I love you, Raine Storm," he says with a possessive edge that sends a shiver down my spine.

"I fucking love you and I'm not letting you go ever again."

31

THEO

Excitement tingles in my chest as I nod at the nurse manning the desk in the ward that Raine has been kept in for the last four days as she's recovered from the worst of her injuries from the crash.

She was lucky. Really fucking lucky.

And fuck am I relieved.

I get to take her home today. Get to tuck her up into my bed and take care of her. That concept isn't something I thought I'd ever be looking forward to.

But I am.

I want to be the one making her soup and bringing it to her in bed. I want to be the one to help her into the shower and reapply her dressings after. Fuck, I just want her.

In my arms, in my life, in my bed.

If I thought I wanted her before all of this happened, I was gravely mistaken. Because watching her almost die in that collision has turned my addiction to her up to the max. If I had my way, then I wouldn't have left this place. I didn't for two days, but once she woke, she looked at me with pain darkening her eyes and I knew what was coming.

She's ashamed of her past, of the things she's done. Been forced to do.

But she shouldn't be.

I'm in love with her.

Her.

Not only her past. Not only her future. Not just parts of her.

All of her.

She's incredible. Strong, independent, wild, funny, intelligent, resilient. Hot. Did I ever mention hot?

My fists clench as the image of her curled up in my bed that's been helping get me through the last few days flickers through my mind again.

Fuck, I can't wait.

Voices hit the second I step into her room, and I find Trudy helping Raine into her hoodie.

My teeth grind at the sight. I should be the one doing that.

"Ah, look. Here is your taxi," Trudy says with a wide smile.

But while Raine's lips twitch in the right direction when our eyes meet, she's nowhere near as excited as her social worker.

I've told her over and over since she woke that I don't care about what's happened. That none of us care about her past. But she can't get past it. She doesn't believe she's good enough for me, for us, for this life, and I fucking hate it.

"All the discharge paperwork has been completed. She's a free woman," Trudy says with a smile as I grab the small bag of belongings Raine's collected during her short stay.

Silence follows her words, and she looks nervously between the two of us.

"I've got this. None of the staff here have anything on Doctor Theo Ashworth," I announce arrogantly, and thankfully, Raine scoffs a laugh.

"There's my girl," I whisper, reaching out to cup her jaw. "Ready to go home, sunshine?" I ask, searching her eyes.

They shutter and she nods. Although if I weren't touching her, I'd have no idea she's done it.

"Okay, well. I'm just getting in the way," Trudy says. "I'll swing by and see you tomorrow, Raine. See how you're settling in."

When Raine doesn't respond, Trudy gives us a lingering smile before dipping out of the room.

I've no idea how she got so lucky for her to have a social worker who seems to trust us, but I'm not knocking it. Although I think Christian and Fiona may have had a helping hand in that department.

"Do you have everything you need?" I ask, glancing around the room and searching for stray belongings.

"Yes," she whispers.

She gets to her feet without my help and shuffles toward the door. While she might be well enough to leave, that doesn't mean that she isn't still suffering from the after-effects of the crash. Her body is battered and bruised. It's going to be quite a while until she's back in full form again.

But that's okay, as long as she gets there eventually.

"Whoa, wait for me."

"I'm not an invalid," she snaps.

"I know that, sunshine. But you're hurting. I fucking hate it. Let me get you a wheelchair."

Without even bothering to respond to that comment, she pushes forward and shuffles through the door.

"Shit," I hiss. Stepping up behind her, I wrap my arm around her waist.

"You don't need to do any of this. I'm—"

"I do," I state. "I need to do all of it and more. You're my girl, Raine. Whatever you need, I'm here for it. Always."

She sighs, letting her head hang, refusing to accept or believe my words.

That's okay. She might not want to hear them now, but one day soon she will, and even better, she'll believe them.

Slowly, we make our way to the lift but before we get there, she pauses at the sign showing what floor all the wards are on.

My heart sinks the second she begins scanning the text before her because I know what—or who—she's looking for.

"It's over, Raine. You don't—"

"Intensive care is on the fourth floor."

"Raine," I sigh.

"I know what you think," she whispers. "But this isn't about you. It's about me, Theo. And I need—" A shudder goes through her. "You just said that you're here for—"

"I meant it. I just don't want you in any more pain than you need to be in."

"I need to see him, Theo. I need... closure, I guess."

It's selfish and ridiculous but hearing that she wants to see him, a guy who's had such an impact on her life, a man she thought she loved once upon a time, makes something tight and painful wrap around my chest.

The only man I want her to think about is me. I want her eyes on me and no one else. It's possessive and over the top but I can't help it.

She's mine.

I'm hers.

And that's the way it's always going to be.

"Okay," I force out, taking a step closer to the lift with her still tucked into my side.

My heart is in my throat as we climb through the building. And I'm not the only one struggling because Raine trembles from head to toe.

I want to tell her that she doesn't need to do this, but clearly, for some reason, she feels that she has to, and who am I to argue with her?

I might know some of the details of her past, of their

relationship, but I will never fully understand what she went through. What he meant to her at one time in her life. All I can do is hold her hand and hope that doing this will help her deal with it all and move on.

We go through the rigmarole of getting buzzed in and the second we turn the corner to his room, the cop guarding it hops up, his eyes wide at the sight of Raine.

"Miss Storm, I'm not sure this—"

"I just need a minute. Please," she begs, giving him her best puppy dog eyes.

He studies her for a beat, but before I can add anything he says, "I'm just going to turn my back and look at the view for a bit. Do not do anything stupid."

"Thank you," Raine breathes, turning toward the door the second the cop looks the other way.

With my hand pressed against the small of her back, I follow her into the room.

Vaughn's been up here since his own surgery the night they arrived, but I haven't been to see the cunt who tried to kill my girl. He's already dead to me as far as I'm concerned.

Monitors, tubes, and more medical equipment than I've seen in my life surround the bed in the middle of the room.

"Oh my God," Raine mutters, moving closer to the waste of space all this has been wasted on.

They should have left him to rot in the front of his car as far as I'm concerned.

"He's sure looked better," I confess, my eyes focusing on his grey complexion.

"Do you think he's going to make it?" Raine asks absently.

"No idea. I hope not."

Her breath catches, but she doesn't argue.

She can't.

He's a piece of shit who's done nothing but ruin her life.

He deserves this. And more.

I've no idea what's spinning through her head as she

stands there staring at him. I'm hoping it's the closure she was looking for, but I can't stop the fear that despite everything, there still might be something there.

I don't do anything or say anything, I just stand beside her, praying that I'm giving her some kind of support.

The seconds feel like hours as we watch his chest rise and fall thanks to the ventilator beside him. How easy would it be to just turn it off?

I'm so lost in my thoughts of how I could end the fucker right here, right now that when she speaks, it startles me.

"Let's go," she says coldly.

"U-uh, yeah."

Glancing down, I find silent tears staining her cheeks. "Sunshine?"

"I'm okay. I just... I need to get the hell out of this place."

"Fuck, baby. You've got it."

If I never return, it'll be too fucking soon.

In only minutes, we step out through the main entrance into the bright winter sun. She winces at the brightness, but she doesn't cower. She also doesn't say anything.

And she doesn't until we're in my car and halfway back home.

"Thank you," she whispers. "I know you didn't want to do that."

"Anything. I told you I'd do anything for you," I promise again, reaching for her hand and twisting our fingers together.

"Why?" she asks, keeping her eyes locked on the passing scenery.

"Why, what, sunshine?"

"Why me? Why all this?"

"Raine," I breathe, a laugh of disbelief spilling from my lips. "Because you deserve it. Because you're everything. Because I lo—"

"You can't," she argues, cutting off my words. "I'm not—"

"You're perfect. You're everything to me."

She falls silent, the air surrounding us turning thick.

"You deserve more than me, Theo. More than—"

"Raine, I know what you're doing and it's not going to work. You can tell me that you're unworthy and not good enough as much as you like, it's not going to change my mind. You're it for me. And I promise that for each time you tell me you're not good enough, I'll tell you that you are five times over.

"I'm not going anywhere, okay? I will do anything and everything to prove all of this to you, starting with making sure you get better. Then you're going to go back to school and you're going to hold your head high because you deserve your place at All Hallows' just as much as every other motherfucker who walks those halls.

"We're going to study together. We're going to do our exams together, and then we're gonna have an epic fucking summer together."

"But—"

"Maybe I'll defer a year," I say before she can say anything about my future. "Millie will need me around no doubt. Then we can start uni together."

"Oh no. No, Theo. No."

"Okay," I concede. "This is all shit for the future. Right now, let's just get inside. I need to hold you so fucking bad."

She glances over as I pull into my space outside the Chapel. All her arguments are right on the tip of her tongue, but my silent warning and her exhaustion keep them from spilling free.

"Come on," I say, killing the engine. "The others have gone out to give us some space to get settled."

Raine studies me before turning to look at the Chapel in the distance. She sighs, and it's full of pain and uncertainty. I promise myself there and then that I'm going to banish both as soon as physically possible.

Without another word, I push the door open and climb

out. Grabbing her bag from the back, I get to the passenger side just in time for her to open the door herself. "Hey," I complain. "I'm meant to do that."

She stares up at me with her big violet eyes and my heart tumbles in my chest.

This is it.

From here on out, it's the two of us against the world. And no other motherfucker is going to stop it.

32

RAINE

Theo watches me, the intensity in his gaze almost too much to bear.

I know he means well. He's been there every step of the way since I woke up five days ago in the hospital.

But I'm not ready for this.

I don't know if I'll ever be ready.

The heavy door of the Chapel bangs shut, making me flinch.

"Home, sweet home," Theo says with a playful tone. But it's lost on me.

"I can't stay here," I say.

"What?" He frowns. "Of course, you can. I'm going to take care of you."

"Theo—"

"No, sunshine. I need to do this. Let me do this, okay?"

"I... okay."

Relief washes over his expression. "Come on, let's get you up to my room."

Weary, I follow him upstairs and into his bedroom. He falters for a second, and I wonder if he's remembering my betrayal. The money I stole. The fact that the last time I was here, was the last time things were okay between us.

"Do you want to sleep?"

"I'm not sure I can."

Every time I close my eyes, I see Vaughn's face.

"We can watch a film. Or one of those trashy TV series Millie thinks I don't know she watches."

"Whatever," I murmur.

Theo pulls back the bed covers and offers me one of his Saints t-shirts. "Need some help getting changed?" he asks.

"I think I've got it." I snatch the t-shirt from his hands. He gives me a sharp nod, but I know he's confused. I can sense it.

Making quick work of changing, I climb into his bed and pull the covers over me.

"I'm going to get you a glass of water and sort out your painkillers."

"Thanks," I whisper, barely acknowledging him.

"Raine, I..." He stops himself and relief flows through me.

I don't want to have the hard conversations yet.

Maybe ever.

Something inside cracked when I saw that truck barrelling toward us. When I accepted that I was going to die.

Only, I didn't.

And now I'm here and Theo thinks everything will just go back to how it was before.

But how can it?

He knows the truth now.

They all do.

And it won't be long before the whole town knows about my dark, sordid past.

I'm not ready to deal with that.

So I do the only thing I can.

I close my eyes and pray darkness will find me.

I wake with a start.

It takes me a second to realise where I am. Whose arm is wrapped around my waist, holding me tight as if he's scared I might disappear at any moment.

I'm frozen in place while Theo snores softly behind me.

It's late, darkness shrouding the room.

I must have slept the entire day away. Which means I need to pee.

Gently, I move Theo's arm away and try to shimmy to the edge of the bed. My body cries out in protest, but I swallow the pain, determined to do this.

Managing to sit up, I give myself a couple of seconds.

A couple of seconds too long.

"What are you doing?" Theo murmurs from behind me.

"I need the toilet."

"Why didn't you wake me? I'll help you."

"I can do it by myself."

"Raine, come on..."

"Fine." I admit defeat because my body is too weak and everything hurts too much.

Theo climbs out of bed and comes around to me. Hair everywhere, a sleepy expression on his face, he looks adorable. "Okay." He bends down a little. "Wrap your arms around my neck."

"What?"

"I'm going to carry you."

"Theo, I don't need carrying. I can—"

"Just humour me, sunshine."

Relenting, I wrap my arms around his neck, and he lifts me, cradling me against his chest. "How are you feeling?"

"Like I got hit by a truck."

"Raine..." He grimaces.

"Too soon?"

"What am I going to do with you?" He gives a little shake

of his head as he carries me into the bathroom, carefully lowering me to my feet.

But he doesn't release me. Instead, he leans in, touching his forehead to mine, and inhaling a shaky breath. "You're here," he whispers.

My heart aches at the vulnerability in his voice. Aches with the desire to fix this—fix us. But I don't know if I can, not this time.

"Can I... kiss you?"

"I-I really need to pee." I pull away, breaking the connection between us.

Dejection glitters in Theo's eyes but he gives me a small nod, stepping back to give me some privacy. "I'll be right outside."

"Thanks."

He leaves, taking the air with him.

Theo is here, and it's all I wanted.

But everything is different now.

I'm different.

And I'm not sure I'll ever find my way back to the girl I was before.

I thought going to see Vaughn would give me some closure. To know he couldn't hurt me anymore. But it only filled me with an overwhelming degree of hurt and anger. He ruined everything.

He ruined me.

And I don't know how to make peace with that.

I manage to go to the toilet and wash my hands. The second I open the door, Theo scoops me back up in his arms and carries me back to bed, laying me down like I'm something fragile and precious.

"Where's Millie?" I ask, trying to keep the conversation away from us.

"Downstairs on the couch. She refused to leave but I didn't want..." He trails off, climbing in the bed beside me.

"She could have stayed in with us."

"I thought you might want some space." He searches my eyes for answers I can't give him. "How's your pain? I didn't want to wake you earlier for your painkillers so you can have them now."

"I think I'll be okay."

"You sure? You don't have to try and put on a brave face, not with me."

"Honestly, I'm fine."

"I know things are fucked up but don't shut me out, Raine. Please."

"I... I just don't understand how you can still want me."

"I told you, it doesn't matter. I love you, sunshine." He cups my face. "I can't pretend to know what's going through your head right now but I'm not going anywhere, okay. It's you and me, babe."

He makes it sound so easy. And part of me wants to believe him, to let go of the past and embrace the future he's offering.

But something inside me won't let me.

"Just tell me what you need." The desperation in his voice makes my breath catch.

"I... I'm tired. Can we talk about this later? When it isn't the middle of the night?"

"Yeah." He gives me a reassuring smile, but it doesn't reach his eyes. "Sleep, sunshine. I've got you." Theo wraps his arm around my waist, dragging me closer, and I let him.

Because while things might not be straightforward between us, he's still here.

I still love him.

And for now, it's enough.

The next time I wake, Theo isn't watching me.

But Millie is.

"You're awake." She bolts out of the chair and comes over to the bed, wasting no time climbing up beside me.

"Hi, what time is it?"

"A little after ten. Theo said it's the trauma."

"He said you slept downstairs on the couch," I say.

"I didn't want to leave in case you..."

"In case I ran again?" She nods and something inside me twists with guilt. "You know me leaving had nothing to do with you, right?"

"I know. But it still hurt. I thought we were friends. I thought..." The hurt in her gaze drives the knife in my heart a little deeper.

"Millie, look at me." She lifts her head and I reach for her hand, twining our fingers together. "My life before I came here was... complicated."

"You could have told Theo. Or me. Or somebody. You almost died, Raine. We almost lost you."

"I'm sorry."

"Just don't do it again." She squeezes my hand, tears clinging to her lashes. "He needs you, we both do."

I don't answer, I can't. Because I'm not sure where we go from here, but I don't want to tell her that.

I'm such a coward.

I always wanted to be a part of something so much but deep down, I never thought I'd get to have it.

Now I have the world at my feet, and I'm scared.

I'm so scared that my past, the girl underneath the bravado and attitude will never be good enough for a boy like Theo Ashworth.

"Do you need anything? A drink? Something to eat?"

"Some water."

"Of course. Here." She gets up and comes around the other side of the bed, helping me to sit up before offering me a glass.

"You have to take your painkillers four times a day. Theo wrote a reminder in his phone. He's taking this whole Nurse Theo thing very seriously." Her smile is infectious and for the first time since waking up a genuine smile curves at my lips.

"I bet the boys aren't very happy I'm here."

"What? Are you kidding? Everyone's so relieved that you're here and you're okay. The girls have been bugging Theo to see you, but he doesn't want you to feel crowded."

"But I thought—"

"What? You thought that they'd all hate you now?"

"Honestly, I don't know what I thought. But I'm not like them, Millie. You all have to know that. The things I've done..."

"Don't matter. You're one of us, Raine. My brother loves you. *You*." She smiles. "And I'm not sure he's ever loved anything except himself."

"He loves you," I point out.

"Yeah, I guess he does. In his own annoying Theo way." Her soft laughter dies, and her expression turns sombre. "Theo said you went to see him... Vaughn, I mean. Do you... do you want to talk about it?"

Pressing my lips into a thin line, I shake my head.

"Okay. But I'm here, whenever you're ready. And if you never want to talk about it, that's fine too. Miss Linley will also be there. She's glad you're okay."

"You talked to her about me?" I ask, surprised.

"I was worried. About you, about Theo. I know she's an adult, but I trust her."

"It's good you have someone to talk to, Mills."

"I have you too, right?"

"Yeah," I whisper.

I can't deny this kid.

Even if I don't want to make any promises, she's impossible to say no to.

"My brother will—" The door opens, and Theo appears

with a tray of food. "Speak of the devil," Millie stands. "I'm going to find the girls. Elliot promised to make me and Abi pancakes again."

"You can stay and eat with us," I say, unsure I'm ready to be alone with Theo again just yet.

"No, that's okay. I'm sure my brother wants you all to himself. But I'll come and check on you later."

"Okay."

"Thanks for keeping her company," Theo says as they pass each other.

The second the door closes behind Millie, the air shifts.

"How are you feeling?" he asks me, setting the tray down on the desk.

"Honestly, I don't know."

He studies me as he slowly advances toward the bed. My breath gets stuck in my throat the closer he comes, until he's right there. Looming over me.

"Hi," he says, dropping to his knees.

"Hi."

"I'm sorry I wasn't here when you woke up, but I really needed to eat. And I wanted to fill everyone in."

"It's fine. You don't need to be with me twenty-four seven."

"Don't do that."

"Do what?"

"Try to play this down. I want to be here. I'm going to be here." Theo reaches for my hair, pushing it out of my face a little. "You're a mess, sunshine."

"Is that your idea of looking after me?" I lift a brow. "Because your bedside manner kind of sucks."

"Do you think you can manage a shower?"

"Yeah, I think so." Theo nods, standing. He starts pulling off his polo shirt and I frown. "What are you doing?"

"I'm going to clean you."

"Theo—"

"Humour me, sunshine. It's taking everything in me not to

drive back to the hospital and not kill that piece of shit myself. I can't control what happened to you, but I can control this. So if you don't want me to do something really fucking stupid, then please just—"

"Yes."

"Yes?" His brows pinch as if he expected more resistance.

"Yes, Teddy." I offer him a small smile. "You can shower me."

33

THEO

Wearing only my boxers, I help Raine out of bed, and with my arm around her waist, we shuffle toward the bathroom.

She's stronger than she was when she woke in the middle of the night, but I know it's going to be short-lived.

She needs this though. She needs to wash the events of the last few days off her skin. I know it won't help with the memories or the pain but it's a start, right?

Raine stands in the middle of my bathroom with my t-shirt hanging from her curled-in shoulders. I've never seen her looking so defeated and I hate it.

I want my sassy, defiant sunshine to come back.

I want her to look me in the eyes and tell me what she really thinks of me. Hell, I'd even take her kneeing me in the balls over this... this... emptiness.

"Okay?" I ask softly as I wrap my fingers around the hem of my t-shirt, needing her permission to drag it from her body.

She nods once but her eyes never meet mine, instead they stay on the tiles beneath our feet.

"Sunshine," I whisper, releasing the shirt in favour of her jaw. "Are you with me?" I gently encourage her to look up. It takes a few more seconds but her eyes finally follow, locking on mine.

The darkness in them makes my breath catch.

"It's going to get better, I promise," I say, resting my brow against hers.

"If you say so," she murmurs.

"Raine," I sigh, wishing I could do more, do anything that would help fix this.

Her palm lands in the centre of my chest and my eyes shutter at the contact. "Don't," she warns. "Just... shower," she says, her eyes dropping again.

With a nod, I go back to her dragging my shirt up her body, revealing the bruises lingering beneath. I saw her get changed when we got back yesterday, but I didn't get a chance to really see her.

"Jesus, sunshine," I whisper, my eyes darting from bruise to bruise, the small dressing on her stomach.

No wonder she's in so much pain.

Raine wouldn't tell me what happened leading up to the car chase that night, but I got the CliffsNotes version from Christian, thanks to his friends on the police force. I know she was at that hotel to pull a job with Vaughn.

I want to believe that nothing happened, but from the haunted look in her eyes, I'm not so sure.

Fuck, it kills me to think about what she's endured over the years at the hands of that sick fuck, but I won't ever force her to tell me anything. I meant what I said, it doesn't matter. When—*if*—she ever trusts me with that information, I'll listen but until then, I'll focus on the only thing that does matter.

Her.

"They look worse than—"

"Don't lie to me. I can handle it. More than handle it." Leaning forward, I press a quick kiss on her brow before dropping to my knees in front of her and tucking my fingers into her knickers.

"Theo," she warns.

I look up at her, and my heart skips a beat when I find her looking down at me. "You'd do exactly the same for me and you know it," I tell her, confident that I'm right.

Something familiar twinkles in her eyes and her lips part as if she's going to shoot back some witty remark about not giving a shit about me, but just before it rolls off her tongue, she bites it back.

"Just you wait until I have a rough match. I'll be cashing in all these favours for you to patch me up. Lean on me," I say as I wait for her to lift her leg. "That's it, babe."

The second I shed my own underwear, I pull Raine into my arms and walk us into the shower. Keeping her out of the spray, I turn it on and get blasted by cold water. It's not until it's warm and I switch our positions and let her stand under the torrent.

A filthy moan rips from her lips as the powerful stream hits her shoulders and despite my desire to keep this about her and her healing, my cock jerks at the sound.

"Good?" I ask, needing to focus on her.

"Yeah," she whispers.

Reaching for a bottle of shower gel, I squeeze a generous blob onto my sponge and get to work. With every gentle swipe of the bubbles, I lean forward and press a kiss to the darkened skin.

I have no idea how to make her understand that the past she's so ashamed of doesn't bother me. But this has to be a step in the right direction.

Once her top half is thoroughly clean, I return to my position on my knees in front of her and continue working. She stares down at me with wide, tear-filled eyes. But at no point does she let them fall.

By the time I stand again, I'm fully hard and ready for action. Not that I have any intention of getting any. But I can't help myself. My girl is standing before me naked and wet. My self-control is only so good.

And she doesn't miss it—not that she could. Her eyes lock on my dick and she stumbles back a little.

"Turn around," I instruct, not wanting her to think I'm expecting anything.

I trade the sponge for shampoo, and I get about washing her hair. My cock brushes against her arse, and every time she moans as I massage her hair, it jerks in excitement, but I never take it any further.

The next time we mess around it's going to be because *she* initiates it. I just have to be patient while she works through all this shit in her head.

She'll get there, I know she will.

I just wish I knew how long it'll take. I want my girl back.

By the time we're done, she's obviously flagging. Turning the shower off, I grab a big fluffy towel, wrap it gently around her body and sweep her off her feet.

"Theo," she shrieks, wrapping her arms around my neck and holding tight.

I sit her on the edge of the bed and step back. "Don't move," I say before rushing back to get a towel for myself and pulling open the bottom drawer of my dresser to reveal Raine's hairdryer and a brush.

"How?" she questions as I plug it in next to the bed and move closer.

"Told you, babe. This is home now. Everything you need is here."

Climbing onto the bed behind her, I gently brush her hair before turning the dryer on and blowing it straight.

By the time I'm done, she's almost asleep sitting up, but I think I've done a pretty good job. Replacing her towel with another of my t-shirts, I encourage her back into bed and lie beside her.

"Thank you," she whispers, her eyes closed, her body exhausted.

"Anything, sunshine. We're going to get through this together, okay?"

She murmurs something inaudible, but I tell myself it was a whispered, 'okay'.

The next two days continue much the same. I might get the odd glimpse of my Raine, but as soon as it emerges, she shuts it down as if she's scared of herself.

She lets me shower her again, but other than more kisses to her fading bruises, that's all she allows me to do.

I get it. I do. But I... I wish she'd start opening up.

There are so many things we need to talk about and until we do, I don't think we're going to be able to move forward.

I know she's scared. Ashamed, even. But I need to show her that she doesn't need to feel that way.

Not with me.

"How's she doing?" Abi asks, jumping up from the table where she was sitting with Liv drinking coffee.

"Same," I say, letting out a resigned sigh.

Dropping into the chair next to Liv, she reaches up and squeezes my shoulder in support. "She'll get there."

"I know," I murmur. "I just wish she'd talk. Tell me about everything she's been through. Exorcise it, I guess."

"She will," Abi says with a confidence I don't feel. "She just needs time. Raine has never had anyone in her life she's been able to trust before. She thinks you're going to run because shit has got hard."

"But I'm not. I'm right here. Right fucking here," I say, my frustration forcing me to slam my curled fist against the table.

"We know. And deep down, so does she. It's just alien to her. She's trying to protect herself and—"

"I feel like a prick for even talking about this after everything she's been through." An exasperated breath rolls through me. "It's just driving me crazy."

"We get it, Theo," Abi says softly, placing a coffee in front of me. "Her past is complex. She needs time to sort through it."

"And having that prick still breathing—albeit barely—can't be helping things. Why won't he just die and put her out of her misery? Fuck," I bark, slumping back in the chair.

"Surely Dad knows someone who can—"

"You are not seriously suggesting what I think you are, are you?" Abi asks Liv, sounding horrified.

"Sure. Why not?" She lifts her shoulder in a shrug. "It's not like he deserves to breathe the same air as any of us after everything he's done."

"I'd do it if I could," I confess. "It was all I could think about when she visited him. Pulling one of those cables and watching the prick die right in front of us."

"Jesus, Theo," Abi breathes.

"Sorry. I just... I fucking love her and I want her to understand what that really means. I don't know what to do. It's killing me."

"Has she said anything to Millie?" Liv asks.

I shake my head. "Not that she's said. She's just... it's like she's shut down and nothing I do will wake her up."

"It's only been a few days, it's still early days."

"I know I'm a selfish, impatient prick."

"You're not," Liv assures me, reaching for my hand. "You're worried. We all are. It's normal. You think she might want to come down for a little bit today?" she asks.

The girls have been asking Raine to come and join everyone for a couple of days now, but she keeps refusing.

I shrug. "I'll ask again."

"Let me," Abi says, pushing to stand, her face set with determination.

The temptation to stop her bubbles right under the

surface, but I hold it back. As much as it'll pain me to watch someone else succeed where I've failed the past few days, maybe it's what she needs.

Some girl time.

"Why don't you go out for a bit?" Liv asks. "Reese and Oak are in the gym. Maybe go and beat the shit out of them. Might help."

My fists curl, the thought of going a few rounds with my best friends filling my head.

"We'll look after her. Go and blow off some steam and leave us to try and talk to Raine."

Sucking in a deep breath, I stare at her for a beat. "Yeah, yeah okay," I say, draining my coffee in three big gulps and pushing to stand. "I'll be forty minutes tops."

"Take your time. We know what we're doing."

I eye her suspiciously.

"Trust us. I'm going to call Tally and we're going to chill. Might watch Magic Mike or something. All those abs are a sure-fire way to cheer up any girl down in the dumps."

"Raine doesn't need to look at a screen for that." Shamelessly, I lift my shirt, showing off what I'm rocking.

Liv barely glances at my stomach. I guess it's nothing she hasn't seen before.

"Go. Go beat the crap out of my boyfriend. Losing always makes him horny as fuck, so you'll be doing me a favour really," she chuckles.

"I'm going to tell Oak that," I warn.

"Go for it. If he's really lucky, I'll make sure I take Reese's edge off while he's in the same room." She smirks.

"Stay away from my little sister," I say darkly.

Liv chuckles again. "Theo, you're in for a world of pain in the coming years. I can't bloody wait," she says, rubbing her hands together in excitement.

"For that, I'm not going to touch your boy," I snap. "Find someone else to do your bidding."

Her laughter follows me as I make my way to the front door. Pulling my phone out, I shoot my sister a message.

> Theo: Heading to the gym. Raine is having girl time. You're welcome to join.

I add that last bit with gritted teeth. But while I might tease Liv about being a bad influence, really, I don't mean it. Millie would be lucky to have a big sister like her.

> Millie: Can't right now. Hanging with a friend. But I'll swing by later. x

Happy that my girls are both as okay as they can be. I head toward where my boys are waiting, the need to cause some pain surging through me like wildfire.

I just have to hope that time with the girls will be as healing for Raine as I know time with my boys will be for me.

34

RAINE

Every day my bruises fade and my wounds heal.

I feel stronger, better. But my mental state only worsens.

I barely leave Theo's room, refusing to see the girls. Even Millie visits less.

Not that I blame her.

I'm not good company right now.

But I don't know how to find myself again.

Theo says and does all the right things. He's patient and sweet and handles me like I'm fragile glass, ready to shatter at any moment.

But I think part of me died in that accident.

A bit of my soul that I'll never get back.

Every night, Theo pulls me into his arms and whispers that he loves me. And right then, in the moment, it feels like he's slowly stitching me back together.

Until the morning rolls around, and I feel as bleak and lost as I did the day before.

Trudy is worried.

I'm still seventeen for another couple of weeks.

If things don't improve, she could push the court to look at my case. I could end back up in a group home.

Miss Linley stopped by yesterday, wanting to talk. But I pretended to be sleeping. I'm not ready to be psychoanalysed. Picked and pulled apart by her.

A knock at Theo's bedroom door, pulls me from the dark thoughts circling my mind.

I don't answer though, hoping whoever it is will go away.

"Raine," Abi calls. "Can I come in?"

When I don't answer, she lets herself in.

"I'm asleep." I roll onto my side, giving her my back.

"The girls and I wondered if you wanted to hang out?"

"Maybe another day."

"Nope. Not going to work, not today." Tally rounds the bed and looms over me. "We've let you stew in here long enough. Either you come down and spend some time with us, or we'll camp out here. But we are having some girl time. It's your choice."

"I said—"

"Here or downstairs?" Conviction burns in her eyes, and I know this is one fight I won't win.

They've gone easy on me, I realise that now. The Heirs and their girlfriends don't pander to people, they bulldoze. They get what they want, when they want it. And it would seem my time is up.

"Fine, you can stay," I relent.

"Wasn't asking for your permission but I'm glad you came to your senses." Her mouth twists with amusement. "You hungry? We brought snacks."

Liv drops a grocery bag on the end of the bed. "I didn't know what you preferred, so I got one of everything."

"You got... why am I not surprised," I murmur, making no move to look in the bag.

I'm not hungry.

In fact, I don't feel much of anything these days.

"Theo and the boys are at the gym beating the crap out of each other."

"Good for them."

"Is that all you've got to say?" Liv arches her brow. "You know they work out half-naked, right? All those hard sweaty abs on display."

"I don't know what you want me to say."

"Anything would be better than nothing."

"I'm tired, I can't—"

"You're not tired, you're hiding." Tally perches on the edge of the bed, taking my hand in hers. "And that's okay. We get it. Honestly, I think I'd be hiding too if I was you. But we want you to know that you don't have to hide from us."

"I'm not hi—"

"Raine." Abi takes my other hand. "It's okay. We know you went through something huge but we're here for you. All of us."

"I..."

They watch me expectantly, waiting for my walls to crumble no doubt.

Strangely, I find myself waiting too.

But nothing happens.

Because I'm broken inside.

I'm—

A rush of emotion surges inside me, catching me off guard. I haven't cried since the day I woke up in the hospital. It was like all my tears just dried up. But my eyes burn now, my throat clogging as everything comes crashing down around me.

"It's okay, Raine. We're here," Tally whispers, pulling me into her arms. "We're right here."

I don't understand what's happening as I sob into her chest, all the pain and hurt crashing over me like a relentless tidal wave.

"I hate him," I wail. "I hate him. I hate him. I hate him."

No one corrects me or tries to ask why. They know I'm not talking about Theo.

No, this is about the trauma and pain caused by the man lying in hospital.

The man who ruined my life twice over.

"Do you want to talk about it?" Abi asks softly, and I lift my head.

"I... I can't."

"Okay, but you need to talk to someone, Raine. You've been through so much. You can't carry all of this around with you."

I nod, because finding words right now is impossible.

"I'm so sorry," I murmur as the tears recede.

"No, we're not doing that," Tally says. "You're our friend. You don't owe us anything, but Abi's right. If you do ever want to talk, we're here. No strings. No judgement."

"Thank you."

I don't think they'll ever realise how much their friendship means to me. Things didn't start off great between the four of us but over time, they all burrowed their way past my defences and the truth is, I don't want to dig them out.

I've never had girlfriends before. Not the kind that don't want to stab you in the back the second you turn around anyway.

"We promised Theo we'd get you to do something other than hide up here and mope. How about we put on a film and binge on some of the snacks Liv brought?"

"I think... that sounds like a really good idea." I smile.

For the first time since waking up in the hospital, a flicker of hope lights up inside me.

I don't know what the future holds.

But maybe, just maybe everything will be okay.

"Shh, she's sleeping."
"How is she?"
"I think she's going to be okay."
"Did she... open up to you?"
"Not really but she cried a lot. I think that's a good sign."

Their whispers get further away as I slowly rouse from a deep sleep. When I finally crack my eyes open, the girls are gone, and Theo is pulling off his hoodie.

He doesn't realise I'm watching until he climbs into bed and lies on his side, facing me. "Did I wake you?" he asks.

"Yeah, but it's okay. What time is it?"

"Like three or something. The boys put me through my paces, and I ache like a bitch. Did you have a nice time with the girls?"

"I cried... a lot," I admit with a small shrug.

"Did it help?"

"You know, I think it did. I've been holding so much in, trying to separate who I was before I came here and the girl I am now. I didn't realise how much it was affecting me."

Theo reaches for my face, brushing the fine hairs away from my eyes. "You are so strong, sunshine. I'm in awe of you."

"Let's be honest," brittle laughter spills out of me, "I'm a mess."

"Then we can be a mess together."

"I... I think I'd like that."

His body goes rigid as he stares down at me with wide eyes. "I think I'm going to need you to repeat that, because I'm not sure—"

"I love you, Theo," I rush out. "I'm in love with you. I have been for a while."

"You love me, sunshine?"

"Yeah, I do."

"Fuck... fuck. I—" The blare of his phone cuts through the air and he mutters something under his breath. "I'll ignore it," he says.

"Maybe you should answer it," I reply when it doesn't stop ringing.

"Fuck's sake. Hello? Yeah, that's me." He goes deathly still, the blood draining from his face. "Yeah, okay. No, that's great, thank you. I appreciate you letting me know."

"Theo, what is it? What's wrong?"

"He's dead. That sick fuck is dead."

"Vaughn is..." The words lodge in my throat as shock spreads through me.

Theo watches me, giving me space to absorb the words.

The truth.

Vaughn is gone.

"He's... he's dead?" My voice trembles as realisation hits me like a wrecking ball.

"Yeah, sunshine. He can't hurt you anymore."

"He can't—" I throw my arms around his neck and bury my face in his shoulder, emotion flooding out of me.

"Shh, babe. I got you. I got you." Theo holds me tightly, stroking his hand up and down my spine as I purge every memory, every bruise, every cruel word.

Vaughn hurt me, used me and betrayed me. But he didn't break me.

Because I'm still here and he's—

"Dead," I breathe, finally lifting my face to Theo's.

He touches his forehead to mine, inhaling a shaky breath. "It's over, Raine. He's gone."

Gone.

Which means I'm free.

I know there's a lot of stuff I still need to deal with. Unresolved feelings and trauma. But I needed this.

I needed to know he couldn't ever hurt me or the people I care about again.

"What are you thinking?" Theo asks, staring intently at me. "Tell me what's going through your mind."

"I... I think knowing he was still alive, that he survived..."

A violent shudder goes through me as I try to find the words to explain what I mean. "You know, before everything happened, I would let myself imagine staying here with you. Being in your life, for real. But I knew it was silly. I knew that one day he'd find me, or you'd discover the truth—"

"Raine, I—"

"No, Theo. Just let me get this out. I'm not proud of my past. But I did what I needed to in order to survive. I've done so many things... Things I wish I could erase. But meeting you, meeting Millie and the girls, hell, even the boys... for the first time, I got to experience what it's like to have a family.

"And I wanted it. God, I wanted it so much." Silent tears roll down my cheeks as I squeeze my eyes shut.

"Raine, look at me," Theo coaxes, brushing his hand along my jaw.

When I finally open them again, I tumble headfirst into him, the love written all over his face.

"I'm right here. Nothing about your past or who you were is going to change that. I fell in love with you, sunshine. The girl you are because of what you've survived. I love all your pieces, even the broken ones."

"Theo—" A garbled sob rushes up my throat as I finally hear what he's saying.

As I finally let myself believe it.

The air crackles around us as he watches me. Gazes at me like I'm the most important thing in his world.

"I'm going to kiss you now," he whispers, his lips hovering right over mine. As if he's waiting for my permission.

But this time, I don't pull away.

Moving closer, my lips curving as the distance disappears between us. I brush my mouth over his, my heart leaping at the small contact.

"Do your worst, Ashworth," I breathe.

And then he kisses me.

35

THEO

I kiss Raine like it's our first and last time all rolled into one. I guess, in a way it is. It's my first time kissing her where she's accepted my words, and my last time before she really understands what being my girl is going to be like.

She loves me.

So it might have taken that cunt taking his last ventilator-powered breath to make it happen, but she said it.

I knew the second I saw the unknown number on my screen that something big was about to happen. I felt it right to the very depths of my dark soul. And the second I heard the words, I knew it was over.

Even before I relayed them to Raine, I knew it was what she needed. That closure she was looking for the day we visited him. She didn't get it then, he was still with us, he was still a risk. A dark shadow blotting out the light. But now... Now, it's truly over and Raine can start her life over without him haunting her.

"Fuck, I missed you," I groan into our kiss, rolling her beneath me.

I'm still gentle, still worried about hurting her more than

she already is, but the way she claws at my back makes me want to forget about all of it.

Eagerly, Raine spreads her thighs for me, allowing me to nestle between them as our kiss grows hotter. I tell myself that if she calls time on this because she's not ready, that I'll be okay. But I think the truth is that I'll probably explode.

Ripping my lips from hers, I kiss across her jaw and nuzzle her neck as my hand slips up her thigh and disappears under the shirt she's wearing.

"You are." *Kiss.* "The most." *Kiss.* "Incredible." *Kiss.* "Person." *Kiss.* "I've ever." *Kiss.* "Met," I confess as my hand pauses on her ribs.

They're more defined from the last week or so of barely eating and I promise myself there and then that I'm going to fix it. I've done everything I've been able to, but now this has happened, something tells me that she's really gonna let me look after her. Including getting her out of this room.

It hasn't escaped my attention that after spending so long dreaming about having her in my room, in my bed that I'm now scheming up ways to get her out of it.

How things change…

"Theo," she cries when I suck on the sensitive patch of skin beneath her ear.

"Love you, sunshine. Love you so fucking much."

Unable to hold back anymore, my hand slides up from her ribs in favour of her breast.

"Oh God," she moans, arching into my touch.

"Is this okay? I don't want to hurt you."

"Yes, yes. It's okay."

I pull back to look at her, to see if she's really telling the truth to find her eyes blazing. Sure, the tears are still lingering but they've been forgotten in favour of this.

Sitting up, I wrap my free hand around her hip and grind into her. It doesn't matter that we're both still in our underwear, the heat of her pussy burns in the best kind of way.

"You're wet for me, aren't you?" I groan, my head spinning with burning need to sink inside her, to reconnect with her in the best way we know how.

"Yes, Theo. Please," she begs.

"You want my dick, babe?" I ask, my signature cocky smirk in place.

"God, you're an arrogant motherfucker." There's barely any bite to her words, not like there used to be and it sure gets swallowed whole when I grind into her again, making her moan as I hit her clit.

"Admit it, you love it. You always have."

"Maybe," she gasps as I sit her up and drag my t-shirt from her body, exposing her incredible tits to me.

"You're so beautiful."

It pains me to do so, but I shimmy down the bed a little, my mouth trailing its way down her body.

"Theo," Raine cries, her fingers sinking into my hair when I circle her nipple with my tongue. "Oh please." She arches from the bed, offering herself up and I can't hold back. "Yes," she squeals as I suck on her. "More... more. I need more."

"You can have everything." I continue to move lower, tucking my fingers into the sides of her knickers when I get there and drag them down her legs. "Look at you," I breathe after throwing her underwear to the floor and spreading her legs. "So fucking perfect. And all fucking mine."

She's soaked. Her pussy glistens in the sunlight streaming in through the windows.

"Yeah. And what are you going to do about it?" she taunts, sounding more like herself with every word she says.

I know she still has a long road ahead, but after days of watching her lose herself more and more, this is incredible.

"What am I going to do about it?" I echo. "This is what I'm going to fucking do about it." I drop to my front, spread her legs wider, and lick her from arse to clit, making her scream and buck against me.

"Theo," she cries, her grip on my hair so tight I'm sure she's going to pull it clean out.

Not that I care.

I am here for this a million times over.

I eat my girl like a man possessed, forcing my name to spill from her lips over and over and I build her up and never let her fall.

"Oh my God, please, Theo. Please," Raine whimpers, her thighs pinned to my ears as I suck on her clit. "Make me come, please."

Sitting up, I wipe my mouth with the back of my hand. "Not yet," I tell her, my voice rough, giving away my own need for her as I stand and shove my boxers from my hips.

Her eyes immediately drop to my cock.

Crawling back into my bed, I take myself in hand. "You want this, sunshine?" I taunt, rolling my eyes up her body, loving the flush that covers her cheeks and chest.

I did that. Me. I drove her to the brink again and again and made her look that fucking beautiful.

"Yes," she whimpers, licking her lips as if she's imagining me pushing inside her mouth.

Shuffling closer, I wrap her legs around my waist and rub myself through her folds, coating myself in her juices.

"Oh God," she whimpers when I circle her swollen clit.

"Missed this pussy."

"So romantic." Her eyes roll.

Dropping lower, I push the tip in and fall over her body, catching myself with a hand on either side of her head. "You want romance, sunshine?" I ask, dipping low so my lips brush hers while our eyes hold. "I love you, Raine Storm. I love you more than I ever thought possible. From here on out, I want you by my side every single step of the way. I don't care if it gets hard, if you fuck up. None of that matters.

"I'll fuck up too, I promise you that. I also promise you that no matter what happens, you deserve this. You deserve to be happy, to have a family, and to be loved."

A lone tear slips down her temple, soaking into her hair.

"Me and you, sunshine. Forever. What do you say?"

She sniffles, her eyes flood with tears she's desperately trying to hold back. "I say yes, Theo. I'll always say yes."

"Thank fuck," I groan before thrusting forward and filling her in one swift move.

"Theo," she screams, her body shooting up the bed, but I quickly put a stop to that by wrapping one hand around her hip.

"Love you, sunshine. You're my everything," I tell her before stealing her lips in a slow and passionate kiss as my hips move at the same agonising pace.

We move together seamlessly. Like we've been doing it our entire lives.

With one hand twisted in my hair, she grips my arse with the other, attempting to make me speed up. She's right on the edge. Her pussy ripples around me, desperate for the release I've withheld from her.

"Theo, please," she begs, dropping her hand to my shoulder and impaling me with her nails.

The bite of pain goes straight to my balls, and I have to grit my teeth to stop from blowing before she falls.

"I've got you, babe," I rasp. "I've always fucking got you."

With my grip on her hip tightening, I thrust into her, ensuring I hit the spot that will send her flying over the edge.

"Oh my God, Theo," she cries when I circle my hips and she finally falls. "Yes, yes, yes," she chants as her body locks up with pleasure, dragging my own orgasm out of me.

"Fuuuuuck," I groan. "Fuck. I love you. I love you. I love you."

Wrapping my arms around her, I hold her tight as we both come down from our highs before flipping us over, putting her on top of me for fear of crushing her against the bed.

No words are said between us for the longest time, but they're not needed. Our bodies said everything that's important right now.

Eventually, though, Raine breaks the silence. "I really needed that," she confesses, making me bark out a laugh.

"Oh, babe. Me too.'

Before she can say anything else, her stomach growls loudly.

"Looks like someone didn't eat enough snacks," I tease.

"I did. You just helped me work them off."

"Do you..." My question trails off, debating whether or not I'm about to push too hard.

"Do I, what?" she asks, lifting her head from my shoulder and gazing down at me with her sex-glazed eyes.

"Do you think you'd be up for a trip out?"

She stills but doesn't immediately say no. "What are you thinking?"

"Burgers."

"Theo, you're still inside me and you're thinking about burgers," she laughs, the sound like music to my ears.

"Yes and no. I'm thinking about feeding you a burger to give you the strength to come back here and do that again."

My cock swells as I think about round two, and it doesn't escape her notice if her raised brows are anything to go by.

"Can we do takeaway? I'm not sure I'm ready for—"

A smile spreads across my lips. The fact she's willing to leave the room, and the Chapel, is more than enough.

"We can do whatever you want."

Raine nods before sitting up, forcing my dick deeper inside her velvet heat.

"Keep doing that and we won't be going anywhere," I chuckle.

"Shower with me?" she asks, awkwardly climbing off me, showing me that despite having a breakthrough, she's still suffering, still healing.

"Now there's an offer I can't refuse."

As much as I want to take her again in the shower, I don't. I'm a good boy and focus on cleaning up so I can fill her growling belly.

"Ready?" I ask once we're both dressed as I have my fingers wrapped around the door handle.

She nods once, but there's hesitation in her eyes.

"Me and you, sunshine. We've got this."

With her tucked into my side, we make our way downstairs. The second we turn the corner we find six shocked faces staring back at us.

They all quickly recover, not wanting to make a big deal about her appearance, which I'm grateful for.

I'm about to explain the reason for this turnaround but she beats me to it.

"Vaughn is dead. It's over," she says, her voice rough with emotion. "We're going to get takeaway."

"So do us a favour and make yourselves scarce when we get back," I tell them as they continue watching us closely before guiding her toward the front door. "I plan on giving my girl the best date of her life."

36

RAINE

"What?" I ask Theo as he stares at me.

"You fucking amaze me," he grins, cutting the engine.

The car smells amazing and I can't wait to get inside and tuck into our gourmet burgers and hand cut fries. But he makes no move to get out of the car, and if I'm being honest, I'm in no rush either.

"Our food is going to get cold," I point out.

Yet, we still both sit here.

I get it though. The significance of this moment—I didn't think I'd get to this point either.

Not while Vaughn was still alive.

Hearing he was gone was like a weight instantly lifted.

He has no power over me anymore, and I get to decide who I want to be and how I want to live my life.

I finally get to leave my past behind.

"Come on, sunshine. I promised you the date to end all dates." Theo shoulders his door and climbs out, coming around to open mine.

We walk to the Chapel hand in hand. My ribs still smart a

little and some bruises feel more tender than others, but I know they'll heal.

Laughter drifts out of the building and Theo rolls his eyes. "Should have known they wouldn't listen to a fucking word I said," he mutters.

"I know you wanted it to be a date but how about we spend some time with them?"

"Yeah?" His eyes light up.

"Yeah." I nod. "Although I'm not sharing my food with them."

"They can order in." He shrugs, his eyes dropping to my mouth.

"Theo," I breathe, desire pulsing inside me.

"What, sunshine?" He advances toward me, backing me up against the wall.

My breath catches as one of his hands rests on the wall beside my head. "The food..."

"This is more important." He dips his head, capturing my lips in a slow lazy kiss that has my toes curling and heart racing.

"Yo, dickhead, put your girl down and get in here," Reese yells, and Theo pulls away.

"I'll tell them to clear out," he says.

"Later." I fist his hoodie, stealing another quick kiss. "I want to hang out with them."

"Okay. But after, you're all mine."

"Always." I smile.

It isn't uncertain or forced, it's one hundred percent genuine. Because I love Theo, and he loves me. And nothing else matters.

"You want us to clear out?" Elliot asks the second we step into the room.

"If I had my way, yes. But Raine wants to hang out."

"Of course she does, we're better company than you," Oak teases, and Theo flips him off.

"Sit," he says, giving me a heated look. "I'll get some plates."

"I'm not sure I like this new domesticated version of him," Reese says. "He's making the rest of us look bad."

"Maybe you could learn a thing or two," Liv lifts a brow. "It's good to see you up and about."

"Thanks. It feels good," I admit. "I know I haven't been..."

"You don't owe us anything," Elliot says, surprising me. "We're just glad the two of you figured it out."

"Fuck me, Eaton. Who are you right now?"

"Fuck off." Elliot growls.

Everyone chuckles.

Everyone except Abi, who peeks over at him with a slight blush to her cheeks. I hope they figure it out soon because they're not fooling anyone.

Theo comes back with our food, placing a tray on my lap and dropping a kiss on my head.

"Fucking hell, he has gone soft," someone chuckles. But Theo doesn't take the bait, making sure I have everything I need before he drops down beside me.

"Could have gotten something for the rest of us," Oakley teases.

"Fuck off, get your own."

I pick at my food. It's good, really good. But my appetite still hasn't fully returned, and I know it'll take a little while until I'm back to myself.

But this, being here with Theo and our friends, is more than I ever could have hoped for.

"When do you think you'll be back at school, Raine?" Tally asks and Theo shoots her a murderous look.

"What?" she balks.

"We haven't talked about it yet," I murmur.

"There's no rush," Theo says.

But the truth is, we need to have the hard conversations. Theo is due to start university in the autumn. And I'll be stuck here, all alone. I'll have Millie, sure. But it won't be the same.

It won't—

"Hey." He nudges me with his elbow. "We'll figure it out, okay."

I nod, forcing a smile.

"It's your birthday soon too, isn't it?" Abi changes the subject.

"Yeah."

"Maybe we can celebrate."

"Oh no, I don't—"

"Guys, come on," Theo groans. "We're supposed to be chilling."

"You're just upset Raine chose to hang out with us and not—"

"Babe," Tally scolds Oak. "Don't push him."

"Well, one thing is for sure," he says. "The Heir chasers will lose their shit when they realise you're definitely off the market."

"All their attention will be on you now, Eaton," Reese adds with a smirk. "I can only imagine the shit they'll pull to try their luck with you. The last Heir standing."

"Fucking idiots." Elliot mutters but I don't watch him, I watch Abi.

Watch the blood drain from her face as if she hadn't realised what me staying in All Hallows' would mean.

"Four months," Oak goes on. "And then we're done with college and have the whole summer before shit gets real."

Tension ripples through the air as Theo glares at him again.

"What? Surely I didn't—"

"It's called tact, dickhead," Reese laughs. "Look it up."

Theo leans in and lets out a heavy sigh. "I know you only just left our room, but can we go back up there? I'm not sure I can survive this without knocking him the fuck out." My brows furrow as I stare at him, and he frowns back at me. "What?"

"You said 'our room'."

A slow smug smile tugs at his mouth, setting off butterflies in my stomach. "You noticed that, huh?"

"Theo, I didn't agree to stay here permanently," I whisper.

His smirk intensifies as he steals a kiss before replying, "We'll see."

I stay at the Chapel for the rest of the week. Hanging out in Theo's room with him or Millie. Sometimes Abi joins us, and we play Monopoly. Sometimes Theo skips class to stay in bed with me where he continues his mission to show me just how much he loves me.

It's amazing—he's amazing.

But I've decided to keep my room in the dorms.

I don't want to be that girl, so infatuated with her boyfriend that she doesn't know how to be alone or do things with her friends.

Theo has been in a sulk about it since I told him my decision, but he's going along with it on one condition—that I let him keep the camera in my room. We compromised, so long as I get to decide when it's turned on or off.

Today, I'm going back to class, and I haven't told him or Millie, but I'm kind of terrified. I know how fast the rumour mill circulates at All Hallows'. If people haven't already learned the truth about me, they'll have filled enough blanks to make my life difficult.

Mr. Porter has reassured Trudy and Miss Linley—and Theo since he demanded to be in that awkward meeting—that any issues will be swiftly dealt with, but I know how vicious the Heir chasers can be.

Especially Keeley Davis and her mean girlfriends.

A loud knock on my door pulls me from my thoughts.

Much to Theo's disapproval, I slept in my dorm room last night. I couldn't really explain it, but I needed some time alone to get my head around everything. I get to have the life I never believed would be mine.

It's going to take a little getting used to.

"Raine, open up." Millie's voice filters through the door.

I open it, and frown. "Hi, what's up?"

"I need to talk to you." She barges inside and closes the door behind her.

"I'm freaking out."

"What, why?"

"Because Marcus asked me to hang out with him next weekend and I don't know what to say."

"Hold up." I shake my head. "First of all, who the hell is Marcus? And second of all, why am I only hearing about this now?"

"He's a boy in my class. And you've been kind of preoccupied." She rolls her eyes like it's obvious.

"You can always talk to me Mills."

"I am talking to you, duh."

"So Marcus... does Theo know—"

"No." She flushed. "And don't you dare say a word to him. I mean it, Raine. I only have you to talk to about this stuff."

"Okay, we won't tell Theo... yet."

"Ever," she murmurs. "It's a miracle anyone even wants to talk to me thanks to my overbearing arsehole of a brother."

"You love him really."

"Yeah, but that's not the point."

"So what is the point?"

"I... I like him, okay? He's smart and funny and he doesn't think I'm a freak show just because I attend group therapy. He gets me," she says with a half-smile.

"He sounds nice."

"He is."

"So what's the problem?"

"Have you met my brother?" she shrieks. "Once he finds out, he'll ruin everything."

"No, he won't. I won't let him."

"And how do you plan on doing that?"

I can think of a few ways, but none are suitable for Millie's ears.

"You can hang out with Marcus and leave Theo to me, okay?"

Millie lunges for me, throwing her arms around me and hugging me tight. "Thank you. I knew you'd understand, you're the best Raine."

My heart swells as I hug her back. I might be hopelessly in love with her big brother, but Millie also holds a special place in my heart, and I'm so happy that I get to be around to watch her grow.

"Can we go to class now?" I ask, gently shoving her off me.

"Isn't Theo walking you?"

"I imagine he'll be here soon, but I don't want to make a big scene."

It's bad enough that everyone stares and whispers whenever I go down to the kitchen. But I keep reminding myself their judgement can't hurt me.

Not after what I've survived.

I grab my bag and follow Millie out of my room. Sure enough a couple of girls pass us in the hallway and immediately drop their voices to a whisper.

"Ignore them," Millie says.

"Oh, I am."

We head out of the dorms and start walking toward the main building.

"You know, my brother is going to lose his shit when he realises— Uh-oh."

I look over just in time to see Theo storming toward us.

"I thought we agreed to meet at your dorm room?" he barks.

"Millie showed up, so I figured we'd get a head start."

"Sunshine..." The warning in his voice sends shivers down my spine.

"Relax, I'm fine." I press my hand to his chest and lean up to kiss him. As I pull away, he anchors his arms around my waist and crashes his mouth down on mine, stealing the air from my lungs.

"And that's my cue. See you later, Raine. Big brother." Millie takes off, leaving me completely at Theo's mercy.

"I should punish you for this." He pins me with a dark look.

"Mmm, what do you have in mind?" I smirk.

"You, me, and some time in the basement."

"So eager to tie me up, Teddy?"

"Fucking desperate." He touches his head to mine, inhaling a deep breath.

"You seem nervous," I say, my chest tightening. Because if anyone should be nervous about what the day will hold, it's me.

"The only thing I'm nervous about is losing my shit with some arsehole who thinks they can talk shit about my girl."

"Your girl, huh? Sounds serious." I take Theo's arm and pull it over my shoulder, tucking myself into his side as we head toward the sixth form building.

"If anyone says anything..."

"I can handle it, Theo. I promise."

"I just don't want anything else to scare you away."

"Hey." I stop and gaze up at him. "I'm here, aren't I?"

"I know but—"

"No buts. I'm here because I want to be here, Theo. I want to be with you."

Relief skitters across his expression, and he ducks down to

steal another kiss. "So I know you're a bad-arse and don't want to make a big thing of it, but I kind of did a thing."

"Oh God, what did you do?"

We reach the building, and he motions inside. Elliot, Reese, and Oakley look up as we enter, and the girls fall into step beside them.

"What the hell is this?" I demand, aware that everyone is staring at our welcoming committee.

"This is us making a stand," Elliot steps forward. "You're one of us now, Storm. Time this place knows it." He turns on his heel and cuts through the morning crowd as the boys follow him.

The girls swarm me, Liv at one side and Tally and Abi on the other side.

"Everyone's staring," I murmur, holding my head high, refusing to look away.

"Let them. They're just jealous," Liv says loud enough that a group of Heir chasers overhear.

"Welcome to the inner circle," Tally winks, lacing her arm through mine. "Officially."

"Officially," I chuckle.

I like the sound of that.

As if he hears me, Theo glances over his shoulder at me and mouths, "I love you."

"Love you too."

Something settles deep inside of me, and for the first time in my life, I feel content. Happy and free.

Because loving Theo means I'm not alone.

It means I have a family.

A future.

And I'm going to hold on to it as tight as possible.

EPILOGUE

Raine

"Fuck, sunshine, I can't get enough of you."

Theo kisses me harder, his fingers curling inside me as I ride his hand. The heavy bass of the music pulses in the air but we're both too lost in each other to care.

It's my birthday party.

I turned eighteen today.

I am officially an adult which means I finally aged out of the system.

We're supposed to be celebrating with our friends, but Theo took one look at me in my skintight black skirt and crop top and dragged me into the bathroom.

"People will be looking for us," I pant.

"Let them look."

"Good plan." I chuckle, covering his hand with my own, directing his movements.

"Someone feeling needy?" he murmurs against my lips.

"You're teasing me. I want to come."

"And you will, when I'm ready to let you." He nips at my bottom lip, rolling his thumb over my clit and finally giving me what I want.

"Oh God," I drop my head back against the wall, drowning in the overpowering sensations.

Theo is so good at this.

At sex.

At knowing exactly how to get me off.

Every day, he learns a new way to make me scream his name and I love him for it.

God, love him.

The last couple of weeks haven't been easy. Even with Theo and the Heirs keeping a tight grip on the rumour mill at All Hallows', my name has still been the hot topic on everyone's lips.

But honestly, I don't care.

The people who matter to me know who I am. They know what I've been through. The rest is all white noise.

"That's it, sunshine. Clench around my fingers, show me how much you want it."

"Yes... God, yes," I moan, writhing against his hand.

Someone knocks loudly on the door and Theo barks, "Fuck off, we're busy."

"Oh my God." I bury my face in his shoulder, biting back a smile.

But they knock again.

"I said... Fuck. Off."

"Ashworth, is that you? Shit, I didn't realise. I-I'm sorry I—"

"Fucking idiot," Theo hisses, dipping his head to lick and suck my neck while he ups the pace. "Can I fuck you?" he asks.

"Yo, lovebirds," Reese's voice filters into the bathroom. "Finish whatever the fuck you're doing and get out here. We want to toast the birthday girl."

"I swear to God," Theo mutters, but the moment is gone. Right along with my impending orgasm.

"Come on, lover boy." I shove him away gently. "We can finish this later."

"I'm going to fucking kill him."

"No, you're not," I chuckle, straightening out my knickers and skirt. "They just want to celebrate with us."

"Cock-block me more like." He pouts, giving me his best puppy dog eyes.

"Come here." I crook my finger and he comes willingly. Wrapping my arms around his neck, I gaze up at him. Hardly able to believe that we're here.

That we made it.

"I love you, Teddy."

"You've really got to stop calling me that."

"You love it," I smile sweetly.

"I love you, sunshine. So fucking much."

"I love you too."

"Enough to let me fuck you in the basement later?"

"So predictable." I roll my eyes, as I steal a chaste kiss. "Come on, my dirty boy. Get me drunk enough and maybe I'll make all your dreams come true."

"What are you doing all the way over here?" I ask Abi sometime later.

I'm a little bit tipsy but nothing over the top. Despite my promise to Theo, I don't want to be out of control. Although the party was invite-only, there's still a lot of people crammed into the Chapel, and I can't help but feel a little on edge.

"I'm not really feeling it," she murmurs, barely meeting my eyes.

"Abs, what's wrong?"

"I..." She lets out a big sigh. "It doesn't matter."

I follow her line of sight, not surprised to find Elliot drinking and talking with a couple of boys from the team.

"You know one of you is going to have to make the first move eventually," I say.

"What?" Her eyes go big, full of panic.

"Come on, Abi. It's obvious there's something going on between you. You dance around each other like magnets."

"He'll never act on it. He's made that more than obvious."

"So you make the first move. Show him that you're not the fragile breakable girl he thinks you are."

"I..." She worries her bottom lip, mulling over my words.

"Life is too short, babe."

"I'm not sure I'm cut out to—"

"Abi." I take her hands in mine. "You're one of the strongest people I know. Elliot would be lucky to be with you."

Her cheeks turn five shades darker, but she needs to know how amazing she is. How resilient and strong.

"Thank you." She gives me a faint smile. "That means a lot."

"I know you think he couldn't possibly want you back, but isn't it better to take a risk than never find out?"

Strong arms wrap around me from behind and Theo pulls me back against his chest. "What are you two whispering about?"

"Nothing," I reply, twisting my head a little to look at him.

"I'm going to go find Tally and Liv." Abi moves around us.

"She okay?" Theo asks.

"Do you think they'll ever get their shit together?"

"Who? Abi and Elliot? Un-fucking-likely."

"But they would be so good together."

"Sunshine, don't start playing matchmaker." Theo grazes his mouth over mine. "It never ends well."

"So... Now wouldn't be a good time to tell you that I think Millie has her first boyfriend."

"What the fuck did you just say?" He rears back, glaring at me.

"And this is exactly why she chose to talk to me about it and not you."

"She... What the fuck is happening right now, Storm?"

I roll my eyes at his theatrics. "Marcus is a nice kid."

"Marcus. And what class is Marcus in so I can hunt the little fucker down and—"

"Stop." I press my finger to his lips. "Millie is almost thirteen. It's going to happen eventually. She deserves to have friends. To experience first love. And she deserves to have a big brother who lets her make her own choices."

"But I—"

"No, Theo. You need to stand down on this one. I promised her I'd handle you."

"Handle me?" His eyes darken. "And exactly how do you plan on *handling* me, sunshine?"

"I can think of a few different ways." My mouth twists with amusement. "But you've got to promise not to bulldoze them."

"I don't like it, Raine. I don't—"

"You don't have to like it, but you have to accept it. Millie deserves that much."

His expression falls and I know I've won this battle. "Yeah, okay. But I want to meet him, and I will be laying down some ground rules."

"I would expect nothing less. Just promise not to kill him with your bare hands, okay? I don't need you getting arrested. I kind of like having you around."

"You like me, sunshine?" Theo smirks and the heat in his gaze sends a shiver through me.

"You're okay."

"Okay?" He barks out a rough laugh. "Fuck, I love you."

"You love me, Ashworth?"

"Yeah, I do. Hopelessly. Desperately. Unconditionally."

He steps into me, so I have to crane my neck to look at him. What I see there leaves me breathless.

Theo might be cocky and cold and complicated, but once he lets you into his inner circle, you quickly realise he loves with his entire heart.

And I never want to lose this feeling.

"You're mine, Raine," he whispers. "And I'm never letting you go."

Abigail

I watch Elliot from across the room, aware that I probably look like a deranged stalker.

But I can't help it.

Whenever he walks into a room, I become hyperaware of him. The raw power he emanates.

The darkness.

Sometimes I think I'm making it all up in my head. This deep sense that we are somehow the same.

I know he doesn't agree. He thinks I'm this shy, meek girl afraid of her own shadow. And maybe to some degree, he's right.

I am afraid.

But not in the way he thinks.

I've lived in the darkness for so long, it's hard to imagine living in the light.

He senses me staring and looks over. His eyes hold the same shadows mine do, and more than anything, I wish I was the kind of girl who could stand beside a boy like Elliot Eaton.

I want to know his deepest, darkest secrets. I want to be the person he turns to when things get to be too much.

I want to be his.

A truth I've been struggling with lately. Especially, since he's made it more than obvious he won't cross that line with me.

He cares about me; I don't doubt that. It's in the little gestures he makes. The way he protects me from a distance. Always makes sure I'm okay. We've struck up a mutual friendship over the last few months as we've watched our friends fall in love.

But I don't want to be just his friend.

I don't want to watch some vapid Heir chasers swoop in and steal him away from me.

A deep frown crinkles his eyes, and I realise my expression must say a thousand words. Before I can stop him, he excuses himself from the conversation and heads toward me.

My heart crashes wildly in my chest as I try not to panic.

"What's wrong?" he asks the second he reaches me.

"N-nothing."

"Your expression just now... You looked terrified."

"I'm okay. Thanks for checking up on me though." I smile, wishing I had the confidence to push the issue.

Wishing I could tell him what I feel in my heart.

"Nobody said anything to you, right? Because I've told you before, if anyone gives you shit..."

"I'm fine, Elliot. I promise."

He jams his hands in his pockets, and nods. "Are you enjoying the party?"

"It's not really my scene." I shrug. "You know that."

"It wouldn't hurt you to cut loose occasionally, nobody will hurt you here."

I drift closer to him. I can't help it. Whether he realises or not, he reels me in. His darkness calling to me.

I gaze up at him, wondering what it would be like to kiss him. We've hugged before, and it was amazing. But I want more. I want to know the shape of his mouths, the taste of his lips.

"Red," he breathes, his body going rigid beneath my touch as I lay my hand on his chest.

I don't know what I'm doing but I can't stop myself.

It must be the couple of drinks I had, or Raine's words of encouragement, or maybe for once in my life, I want to know what it feels like to get the boy.

I lean up on my tiptoes and brush my lips over his, kissing him.

I'm kissing Elliot and it's everything I ever dreamed of.

My heart careens beneath my ribs, my body trembling as I curl my fingers into his black shirt, trying to get closer.

"Abi," he murmurs, pulling away slightly as I lean in, smiling.

"I've wanted to do that for so long," I admit, opening my eyes to look at him.

But he isn't smiling.

Not even a little bit.

"E-Elliot?" I whisper.

He steps back, putting some distance between us. "You shouldn't have done that."

"It's not how I thought our first kiss would go either but I—"

His eyes shutter as he inhales a deep breath. When they open again, what I see there makes my stomach tumble.

"Elliot?"

He doesn't answer me, but his silence speaks volumes.

He doesn't feel the same.

All this time, I thought he was keeping me at arm's length because he thinks I'm too pure and innocent for him, it never occurred to me that he might not feel the same.

Oh God.

Tears burn the backs of my eyes as the weight of what I

just did crashes down on me. "I need to go." I spin on my heel and take off toward the front door.

I can't be here.

I can't stand to see the rejection in his eyes.

"Abi, wait," his voice rises above the music. But I don't stop.

I don't stop until I burst through the doors and into chilly night air.

My phone starts ringing and I fumble to get it out of my bag. Tears drip onto the screen as I frown at the number.

"Maureen?" I answer. "What's wrong?"

"It's your dad, sweetie." Sadness fills her voice and something inside me cracks.

"Abi," Elliot booms and I turn around to find him in the doorway looking all kinds of pissed off.

"Abi, are you still there?"

"I'm here," I whisper, bracing myself for the words I've been dreading.

The words I know will change everything.

"I'm so, so sorry," she says, and I drop the phone, pain shattering through me.

"Abi, what the fuck?" Elliot catches me before I crumple to the ground. "What's wrong? What happened?"

I meet his cold stare, as I say the words I hoped I'd never have to say.

"He's dead. My dad is dead."

Elliot and Abi's story continues in the SAVAGE VICIOUS HEIR DUET.

SAVAGE VICIOUS HEIR SNEAK PEEK
HEIRS OF ALL HALLOWS' DUET FOUR

Chapter One
Abigail

Rain pelts down on the umbrella someone holds over me, the wind howling around us.

It's a miserable day.

Cold. Dark. Bleak.

But it matches my mood. The endless stream of tears rolling down my cheeks. The angry storm battering my insides.

I feel like I haven't taken a breath since I heard the words.

He's gone.

My father. The one person I had left in the world.

I always knew this day would come—sooner than it should have because of his ill health—but I didn't know.

I didn't—

"Abi," Raine gently squeezes my arm. "It's time."

"W-what?" I blink at her. Empty. Hollow.

Numb.

"The rose." She motions to the open grave. The dark black hole they lowered my father's casket into.

I take a step forward, and another. "Goodbye," I whisper,

throwing the lone stem into the abyss, watching as it disappears.

"We should get you inside," she says, wrapping her arm around me. "This storm isn't going to pass anytime soon."

I nod, letting her lead me away.

Wondering when the pain will stop.

Wondering how I'll ever piece myself back together after this.

I don't know how long I've been sitting here, hiding in my bedroom. But eventually, a knock pierces the silence. My sanctuary.

"Abigail?" a soft voice calls. "It's me." Olivia slips inside. "There you are." She offers me a sad smile. "We were worried."

"I... I can't."

"I know, gosh, babe." She hurries to my side and takes my hand in hers. "I know. Can I get you anything? Something to eat? Drink?"

Something to take it all away, I swallow the words.

She would never do that though. Maybe her boyfriend's friends Theo and Oakley would. Give me a pill to tamp down the pain. But not Liv. Not Tally or Raine.

My friends.

The only people I have left expect Maureen, my father's carer. And now he's gone, I suppose she'll—

I shove down the wave of grief before it consumes me fully.

After losing my mum in the accident that left me scarred and ruined, I thought I knew pain and loss. But this feels different. Even though I've had years to prepare, losing my father has broken something inside me. Fractured me apart in ways I can't even fathom.

It wasn't time.

We didn't have enough time.

Yet, he's gone.

He left me.

And now I'm alone.

"You're not," Liv says, and I realise I must have said that last part aloud. "You have me and Tally and Raine. The boys too. And Elliot—"

I go still at the mention of his name.

Elliot Eaton.

The boy I've spent weeks fantasising about. Falling for the idea that there could be something between us, that maybe the strange tug I feel in his presence was reciprocated. That, maybe if, one day, I was brave enough to pull on that tether, he would pull back.

He didn't.

And I should have known. I should have known that someone like me wouldn't be the kind of girl Elliot Eaton wants.

At least if one good thing came from all of this... this hurt, it's that we can pretend it never happened.

We can pretend I didn't kiss him that night.

"Abi?" Liv gently nudges my arms, pulling me from my maudlin thoughts. "Tell me what you need."

"I want to sleep," I whisper over the hoarseness of my throat.

"But the wake—"

"Tell them, I'm sorry. But I can't. I can't go down there."

"Do you want to stay here? I can take you back to my house or—"

"It's fine. I'm fine." The lie turns the air thick and heavy. But she doesn't argue.

Instead, Liv helps pull back the covers and gets me settled. "I'll stay with you," she says, but I shake my head.

"Alone. I want to be alone."

Another lie.

But one I need to tell to shore my defences, to protect myself. Because while she might be my friend, while they all might be my friends, one day, they'll leave.

Just like everybody I love does.

"Abigail, I'm so very sorry for your loss," Mr Porter says.

"Thank you. Is my room ready?"

"Abigail, I—"

"Please, Mr Porter, I can't stay in the house. I can't... be there." Panic floods my voice as blood roars in my ears.

It's been two days since the funeral. A week since my father passed. And I can't spend another second rattling around in that big empty house.

He's everywhere, in everything. Haunting me.

When the headteacher of All Hallows' doesn't answer, I add, "Please, I'm begging you. Money isn't an issue, you know that."

Ironic really, that my father, as a well-respected judge, earned more money than we could spend. But it couldn't save him.

It couldn't cure the disease addling his body.

"Fine, yes. Of course. You can move into the dormitories."

"Thank you. Thank you." Relief sinks into me as I wipe my eyes.

I'm surprised I have any tears left to fall. It's all I've done for days. Cry and sleep and cry some more.

After the wake, the girls wanted to stay with me, but I didn't want them too. I couldn't bear it. The pity in their eyes, the utter hopelessness.

Besides, I don't want them to know that I'm slipping. Falling into old habits and dark places. And I definitely don't want Elliot to know. I don't want him to try and intervene and play that big brother role that I so obviously mistook for something more.

I inhale a shuddering breath, thanking Mr Porter again. "When can I move in?"

"As soon as—"

"Today," I blurt out. "I already have my things."

"Okay, okay." He concedes. "Mrs Danvers will get you settled. Let me call her."

He does and I wait. Desperate to get to my new room—my new home I suppose.

The house is legally mine now as are most of my father's money and assets. But I can't think about that yet. Can't deal with any of it.

All I want to do is sleep and forget. Just for a little while. Until the pain recedes and I feel like I can breathe again.

"She'll be right over," he says, standing. "As for your class schedule, I'll speak to your teachers. See if we can make some allowances, maybe look at coursework extensions."

"Thank you."

He gives me a small nod. "Your father was a good man, Abigail. His absence will be felt by all of us."

There's a small knock on the door and I'm saved from having to say anything else when the dorm aunt Mrs Danvers appears.

"Oh, Abi." She rushes over to me and takes me by the shoulders. "I'm so very sorry."

"Thank you."

"Come on, let's get you settled. I have a lovely quiet room for you in the Bronte Building."

"Take good care of her," Mr Porter says.

He's never been an easy man to deal with, but his words seem genuine.

People liked my father. An intelligent and revered man, they respected him. Even if he didn't always make the right choices. Like trying to secure my future by marrying me off to Reese Whitfield-Brown.

I suppress a shudder.

It was an act of desperation. To make sure I had someone to take care of me when he was gone. But Reese and I weren't right for one another and when I realised he had fallen in love with Olivia, I begged my father to change his mind.

And for a while, I thought that maybe Elliot would—

No.

I shut down those thoughts.

I was wrong.

I misread everything. Every glance and touch and whisper between us.

While I was looking at him like he might be the one to keep my heart safe, he was looking at me as nothing more than a sister. A friend. An obligation.

I follow Mrs Danvers out of the building and across campus toward the dorm buildings. All Hallows' is a beautiful place steeped in history and tradition. But it also houses some dark secrets. Whispers of secret societies and twisted games. It's no surprise though, when some of the richest, oldest families in Oxfordshire send their children here.

Lawyers, businessmen, politicians, they are the country's future leaders.

I never cared before, happy to hide in the shadows and avoid people's stares. But then I befriended Olivia Beckworth, and she pulled me into her life. Their lives.

The Heirs of All Hallows'.

But the rumours and gossip do Reese, Theo, Oakley, Elliot injustice. Entitled and arrogant and dangerous, they are. But they're also loyal and strong and protective. And if you're welcomed into their inner circle, you're one of them.

You're family.

But after making the vital mistake of kissing Elliot the

night I discovered my father had passed, I fear everything is ruined now.

He's the last Heir standing.

The only one of them not in a relationship. And when he does finally meet someone, there'll be no room for me in their circle of eight.

So it's better really; better that I cut myself off and accept my fate now.

I'm not one of them, not really.

And I never will be.

But it was nice to pretend, for a little while, that I belonged.

"Your room is at the end of the hall and around the corner, next to the fire escape. So you'll have plenty of space."

"Thank you."

We slip through the door separating the main hallway and small hallway where my new room is. She's right, it is out of the way. Almost in its own annex.

"Here's your key." I take it from her, and she offers me a sad smile. "If you need anything—"

"I'll be fine, thank you." I unlock the door and push open the door.

"It's a little bigger than most of the rooms but given the circumstances..." She trails off, understanding glittering in her eyes.

"There's no guidebook for this kind of thing, Abigail. But you have people who care. If you ever need to talk, you can come to me or Miss Linley. And I'm sure the girls are all eager to help in any way they can."

I nod too weary to reply.

"Okay, well, I'll leave you for now. Take all the time you need."

"Thank you."

She hesitates but doesn't say whatever is on her mind. So I step further into the room and close the door behind me. It's a nice, bright space, daylight pouring in through the window overlooking the campus grounds but it feels all wrong.

I throw down my bag and march toward it, lowering the blinds first, and then yanking the heavy curtains shut, plunging the room into darkness.

Turning, I walk over to the bed and fall down onto it, curling myself around one of the pillows.

Then I close my eyes and pray sleep finds me.

Elliot and Abi's story continues in the SAVAGE VICIOUS HEIR DUET.

ABOUT THE AUTHOR

Two angsty romance lovers writing dark heroes and the feisty girls who bring them to their knees.

SIGN UP NOW
To receive news of our releases straight to your inbox.

Want to hang out with us?
Come and join CAITLYN'S DAREDEVILS group on Facebook.

ALSO BY CAITLYN DARE

Rebels at Sterling Prep

Taunt Her

Tame Him

Taint Her

Trust Him

Torment Her

Temper Him

Gravestone Elite

Shattered Legacy

Tarnished Crown

Fractured Reign

Savage Falls Sinners MC

Savage

Sacrifice

Sacred

Sever

Red Ridge Sinners MC

Crank

Ruin

Reap

Rule

Defy

Heirs of All Hallows'

Wicked Heinous Heirs

Filthy Jealous Heir: Part One

Filthy Jealous Heir: Part Two

Cruel Devious Heir : Part One

Cruel Devious Heir : Part Two

Brutal Callous Heir : Part One

Brutal Callous Heir : Part Two

Savage Vicious Heir : Part One

Savage Vicious Heir : Part Two

Boxsets

Ace

Cole

Conner

Savage Falls Sinners MC